All for a Sister

All for a Sister

A NOVEL

ALLISON PITTMAN

Tyndale House Publishers, Inc.
CAROL STREAM, ILLINOIS

Visit Tyndale online at www.tyndale.com.

Visit Allison Pittman's website at www.allisonpittman.com.

All for a Sister

Designed by Ron Kaufmann

Edited by Kathryn S. Olson

Published in association with William K. Jensen Literary Agency, 119 Bampton Court, Eugene, Oregon 97404.

Library of Congress Cataloging-in-Publication Data

Pittman, Allison.
All for a sister / Allison Pittman.
pages cm
ISBN 978-1-4143-6682-1 (sc)
1. Heirs—History—20th century—Fiction. 2. Inheritance and succession—Fiction.
3. Hollywood (Los Angeles, Calif.)—Fiction. I. Title.
PS3616.I885A77 2014
813'.6—dc23 2014005565

Printed in the United States of America

20 19 18 17 16 15 14
7 6 5 4 3 2 1

ACKNOWLEDGMENTS

I cannot say enough about the fabulous people at Tyndale, who continue to let me follow the story trails wherever they lead. Nor can I ever express how grateful I am for my agent, Bill Jensen, a font of wisdom in all questions great and small.

Thank you, family—Mikey and the boys—for being so supportive and, more important, self-sufficient!

And here you are . . . my Monday Night Group and the PITT crew . . . reading first words for the first time. It's only because of your amazing love and support that I finally felt strong enough to go this one "alone." But not alone, really. Because above all else I must honor my Lord and Savior, Jesus Christ, and the Holy Spirit who sustains me.

LORD, you alone are my inheritance, my cup of blessing.
You guard all that is mine.
The land you have given me is a pleasant land.
What a wonderful inheritance!

PSALM 16:5-6 (NLT)

CHAPTER 1

CELESTE, AGE 20

LOS ANGELES
1925

CELESTE WALKED BACKWARD through the house, a lifetime of poise and confidence in every step.

"Perhaps something here? On the stairs?" She ascended four steps, then turned, striking a dramatic pose along the banister, one leg stretched provocatively from her fringed skirt.

"That's a nice one, Miss DuFrane." The photographer, Jimmy from *Photoplay*, seemed more indulging than enthusiastic. "But I think we're looking for something to bring out more of the ingenue, you know what I'm sayin'? A little more starlet, little less 'Jazz Baby.'"

Celeste frowned—really more of a pout, and really rather pretty. "I don't want to come across as another Mary Pickford."

"Well, you ain't no Clara Bow, neither. Why don't we think about goin' outside? Some fresh-face-in-the-garden action?"

She dropped her pose and clomped down the stairs. "Is that what Mr. Lundi requested?" Indeed, it sounded exactly like something Roland Lundi would say.

Jimmy pushed his hat back, revealing a rapidly receding hairline. "Look, he's your agent. I just got the memo. 'Meet the untold story of Celeste DuFrane.' Already sounds like a headline, don't it?"

It did, but not one she relished. There was a reason the story hadn't been told—not even to her. Besides, it wasn't Celeste's untold story; it was her mother's, kept in the shadows until the reading of her will. Celeste's story was simple: a beautiful little girl wants to be a movie star . . . and she is. No rise from poverty, no brave tale of immigration, no miraculous discovery in a mundane talent show.

"Follow me, then." She brushed past Jimmy and walked with a measured, swaying step, leading the way through the kitchen, where Graciela's warm, welcoming face looked up from the ever-growing pile of colorful sliced vegetables on the counter.

"Will your guest be joining us for lunch, Miss Celeste?" She spoke with an exaggerated deferential tone, her accent almost comically pronounced, the way she did when she meant to play the maid.

"Él no es un invitado," Celeste said, her Spanish as perfect as Graciela's English. She grabbed a slice of sweet red pepper and bit into its crispness without ever breaking her stride, continuing toward the double French doors leading to the patio, where she stopped short and allowed Jimmy to be a gentleman.

"That part of the mystery?" he said, holding the door wide. "Are you the maid's secret daughter?"

"You got me." Her voice dripped with uncharacteristic sarcasm, but it built up the wall Roland told her to build. She wasn't to say a word until he arrived. With the mystery woman.

Jimmy took the hint and said nothing more until they were standing in the middle of the garden, surrounded by Graciela's perfectly tended roses, their feet resting on the pink cobblestones that intersected the velvet-green grass. It was a day that carried the ocean on the breeze, and Celeste lifted her face to it, breathing deep.

"Aw, that's beautiful," Jimmy said on cue. She knew her blonde hair, freshly styled, shone in the sunlight, and when she closed her eyes, her carefully applied makeup was its own work of art.

Soon enough, Celeste heard the sound of the shutter, and she opened her eyes.

"Look, you're a beautiful girl, but I'm not seein' a story, you know what I mean?"

"How can you say that?"

"California princess. You wanted your own house. You got your own house. You wanted to be in the movies. You're in the movies. Maybe if you were a star—"

"I have a film premiere next week."

"You the star?"

"Third lead."

He touched the rim of his rumpled hat in mock salute. "Have Lundi give me a call when you're playing Chaplin's lover, and we'll talk. Meanwhile—" he hoisted up his camera—"if this turns out any good, maybe I'll put something together about our California girls. Homegrown, not like the Swede I'm shooting later."

Celeste worked her face into a smile and balled her fist as if that could keep *Photoplay* from slipping through her fingers. "I understand."

Rather than leading him back through the house, Celeste pointed Jimmy toward the side gate, where the sad-looking jalopy she'd spotted upon greeting him waited at the edge of the drive to take him away.

Back in the kitchen, Graciela was arranging a platter with slices from a fresh-baked chicken. She glanced up, then looked around expectantly.

"He left," Celeste said, leaning against the counter and picking at the carcass with delicate fingers. "He said there wasn't a story."

Graciela tsked but said nothing.

"Mother confided everything in you—toward the end, I mean. So tell me, what can I expect? What do you know about this woman?"

"*Nada.* Not much more than you already know. She's been in prison—"

"Because of what happened to my sister."

"*Sí.* And now she's coming here."

"A prisoner. Here. What are people going to think?"

"It's none of their business, *mija*. That's why you did good to send that *periodista* away. *Familia, verdad?* Like your mama always said, secrets don't hurt anyone until they get away."

"Easy for Mother to say. She's dead."

"Dios la tenga en su gloria," Graciela said, crossing herself and punctuating the gesture with a kiss to the tips of her fingers.

"Oh, sure," Celeste said, "she gets to rest in peace, while the rest of us—"

The three-tone chime of the front door interrupted her thought.

Normally it fell to Graciela to greet guests and visitors, but this time Celeste waved her off. The sound of her high heels bounced between the shining tiles and the high ceiling, a sound that she had always found both powerful and reassuring. At the entry hall, she paused for just a moment to check her face in the mirror. She took a deep breath, grasped the door's brass handle, and opened it wide.

"There's our girl," Roland said with the affection of a favorite uncle. He stood, hat in hand, wearing a crisp, pale-blue suit, accessorized with a blue-and-gold cravat, his black hair slicked to perfection. Once over the threshold, he greeted Celeste with a kiss to her cheek and whispered, "We need to talk. Just you and me."

She nodded, feeling completely incapable of uttering a word as the woman standing behind him came into full view.

She was smaller than Celeste had expected. In the movies, evil women were always large and looming, casting shadows across entire rooms. They had untamed hair; square, widely spaced teeth; and nostrils that flared to accentuate a maniacal grin. But this girl—or woman, she supposed—seemed perfectly pleasant. Potentially pretty, even, with a bit of makeup and some decent clothes. She wore a cheap dime-store hat that sat on her head like a brown, overtipped bowl, and beneath it, more brown in the uneven tufts of hair. The haircut must be new, Celeste surmised, because the woman's fingers fidgeted with the ends of it under her scrutiny. Celeste had done the same thing last year when she finally succumbed to fashion and had her own blonde tresses bobbed.

"You must be Dana," she said at last, remembering that manners must always trump fear.

"I am," the woman said, holding out her hand only after Celeste's second prompting. It was small and rough and cold, and Celeste found herself tugging to bring her inside.

"Welcome," she said. "We have a saying here. *Mi casa es tu casa.* It means, 'My house is your house.'" She let forth the last of her nerves in a giggle. "I guess, for us, that's really true."

Not even the slightest hint of a smile tugged at Dana's lips. "I'm sorry for that." She spoke as if unused to any form of conversation. "I had no idea . . ."

"And there's my spicy chickadee," Roland said, injecting himself into the dialogue.

"Bah!" Graciela brushed right past him and, without waiting for permission, wrapped the frail stranger in her soft embrace, muttering a message of welcome and blessing. Pulling back slightly, she said, "*Venga conmigo.* Come with me, upstairs. Your room is ready, and you can take a nice bit of a rest before lunch."

Dana looked to Celeste and Roland for permission.

"It's all right," Celeste reassured, eager to be released from the discomfort of this introduction. Perhaps it would be best if they got to know each other in increments. Neither she nor Roland spoke as they watched the two ascend the stairs, Graciela carrying the single satchel and Dana following behind, head down, hands limp at her sides.

"So," Roland said when the others were clearly out of earshot, "no *Photoplay*?"

"Thank goodness." She gave him a sidelong glance. "You've had better ideas, you know."

"Indeed I have. In fact, I had a better one on the train. Shall we?"

He took half a step, and she took the hint, escorting him to the room that had been her father's office. She was in the process of having the whole place redecorated. White—walls, carpet, furniture—with heavy curtains and a wall left empty to serve as a screen for intimate viewings. She sat and he followed, taking a cigarette from his breast pocket and lighting it with the ornate crystal lighter on the low, glass-topped table.

"You made me look like an idiot," Celeste said as Roland busied himself with the smoking ritual. "They didn't even send a reporter, you know. Just a photographer. What's a photographer supposed to do with an untold story?"

"Forget about them," he said through a first puff of smoke. His voice was low and rough, perfectly matched to the faint crackle of the burning tobacco. "We're going to tell that story ourselves."

"Good luck. After today, I'll be lucky to get my picture in the funny papers."

"Listen, sweetheart. We're going for something much bigger than the papers. This story?" He used his cigarette to trace a rectangle between them. "It's got silver screen written all over it."

CHAPTER 2

THE WRITTEN CONFESSION OF MARGUERITE DUFRANE, PAGES 1–12

TO MY SWEET GIRL, Celeste, who has been always the delight and sustenance of my life, I take its waning days to tell you all. It is a rare thing indeed when the counsel of almighty God intersects with that of our given laws, and a declaration brings both condemnation and release. But such has occurred. Although I write this at the insistence of our attorney, Mr. Christopher Parker, Esquire, the confession I write here is nothing short of what I have professed to our Lord. I am assured of his forgiveness in all I shall reveal, and I can only hope to secure your own. And as to others against whom I have sinned—and they are many—I can pray they will not begrudge me God's mercy, as most have already met him in glory. All except her, for all I know.

The witnessed signature at its end will show this to be the final testament of my life.

You should know, darling girl, that we welcomed your arrival with all the blessed relief and anticipation any child has ever known. As well, you should know that before you came into our life, we had another little girl named Mary. She had a beautiful cap of soft blonde-white curls, and we called her our "Little Lamb." There are features the two of you share, but she had none of your fire. She was sweet and shy, if such could be said of an infant. In our short time together, I don't remember her ever making a sound that could be heard from the next room. We kept chiming clocks in every room of the house, lest we'd forget to feed her.

And, oh, how Calvin adored her. He would touch her sweet cheek and entwine his fingers in hers. Even though he risked the wrath of both myself and the nurse, as his fingers were always dirty from his adventures in the garden, he could not stay away. Perhaps, dear one, that is why the two of you always experienced such strife. As excited as your father and I were when you arrived in our lives, Calvin never completely shared our adoration. You would never be our lovely Mary, our Little Lamb, even though your brother often teased you about being the living ghost of that phantom child. If you could only understand how I have longed to meet her again in heaven. That day draws ever nearer. And yet, for much of your life, through my own diligence, exactly how she left this world was never spoken of in your presence. Nor anyone else's, for that matter, after a time.

So I begin.

Deep in your earliest memories I'm sure you remember our house in Highland Park. It had been in my family for three generations, built by my grandfather as the first symbol of his wealth. Your own father never liked to acknowledge that our money came from my family. While it's true he made an acceptable salary as an academic, it was my money that kept us afloat in society while he fiddled with his chemicals and filed his patents and delivered the occasional lecture. Inventors have been known to become rich, but it helps tremendously if they already are. Ask Mr. Edison, should you doubt.

I married your father, Arthur, because I immediately, deeply loved him. At the time, I didn't recognize this as a spell he was so adept at casting. He was handsome, and humble, and so passionately intelligent. He had a way, in our courting days, of making me feel like I was the only woman in the world. The only woman who ever had been. Unconcerned with the confines of propriety, he kissed me sooner than he ought, bedded me before our marriage, and once he was properly installed as the man of my house, failed to see me again. Always, he wanted something more; it is what drove him through his world of discovery. Unfortunately, it was what drove him into the beds of countless others.

Until you came along. You, my Celeste, centered him. Settled him. Perhaps because, from the beginning, it was obvious you were his equal in intelligence and curiosity.

But I digress.

I loved that house and I loved your father, despite the eccentricities that would forever set us apart from our Chicago circle. I believe all of our friends saw him as somewhat of a novelty. Always doodling his formulas and leaving the room in sudden fits of genius. But he had the appetites of a man far above his natural status. The best foods, the finest wine, the most beautiful women. Yes, I can tell you this now, as he is gone and your memories of the good, loving father that he was are in no danger. He never made any attempt to hide the fact that he pursued me relentlessly because of my beauty. The portraits of my youth will attest to that. There was a carnality to him that he kept hidden under his intellectual pursuits. So entranced was I with the latter, I feared what might happen should he not have that distraction of the former. While he satisfied his appetite in beds other than our own, there were only two circumstances in which I feared the ramifications of his unfaithfulness.

The first was in the spring before you were born, when our little family consisted of only myself, your father, Calvin, and our

Mary. With the absence of all but the most distant relatives of your father's in St. Louis, Missouri, we filled our home with friends—sometimes little more than acquaintances—for all celebrations. It was a large house, you remember, built for grand occasions, and in those days there was nothing I liked better than a house full of music and people, dining and drinking with games of charades and pass-the-slipper. Old-fashioned, I know, especially in light of today's modernity of phonographs and dancing. And perhaps unconvincing, given that you've only known my proclivity for solitude.

There was a woman—vapid thing, divorcée—who had nudged her way into our group by refusing to vacate it even after her husband so publicly and disgracefully abandoned her. Mrs. D—— should suffice, as I can tell you now that nothing ever came of it. Sometimes I wonder if the poor woman even knew the qualities she exuded, always hanging about with such a wanton gullibility. We all worried that our husbands would succumb, falling to some great, unfulfilled masculine need. I more than others, I suppose, for I'd suffered the storm of infidelity. I knew the signs to look for, the slight touch, the gaze that lingers too long, the mad scramble to be near one another that they might be thrown together accidentally during one of our silly games.

And so it was that night in October. We hadn't given any sort of party since your brother's birthday three months before, largely because of my suspicions of your father and Mrs. D——. How silent our house! Calvin content with his puzzles and little Mary quiet as a pillow wherever she might be. Quiet, too, as your father was so often away, sometimes spending entire nights in his lab, perfecting the components that would eventually bring us here to Los Angeles. Or so he said, and I refused to give myself over to doubt. Besides, Mrs. D—— was having a flagrant affair with a star tenor in our Metropolitan Opera, so my fears were kept at bay.

Thus when my birthday came around, I decided to throw a lavish affair in our very own home. I ordered a cake from a local bakery and, rather than taxing our kitchen staff, arranged to have the food catered by Kruger's. In lieu of a formal dinner, I opted for a series of heavy hors d'oeuvres so those in attendance could eat and mingle at will, myself included. Two hours before the first guest was due to arrive, I was called to the kitchen. Mrs. Lundgren, one of our regular staff, was too ill to work—a complaint I'd grown used to. In fact, just weeks before, I'd included five extra dollars to finance a visit to a doctor, but we both knew our places well enough to never speak of it.

In her stead, she'd sent her daughter, Dana. The girl was about twelve years old, I'd say, well old enough to enter service, though her mother seemed bent on another course. She wore her mother's uniform—black dress with the high collar and lace pinafore. I'll never forget how the garment hung on her, so thin she was.

It wasn't as if the girl had never been to our house before. She'd come often enough when we had heavy cleaning to do and need of an extra set of hands. Even more often in the months previous when her mother had fallen prey to illness. But never on a formal occasion.

"Mama's taught me everything," she assured me, carrying a tray and addressing imaginary guests to my satisfaction, so I put her to work.

Just as well, because the gaiety in our house that night would have masked untold blunders. Mrs. D—— and her tenor entertained the crowd—he, singing; she, plunking away on the piano; and the both of them carrying on like lovers in a matinee. Your father told one version or another of his favorite jokes, and our house felt so much like a home, I wanted the children to be a part of it. I went upstairs myself to fetch them down, little Calvin looking so sweet and sleepy as he walked behind me, and my sweet Mary with her soft, drowsy face against my shoulder. I paraded them around shamelessly to be petted and coddled, perhaps as my pronouncement to the room that my husband had responsibilities here that far outweighed the rewards of any dalliance.

Looking back now, I see that I needn't have worried so much about my husband's eye roving about our party guests. On the contrary, he seemed completely devoted to our protégé, Dana, assisting her with the heavy silver trays, holding the kitchen door open, and whispering *somethings* into her ear during the odd moment when she appeared overwhelmed by her duties.

How easily I suppressed my fears. She was only a child, after all. Young enough to be his own. And the child of a servant, no less. No matter what my husband's failings might have been in his ability to be faithful to me, he was married to the idea of being part and parcel to some manner of aristocracy.

So when the hour struck late, and all the guests had left, and a bitter cold rain began to pummel the house . . . And when little Dana stood, so thin in her mother's dress, without any sort of coat whatsoever . . . And here we were with a house so huge and warm . . .

"Let her sleep in the nursery," your father said, bending low to speak. "In the night nurse's bed. She'll catch her death out there."

I told him he was right, of course. Just another reason why we should have kept a nurse full-time, for these nights when I'd be too exhausted to care properly for the children. Mrs. Gibbons, our only live-in staff, was good enough to make a bottle, which was still kept warm, wrapped in a tea towel, and I fed it to my Mary as I watched the girl rummage through a forgotten cabinet to find some suitable gown to sleep in.

"She's awfully sweet," said the girl—Dana. *Dana!* I must resign myself to the use of her name. I remember her thin, cold hand hovering near Mary's head, hesitant to touch.

I mumbled an agreement as I rocked her, drinking her in as she sucked on her bottle with those heavy, drooping eyes.

"And very lucky, to have all of this."

I took my eyes away from my drowsy child to look at this girl, her bony frame draped in faded, yellowed cotton, surrounded by all the silk and eyelet lace trimmings of the nursery. She, Dana, had been a little one just like Mary, though she'd no doubt suckled at her mother's breast, as was more fitting the poor. If I remember correctly, she'd been no more than two years old when her mother came to work for the family after her father's—if we are to believe the stories—absentee death on a river barge. Her mother had presented herself with the title of *Mrs.* as would befit a married woman, but one could never tell for sure.

I told her it wasn't luck, keeping my voice soft and even so as not to disrupt my daughter's oncoming slumber. We are born into the life God designed for us to have. He has a purpose, a plan for my little one, just as he has a plan for her.

"Do you really think so?"

How can I faithfully describe the way those words were spoken? By their construct, I know they were meant as a question, but there was no hint of inquiry in her pronouncement. No desire for a response. No curiosity. More like a simple resignation with a hint of bitterness. And flat, as though she'd spoken them into an empty tin.

I told her it wasn't a matter of my thinking so; that it was in the Bible.

"Where?" she challenged. "Where does it say in the Bible that God wants some of us to be rich and others not?"

I had to confess that I didn't know exactly, but it had to be the case, for such was the world. How could the rich be charged to feed the poor if there were no poor to feed?

"Still, it doesn't seem fair, if we're all his children." Throughout our talk, she roamed about the room, touching all the pretty things. She'd plucked a small, square pillow from Mary's crib, a pretty thing made of pink silk, covered with lace and small pearl buttons. "Could you choose? Could you bear to have one of your children grow up here and send the other one off to live down by the slaughterhouses?"

I'd grown uncomfortable with the conversation and told her so, at which point she looked stricken and apologized profusely.

"Mama always tells me I think too much. No future in that for a girl."

By this time the nipple had fallen completely away from Mary's sleepy lips. I handed the bottle to Dana at first, thinking she might take it down to the kitchen, but reconsidered, given her dishabille. Instead, I asked her to set it on the tray table at the top of the hall, just a few steps away, to be gathered by the housekeeper in the morning. During those few moments of her absence, I held my sweet Mary to my heart, rubbing her warm back to coax out the last air bubble, then laid her down in her crib and pulled her soft wool blanket up as a guard against the cold night.

Dana returned and stood beside me, and for a moment we looked down at my daughter together, and some force compelled me to reach my arm around her. I haven't touched many people in my life, and something about that moment sent rather a shock through me. The thinness of her shoulder blade, so different from my own healthy, soft girl. I made a promise to myself, then, to make right what I could. To better provide for her mother, so her mother could better provide for her. It is a promise I kept, though differently interpreted from what I imagined.

After wishing her a genuine good night with a kiss to her cool temple, I escorted her to the bed in the small alcove adjacent to the nursery and tucked her in, returning soon with a thick down comforter.

When I finally retired, my husband was already sleeping soundly, such as he did after a night of too much wine, but I remained awake for the better part of an hour, listening to the steady pounding of rain against the window.

Perhaps, I thought, *I could bring the girl here to live. There's another room off the kitchen she could share with her mother. Show her kindness and generosity to soften her bitterness.*

And then I drifted off into the sweetest sleep. Better than any I've had since. Dreamless and deep.

Then, that sound I'll never forget. How it haunts me still. More of a wail than a cry—so unaccustomed in our quiet home. It tugged me from my blissful depth, slowly, hand over fist, my mind heavy with sleep. I turned my head to see my husband's empty pillow, his place in the bed exposed and cold.

I spoke his name in case he was waiting in the shadows, but in the absence of a response, I heard the wailing again. Louder this time, and mournful, a duet with my husband's own voice. Fully awake now, I sat up and trained my ear. It was the nursery. Of course it was, dear Mary with a stomach pain, crying out having woken to a stranger.

Without a thought to putting on a robe or slippers, I ran toward the nursery, each step stealing any hope that this was a matter so simple as a sour stomach. Those were not the cries of my child, but the girl just down the hall. And my fickle husband out of bed—

Oh, how the hall stretched before me. Miles of paint and photographs and that runner Calvin was always tripping over.

When I finally arrived, the door was open, and there was my husband, wearing only the trousers of his pajamas, his hair disheveled, and a look of sheer panic on his face that stopped my heart. His mouth moved as if to speak, but no words came out.

Still the wailing continued, and from behind him stepped the girl. She'd lit a lamp, and her borrowed gown, thin as it was, made a cotton halo around her frame. It was torn at the shoulder, open, exposing her breast. Or, at least, it would have exposed it if not for the fact that she clutched some small bundle. It took a moment for my eyes to adjust to the sight, and then I realized what she clutched was my Mary.

It made no sense, that she would be holding my child. That he would be in the room. I rushed forward, screeching for the girl to give me the baby. By now her wails had taken form—*"I didn't . . . I couldn't . . . She wasn't . . ."*

I grabbed for my baby in a manner I never had, like she was a sack of something needed in the kitchen, and indeed in doing so found her to be heavier than I remembered. Heavier than she was in sleep. Heavier than she was in life. My entire body dropped with the weight of her. Straight to my knees I fell, cradling her, holding her close, praying with every breath she'd never have.

CHAPTER 3

DANA VISITS THE OFFICES OF ROLLING ARTS ENTERTAINMENT

CULVER CITY, CALIFORNIA
1925

HE SAT ON THE OTHER SIDE of the desk. Staring, not speaking, while the clock ticked another five minutes gone. Dana stayed perfectly still in her wooden chair, knowing the slightest movement would send an echoing creak into the musty, solid silence.

He spoke, not taking the thin cigarette holder from his lips, and it bobbed with each word. "Do you know who I am?"

"Celeste said you make movies."

"That I do." His voice was deep, his words clipped. German, she would have thought, though she knew nothing about Germans other than the fact that they were the enemy in the war. Later, Celeste would relay that he was, in fact, Austrian. Which meant even less. He seemed too old to have been a soldier. His hair, short and a jumble of colors ranging from near blond, to brown, to gray, sprang stick-straw-straight above a tan, angular face. Werner Ostermann, according to the name on the brass plate on his desk, and on the door, and on the small scrap of paper folded neatly in her pocket.

"And you want to make a movie about me."

"That I do."

He gave no verbal elaboration, only bored his gaze deeper. Instinctively she reached for her hair to stroke the long tresses, seeking the comfort she'd always found in their weight, but her fingers found only the soft, curling fringe peeking below her hat. Slowly, she returned her hand to her lap, pleased at having done so without eliciting the tiniest noise from the chair.

"I suppose I don't know how that is possible."

His lips spread into a thin grin, and he removed the cigarette holder, balancing it across a shallow dish on the corner of the paper-strewn desk. One dropped ash, and the entire small office would be in flames.

"Nothing more than a thousand pictures shining on a screen. And each picture tells a story."

"I don't have a story."

"I disagree."

She wanted to argue. After all, she'd been to a movie. Three, in fact, just since her arrival in California. One about a man who meets Jesus and races chariots. Another about a woman who walked a tightrope and rode white horses in the circus, and the last about a hideous monster lurking in the shadows of a castle. That one she couldn't watch, except from between the thin slit of her fingers as she covered her eyes. Celeste had been squealing beside her. *"Dana! Dana! You're missing the best part!"*

"I've done nothing for anybody to see," she said, fighting hard to keep her voice above a whisper. "What could you possibly put on film?"

He held his hands in front of his face, angling them against each other until he'd created an open square through which he looked at her with one eye and said, "Take off your hat."

"My hat?" she questioned, but obeyed.

He stretched his arms out farther. "I can see the entire story in your eyes. With a camera and some music, I could make a movie just right here. But—" he dropped his hands—"only I would understand it, and art must be shared."

She turned the hat over and over in her hands. "I'm not art."

"That remains to be seen. But Celeste is. Your story. Her face."

He slammed his hand on top of the desk as if delivering a verdict. Dana flinched at the gesture, nearly dropping her hat. It really was a beautiful thing—a bell-shaped dome, a flipped rim, and a wide blue ribbon punctuated by a perfect silk flower. She put it back on her head, not bothering to look for the perfect angle the way Celeste had taught her, and sat up straight.

"Why do you need me, then? You know the story. I hear it was in all the papers."

In answer, he picked up a handful of folded newspapers and held them aloft. "These tell me nothing. They have no heart."

"Neither do I." She said it with convincing flatness, or so she thought.

Ostermann let out a short, bitter laugh. "So dramatic. Perhaps you are the one to be the actress in the film?"

He was joking with her, of course. Something she was still training her ear to detect.

"What do you want to know? They say I killed a child. They put me in prison. And then they let me out, and I came here. All that time between—twenty years, Mr. Ostermann; more than half my life—nothing happened. I went nowhere, saw no one, did nothing. Who would come to the theater to see an empty screen?"

"There is no such thing as *nothing*. You tell me, all of this nothingness. Surely I am not the first to ask?"

Far from the first. There'd been a journalist in Chicago, and even two on the train, pestering her with questions. How did it feel to be free after all this time? What did she want to do? Where did she want to go? What was the connection between herself and the lovely Celeste DuFrane? Their queries pelted her like stones, chipping away at the wall she'd built around her—far higher and stronger than those of Bridewell, though nobody called it that anymore. It was the Chicago House of Corrections, officially. Bridewell, nothing but an old, sentimental term of affection. A nickname carried from those who knew her before the fire. A safer name for a place to put children.

These questions, however, felt different. Ostermann's office was close and plain and gray, lit only by a small window high up on the opposite wall. Under his scrutiny, she felt the space closing in, and the odd comfort of the confinement frightened her.

"Will you leave the door open? So I can leave if I want?"

"Of course." His expression lacked any hint of triumph as he stood, walked out from behind his desk, and spoke curtly through the opened door. Within seconds, the capable, sturdy woman who had greeted Dana in the outer office came in, carrying a small notebook and a sharpened pencil. "This is Miss Lynch. She will be taking notes as you speak. Is that all right with you?"

"Of course," Dana said, purposefully repeating his words, trying to match his tone. She turned to acknowledge Miss Lynch, who sat in a chair to the left and slightly behind her. In the meantime, Werner Ostermann settled himself back behind his messy piles and lit a fresh cigarette.

"Do you mind?" Dana said, emboldened. "I'm not used to the smell, and the smoke burns my eyes."

He said nothing but stubbed out the offensive thing.

"Thank you."

"Proceed." He opened his hands toward her, inviting.

Again the clock ticked silence, the only other sound being the soft clearing of Miss Lynch's throat.

"Where should I begin?" Dana's voice was little more than a whisper, so soft she could feel Miss Lynch craning closer.

"I believe it was Oliver Twist who began with his birth, but I don't think we need to go back that far. Perhaps the night you were arrested?"

She shook her head. "I don't remember much about that." It was a truth that had not served her well at the time of her arrest, and after all these years, it wasn't a truth at all.

"Perhaps, then, a memory from before?"

Before she went to prison, he meant, but those memories were equally shrouded. Still, she closed her eyes and took in a deep breath, seeing a small, pale hand pushing aside a curtain.

"My mother and I lived in a small apartment on the third floor above a grocer. . . ."

CHAPTER 4

EXTERIOR: A narrow, dark street in an impoverished neighborhood. A woman, young but moving with a stooped gait of fatigue, makes her way, carrying a shopping bag. She stops for a moment, observing a father buying a bag of toasted chestnuts for his daughter. It is a touching scene, and the woman appears wistful before summoning new courage and beginning a tedious climb up a set of narrow steps attached to the alley side of a dark brick building.

INTERIOR: The apartment is shabby and plain but clean. A small table, two chairs, a stove, and a single narrow bed in the corner. A girl, almost a young woman, bustles about, setting the table with two simple plates and two glasses. She pours milk into the glasses, but only until each is less than half-full. She looks with longing, obviously wishing for more, but when the door opens, she puts on a mask of contentment and says, "Mother!" before rushing to embrace the woman from the street scene.

1904

"DARLING!" MAMA CALLED from the doorway. Her voice had the ring of enthusiasm, but one of obvious effort. Her eyes, the same pale blue as Dana's own, appeared mismatched with the cheerful greeting and the smile. She glanced at the bed in the corner with a touch of wistfulness; then her eyes darted back to Dana and grew a little brighter. Immediately Dana wished she'd poured all of the milk into one glass to give to her.

"How was the party?" Dana asked as she pulled out a chair, eager to see Mama off her feet.

"Too much. So lavish for a boy just seven years old." Mama still spoke with a trace of her Swedish heritage, though she'd been born right here in America, not ten blocks from this very room. "Toys and toys and toys, and a table twice the size of this room filled with every kind of sweet."

"You look so tired. They should have let you go home. I could have come and taken care of the baby."

"You know how particular Mrs. DuFrane is," Mama said, running an absent finger along the edge of the empty plate.

"And how is the baby?" Dana had only caught the quickest glimpse of her—a pink-faced thing—as Mrs. DuFrane carried her in a brief tour around the festivities.

"Sweet." But it took her a while to say it, only after closing her eyes and opening them to focus on the plate in front of her. The sight of it proved to be invigorating, as a new cheerfulness took hold. "And speaking of *sweet*, I've brought home several little things left over from the party. Chocolate-filled crepes and fruit tarts and a dozen cinnamon-dusted cookies."

"For supper?"

"Why not? Even paupers ought to be able to eat like kings every now and again."

Dana eyed the shopping bag, imagining the treats within, and unrolled the top, extracting three paper-wrapped packages. "Which are the crepes?"

"That long, flat one, I think." But she was hardly paying attention.

"Which would you like then, m'lady? Crepe or tart or—?"

"You know, I am not very hungry."

Though it might have been a trick of the rapidly fading light, Dana noticed that her mother was not only pale, but slightly green.

"Can I get you something else, then? There's bread left, and a little butter."

"No. I think I need to just lie down for a while."

"You don't have to go back to the house?" Though not a regular occurrence, Mama was often required to sleep in the small room off the baby's nursery, mostly on nights when one of the DuFranes' social engagements would render Mrs. DuFrane incapable of rising in the night to care for the child's needs. Dana hated those nights, when she was left alone in the apartment, no matter how safe and cozy a home Mama had created. It would be so much easier if they could simply live in one of the rooms in the vast, sprawling house. But Mama promised, always: *"Not much longer. Just until the baby isn't a baby. And then I'll find us something better."*

Now Mama shook her head, her lips held especially tight. "No going back tonight. It's a staff holiday in honor of the boy's birthday."

"How nice." Dana grasped her growling stomach in anticipation of the treat, and her mother almost laughed.

"Here." Mama poured her milk into the other glass. "We will get another bottle tomorrow morning."

After finally removing her hat, Mama made a slow trek to the bed in the corner of the room and curled up on it. Her eyes almost immediately fluttered closed.

Meanwhile, Dana happily, hungrily indulged in the treats—one of each—before reluctantly wrapping the rest in the paper bag to be put away until later. By now the room was growing dim, and she took a match from the matchbox, prepared to light the lamp, but took one look across the room to where her mother rested so peacefully. Reconsidering, she replaced the match, set the lamp down, and retrieved a thick but worn quilt from a steamer trunk at the foot of the bed. This she spread out on the floor alongside the bed, then lay herself down upon it, flat on her back, staring up at the ceiling. After a few moments, her mother's hand came into her frame of view, beckoning, and Dana rose first to her elbows, then straight up. She moved to the foot of the bed and gently removed her mother's shoes before curling up beside her, spreading the quilt over both of them, and waiting for the room to grow dark.

"Are you even listening to me?"

Ostermann's eyes had closed soon into her narrative, but Dana had continued to speak. She'd all but blocked memories of her mother. Useless things, serving only to mire her in the competing agony of resentment and guilt.

"*Crêpes au chocolat,* apple tarts, and some sort of cookie." He counted them off on his fingers as he spoke, pausing on the third. He opened one eye to look past Dana to Miss Lynch. "What kind of cookie, exactly?"

Miss Lynch flipped back a page in her notebook, brow furrowed. "Cinnamon-dusted," she said with all the authority of having been in the little apartment that evening.

Both eyes were open now, so dark and brown as to make Dana wish he'd close them again.

"It is Miss Lynch's job to listen. It is my job to see. When you speak, do you not see everything laid out as if on a stage before you?"

"Yes," she admitted, wondering for the first time whatever had happened to all those modest furnishings, those few possessions that had made their apartment a home. Perhaps even today strangers ate supper on those very dishes, sat at that table so long ago abandoned.

"You have the benefit of memory. I have the gift of vision. You remember; I create."

"Should I be writing this down?" Miss Lynch interjected from the corner.

Ostermann arched an eyebrow in response, prompting Miss Lynch to quietly tuck the pencil behind her ear.

"There's a lot I don't remember. And I'm afraid—"

He held up a finger, interrupting her, and ordered Miss Lynch back out to her desk.

"What is this? You are afraid? Are you not safe now, with a home?"

She was, though she didn't know what she was meant to do here in this bright, sun-filled place when she'd known little more than shadows for the better part of her life. What she feared most was the phenomenon of mere minutes ago, when she spoke aloud of things she'd long denied herself permission to remember. How real it all was—the softness of the quilt, the heaviness of her mother's eyes, the sweet burst of sugar. If she continued to tell her story, other memories would take on such dimension, none so pleasant. She would be once again cold and damp, helpless and hungry. Thin with illness and bent with fatigue. All those things they'd said to put behind her would spring to life in this little office, her fidgeting releasing the creaks in the chair.

Ostermann must have grown impatient for an answer, because he'd walked out from behind his desk and now crouched next to her, folding his tall frame until his dark eyes looked up into hers.

"Were there times," he said, "ever, when you wanted to scream?"

She nodded, muted by the same timidity and fear that had always plagued her.

"Well then—" he took her hand within both of his, a touch she couldn't have anticipated, and so unfamiliar she couldn't think to pull away—"we will shout together."

CHAPTER 5

CELESTE, AGE 5

1910

DADDY SAID THE HOUSE looked like a palace, but Celeste didn't see it that way. There was nothing tall or pointy, and no forest or land or tall, narrow windows for a princess to look out of.

She told him so, and he said, "Not a *castle*, my dear. A *palace*. Like from *Arabian Nights*. Someplace a sheikh might live, all spread out with plenty of room for his harem."

"What's a harem?"

Celeste's question drew a disapproving look from her mother. Not for her so much as for Daddy. "There's been quite enough of that, I daresay."

"Come on," Daddy said, drawing the word out and lifting Celeste up into his arms. They'd taken a train from Chicago and a car from the train station and now stood under the blazing sun, its light glancing blindingly off the whiteness of the house. "Land of milk and honey, this is, and we're going to make more money than you ever thought about."

"Unless you're getting some hidden increase in salary," Mother said, "I don't see how much will change. And besides, you know it's garish to speak of such things."

Mother was trying to sound like money didn't matter, but Celeste knew that couldn't be true. She knew they had lots of it.

From her perch near her father's shoulder, she could better see the grounds between the house and the low, stone wall surrounding it.

"What kinds of trees are those?"

"They're palm trees, stupid." This from her older brother, Calvin, who at nearly thirteen was an expert on just about everything.

"They're too little to be palm trees." She'd seen palm trees before, in picture books, and they were always tall up to the sky.

"So they're short palm trees." He walked with his head held low and his cap pulled over his eyes. He'd been complaining since the day Daddy said they were leaving Chicago, no matter how much their parents tried to convince him that there would be new friends to play baseball with in California.

"Are they going to grow tall?" She leaned close to whisper her question in Daddy's ear so Calvin wouldn't call her stupid again.

"We'll have to wait and watch and see."

They'd arrived at the front doors—two of them, side by side, with big, silver nails poking out in patterns. One of them swung open before her very eyes, revealing a dark-skinned woman with a single thick, black braid wound around her head like a crown. She wore a dark dress with a starched, high-necked white pinafore.

"Bienvenido, señor." She dipped her head toward Celeste's father. *"Y señora,"* her mother.

"Graciela," Daddy said, and when he did, his tongue trilled in his mouth in a way Celeste had never heard before. He went to put his hand on her shoulder, as if the two of them were cohorts in welcoming the family to the house, then took it away with an air of nervousness Celeste had never seen. "This is my wife, Mrs. DuFrane; and our children, Calvin and Celeste."

Graciela greeted each, keeping her hands folded primly as she acknowledged Mother, then shaking Calvin's and softly touching the silkiness of Celeste's blonde curls.

"So pretty," Graciela said, smiling, revealing a row of perfect white teeth.

"Thank you." Celeste drew closer to her mother.

"I assumed I would be in charge of hiring the staff," Mother said, her words tight.

"Graciela was employed by the previous owners. Practically came with the house."

"Does she even speak English?"

"Yes, ma'am," Graciela answered for herself.

"Do you cook?"

"Yes, ma'am. I have a lunch ready for you in the kitchen, whenever you would like."

Her words flowed like water, like the perfect draw of a warm bath, the syllables splashing and lapping, one into the next. Celeste had to listen close and think back to make sure she understood. *Lonsh. Keeshun. Lonshrrrrreadyforrryoueeenthekeeshun.* She repeated the phrase softly, trying her best to match Graciela's pronunciation.

"Stop that." Mother's words sounded like hisses. "It's rude."

"Oh no, señora. Haven't you heard that imitation is the most sincere form of flattery?" She reached out softly, placed the backs of her fingers against Celeste's cheek. "You are quite the little mimic, *mija*."

"Don't touch her." Mother grabbed Celeste's arm and yanked her daughter roughly to her side.

"Perdóname." She sounded gracious, not chastised, though

she stepped away. Keeping a distance, she turned to Calvin and smiled brightly. "Are you hungry, young man?"

"Not especially."

"Liar," Celeste erupted. "You said your stomach was grumbling on the train."

"Shut up."

"You did!" She looked to her parents for justice. "Remember? He wanted to buy a bag of peanuts and you told him no. But then he snuck off anyway—" she turned to Graciela—"and he said he was going to buy a schnitzel with his pocket money, but then he couldn't find anybody. Don't they have those here?"

"That's enough." Daddy picked her up and brought his nose to hers. "All that matters now is that we are home. Would you like to see your new room?"

"I liked my old room."

"You'll like this one too. I promise." He turned his head. "Marguerite? Would you like Graciela to show you the kitchen?"

Mother touched her hand to her brow. "If it's all the same to you, I think I'd like to lie down for a while."

"Of course, darling." He deferred. "Graciela, if you'd go to our room and prepare it for Mrs. DuFrane to take a little *siesta*?"

He set Celeste down again, took her hand, and led her across a wide, shiny floor of different-colored tiles that made her footsteps echo. She heard Calvin clomping behind them, but when they came to the spiraling staircase in the middle of the entry, he pushed ahead, running up the steps two at a time and, once he got to the top, jumped up and down, begging their father to let him slide on the banister to the bottom.

"Not now," Daddy said, laughing. "No need to crack your head on our first day here."

At the landing, he steered them to the left, where two doors, one pink and one blue, waited on either side of the hall.

"Guess which one is yours, silly Cel—"

But she had already broken away and was flying headlong toward the door. She grasped the brass knob and turned, seeking permission to open it when Graciela and Mother came into view.

"Can I open it?"

"And you, too, Calvin," Mother said, shooing them on. She seemed a bit rejuvenated by their enthusiasm and came to place her hand on the knob too, so they could open it together.

"Ooooooh." It was all Celeste could say at the vision that awaited. She knew they'd shipped some of their things ahead; she'd had to pack and say good-bye to several of her favorite toys and dresses nearly a month before. But here they were now—her dollhouse and all its furniture, just how she liked it, and a shelf with all her books, and her tea table and chairs. But there was also a sweet, small china cabinet holding her best, most delicate dishes, and a new rocking horse much larger and finer than her other baby one. The bed was a dream, with four tall posts and white, gauzy material draped between them. The coverlet—pink satin with white stitching—and enough pillows to burrow under.

"What do you think, princess?" Daddy, hat in hand, filled the doorway.

Celeste spun in a slow circle, taking it all in. The forest mural painted on the wall. The freestanding easel with a real chalk tray and eraser. The lavender toy chest with who knew what treasures within. And her favorite dolls, all sitting pretty on the upholstered window seat. It was all too wonderful for words, so she simply ran and wrapped her arms around her father's cedar-trunk legs and then approached her mother with a more restrained, ladylike embrace.

"Go look out the window, darling," Mother said, and Celeste obeyed, her feet barely touching the rose-colored carpet. She clambered up onto the seat and pushed the sheer covering aside. The backyard below looked like some sort of fairies' meadow, with lush green carpet and fountains and flower beds. Best of all, a small, pale-yellow house in the corner, with a real picket fence and a tiny cobblestone walkway.

She clapped her hands in rapture. "A playhouse!"

"And one you can play in all year round," Daddy said, "because there's never any snow."

That gave her a little bit of a pang because it was fun to play in snow, sometimes.

"Enough of this girlie baby stuff," Calvin complained. "Can I see my room now?"

"Sure, sport," Daddy said, and though Celeste was loath to leave her own paradise, she picked up one of her dolls—a lovely, pretty thing with long black hair and bright-blue eyes—and lingered on the outskirts of the family as they huddled in the doorway of her brother's room, listening to him go on about a new baseball mitt and an electric light for his desk and a special wicker basket for all of his dirty clothes. It was nice to hear him not being grumbly for the first time since the announcement that they were leaving Chicago, but she didn't want to pretend to care about his things any more than he pretended to care about hers. So step by slow step, she inched her way back down the hall, until she met up with Graciela, quietly shutting the door to the big room at the opposite end of the hallway.

"What did you think of your room, *mija*?"

Celeste looked to the left and the right before approaching. "My name is Celeste, remember?"

"Oh yes." They were now both at the top of the stairs. "*Mija* just means little one—little girl."

Celeste took a moment to study the woman's face. Her eyes were wide and brown, darker than any she'd ever seen, and the brows above them were black, like her hair, and thinned to pretty arches. Her nose had a little hook right at the top of it; her lips were full and pink, like she'd just eaten a strawberry. And her skin—the color of cocoa after Mother had added a generous bit of milk. Graciela looked old enough to be a mother too, but Celeste knew better than to ask if she was one. It made women sad, Mother said, to ask such things.

"Are you hungry, Celeste?"

Celeste nodded and clutched her doll.

"Then why don't you and I go downstairs to the kitchen and you can help me. Would you like that?"

Celeste nodded again and reached for Graciela's hand, as she was never to walk up or down stairs without holding a grown-up's hand, unless they were the stairs at home, and this didn't feel like home yet. Graciela seemed reluctant at first, even looking over her shoulder toward Calvin's room, but then gave a quick squeeze before the two took the first step.

En route to the kitchen, Celeste got a glimpse of their new parlor, and her father's office, and a dining room, all with the familiar accoutrements and furnishings of their previous house. It was then, too, that she noticed a particular hitch to Graciela's step, reminding her of a boy back home who had one leg longer than the other.

"Why do you walk like that?" After all, Mother never warned against asking *that*.

Graciela didn't stop walking. "My leg was hurt, a very long time ago."

"How?"

"That is not a story for today, *mija.* Let's get to know one another better first."

"Why do you talk like that?"

Graciela looked down, amused. "Like what?"

"You sound different."

"I suppose it's because when I was a little girl, like you, I spoke Spanish. Only Spanish. I didn't learn to speak English until I was already a grown-up. So the words in my head are one language, but in my heart, they are another, and when they meet in my mouth, I suppose they get all tangled up."

"I think it sounds beautiful."

Graciela gave her hand another squeeze, then let go, making an abrupt turn. "This way."

While the rest of the house had the comforting advantage of familiar furnishings, the kitchen was unlike anything she remembered of home. For one thing, it was full of sunshine, with large, paneled windows looking out onto the fantastical backyard. She could see the playhouse from here, and her eyes darted over to the door that would lead straight to it, but she'd promised to help Graciela.

"What shall I do?" Celeste asked, watching the woman open the door to the largest icebox she'd ever seen and pull out a tray covered by a white cloth.

"We're making *tortas,*" Graciela said. She removed the cloth from the tray, revealing an array of sliced meat and cheese. Then she used the cloth to protect her hands as she opened the shiny oven to pull out a pan filled with delicious-smelling breads—each smaller than a loaf but bigger than a roll. She reached high into a cabinet above to bring down a pretty cut-glass bowl, then left to return shortly with a large jar of floating colors.

"*Verduras encurtidas.* Pickles. Cucumbers and carrots and peppers." She opened a drawer and took out a long-pronged fork. "Fish them out, please, and put them in the bowl."

She helped her up onto a tall stool, and Celeste dove in, at first clumsy with the unfamiliar task, but soon pleased with the colorful display. Meanwhile, Graciela sliced the breads and stuffed them with the meats and cheese, making a pyramid on the tray. She hummed a tune as she worked, one Celeste had never heard before, but after a few measures, she picked it up and began to hum along. Graciela seemed startled at first, and paused before smiling encouragingly and continuing on.

"What are those called again?" Celeste asked when the last of the little loaves had been stuffed.

"*Tortas.*"

"*Tortas,*" she repeated. "And these?"

"*Verduras encurtidas.* Pickled vegetables." Then, taking the fork from Celeste, she speared a chunk of vinegary carrot. "*Zanahorias.*"

Celeste repeated the word, then bit into the delicious, crunchy piece.

"*Pepino,*" she said, handing over an herb-crusted piece of cucumber.

"*Pepino.*" These were her favorites back home, and the taste linked the two kitchens. Then Graciela offered a long, red, shiny strip of something unfamiliar.

"*Pimiento.* A pepper, but it's sweet, not hot."

Celeste held it gingerly between her thumb and first finger. "*Pimiento?*" The color was vibrant and inviting, and she was about to bring it to her lips when Mother's voice invaded.

"Just what are you doing?"

"Señora DuFrane. Miss Celeste is such a good helper. And so smart."

Celeste beamed with pride, hoping some of the praise would warm Mother's disposition.

"You shouldn't run off like that," Mother said, slightly deflated.

"I didn't run off, Mother. This is our home."

"Yes, of course it is." She crossed over into the kitchen and placed a warm, dry kiss on Celeste's cheek.

"Pimiento," Celeste said, dangling the strip of vegetable between them. "It's a pepper. Only it's sweet, not hot."

Mother's eyes looked sad for just a second; then she opened her mouth wide, and when Celeste dangled the pepper into it, she snapped it shut, cutting the pepper in half.

"What does it taste like?"

Mother was chewing, looking quizzical. "You tell me."

Enthralled, Celeste popped the remainder into her mouth, and her senses immediately flooded.

"What do you think, *mija*?"

It was new and fresh and sweet. She looked from Graciela to her mother and said, "It tastes like California."

CHAPTER 6

DANA GOES FOR A DRIVE AND LEARNS TO HOLD ON TO HER HAT

1925

DANA HEARD THE CLATTER of shoes on the marble floor and braced herself.

"Just a minute! Just one more minute. I can't find my scarf!"

Dana smiled but remained silent. She wasn't one to holler in the house, not the way these walls echoed. And what would she say? It wasn't her place to grant or deny permission. There was a narrow, upholstered bench in the entryway by the front door. Dana sat down on it and commenced fiddling with her pocketbook. It was a small bag made of some sort of thick, tapestry-like material, with a gold-plated clasp. Nothing in it, really. Just a handkerchief, a drawstring pouch with a few coins, a small mirror, and a new lipstick. But Celeste had insisted that every girl needed to carry such things and that they needed to be carried in a pocketbook. As in everything else, Dana acquiesced.

Clatter. Clatter. Clatter.

Celeste arrived, a frothy vision in a dress of sea green and a long, gossamer scarf knotted at her throat, flowing down. How one could ever misplace such a thing, Dana didn't know. But then, for Celeste, things of beauty were not so rare.

"I'm ready!" Announced as if some great accomplishment. She stopped short in front of the large mirror in the hall for a final inspection. She wore her hair in a bob of soft curls, dark-blonde and perfectly set. She dropped a hat on top of them and tugged it down, studying the result from every angle, then turned. "Well?"

"You look lovely," Dana said, as expected.

Celeste pouted. "Wish I could say the same to you. Honestly, would it kill you to use a little bit of rouge? It's one thing to be fashionably pale, but you look absolutely dead."

Dana shrank under the younger woman's scrutiny and reached for her long-shorn hair.

"I'm sorry." Celeste moved to reach for Dana's arm, but Dana leaped to her feet before she could be tugged up and made a show of smoothing her dress.

"I didn't think," Dana said. "I don't know quite what to do, I suppose."

She found herself looking in the mirror, Celeste peeking out from behind her.

"That's understandable. But I can teach you if you want. Just a little bit to pretty you up. Make you look more modern. Younger, even."

"Do I look that old?"

"Sweetie, you're thirty-two. You *are* old. But right now, we're late. Come on."

Celeste took her hand in an inescapable grip and hollered something in Spanish before opening the door and pulling Dana outside, where an automobile waited at the edge of the short-cropped green lawn. It was the color of pale butter with bloodred leather upholstery and chrome trim that reflected the sun.

Dana eyed the empty seat behind the steering wheel. "Who is going to drive?"

"Silly-nilly." Celeste broke free and ran ahead. "I am! I'm twenty years old, you know."

Dana followed reluctantly. "Are you sure?" She'd only known Celeste for a short time, and she knew even less of automobiles, but nothing she'd seen of either made it a good idea for them to be joined together. "What about Mr. Lundi? He drove us yesterday."

"Roland is otherwise engaged." By this time she had started the car and was gripping the wheel. "Or that's what his secretary told me. *Otherwise engaged.* The coward, unless he's meeting with someone from Metro-Goldwyn. But we'll see. Are you ready?"

Before Dana could respond, Celeste pounced on the accelerator, and the two women careened into the street. Dana clutched her hat to her head, wondering how it was that Celeste's remained so perfectly perched.

"Tell me again how he seemed."

"Who?" Dana said, distracted by the neighborhood shrubbery that seemed far too close.

"Funny. Who do you think? Ostermann. Did he seem interested?"

"He listened quite closely."

"That's not what I mean." She steered the car around a corner, bringing it to a chugging near stop before roaring straight again. "The movie. Do you have any idea what it would mean to me if he went through with it? To have him write and direct a film specifically for me? What am I saying. Of course you don't. You've practically been in a cave—"

She took her eyes off the road and turned to Dana, reaching out to pat her leg. "You know what I mean, darling."

"It's fine," Dana said, pointing out the lorry come to a dead stop in front of them.

"Honestly, it would be hard for anybody to understand—anybody not in the film business. Can you understand, though, how very much I want to be a star?"

"Like that Mary Pickford?"

It was the wrong thing to say, and Celeste expressed her disagreement with a sharp swerve to the left and a fresh acceleration. They were out of the neighborhood by now, practically flying down the open road en route to the studio. The speed picked up the gossamer scarf and sent it billowing back and away from Celeste's neck, like the tail of a kite. Dana clutched at the door lest she fly with it.

"America's sweetheart, my aunt Pansy. She's not even American, you know. She's Canadian. Those sausage curls, like she's some sort of stunted schoolgirl. And I swear, if Lundi books me to play one more wide-eyed farmer's daughter—"

The blare of an approaching vehicle's horn kept Celeste from finishing the thought. Dana's stomach flipped over, and since she couldn't leap out of the car to save herself, she'd try to save the conversation instead.

"I'll tell him everything. And when I do, he'll want to tell everybody."

By the time they arrived at the studio gate, Dana felt a thin sheen of sweat on the back of her neck, and she took the blessed moment when Celeste chatted with the guard to exhale the breath she'd been holding for most of the twenty-minute drive. As Celeste maneuvered the car through the studio grounds, a host of people either waved in greeting or dove out of the way—or both. She parked the car in front of the low-ceilinged, plain white building labeled *Offices of Rolling Arts Entertainment*, Werner Ostermann's production company.

Celeste took a mirror from her purse and checked her lipstick and her hair, smiling at different angles while batting her eyes. In a spirit of camaraderie, Dana did the same, holding her little square mirror far enough away to be able to see most of her face. The brisk ride had brought a hint of color to her cheeks, and her hat managed to drift a bit to a most becoming angle. With an unsteady hand, she pulled the lid off the tube of lipstick and touched it to the center of her bottom lip.

"That's it," Celeste said with a gentleness Dana had never heard from her before. "Just at the bottom, where your lips are their fullest? And then the top. Then do this." She mashed her own vermilion lips together, hiding them into one thin line, then popped them out again. Dana followed suit, feeling more self-conscious about this act than she had the actual application.

"Perfect," Celeste said, and a quick check to her reflection brought Dana to the same conclusion. Maybe not perfect, but better. Brighter.

She almost smiled, saying, "Thank you," as she fastened the clasp on her pocketbook.

A young man wearing something like a uniform had arrived to open the car door for Dana, then ran to the opposite side to do the same for Celeste, who acknowledged him with a singular movement that encapsulated a wink and a shrug and a curtsy. He tipped his hat and waggled his eyebrows and muttered something about getting behind the wheel of that chassis sometime, prompting her to slap him playfully on the shoulder before beckoning Dana to follow.

"Ma'am," he said with all the deference a young man would have for his elder. Still, Dana kept a wide berth as she passed.

Inside the tidy office, Miss Lynch looked up from her typewriter, her expression not changing in the least.

"Good afternoon, Miss Lundgren." Then, noticing Celeste, her face lit up. "And Miss DuFrane! What a wonderful surprise to see you here."

"Hello, Kippy." Celeste extended her hand. "We're here to see Mr. Ostermann. Is he in?"

"Just one moment." She stood, tucked a pencil behind her ear, and made brisk work of walking from her desk to the door with his name printed in thick, black letters on the clouded glass.

We? The thought of telling her story, in all its detail, in the presence of this girl of all people was enough to freeze every unspoken word. Dana swallowed, summoning her courage. "I don't think it's a good idea for you to come in with me."

"Really? I think it would be marvelous. Especially if he decides to let me star in the picture. I'm a part of it, after all."

"You're not a part of what I'm telling him. These are things—events—before you were born. And after, I suppose. Still, they've nothing to do with you."

"But if I'm to play you—"

"Eager as ever, I see." Werner Ostermann stood in the doorway to his office. His shirtsleeves were rolled up to the elbow, and an unlit cigarette dangled from his fingers. "Casting yourself before there is even a script?"

"Well, a girl can't wait around forever, can she?" She held out her hand, sending a cascade of bangles clattering toward her elbow as Ostermann brought it to his lips.

Dana offered no such opportunity, but he greeted her with no less warmth before returning his attentions to Celeste.

"I had lunch with Frank Borzage yesterday, you know. He said you did fine work in *The Dixie Merchant*."

"Just a bit part," Celeste said, pouting. "But I know I could do more, given the opportunity."

"Time will tell." He spoke with the gentleness of a father, closing the conversation but leaving plenty of room for hope, as was evidenced by Celeste's triumphant grin.

"It will indeed."

"Now, I will be occupied with Miss Lundgren for the next hour or so. Do you have something to do while you wait?"

"Oh." Her pretty lips formed the letter and the word. "I thought I might . . . That is, I was wondering if I couldn't sit in."

"I don't think that would be a good idea," he said, much to Dana's relief. She couldn't help but feel her own twinge of triumph. "Wait here." He disappeared into his office and immediately returned with a book. "Publishers are always sending me these things. Who has time? You read it and let me know if it is a good story or not."

"Oh," Celeste said again. "All right." She took the book and held it as if experiencing the sensation for the first time. Dana felt a familiar twinge of jealousy. Imagine, someone inviting you to read a book. A brand-new one, just given away.

"And you can sit at Miss Lynch's place, if you like. If Lon Chaney calls, take a message."

"Yes, sir, Mr. Ostermann." Celeste seemed far more pleased at the idea than did Miss Lynch, who plucked five sharpened pencils from the clay cup on her desk before holding the door to let Dana pass.

Not until she crossed the threshold did Dana realize she'd been waiting to return to this room. It was, to date, the one place in California where she felt comfortable. Celeste's home was nothing but one wide-open space flowing into another. The streets outside were loud and crowded. Even the sky loomed too large to feel like it could pin itself at the corners and hold creation. Ostermann's office was small and somewhat dark. Easier for her eyes even after Miss Lynch lit the lamp in the corner where she sat. It smelled of paper and cigarettes—warmth. The chair she'd occupied before waited for her again, and without being asked, she sat down.

"You are doing well?" Ostermann asked as he settled himself behind his cluttered desk.

"Yes, thank you, Mr. Ostermann."

"Call me Werner. And you and Miss DuFrane? You are getting better acquainted?"

Dana nodded. "She's not . . . home, very often."

"Youth," he said, then immediately looked uncomfortable. "But to matters at hand. What shall we talk about today? Would you perhaps like to tell me about the night you were arrested?"

She felt herself grow cold, her blood as frigid as the rain that had pelted the windows during the storm that night. He'd asked the same question at their last meeting, and the purposefulness behind the question proved he hadn't simply forgotten. It was some sort of a trick. A trap, maybe, but she took a familiar step aside.

"I told you already. I don't remember much about that." Though she did, every detail. The color felt thick upon her lips, and she dared not close her mouth lest she not be able to open it again. "Only what's been told to me."

"No, no. Tell me only what you know. What you remember and what you saw and what you heard. I need to see this all revealed through your eyes. Perhaps something about the trial."

"There was no trial, Mr. Ostermann. If there had been, perhaps there'd be no story at all."

"But there had to have been—"

"An inquest. A coroner's inquest in the DuFrane home, because Mrs. DuFrane was too distraught to leave the house. Right there in the front parlor, where I'd been serving tea just a few days before."

And here, finally, she would have the chance to speak.

CHAPTER 7

INTERIOR: A well-appointed parlor decorated in a lush Victorian style. Center is an ornate wooden table, long and narrow, where three distinguished men wearing dark suits sit in a line. The man on the far left is the county coroner. He is reading aloud from an official-looking dossier.

CLOSE-UP: Typewritten certificate of death.

FOCUS: *Cause of death: suffocation.*

CUT TO: Young Dana, set apart from the gathered company.

CUT TO: Mr. and Mrs. DuFrane, she draped in magnificent Victorian mourning clothes. She has collapsed in her chair and weeps into the handkerchief proffered by her husband.

CUT TO: Young Dana, obviously watching, her expression inscrutable.

1904

"WE WILL NOW HEAR the testimony of Mr. Arthur DuFrane," the judge intoned.

Mr. DuFrane, handsome in a perfectly tailored black suit, carefully extricated himself from his wife and stood before the illustrious trio, where he was told to recount all that he could to exact detail.

"There was a horrific storm, if you remember," Mr. DuFrane said as a lead-in to his testimony.

Mama said he was a scientist—an inventor and professor, too—something Mrs. DuFrane's family highly disapproved of. Now he addressed the three men at the table as if they were schoolboys, and they seemed no less pleased.

"The storm is not relevant," the judge said.

"My apologies. I was simply trying to be thorough. My recollection is somewhat handicapped, as we had hosted a social event, and my head was not entirely clear when I retired. I'm afraid that makes for a restless night's sleep. The storm woke me, is what I meant to say."

"And that is why you went to the girl's room?"

"If you are referring to my daughter's room—the nursery—yes."

The judge acknowledged Mr. DuFrane's clarification, but with a skeptical eye.

The man to the right of the judge had been introduced as the prosecuting attorney, and he asked his questions with a formal reserve.

"You felt a need to check on her, even though the accused occupied the same room?"

"With all due respect," Mr. DuFrane said, though he didn't sound like he held much respect at all, "Dana is not an experienced nanny. It is not unheard of for a father to ensure the welfare of his children."

"Just tell us what you saw," the judge said with an impatient check of his watch.

Mr. DuFrane looked at Dana as if begging for mercy of his own, and she wished beyond all that she could grant it. Unfortunately, she had no power to absolve him of the sort of accusations she didn't fully understand. In fact, she'd been forbidden to speak—in her defense or his.

In that moment of silence she felt herself back in that room, lit by intermittent flashes of lightning, but otherwise dark. She could feel the baby next to her small, bare breast, as she prayed her life would be strong enough to transfer warmth. Skin to skin, the way her own mother used to do on the coldest winter nights. But there was no warmth and there was no breath—only cold, dead weight.

Mr. DuFrane's version was almost as cold. "She was standing near the crib. Holding the baby."

At this, Mrs. DuFrane cried out, "She killed my baby!" calling the judge to vigorously rap his knuckles against the table.

"If you cannot contain yourself, Mrs. DuFrane, I shall have no choice but to exclude your presence from these proceedings."

Not for the first time, Dana wished her own mother could be in attendance so that she, too, might cry out on behalf of Dana's life. It had been explained to her, however, by the judge himself, that only those who were witnesses to the event, or who held any medical expertise, would be allowed to testify. As her mother hadn't arrived at the house until well into the morning, after somebody had thought to send for her, she held no place in either category.

The prosecuting attorney asked, "Did the accused say anything to you?"

"She was deeply upset. Crying in an uncontrollable fashion. Nothing intelligible."

"And did you have an occasion to examine your daughter?"

"I did."

Dana remembered the moment. He took the baby from her so gently, as if equally afraid of hurting her as the baby. She remembered the touch of his knuckle against her bare skin. No man had ever touched her before.

"And she was, in your opinion as a man of science, deceased at that point?"

Only the quickest clench of his jaw and a rapid succession of blinking betrayed anything other than a biological conclusion. "She was."

"If I may interrupt," the coroner said, looking up from a sheet of paper rife with handwritten notes, "in our initial conversation, you mentioned an unusual marking on the baby's face. Do you recall?"

"I do."

"Can you explain? Describe?"

He glanced at Dana again, his eyes clearly pleading for forgiveness, and she turned away, only to find Mrs. DuFrane staring at her with murderous fury. Shivering, she wished—if nothing else—she might never have to see that woman again.

"It looked like lace," Mr. DuFrane said with a catch in his voice that made him stop midsentence and repeat himself before answering what would surely be the next question. "Like the lace of one of her pillows."

"And where was that pillow found?"

"It was in her crib. In Mary's crib."

"Had it been there when the child was put to bed?"

"Honestly," he said as if to give weight to his words, "I don't know."

Mrs. DuFrane could contain herself no longer. "No! No, it wasn't!" She pointed a shaking, accusing finger at Dana, and it seared through her like a lance. "I saw her holding it, saying how unfair it was for my baby to have such pretty things! I saw it in *her* hands! And then—"

Once again, the judge pounded on his table, and Mr. DuFrane went to his wife's side, took her in his arms, and soothed her as he would a child.

"Take her out," the judge ordered. Mr. DuFrane complied, leaving Dana alone to face the trio in the echo of a mother's grief.

CHAPTER 8

CELESTE, AGE 6

1911

NO SNOW. Ever, ever, never. She sat on her window seat, face pressed against the cool glass pane, and looked out over the lush, green yard. Behind her, Graciela could be heard humming a familiar tune as she spread the quilted coverlet.

"*Cómo se dice* snow *en español*, Graciela?"

"Nieve." She embedded the tune in her reply.

She wondered if Graciela had ever seen snow, and asked. *"Alguna vez has visto la nieve?"*

"*Sí.* When I was a little girl, like you. We lived in a village in the mountains."

"Did you make snowmen?"

Graciela chuckled, a sound as warm as the day, prompting Celeste to turn around to look at her. Her dark hair was tucked into a neat bun at the nape of her neck, wrapped by a rope of thick braid. From the number of times the woman had attended to her bedside during late-night illness and nightmares, Celeste knew it descended well below her waist and always smelled sweet.

"El coco," she'd said when Celeste asked. Coconut.

"El coco." For months she begged for the coconut-scented shampoo, but Mother would buy nothing but Canthrox. Sometimes, though, when Mother was away, Graciela would bring her brownish bottle of sweet-smelling soap and wash Celeste's hair—even if it wasn't a Saturday. On those nights she would sleep with her hair splayed out on the pillow, rather than her usual neat plait, and be lulled to sleep by the warm, sweet scent.

"No, *mija*," Graciela said, arranging a few of Celeste's favorite dolls on the pillows, "always too much work to do."

Celeste sighed and turned back to the window. "I miss snow," she said, though already the memories of those bitter-cold afternoons were fading. "Mother says it doesn't feel like Christmas without it."

Graciela made a sound reserved for conversations about Mother, something like a puff of steam, and muttered, *"Qué fría"*—something she often said even when they weren't talking about the cold.

"How long is it until Christmas?"

"Nine days," Graciela said.

Celeste translated *nueve* in her head but said nothing. That Graciela taught her little phrases and words was a wonderful secret they shared. She was about to ask more questions, whether Santa Claus would remember to find her here, whether or not she would really get the pony Daddy promised, or whether Graciela would take her to the store to buy a gift for her horrible brother, when movement in the backyard called her attention.

It was her father, looking handsome as always in a brown tweed jacket and a new cap pulled down over one eye. Another man followed, carrying a large, square black case, and there were also two women with bright-colored dresses peeking out from under woolen coats they clutched closed beneath their chins.

Curious, she pressed her nose against the glass, mindless of the smudge. The women stood on either side of her father, each with a gloved hand on his shoulder. One puffed at a cigarette held in a long, thin stem; the other tilted her head back in a laugh that carried itself like a galloping horse right up to Celeste's ear.

She sensed Graciela behind her. *"Qué pasa?"*

"Daddy," Celeste said, and though her own voice coming from so far away surely could not compete with the laughter of the woman beside him, her father looked up. He touched the brim of his hat and, in so doing, shrugged the women away. They, in turn, looked to see what had called away his attention, shielding their eyes beneath their velvet hats.

"Do you know them, Graciela?" Perhaps they'd attended one of the grown-up parties Celeste had witnessed from the top of the stairs.

"Mujeres fáciles." Even without translation, Celeste knew this was not a compliment.

In the backyard, Daddy was motioning for her to come down, and the lady with the cigarette twisted her lips, not pleased.

Celeste looked to Graciela for permission. "Should I go?"

"Sí." She took a thick, warm sweater from the brass tree standing beside the bedroom door and popped it over Celeste's head. "And I'll make some hot chocolate for you to have with your lunch later."

She gave the little girl a soft tap on her bottom, their unspoken permission to run in the house—granted only when Mother wasn't home.

On this day, she had gone back to Chicago, she said, to sell their old house. According to the arguments that echoed throughout *this* house, their former home was a fortune of bricks and emptiness, part of an old life that neither wanted to remember.

It was impossible to tell which parent was more angry, or why either of them cared, but in the end it had been Mother to pack her bag and board a train, saying it was best to keep such things in the family.

Celeste ran to the stairs, then waited for Graciela to descend before climbing onto the banister and sliding down the varnished wood. Once she landed safely on the bottom step, she clattered through the entryway, delighting at the echo of her footsteps, and tore through the kitchen, pausing only long enough to take a pinch of ginger cake left on a plate on the counter.

Outside, the air was cold, with a hint of salt from the ocean that Mother said they couldn't visit again until spring. The two women were sitting on the little iron bench flanked by empty rosebushes, their heads tipped together as if conspiring. Celeste's father and the other man worked together settling a camera atop a tripod. She wanted to tug at his coat to get his attention, but she knew he didn't like to be disturbed when he was working, so she moved to put him between herself and the women and waited for him to notice her.

"Sure we don't need more light?" The other gentleman crouched to look through the lens.

"This is perfect," her father said with an air of authority that made Celeste go to her toes with pride. "Too much, and the color would bleed into the reflection."

"So you're saying we'll only be able to make movies on hazy days?"

"I'm saying we'll develop screens and shades, but that will have to come with initial investors. For now—"

He'd taken a step back, bumping right into Celeste, and bent to sweep her up in his arms.

"There's my girl!" He carried her over to the little iron bench, holding her high enough that the two women had to crane their necks to look at her. "Which of you two ladies wants to play Mother?"

Their faces froze into crimson-lined smiles, and one of them managed to speak without seeming to move her lips at all.

"You never said anything about working with a kid."

"Adorable as she is," the other added quickly.

"I want to capture as many different scenes as I can," Daddy said, hitching Celeste closer to his side. "Including action and high motion, and I don't fancy either of you running with abandon through the yard."

"I told you already I'd do whatever motion you wanted," the woman with the cigarette said. She reached out and pinched at Daddy's pant leg, making Celeste want to kick her hand away.

"Making you not quite the ideal mother material, I suppose." He set Celeste down on the ground and pointed her toward the other woman. "Celeste, sweetheart, this is Edie."

"Abby," she said, darting her eyes first up to Daddy and then down to Celeste.

"Sorry."

"Charmed." Abby held out her hand, and at her father's prompting, Celeste shook it.

"Now," Daddy continued, "I'm going to be filming . . ."

"Nadine," the woman prompted.

"Nadine, over by the trellis. Abby, if you wouldn't mind, maybe add a touch of color to my girl, just the lips and cheeks?"

"Of course." But she looked like she minded quite a bit.

Celeste took the abandoned seat on the bench and watched over Abby's shoulder as Daddy helped Nadine out of her coat, despite the woman's protest of the chilly temperature.

"I'm not asking you to trek across the Klondike," he said.

"I need to capture the color of your dress. Any camera can pick up a black coat. There, over by the hibiscus, please." And when Nadine looked confused, he took her elbow and turned her toward Graciela's pride and joy—the perpetually bright, flowering plant in the corner of the garden.

"Hey, kid," Abby said. "Look here."

She'd taken a small jar out of her purse and held it open in the palm of one hand, the fingers of the other dipped in. "Do this." She spread her lips into a long, thin smile, and Celeste did her best to imitate it and not back away when Abby touched her rouge-tipped fingers to her cheeks. "Now blend." She demonstrated by rubbing her own fingers in a circular motion on her already-pink cheeks, and once again Celeste mimicked the action.

"Mother wouldn't approve," Celeste said, hoping not to rub it all away.

"Well, I ain't a mother. Now pucker. Like a kiss."

Celeste did so and, without prompting, squeezed her lips together to work the dabbed-on color to a perfect tint, though Mother would have had a much different way to describe it, using words that Celeste dared not even think.

"Can I see?"

"See what?" Abby applied an unnecessary layer to her own lips before screwing on the lid.

"Me. Can I run inside and look in the mirror?"

"Here." She reached inside her purse again and produced a small compact, from which she withdrew a circle of powder-flecked cotton and dabbed at her nose. Celeste took the proffered mirror and saw her own familiar face, now enhanced with new color, and puckered her lips again.

"I look like a lady in a magazine," she said, in awe of this new beauty.

"You got a ways to go before that." Abby took the compact away, snapped it shut, and turned to look at the scene behind her. "That one—*she* could be in a magazine."

Celeste leaned forward, wishing her father would move out of the way so she could get a better view. She tugged at Abby's sleeve. "Do you want to go up on the patio? It might be a little warmer."

"Sure. Heaven forbid, I suppose, we could wait inside."

"I can't invite strangers in."

Abby gave a short laugh. "Good policy, sister."

Making a wide arc around her father and the cameraman, she led the woman to the covered patio, where they sat on cushioned rattan chairs facing the yard. From here, she could see everything. The cameraman's arm worked furiously, turning the handle on the wooden box, his head buried beneath a square black cloth.

"That's it," Daddy was saying. "Now touch the flowers. Go ahead, lean in and smell it; then look at me."

Nadine followed his instructions, running her tapered fingers across the blossoms as if encountering such a thing for the first time in her life. She looked over her shoulder. "Can I pick one?"

"Of course," Daddy said, and Celeste drew in a sharp breath. Not even Mother touched any of the flowers in the garden without Graciela's guidance.

Nadine plucked a flower from the bush and turned to face the camera. She held it up to her nose and then ran the petals across her lips as if they had somehow contributed to the stain. Even from this vantage point, Celeste knew she wasn't looking at the camera, but at Daddy. She held her head down somewhat and looked up, her eyelids heavy, almost like she was sleepy.

"Hussy," Abby said, and while Celeste didn't recognize that word any more than the Spanish term Graciela had used when they were looking on from upstairs, once again the tone was unmistakably insulting.

"Beautiful," Daddy said, straightening his stance and putting his hand on his hip.

"Why, thank you," Nadine said. She'd removed her hat along with her coat, revealing chestnut-colored hair coiled and pinned at the nape of her neck. She took the flower now and tucked it just above her ear, thrusting her bust forward as she did so.

"How does that look?" she asked, tilting her head to give the best possible view.

"Beautiful," Daddy said again, but slower this time. "Blow me a kiss, sweetheart. Right to the camera."

Nadine complied.

"Now a little twirl."

And she twirled. Her plum-colored skirt fluted out toward the hem, and she staggered just a bit when she stopped, facing the camera. She giggled like she was one of Celeste's schoolgirl friends rather than a grown woman.

"Sorry about that. One more spin and you'd have to come catch me. I guess I didn't miss my calling as a dancer after all."

"Sweetie, you don't miss anything," Abby said, though far too softly for Nadine to have heard her.

When Daddy said, "Cut," the cameraman's arm stopped its motion, and he stood straight, emerging from the black cloth covering.

"What do you think?"

"What do I think? I think it's a good thing your kid's in the audience."

Daddy laughed and turned toward the porch, opening his arms. "Come here, Celi!"

At any other time, Celeste would have run to him, sometimes

making him tumble under the force of her jump into his embrace, but the scrutinizing eyes of Abby and Nadine slowed her steps, and it felt like she was walking in wet sand rather than the small-stoned path that trailed through the yard and garden. When she finally reached him, he took her hand, called for Abby to follow, and walked her to the brightly colored playhouse in the corner.

"Now—" Daddy squatted down to her eye level—"I want you to look right out at me and say, as clearly as you can, 'Come find me, Mama!' Then duck into your playhouse and shut the door."

"But Mother isn't here," Celeste said, looking into his eyes for some sign that he was telling a joke.

"That's me," Abby said, not sounding at all thrilled. "I'm the mama."

Celeste cupped her hands around her mouth and came in close enough to smell her father's shaving soap. "She's not my mother, and I don't like her."

"Oh, darling." He hugged her close and nuzzled his moustache in the crook of her neck, tickling in the way that usually made her laugh, then pulled back to his arm's length. "We're just pretending. Like you do with your dolls, how you pretend to be their mother? Think of it in reverse. You're a real little girl, and she is like a great big doll."

"Now that I like," Abby said.

Celeste scowled at her. "Nobody asked you."

Daddy strengthened his grip to get her attention. "Be kind. We're only going to play for a few minutes. You will say, 'Mama! Come find me!' then hide in your playhouse. When I call to you again, you will come running out, look at Miss Abby, run up to her, and hug her."

Celeste pondered this for a moment. "If I want her to come

find me, why do I open the door at all? Why don't I stay inside and hide?"

"And that," the cameraman said, "is why you're some kind of scientist and not a director."

Daddy chuckled and stood. "What do you suggest?" His question was no doubt directed to any of the grown-ups standing around them, but it was Celeste who answered.

"She should come look through the window and pretend not to see me. And then—" Celeste moved away from her father and stood next to the playhouse—"pretend to look and say, 'Cel-leste? Where are you?' And *then* I'll come outside because I'll think I fooled her."

Daddy's look of pride warmed her more than any sun ever could.

"How did you think of all that?"

"That's how Graciela plays." She didn't mention that sometimes she pretended Graciela was her mother.

"Well, then, that's how we'll do it." Daddy told the cameraman to set up the next shot and told Abby to take off her coat and hat, making her look like any other mother out playing with her daughter on a lovely day. He bent back down to Celeste and kissed the tip of her nose. "You look beautiful, sunshine."

She felt beautiful just because he said so, and determined to do the very best that she could to please him. Soon the cameraman's arm was turning the handle, and at her father's direction, she stood in front of the playhouse. Looking past Abby's sullen figure, she saw Graciela standing in the open kitchen door, looking on. She wanted to break away, run into her soft folds, and inhale the familiar scent of coconut and flour, but the sound of the camera took over, and instead she smiled, giving license to her fantasy, and pressed her lips together before saying, "Mama! Come find me!" exaggerating every word and giving a little shrug and a giggle before ducking into her playhouse. She gave one long, sneaky look from behind the door before closing it.

From the semidarkness inside, she could hear Abby shuffling around outside, apparently not doing anything the way Daddy told her to because he kept saying the same things over and over.

Then her face filled the window, blocking out the light, invading the familiar smell of musty lumber with that of a heavy perfume.

"Hey, kid. Don't make me look bad."

Celeste couldn't imagine what she meant by that, and she wished she could stay inside her playhouse until her real mother came home. Or until Graciela called her in for lunch and hot chocolate.

"Act like you're looking for her," Daddy was saying. "Put your hand up, like this. No, like this, like you're searching. Like this." And then, with an air of frustration, he summoned Celeste outside. Although it wasn't exactly how they had planned, Celeste popped her head out the window and said, "Here I am!" her eyes finding Abby rather than the camera. Then she swung open the door and stood in the threshold.

"Go to her," Daddy said.

Celeste brought her hand to her mouth as if to stifle a giggle, knowing it would hide the movement of her lips from the camera. "She needs to kneel down, or they won't see me."

"Get down, Abby," Daddy ordered.

There was nothing about the woman's expression that made her look like a loving mother. "I'll get my dress all dirty."

"I'll pay for the cleaning."

Reluctantly Abby knelt in the soft grass.

"Oh, Mama." Celeste took two small steps and wrapped her

arms around Abby's neck, gently turning their bodies so that she could face the camera head-on. She looked straight into the lens, then up at the sky, pretending to thank God for giving her such a wonderful mother, not letting go until Graciela called her in for lunch.

CHAPTER 9

THE WRITTEN CONFESSION OF MARGUERITE DUFRANE, PAGES 13–24

IT DOES NOT ESCAPE my attention that whatever respect you may have for me will be exhaled forever away before you reach the end of this writing, if indeed I have the courage to write all of the truth as I have been instructed. There are some secrets that are best taken to our graves. For example, did you know that your father had a dwarfed sixth toe on his left foot? Of course you didn't, as his vanity and propriety never allowed him to be barefoot in any kind of company—not even that of his loving family. I myself only got a glimpse of the thing on sporadic occasions and learned early in our marriage never to comment on it, lest I raise his ire and prompt him to comment on my own flaws. It may seem a silly thing now, but I believe his quest for education and influence came from the constant reminder of his imperfection. The night your brother announced that he was going to sign up to fight in the War, I told your father it was too bad that polydactyly (for such the condition is named) was not an inheritable trait, as it might have made Calvin unsuitable for service.

"How do you know that term?" he asked, as if I had no right to speak it. "Whom have you shared this with?"

I told him nobody, that I'd merely come across it in a medical book when I first took the children to our city library.

Nothing, though, would assuage his anger, and as I recall, he didn't speak to me for nearly a week.

But listen to me, waxing on about something of so little consequence. Stalling, I suppose. Or distracting myself, as I have always done since Mary died. I barely left the baby's room for weeks, only for the funeral, and of that I have very little recollection. I slept on the floor; I didn't eat. Your father has since said he feared he would lose us both.

The first clear memory I have after putting my Mary to bed is the sight of your father's face, close to mine, waking me from a midafternoon stupor to tell me her death had been ruled a homicide, and the girl was locked up in jail. I don't know what I'd been waiting for—some obscene fear that she might return with that envious hunger I'd seen and take the rest of my family away, perhaps.

I got up, took a bath, dressed in something fresh and clean. I went down to the kitchen and ate anything I could find. For weeks neighbors had been bringing meals—roasted chicken and hams and cakes and breads. I'd refused plates of food and bowls of soups, and now every uneaten morsel gnawed at me. I remembered what it felt like to have my belly full with my child, and I thought maybe I would be able to fill myself up again and bring her back. I pulled platters from the icebox and rummaged through the pantry, tearing at food with my bare hands, barely swallowing one bite before stuffing my mouth with another.

Mrs. Gibbons found me and offered to heat something proper, but I sent her away. To the market, I'd said, to get something fresh. Fruit, perhaps, or some sweet berries to mix with cream to take away some of the staleness of the leftover cakes.

I ate everything, tasted nothing. Not even the sound of the front door's bell deterred me. After all, I'd been hearing it for weeks. Well-wishers and officials and I don't know who all had dropped by, and I'd ignored them. It rang and I ate, caring no more about what or who might be on the other side than I did about the stains of congealed grease on the cuffs of my clean dress. Whoever it was would go away, and certainly had, I reasoned, when the ringing finally stopped. But then a small voice came to me as I shaved a slice of cheese.

"Mother?"

It was, of course, Calvin, looking properly dapper in his school clothes, wearing the black velvet band around his sleeve as his testimony of mourning for his sister. He seemed such a big boy, but no more a part of me than any other child. I hadn't touched him since the night I kissed his head, having dismissed him from that awful party. Vaguely I remembered hearing his voice on the other side of the nursery door, your father telling him that Mother wasn't feeling well yet and that she would be better soon. *Soon* has little meaning to a child's mind, and he eventually stopped coming to the door. I couldn't remember the last time the boy had even crossed my mind. His very name eluded me in that moment, and I simply stared until all the letters tumbled into place and I could say *Calvin* with some confidence.

"There's a lady at the door."

A lady?

"Mrs. Lundgren."

The food in my stomach worked itself into a panic, and I clutched to keep it still. Fearful it would spew out if I opened my mouth, I held my jaw clenched and told him to send her away.

"She asked for Father, and I told her he wasn't home. And then she asked for you, and I said you were sick, so then she just told me she would wait for Father."

She *told* him? As if she had any right to tell anybody anything.

"Are you feeling better?" My little man stood, his eyes taking in the mess of soiled dishes and platters scattered throughout the kitchen. It's then that I noticed the circles under his eyes, his pale skin, and a mixture of fear and sadness that should have been far beyond his years.

I told him to go upstairs and play, handing him the slice of cheese, which he took with dubious thanks. I assured him I would speak with Mrs. Lundgren once I'd had enough time to put on the kettle for tea and that he shouldn't give the visit another thought. This pleased him, and he bounded up the kitchen stairs, whistling a popular tune of the day. It was the first bit of life I'd seen since putting my Mary to bed that night, and I watched and listened, hating him for every bit of it. I suppose that, too, is a confession I hadn't foreseen making in this document, but there it is. Once his existence came back to my realm of consciousness, I resented his very being. Every breath he took was one Mary would be forever denied. Never again could I smile at my baby girl, so I refused to smile at him. My daughter was cold, and I adopted the same frigidity. It seemed grotesquely reasonable at the time, and his father experienced no such interruption to his affection, so I left them to each other's good graces.

Not forever, of course. When you came into our lives, darling Celeste, you brought life with you. But in that dark time, those months stretched out between Mary's death and your birth, poor Calvin had little more than a shell for a mother. And yet, remembering the blackness in my heart, I wouldn't dare to wish to return and make things right. I couldn't change a thing, you see, because if I did, I might not have you.

I did not, of course, put on a kettle of water to make tea to share with Mrs. Lundgren. Instead I poured a glass of cold buttermilk, drank it down, and waited for the rest of my food to settle while I used a soiled towel to attempt to clean my face and hands. Mrs. Gibbons had a small room behind the kitchen, and I popped in there long enough to inspect my dress and hair in the oval mirror above her washstand. The gauntness of my face was somewhat surprising, as I'd always had such rounded features; and my hair, for all its neatness, was dull, like that of an old woman. All I really cared about, though, was that there were no traces of crumbs on my bodice, nor any particles trapped between my teeth, and a close inspection granted that assurance.

The sound of a mighty battle being waged with wooden soldiers drifted from Calvin's room upstairs, and I prepared myself for a battle of my own as I walked to the entryway to see just what Mrs. Lundgren could have to say to us. Upon seeing an empty hall, I felt a surge of relief, thinking the woman had come to the end of her patience and left, but then I saw a shabby coat and fashionless hat hanging on the brass tree, and I knew Calvin must have invited her to wait in the parlor. Certainly, knowing her place in our home, she wouldn't have invited herself to such a privilege. I hated him even more.

Shoulders straight, I walked into the parlor to find her sitting—*sitting*—with her hands in her lap, staring at the floor. I allowed myself the luxury of staring at her, this woman whose child had killed my child. Were I of a lesser species or lower class, I might have lunged at her. A life for a life, as God once instructed his people. But then she looked up at me, her gaze like iron, and we took turns stating facts.

"They may put my daughter in prison."

Your daughter killed my child.

"She's little more than a child herself."

I had no response to that, so I simply asked her what she meant by coming here.

"I'd hoped to speak with Mr. DuFrane."

I told her he wasn't at home, having no other information to add. Whether he was at his lab, or at the club, or swinging from a skyscraper, I had no idea. I couldn't be sure he'd been here this morning, or the night before, but I had no reason to indulge that level of detail, and I had no answer to her query as to when he would return. I did, however, tell her that I thought it highly improper for her to come to call on Mr. DuFrane when all matters of the household should clearly be handled by me.

"I'd heard you weren't feeling well."

When I asked her who'd said such a thing, she said, "Everyone," with an unsettling shift to her eyes.

I pointed out that I was obviously well enough to meet with her now and insisted upon a response to the order of her business.

She looked up at me—and I say *up* because in all this time I'd refused to sit with her and she apparently lacked the training to know that, again, given our social differences and the fact that she was a sometime employee of our home, she should be the one to stand in my presence. Her gaze, however, seemed to bring us to an equal plane, and without a trace of humility, she said, "I've come to ask you to help me bring her home."

My knees threatened to buckle, and I clutched the back of the sofa to retain my place of superiority.

"My daughter. My Dana. You have to help me bring her home."

But she killed my child.

"She didn't. She couldn't have. And as a mother, you have to realize that. They wouldn't let me testify at the hearing, since I wasn't a witness to . . . whatever happened." She at least had the good sense to look embarrassed. "My hands are tied, you see. But you, or Arthur—I mean, Mr. DuFrane—he was there."

The sound of her voice saying my husband's name brought

my too-full stomach to roiling again, and I held my fingers to my lips in an effort to stem the sickness within before asking if that, then, was the reason she particularly wanted to visit with him instead of me.

"Yes," she said, looking a little sick herself. She picked at a pill on her wool skirt, her roughened hands snagging on the fabric. "I have heard his account. I was allowed to read his testimony, after. Nothing he says implicates Dana as having done anything . . . wrong."

I repeated again the only truth that mattered to me. My child is dead. And then I asked her to leave.

"Please," she begged. Her eyes filled with tears and she held her hands as if addressing me in prayer. "I need my daughter."

More than I need mine?

She hesitated long enough that I knew she was considering her answer, which tipped my emptiness to fury, strengthening me in a way peace never could. I didn't ask her to leave again; I ordered her to do so, stepping back to make a wide berth and stretching my arm in a grand gesture toward the door.

She stood. "I wish there was something I could do to bring your Mary back. I have prayed every night to wake up and find this all to be a dream, but there is nothing I can do. I cannot bring your little girl back to you. But please listen to me—hear me as a mother. You could bring *mine* back to *me*. One word to the judge, and there wouldn't even be a trial. Certainly you don't believe that my Dana—"

I covered my ears, insisting that she stop. Surely she didn't expect me to extol Dana's virtues, not when I'd seen her to be a selfish, covetous girl. I told her about that evening, how Dana had touched everything in my baby's room, complaining how unfair it was that some had more than others.

"You are certainly misremembering. She is a good girl; you know that. You have known her since she was—"

A baby, I completed. And she's obviously grown up with a bitter spirit that has fooled us all.

Something changed in her expression as I spoke, a hardening I hadn't anticipated and couldn't explain. First her lips stretched thin, as if reinforcing themselves to hold back what she wanted to say, and her eyes—a distinctive grayish, mossy color—narrowed, one more so than the other.

"I can see that you are too steeped in mourning. I will wait and talk with Mr. DuFrane. I don't think any of us will want this to end with any more unhappiness than it needs to."

There it was, an unmistakable threat. Her gaze made me uncomfortable, and I felt every advantage I had of wealth and power and grief begin to slip into weakness. On the cusp of acquiescing, I looked away, intending to gather my thoughts and my strength. It was a fleeting moment, and I will always wonder if it didn't happen by her express design, but there was something in her stance: the way her posture formed a sway to her back and her hands rested protectively across her stomach. I'd held my stomach in just such a way too, grasping at the phantom remains of my murdered child. But Mrs. Lundgren had no such haunting. I knew in that moment she had a thriving life within her, and a fresh wave of injustice washed through me.

Without a trace of doubt, I asked her when her baby was due.

At first, she looked guilty, almost ashamed, and I suppose that is only fitting, given that she was not—as far as I knew—married, not to mention she was in the presence of a woman who had so recently lost an infant child. What was it her wretched daughter had said that night? That if we are all God's children, it didn't seem fair for some to have so much and others so little. Yet here we stood, two of his children. I with my child ripped away, and the mother of the murderer poised to be comforted with new life. In just a few months' time, she would have two thriving, healthy children, and I would forever have only one.

"End of April," she said, "as far as I can figure." She spoke it as a fact, devoid of any sense of joy. Further proof that she did not deserve such a blessing.

I confided in her that I would never be able to have another child, something that had been a confidence held between Dr. Hudson and myself. For reasons you might understand later, when you are a married woman with a husband of fleeting interest and questionable fidelity, I hadn't even shared this with your father. The successful end to my pregnancy with Mary had been an unquestionable miracle, one I should never again presume that God would perform. Just one of many secrets held between myself and the Almighty, as Arthur and I continued with the responsibilities a wife and a husband owe to one another. I counted it as divine cruelty that my own coupling would result in nothing but fruitlessness, while here this woman comes to my home, walking right past the black wreath of mourning on the door, with her belly full of blessing.

Something held my tongue from asking about the father, perhaps because I had no business sullying my own propriety with such knowledge, perhaps because it was none of my business, or—and this I now embrace—perhaps because I did not want to think there was a third party to involve in the idea so recently sprouted in the dark soil of my mind.

A life for a life. God's ancient words threw off the taint of revenge and took on the shadow of promise. I summoned the last vestiges of my strength to tug one corner of my mouth into a smile and, with an air of grace that galls me to this day, I invited her to, once again, sit down.

Then I left her to make a pot of tea, emptying the last bit of my grief feast into Mrs. Gibbons's small commode while the water boiled.

CHAPTER 10

DANA GOES TO WARNER BROTHERS

1925

"IT'S A COMEDY," Celeste was explaining as she took the pins from her hair, leaving a cap of curls, which she brushed and fussed into a honey-colored froth. "I play—what else—a shopgirl, only this time I'm not just in the background. I get to flirt with the leading man with dialogue and everything. And my name is going to be on the final credits slide, and I even get to have a part in the big chase scene at the end. Isn't that exciting?"

Dana picked up a small jar of cream from the dressing table Celeste shared with two other girls and twisted off the lid.

"That's for later," Celeste said. "Cold cream. When it's time to take all this off." She picked up a pencil and set to darkening the already-black rim around her eyes. When she had finished, she dusted her face a final time with a lavender-tinged powder, leaving an unnatural, death-like shade that conjured up painful memories.

"Dreadful, I know. Papa was working so hard to develop a film that would shoot a more realistic color. Did you know that? He was onto something, too."

Somebody opened the door and barked, "Five minutes!" causing a flurry of powdering and primping.

Celeste turned to her. "How do I look?"

Dana smiled. "Grotesque. But beautiful."

"Here." Celeste handed her a small sewing basket. "If anyone asks, you're my seamstress. This skirt they put me in is so big, I might need you to take it in a stitch or two at the waist, or else I'll be in my bloomers behind the counter."

Wordlessly, Dana took the basket and commenced following Celeste through a labyrinth of dark hallways, brushing up against one person after another, incurring a "Watch it, sister!" as if their brush against each other had been a serious impediment to progress. Still, she felt right at home in the darkness of the passageways and perfected a narrow-shouldered posture, angling her body to the narrowest space between the wall and those coming against her. Soon, no one noticed her at all, and the sense of invisibility settled over her with a comforting familiarity.

The feeling disappeared, however, the moment Celeste's steps stopped and she turned with a dramatic flair, announcing, "Welcome to the fabulous world of movies, movies, movies!"

Dana took her first step into this "fabulous world" with her breath held tight. The ceilings were vaulted at least three stories high above a wide space without windows or walls. A cacophonous sound of carpentry and machinery competed with that of a dozen groups of musicians playing inharmonious tunes. Occasionally a voice would make its way above the din, though its shouted words were swallowed up.

Celeste took Dana's arm and drew her close. "Exciting, isn't it? We're over on stage 8."

As there didn't seem to be any clear pathways or direct organization of movement, Dana sidled her steps closer to Celeste's and allowed herself to be maneuvered through the teeming mass. Scattered throughout the cavernous space were different little rooms set up like a series of three-sided boxes.

"That one's for a Western," Celeste said, pointing to a space paneled with rough-hewn planks. A bar ran most of the length of it, with several stools and a plethora of bottles and glasses on the shelves above. Two men dressed as cowboys were squared off, ready to fight, while a man not three feet away shouted directions about how many blows should land before one or the other took a fall. "I've been in three of them. Westerns, that is. One time playing the sheriff's daughter. I got to spend an entire day crouched under a desk while they dropped all kinds of dust and lumber scraps on top because the bad guys were blowing up the jail with dynamite."

"How exciting," Dana said dutifully.

"I was eleven, and even then I thought, what a silly thing to do, blowing up the jail. Sure, the wall collapsed, but the bad guy could have been killed in the explosion, right? I mean, prison might be awful, but is it worth getting killed over? But then, it's the movies and—" She clapped her hand over her mouth, shadowed eyes wide above it. "Oh, my. I am such a doodle-head."

Her fingers muffled the words, but her meaning couldn't have been more clear. Dana felt a small sting just at the base of her neck, and it spread up and around in an instant. Not exactly shame, but embarrassment, and her mind reached for the words to apologize to this pretty, young girl for even having to consider such ugliness in her conversation.

"It's all right," she said, taking half a step, hoping that would be enough to move them forward. "You shouldn't worry yourself about such things."

Celeste dropped her hand and cocked her head, giving Dana

a look of pity that hammered a blow more devastating than any careless phrase ever could. "Still, it was thoughtless. I forget, sometimes, that you were ever . . . there. Although I don't know how I can because why else would you be here? If it weren't for Mother—"

"Action!"

The voice blasting through a megaphone startled Dana so that she jumped, nearly dropping the sewing basket. Thankful not to be scrambling for needles and pins beneath the sea of footsteps, she gave Celeste's arm a tug, silently forgiving her for the unintended slight and urging the two of them past it.

Stage 8 turned out to be smaller than most of the other spaces, nothing more than a set of shelves with sundry dry goods stashed upon them, and again a countertop running the width of the floor. Except for the absence of the stools, it looked like little more than a refined saloon.

"Now, just stand back and stay quiet and nobody should bother you." Celeste nervously combed her fingers through her hair, shifting her eyes to the left. "That's my director over there. If this goes well, I could be looking at playing second lead in his next picture. So wish me luck."

"You'll do fine," Dana said, feeling surprisingly maternal.

"*Fine* ain't gonna cut it. I need to be absolutely effervescent. Do I look effervescent?"

How she looked was terrified, the brightness of her eyes more like a feverish fear, and her smile a little too wide, but Dana didn't have it in her heart to say so.

"You're the most effervescent person I know," Dana said, pleased to see Celeste transform into a creature of confidence.

In the next minute, Celeste was swept away in a tide of people who bustled about, positioning her just so behind the counter, turning her face to and from different angles, looking up, looking down, while the man she'd identified as the director shouted orders to the man behind the camera, the man adjusting the light, and some poor, trembling girl holding a thick stack of papers. Dana took an extra step back, lest the man take it in his head to yell at her, and heard a familiar voice just over her shoulder.

"You are here to watch the action today?"

She looked up to see Werner Ostermann, thankful that he had spoken to her first, as she might not have recognized him outside the familiar setting of his office.

"What are you doing here?" Immediately she felt ridiculous, acting as if she had the right to question anybody about their presence. She quickly apologized for her gaffe, adding, "I suppose you can be anywhere you wish."

"Not always." He took a generous step back and encouraged her to follow. "Newton—" he inclined his head toward Celeste's director, who was now in the process of reducing the poor script girl to tears—"would throw himself into a fit if he saw me. We do not get along."

Dana ventured a look over her shoulder. "He doesn't appear to get along with too many people."

"He is a man of limited talent and great ambition. A combination, I fear, that keeps him in a perpetual state of foolish tyranny."

"Celeste hopes to make another movie with him."

Werner looked over her head, studying the scene behind them. "She can do better than him. She's an extraordinary talent, that girl. Watch her."

Obediently, Dana turned around, just as Mr. Newton called for action, and a rather plain-looking man walked onto the set, where Celeste stood, her back to him, busying herself with the goods on the shelves. He rocked on his heels in an exaggerated style, puckered his lips to whistle, leaned on the counter, and finally, with an exasperated air, slammed his palm on the little silver bell on the countertop. At which point, Celeste, in a startled flurry, tossed a handful of garments into the air and turned, her hand against her chest as if to calm her heart.

Dana laughed at the expression on her face and the man's reaction as he attempted to help her gather up some of what had been dropped, lifting a skimpy negligee, which Celeste snatched away, scandalized, saying, "Get your hands off that!"

In the next instant, though, she was holding the same garment up against her, her face completely transformed into a coquettish invitation, and said, "Unless it's exactly what you're looking for."

Here, the young man turned, slowly, while Mr. Newton shouted, "To the camera! To the camera! A little more . . . a little more! And—now!" The actor raised his shoulders in an exaggerated shrug, while Celeste continued her flirtatious posing behind him.

"Cut!" Mr. Newton yelled, and everybody exhaled collectively.

"And this is how it is done," Dana said, so caught up in the moment, she'd forgotten that anyone was close enough to hear her.

"Deceptively simple," Werner said. "But now watch. Celeste will do that bit where she holds the nightie up over and over again, until Newton is pleased with the shot. And since he is somewhat of a letch, that could be all afternoon. Come." His fingertips brushed just above her elbow. "Are you hungry? How about a sandwich and a cup of coffee?"

"I don't know," she said, fighting the urge to pull away from his touch, though every nerve within her scrambled at the intrusion. "Celeste told me to wait here."

Werner motioned for the script girl to come to them, and she obliged, covering the short distance with rabbit-like steps. "Tell

Miss DuFrane that Werner Ostermann would like to meet with her in the canteen when she is finished shooting for the afternoon."

The girl's face dawned with realization, and she nodded for all she was worth. "Yes, yes, of course, Mr. Ostermann."

He leaned closer. "And tell her within earshot of Mr. Newton."

This seemed a terrifying notion to the girl, but Werner simply laughed and sent her back to her spot.

"Now," he said and started walking, leaving Dana little choice but to follow.

If she'd had it in her mind to disappear within the busy studio again, nothing but disappointment awaited. Werner couldn't take more than a dozen steps without somebody stopping him to ask a question or hand him a business card. On two occasions he was invited to dinner—or *something*—by some beautiful woman, and these were the only of their interruptions to give Dana more than a passing glance. She withered under their scrutiny, acutely aware of the plainness of her face and the silly mending basket still clutched in her hand. Werner entered each conversation without introduction and left without comment. Because of his height, she was forced to take three steps to his every one and was nearly breathless by the time they emerged through the door and out into the blinding sunlight.

Immediately she stopped, cupping one hand across her eyes, the pain ringing across the top of her head.

"Are you all right, Dana?" She sensed that he was several steps away.

"It still takes me by surprise," she said, waiting for the dancing orbs to allow her the confidence to proceed.

"I know what you mean." He was beside her now, and touching her again at the same place on the back of her arm, but this time she never thought to pull away. Instead, she gave herself over to be guided, blind at first, but eventually acclimating, and by silent, tacit agreement, he took his hand away, walking slowly beside her, matching her step.

Eventually he opened a door and ushered her across a threshold into yet another cloud of noise—hundreds of conversations underscored by the clatter of cutlery. The scent was indefinable, yet familiar. Food and coffee.

She followed Werner in a serpentine path to a table against the far wall with a tented board that said *Reserved.*

"It's reserved for me," he said almost shyly, pulling out her chair.

Before he himself sat down, a lanky youth sporting a crisp, white apron was at the table, pencil poised to notepad. After a brief consultation, he took down an order for an egg salad sandwich and tea for the both of them.

"I've never actually had egg salad before," Dana said, feeling childish the minute the words came out of her mouth.

"I can imagine there is a lot in the world that is new to you." He reached into his pocket for a cigarette, and given that everyone around them was smoking, she didn't feel she had the right to ask him not to. Mistaking her interest, he held the slim box out to her in invitation.

"No, thank you. I feel like I am breathing in enough just from the air around me."

Werner chuckled but made no move to stub it out. "Tell me, then, what else is new to you? What has taken you by surprise?"

Initially, it was the bluntness of his question that took her by surprise, and she took a long look around the room, searching for the answer.

"The noise, I suppose. And it seems like everything moves so fast. Cars . . . and people."

"And you had no idea what to expect?"

She leaned forward to whisper, "Like I told you, I'd never even seen a motion picture. So when I see all of that—in there—it's hard for me to understand."

He'd just taken a drag of his cigarette, and the smoke curled up from his half smile. "They are just stories. Certainly when you were a very little girl, you had storybooks. With pictures?"

"Yes," she said. One about kittens—a family of them—who got lost in the garden. But she didn't go into any such detail here, feeling foolish enough as it was.

"A movie is nothing more than such a thing. But thousands upon thousands of pictures come to life to tell the story. Some of them silly, like what we just saw with Celeste. Nothing more than a series of jokes strung together to make people laugh. Or sometimes romance, because everybody loves a lover."

Just then the young man came with two steaming cups of tea and the sandwiches, all of which was set on the table with precision. He was about to leave when Werner beckoned him to stay. "In case the lady wishes to change her mind," he said, instructing Dana to taste her sandwich. She obliged, having taken a moment to observe the pastel-yellow paste between the bread, thinking it was the prettiest bit of food she'd ever seen. With the first bite, she immediately appreciated the softness of the white bread, but with the second, the fresh, somewhat-tart taste of the egg spread delighted her, and she said so through an indelicate mouthful.

"Very good," Werner said, handing a folded bill to the waiter with instructions to keep the change and bring another sandwich wrapped in waxed paper. "Next time I will remember to ask for a slice of tomato."

"I've never had a tomato," Dana said, chewing thoughtfully.

"Ghastly." His sandwich remained untouched as he finished his cigarette, and with her own half-gone, Dana was tempted to snatch it off his plate. "That will have to be a priority for our next meal."

The last bite lodged in her throat at his words, and she took a sip of the scalding tea to wash it down.

"It seems a small price to pay for your story. After all, some writers get paid hundreds of dollars for such things, even the genius whose muse led him to pen the very scene that has Miss DuFrane currently making love to a camera while surrounded by cheap prop underwear. We can write a tomato into your contract, if you like, and let that shifty little agent of hers take a look at it."

"I think it would be a waste of your time," Dana said, trying to resurrect the pleasure she'd felt at the beginning of the meal.

"And why is that?"

"You said people like stories that make them laugh. Or have romance. I'm afraid there's none of that in mine."

Finally he stubbed out his cigarette in a small tin dish. "They also love a good hero. A survivor. Someone who overcomes injustice and lives to face the world. Out of the grave. Back from the dead. Risen from the ashes. However you tell it."

She listened intently, picturing herself as being worthy of those words. Yes, she had survived, but what other choice did she have? And the only grave she knew of was the one where baby Mary lay, and her mother, for all she knew. There would be no laughter, no romance mixed in with these ashes. As to injustice—well, that would need more than a thousand pictures to capture.

Still, for the first time since their initial interview, her curiosity was piqued. "What would it look like?"

She'd caught him midbite, and he looked at her questioningly.

"I saw all of those different little stages, and I'm just wondering, what would my story look like?"

"I'm counting on you to tell me."

CHAPTER 11

TITLE CARD: Far from the night of hearth and home, peaceful slumber brings comfort to the souls of the innocent, for such is the heart of children in the eyes of God.

CLOSE-UP: Neat, white letters above the barred window of an interior door: *Children's Dormitory.*

INTERIOR—CHILDREN'S DORMITORY: It is a long, dark room, its contents barely discernible by the pale light coming through a barred door. There are twelve beds aligned in neat rows, a narrow aisle between them. Small, sleeping forms—some peaceful, some restless—under thin, worn blankets.

CLOSE-UP: A small, freckled girl, her face scrunched tight in sleep.

CLOSE-UP: A little girl clutching a ragged cloth doll.

CLOSE-UP: A little girl with shorn hair, sleeping with her thumb in her mouth.

CLOSE-UP: Dana, lying on her back, hands folded, staring up into the darkness.

INTERIOR: A long, dark hallway. The wide, shadowed figure of an imposing, heavyset woman, walking, dragging the end of a short baton along the wall. Her wide, utilitarian face is set in a menacing scowl; her hair secured in a knot squarely atop her head. Mrs. Karistin—children's matron. Stern, unyielding, relentlessly cruel.

1906

DANA NEVER KNEW for sure if she awoke before the footsteps or if they drew her from her sleep. In either case, their strident cadence engaged her first sense every morning, before she opened her eyes to the thin, amber light streaming from the hallway.

"Awake and alive, girls. Awake and alive." The familiar morning command of Mrs. Karistin echoed at the edge of the darkness. Dana opened her eyes but kept her body perfectly still, as the slightest movement threatened to bring the chill of the morning into the cocoon of warmth she'd spun during her sleep.

"Stupid old hag."

The whisper came from the next bed and forced Dana to pull her thin, gray blanket below her chin in order to respond. "Hush." The word was not much louder than the sound of Mrs. Karistin's skirt brushing along the brick wall, and it was not intended to defend the woman's honor.

"Well, she is," the girl insisted. She'd arrived only two days before, brought in thin and dark with dirt.

"Awake and alive, girls. Let me see you." For a moment, the silhouette of Mrs. Karistin filled the narrow door, creating a solid shape behind its metal bars. She was as tall as any man, with a figure like a block of cheese—her shoulders, waist, and hips the same intimidating width. Even her profile yielded no disruption to the straight planes of her body. What a relief it must have been for her to take on the job of a prison matron, to wear the formless, gray woolen dress with its long, straight sleeves and sensible belt, sparing herself the false accommodations of corsets and bustles and wide mutton sleeves. For all the children knew, she wore this uniform to church on Sundays and to the theater with Mr. Karistin, if such a man existed.

Dana knew enough of Mrs. Karistin's routine to close her eyes tight, because the minute she said, "Let me see you," the room flooded with light as she flipped the switch on the wall outside, followed by the disgruntled sound of waking girls.

"Up and dressed, girls. Ten minutes. Up and dressed." Mrs. Karistin punctuated this command with a clack of her leather-clad baton over the bars of the door. A gesture she would repeat when there were six minutes left. Then four. Then two, until finally to the back of the head of any girl not dressed, with her hair combed and braided neat, standing squarely at the foot of her crisply made bed. It wasn't a hard blow to the head, not enough to knock a girl to her knees, or even be felt much by the end of the day. But enough to make her elbow her way to the washbasin and be the first in line to splash her face with stinging cold water, or maybe sleep with her shoes on.

Having awoken in this place for nearly a year, Dana had mastered the routine. She swung her stockinged feet over the side of the bed, where her shoes were waiting to be filled and laced. While the other girls lined up at the washbasins, she got out of bed, pulling her blanket up with her and smoothing it in long, sure strokes. Her dress lay at its foot, spread out like something a little girl would fold over the form of a paper doll. It was a trick she'd learned from an older girl during her first weeks here. It not only kept the dress from wrinkling, but it also provided an extra layer of warmth during the winter nights.

She could use that warmth right now, as she shivered in her thin cotton shift. But then she'd run the danger of getting her sleeves wet while she washed, which would mean red, chapped skin for days after. So, half-dressed, she went to the washbasins, which, by now, were vacated by the younger girls, and pumped fresh water into the waiting bowl. She'd learned it was coldest right from the spigot, so she let it sit while she removed her nightcap and ran a damp hand over the hair she'd carefully brushed and braided the night before.

"You look like a granny with that thing." The new girl—Carrie, she remembered—stood behind Dana, hugging her arms around her own thin frame. Her skin was dark, close to the color of the gingerbread cake Mama used to make at Christmastime. Two small bruises, suspiciously the size of a man's thumbprints, were making their last stand just below the girl's bony clavicles.

"It keeps your hair nice." Dana tried not to look at the matted nest that created a dark cloud around the girl's sharp face. "So you don't have to take time to brush it in the morning. And then, when it's warmer and there's bugs in the bed, it keeps them out."

Carrie swiped her arm—wrist to elbow—under her nose and lunged for the vacated spigot next to Dana. "I don't know about you," she said, pumping vigorously, "but I for one don't plan on being here this summer."

Dana pretended not to hear as she cupped her hands beneath the surface of the icy water and brought her face low to splash it clean. Just what kind of dirt had accumulated there throughout the night she couldn't imagine, but that was the rule. Face washing, three times a day: in the morning, after the noon meal, and before bed. It was best in the summer mornings, after a long, sticky night in the airless room, and agreeable after lunch, because it meant another day was half-over. And while frigid winter mornings made the washup nearly intolerable, it was far, far worse at night, because after the cleaning came the darkness.

Eyes closed and face stinging, Dana reached blindly for the towel she knew to be hanging just in front of her to the left. Not finding it with her fingers, she opened her eyes to see the ragged, grayish cloth folded around Carrie's nose. When she'd finished blowing, she held it out, saying, "Do you need this?"

"I'm fine, thank you." Dana rushed back to her bed to dry her face on her blanket. It was somewhat cleaner, anyway.

"Two minutes, or you're too late!" Mrs. Karistin fixed her key into the lock, and the familiar groaning of the opening door spurred the girls into quicker action. "Two minutes, or too late!"

Dana dropped her dress over her head and threaded her arms through the sleeves. With stiff fingers, she tied the closure at the back of her neck, then smoothed the front, hoping to generate some warmth from the wool. Satisfied, she took her place standing at the end of her bed, arms straight at her sides, eyes forward, and waited for Mrs. Karistin's inspection. One by one, the other girls took their places. The smallest one, directly across from Dana, stood stock-still, chin quivering. She couldn't have been more than ten years old, and she'd cried morning, noon, and night since her arrival six days ago. Dana still didn't know her name—the girl hadn't spoken a single word—but Dana knew she'd been arrested for breaking into a blacksmith's shop to steal coal.

Mrs. Karistin made sure to inform them of each new arrival's transgressions.

At that moment, having announced, "Time has ticked, girls. Time has ticked," the big woman made her way down the narrow aisle between the bunks, turning her square head slightly left, slightly right, greeting each girl in turn.

"Apple Thief . . . Pickpocket . . . Window Breaker . . ." She stopped at little Coal Grubber and clasped her hands behind her back, rocking on her heels.

"Tears again today? Poor little Coal Grubber. Tears again today." And then she moved on, as if she'd given sufficient affection, stopping again to grip Carrie's pointy chin in her heavy, cigar-shaped fingers. "And what to call you, my little fresh face? What to call you? From the looks of it, I could call you Bramble Head, but there's no crime in that. At least not out there." She jerked her head in the vague direction of the window high on the wall. "In here, though, we don't like our girls running around like they're two steps off the street. We're here to help you, turn you around, as they say. Turn you around. Looks like your first lesson today will be with a comb, if we've got one up to the task. Might have to go with a razor." Mrs. Karistin smiled at that—a rare sight that revealed a uniform row of small, gray teeth—and drew Carrie closer. "But I suppose you might be more comfortable with a razor after all, wouldn't you?"

"Her name's Carrie," Dana said, unable to take the sound of the woman's voice any longer. It was deceptively high and sweet, like it had been designed to read fairy tales, but with a singsong quality that conjured nothing but revulsion and fear. Sensing new prey, but not dropping her grip on the first, Mrs. Karistin whipped her head around, her smile taking on a sinister quality.

"Well, good morning, Baby Killer. Imagine that, opening your mouth when you've no reason to speak. Imagine that." She turned back to Carrie. "Looks like you've found yourself a new friend, Carrie." She stopped for a moment and looked up, as if considering. Practicing, before adding, "Cutter. Carrie Cutter. Yes, I think that's just perfect for you."

Breakfast was, by far, the best meal of the day for the young inmates at the old Bridewell Prison. It was the only meal to be prepared fresh every day, with mounds of fluffy white eggs, steaming biscuits and gravy, or porridge, the inconsistency of which could be forgiven with the sprinkling of sugar and cinnamon, and sometimes great chunks of cooked apple. Lunch was often little more than bread and cheese and canned fruit, and supper a bowl of some stew that had been set to simmer throughout the day. But breakfast, with its strips of bacon or fat little sausages, felt like a meal a girl could get in a real home.

Even so, it didn't compare to the sumptuous feasts Dana had enjoyed when she was first taken away, when she'd lived in the cozy cell at the back of the Highland Park police station. There, some kind sergeant's wife had brought her a piping hot meal three times a day on a plate covered with a blue-checked towel. Cookies sometimes, too, though Dana pocketed those to give to her mother on her frequent visits. It was the best food she'd ever eaten. The most abundant and reliable, and she'd swallowed a good bit of guilt with every bite.

In those first days, Mama promised, over and over, that everything was going to be all right. That she would talk to Mr. DuFrane. She would make him understand, convince him to talk to the police, the judge, whoever he could, to let Dana come home to her.

"He has money," she'd said. "You would be surprised, my girl, how important money is in this world."

Then, one day, Mama didn't come to visit. Or the next, or the next. On the next, they brought Dana here.

This morning they had great slabs of fried cornmeal, served with a slice of bacon and hot, sweet tea in their battered tin cups. Coal Grubber could only look at her food with distrust, until Dana took a bite, proving its harmlessness. Even then, the girl nibbled with such deliberate slowness that Dana feared she might not finish before the bell rang to send them to their morning lessons. Or, worse, that Mrs. Karistin would come and take her plate away, consuming all that remained in a single, furtive swipe.

"Eat," Dana urged, tracking Mrs. Karistin's movements.

"If she won't, I will." Carrie reached her fork across the table in an attempt to spear a slice of bacon, but at the last minute, Coal Grubber snatched the plate away, her little brows knit in defiance. Up and down the long, narrow table, the girls laughed and cheered her on, and for the first time, she didn't appear to be on the verge of tears. In fact, she smiled in a way that made two tiny ridges appear on the bridge of her nose, and she attacked her breakfast with an almost-carefree abandon.

After breakfast the girls spent an hour with Mrs. Poole, a thin, pinched-face woman of indeterminate age, who read exactly ten pages of *What Katy Did.* It was Dana's third time to sit through the novel, and she liked it even less with each repetition. She much preferred the third in the series, when Katy experiences her adventures in Europe, but her favorite book by far was *Little Women*, with its cozy family of a mother and daughters and all their promising futures.

Once she'd read the final page for the day, Mrs. Poole wrote a question on the small blackboard at the front of the room. *Why is Katy a brave girl?* Dana, being one of the older girls, was charged with handing out the copybooks and pencils as the girls were instructed to turn to the next blank page to write an answer to the question. The littlest girls, or those who could not write, needed only wait for a few moments and Mrs. Poole would write a sentence on the board for them to copy ten times over. Something like, *She is brave because she has learned to walk again.*

"I don't think she's brave at all," Carrie whispered, refusing even to open her copybook. "I think she's a stupid girl who deserves to be crippled forever."

Dana ignored her and began writing the same answer she'd written the last time Mrs. Poole asked this question.

"Besides, it doesn't make you brave to learn to walk. Anybody can walk. It's what—"

Whatever thought she'd prepared was lost in the sharp, stinging sound of Mrs. Poole's hand squarely against Carrie's cheek.

"We do not talk during lessons." The woman held the novel clasped to her breast like some treasured companion and stormed back to the front of the narrow classroom.

Dana ventured a guarded look at Carrie and felt her own face burn at the sight of the palmprint forming on the dark, taut skin. The girl's eyes welled with tears, no doubt a reaction to both the pain and humiliation of the reprimand, and they splashed—two, three, four—onto the red cardboard cover of the copybook.

Feeling the kindest thing would be to look away, Dana did just that and drew a deliberate, black slash through the sentences she'd written. She moved the dulling point of her pencil to the next blank line and wrote: *We don't think she is brave at all. We think she is stupid and deserves to be crippled forever. It doesn't make you brave to walk. Anybody can walk. Sometimes it's more brave to sit still.*

She touched the blunted end of her pencil to her chin and looked out the window. Unlike those in the dormitory, the windows in the classroom were tall and wide, with only two thick bars running from top to bottom to indicate that the girls weren't just students in some impoverished academy. Though the barren trees and the thin layer of muddy snow still bore the banner of winter, the sky was a clear, endless blue, what her mother used to call a "sneaky sky," able to trick a mind into expecting warmth and blossoms and sweet new grass.

Later, in the hour before lunch and then again at three o'clock, the girls were permitted to go outside for half an hour under the watchful eye of whatever matron had drawn recess supervision duty. Here they had the chance to intermingle with the boys, sometimes sparking reunions of brothers and sisters who had been brought in for their cooperative crimes.

Those who knew how to play—the little ones who'd been to school or the older ones who still remembered—would engage in squealing fits of tag or freeze. They weren't permitted ropes for jumping (Mrs. Karistin liked to tell them that all the ropes were used for hanging), and there was never a continuity of interest to organize any real sport.

Dana preferred to watch from her favorite seat on a black iron bench, her face turned to the sun. She'd been too stunned to play when she first arrived, and with Mrs. Karistin's insistence on calling her Baby Killer, the children were too afraid to invite her to join their games. Now she felt simply too old and took on the role of secondary caregiver, helping up the little ones when they fell, dusting their dirt and, later, washing their wounds, even when they trembled at her touch.

This afternoon, Coal Grubber's cheeks, finally dry of tears, glowed a healthy pink as she and others enjoyed a squealing game of blindman's bluff in the chilly, early-spring air, waving her arms and chasing Apple Thief, who looked nothing like a girl driven to this place by hunger. Tomorrow, Dana knew, they might be gone, each having served her juvenile sentence for her minuscule crime. Nobody stayed long. Nobody but her.

"Did you really kill a baby?"

Carrie had come to sit beside her. She'd twisted her hair into a number of braids and now tied scraps of red cloth at the bottom of each one. Wordlessly, she handed a scrap to Dana and turned, allowing Dana to braid and tie the back.

"Did you really cut someone?"

"Sure did." She sounded proud. "My uncle. He was trying to touch me in *that way*, and I wasn't having none of it, and he chased me into the bathroom, and I got ahold of his razor. And I cut him." She turned to look at Dana and made a slicing motion that started from the corner of one eye and extended clear to her ear. "There to there. So much blood, like you've never seen. He was screamin' and chokin' the life out of me when my mama found us."

"Is he in prison too?" Dana took a new tuft of hair, so much softer than she'd imagined it to be, and began plaiting.

"Nope. Because they said he didn't do anything. But I'm going to be here for a whole month."

Dana's hands went still. "How do you know that?"

"Because that's what the judge say." She handed a scrap of ribbon over her shoulder. "You never did answer me. Did you kill a baby or not?"

No one had ever asked her so bluntly, nobody with any authority, anyway. Only the terrified children, and Mrs. Karistin when she was feeling especially menacing. To the children, she said no, so their fears would be assuaged; to Mrs. Karistin, she said nothing, so she'd have no satisfaction. But Carrie, she knew, would not be satisfied with either.

"I wouldn't be here unless they thought I did."

"But did you?"

She tied a small, red knot. "No. I don't think so."

Carrie made a low humming noise that made Dana feel, for the first time ever, that she might have a sympathetic ear, which disappeared quickly with her next question.

"Are they gonna hang you?"

"Why would you ask such a thing as that?"

"Because that's what happens to killers. They say, 'You shall hang from the neck until you are dead.'"

Dana swallowed, with each word imagining the feel of a rope. "I—I don't think so."

"Well, then, how long are you going to have to stay here?"

"Nobody ever said. How do you know all this?"

Carrie turned around fully, clearly frustrated with the conversation. "Weren't you paying attention? At the end, the judge pounds his hammer, and he says, 'I hereby sentence you to a month's hard labor.' Or 'For this crime, you shall spend no fewer than five years in the correctional facility.' Or 'I sentence you to prison for the rest of your natural life.'" She delivered each sentence in a deep, authoritative voice. "You went before a judge, didn't you?"

"Yes. But he never said anything like that."

"So you had a trial?"

Dana nodded. "In the DuFranes' parlor."

Carrie's eyes went wide. "In a *parlor*? You can't have a trial in a parlor. It needs to be a courtroom, with a jury and—"

"How do you know all this?"

Her face beamed with pride. "I have a cousin who lives in Cleveland. We lived there for a year or so. Anyway, he's going to be a lawyer, and he works running messages to the courthouse. And sometimes, last winter, he let me sit in and watch with him because it's warm in there. They have balconies up top for when it's a Negro on trial, but when it's a white man, ain't nobody up there. So I watched them all."

"Maybe they just don't know what to do with me. Maybe they haven't figured out yet if I'm guilty or not."

"How long have you been here?"

Dana thought. "Two Christmases."

"Well, that's plenty of time. You need to talk to the warden."

"I tried, once." Last spring, after waking from a nightmare in which her mother was being swept away in a raging river. Certainly, she thought, Mama had been trying to see her. "Mrs.

Karistin told me that when Mr. Webb wanted to see me, he would see me. And that's the way it works here. 'Two thousand souls under this roof, he don't have time for none of your beans.'"

Carrie laughed. "I'm sorry. It's not funny, but you sound just like her."

Dana smiled. "I've had time to practice." She motioned for Carrie to turn around, then finished the last braid. "There. Much better."

When Carrie turned around again, her face was serious beyond her years. "I bet my cousin can help."

It was the first bit of hope since the last visit with Mama. "Do you really think so?"

She nodded solemnly. "He's the smartest person I know. I'm going to tell him all about you. But you have to tell me, true." She leaned forward and held Dana's gaze as if building a new wall around the two of them. "Did you kill that baby?"

"No." Nothing else to add.

"But that baby died?"

"Yes."

"Did you ever tell that baby's mama that you were sorry it died?"

"*She.* She died. A little girl. And no. They wouldn't let me talk to her."

"You have to do that. Write her a letter. Rip some pages from the copybook, or ask the teacher who read the story today. Ask her for paper and an envelope, and write to that lady. Do you know her name?"

"Mrs. DuFrane."

She could hear her mother's voice. *"Mrs. DuFrane needs me to work late tonight. Lock the door."*

"And you said there was a judge? Do you know his name?"

Dana started to shake her head, then recalled the smallest

snippet of a memory long buried, and she reached for Carrie's hand, as if that grip would help her hold it. "The day they took me out of the cell at the police station, and the officer on duty didn't want to let me go. He said . . ." She closed her eyes, trying to remember the exact words. He was an older man, and sweet. Like she'd always imagined a grandfather to be, and they'd sometimes played cards in the late afternoons. "He said, 'This is highly unusual.' And then the man who came to get me said, 'It's orders direct from Judge Stephens.' And he had some piece of paper."

"Then you need to write to that judge."

Dana exclaimed, "I will!" and threw her arms around the girl who would be her friend for a whole month. Giddy with possibility, she bent her head to Carrie's, and the two conspired as to what, exactly, she should say. Soon there was a third.

"Look at you two." Mrs. Karistin's face was close enough that Dana could smell the grayness of her breath. "Thick as thieves, as they say. Not that it applies to the two of you. Gotta change that, don't we? If thieves is thick, what do we have when we got a cutter and a killer?"

Carrie kept her eyes focused on Dana and said, "Friends."

CHAPTER 12

THE WRITTEN CONFESSION OF MARGUERITE DUFRANE, PAGES 25–38

OH, MY DARLING GIRL, do you have any memories at all of our house back home? By "home," of course, I mean Highland Park, where the nicer houses—like ours—had such lovely architectural idiosyncrasies. It has taken me your lifetime to warm myself to the sprawling vanity of Los Angeles. Here, it seems, walls are but a nuisance to the sunshine, and all the rooms are vast and light, with no place at all to keep a secret.

I remember, once, when Calvin was a very young boy—no more than three—and he'd taken to hiding and waiting for your father and me to seek him. He was quite unsophisticated at first, huddling behind potted plants or lying wait in coat closets. Once he folded himself into the cabinet under the kitchen sink, and poor Mrs. Gibbons nearly died of fright when she opened the door to retrieve the box of soap flakes. Soon, though, he ventured further into the house. Deep into the coal bin, high into the attic, until one day he disappeared altogether.

I wish I could report that I'd been terrified, my heart stopped with fear, the house filled with my hysterical cries, or something more fitting of a mother. But I was exhausted that day. In fact, it might have been during the early stages of my pregnancy with

Mary, and insufferably hot. It was close to four o'clock, that difficult time between Calvin's nap and your father's coming home from work, and I was resting with a cool cloth covering my eyes when I felt his hot little breath against my cheek.

"I'm going hiding. Count to ten and come find me."

I told him I'd be along, though I planned to dispatch your father to the task as soon as he arrived home, but I fell asleep and he, not wishing to disturb me, went directly to his library, looking over his papers or some such thing. I came downstairs having heard the bell for supper, and we were both halfway through the soup before remarking that Calvin was awfully late coming to the table. We sent Mrs. Gibbons to fetch him down, but she returned claiming not to have found him in his bedroom, or the playroom, or even outside.

I'll never forget your father's instant response. He tugged the napkin from his collar and stormed away from the table, bellowing our son's name until I feared he'd shake the chandeliers. Then, and only then, did I remember that I was supposed to have found him.

I was quickly at Arthur's heels, echoing his calls, and in between reassuring him that the boy was simply hiding, as he always did. I did not mention my own lapse, as your father already thought I greatly exaggerated the symptoms of my pregnancy. Understandable, perhaps, because he did not know the depths of my fragility.

High and low we searched, your father still clutching his dinner napkin, both of us shouting so loud we might not have heard Calvin if he did call out. Inside every closet, behind every door. Cabinets and wardrobes. Under beds, beneath the covers, until finally we came upon the linen closet at the very end of the hall. This was not an ordinary linen closet, as it had been constructed shortly after the death of my parents, when your father and I became primary residents of the house. Behind it was a door, and behind that door a series of rooms that had been servants' quarters back when families of privilege employed such persons to stoke fires and polish silver and curry horses. Every new invention, it seemed, made one more person unnecessary, and your father, quite frankly, was never comfortable with such displays of wealth, and so we learned to make do with a single live-in domestic. If I'd held my ground and convinced him to allow a permanent nanny, I might have been spared the devastation of Mary's death. . . .

But I digress within my digression. We went to that closet, opened the door, and heard the faintest sound from the other side. It was clear the linens had been disturbed on the shelves, and Arthur began throwing them to the floor, calling Calvin's name. Finally I spied a tiny finger poking out through a loose board at the back.

Calvin!

I fell to my knees and your father dropped beside me. We pushed on the board as the boy himself must have done earlier in the afternoon. Cheap particle stuff that it was—barely a step above cardboard—it gave way, and Arthur was able to push and bend it enough to allow our son to crawl out from underneath and join us, red-faced and sobbing, on the other side. I remember feeling a strange mix of anger and relief at having found him, and while he was still crying, I took him in my arms and praised him for being such a good hider.

"You didn't come find me." His words were wet with tears.

I buried his hot little face close to my heart and breathed hushes into his sweaty head, hoping his father hadn't heard. I assured him that we'd found him now, hadn't we? That was a very mousy place for him to go, and we were far too big to follow.

"I called and I called, but you didn't hear me."

"Enough of this," Arthur said, throwing sheets and towels onto the shelves with no regard to folding or order. "Get downstairs for dinner, and we'll have no more of hiding for quite some time."

The next day, carpenters came in to make reparations, and I didn't give the incident another thought for years, until the afternoon that woman stood in my parlor, pregnant, insisting I find some way to secure freedom for her daughter.

I sent her away that day with a promise to think and to pray about the best course of action to take. No sooner had the door shut against the evening streetlights than I was at my correspondence desk, searching my address book for the name of the carpenter who had repaired that linen closet. For the first time, I was truly grateful that Arthur chose to leave the lion's share of the day-to-day operations of the house to me. The man himself hadn't written a check or opened a bill for most of our marriage.

Two days later, knowing Arthur would be at a university faculty meeting well past the dinner hour, four strong Italians went to work on my project at the end of the upstairs hall. Leaving them to their labor, I stepped out—dressed in my blackest dress and finest hat—to take care of another matter entirely.

Judge Stephens and my father had been friends since the two met in law school before he even met my mother. Not that Father ever worked as a lawyer; it was just something young men did while they waited to be old enough to be trusted with their family businesses—my cousin Eugene has carried on that tradition brilliantly. Still, he and George Stephens had remained a fixture in my childhood—holiday outings and family dinners. He delivered the eulogy at my father's funeral, and before my mother died, he oversaw the writing of her will, to ensure that every bit of my father's money went to me and not the passel of worthless cousins who'd been waiting with bated breath for her passing.

For all I knew of Judge Stephens—and I carried a wealth of information that had seemed such a burden until this very afternoon—I did not know the extent of his power, or if his appointment would bring him anywhere near the case pending against the girl who had killed my daughter. I'd been too distraught to receive his visit in the days after Mary's death, but I clutched a note written in his familiar hand on thick, official stationery assuring me he would do for me whatever I needed during this horrific time.

This was the evidentiary promise I took with me to the courthouse and presented to a series of secretaries, each less inclined than the previous to grant me access to my longtime family friend. Finally, the one separated from him by a mere wall bade me sit and wait while she consulted his schedule and then poked her head through a clouded-glass door. Then the man himself came out, taking me in a fatherly embrace I neither expected nor welcomed, and ushered me into his office, instructing his secretary to send word that he would be late to court.

"Our little Margi." He'd always had the deep voice of an old man, giving me an idea of what my father might have become had he lived another decade. Indeed, he and Father were the only ones ever to call me by that nickname, and in that moment I cringed at the endearment as I tried to shrink away from his touch.

I said, Hello, George, as soon as I could politely extricate myself and take the seat offered to me opposite his impressive oak desk.

"I'm so sorry about the baby. I came to visit. Did your husband tell you?"

He spoke of your father in a way that showed me he disapproved of my choice of husband as much as my family had.

I asked his forgiveness and indulgence, as I hadn't felt up to receiving visitors, and even in that moment I felt my strength begin to waver. But then I glanced around his office, seeing all manner of framed certificates on the walls, and shelves lined with thick, leather-bound books. No fewer than three robes hung on a brass tree behind him. I'd never had the opportunity to see him in his robes, but I imagined he would disappear within them, he was so thin.

"I've followed the story in the papers, of course. I understand the girl is still being held at the police station, special guest of the officers until a trial date is set?"

I told him I wasn't at all concerned with where the girl was living, and he switched his tone from brisk advocacy to concerned confidant.

"There's been no one to post bail, as I understand it, though it seemed to me a moderate amount."

My stomach lurched at the very thought of a price being placed on the life of my daughter, but I hid my illness by leaning forward in my chair, as if hanging on his every word.

"And I do hope, my dear, that you will find comfort in the verdict of the coroner's inquest. Accidental death. I highly doubt any formal charges will be brought against the girl. She is, after all, merely a child herself. I imagine her grief is surpassed only by your own."

Oh, how he was poised to continue a monologue concerning that "poor girl," and I somehow kept myself from lunging across the desk to strangle any further words of misplaced pity. The best I could do was interrupt him, which I did, asking just why such a verdict would bring comfort.

"Why, to realize that you hadn't opened your home to any premeditated evil. And that you have no need to fear we are turning a killer back out onto the streets."

So this was it. I ran my fingers along the fold of his letter, pressing the crease to knifelike sharpness. And we were all supposed to simply go on with our lives?

"Darling Margi." He came out from behind his desk and took the seat next to me, leaning forward as if to grasp my hand. "It's the kindest way, sparing all of you from a trial. Imagine having to testify about that dreadful night, reliving it over and over again."

I asked him if he didn't think I already lived that night over and over. Along with the earlier evening when I allowed that girl to sleep in my daughter's room. Or the earlier afternoon when I allowed her in my home. Or the previous day when I informed her mother we'd be happy to let her help serve at the party.

"Of course you do. And it might be that you always will. But I've a strong suspicion the prosecution won't want to risk ruining another child's life. Let alone the unfavorable press."

Even he seemed embarrassed by that last bit, and I held my tongue. I'd seen the papers, too. The overwhelming sympathy for this poor girl being held prisoner by the cruel, relentless, punitive wealthy family. I suspected Arthur shared the same opinion and, like the rest of the city, would like to see this all behind us. Only I could see that it would never be behind us at all. The joy of Mary's life and the stabbing pain of her death crippled me, and I pressed George's letter into his hand, reminding him that he'd promised to help me in any way he could.

"And I will," he reassured. "Anything."

I'm glad I couldn't see the smile that crept upon my face, for while I strove to appear grateful, a darkness tugged at my heart, destroying any hint of true graciousness.

I told him I didn't want to go through a trial, and when he attempted to reiterate his reasons for believing there wouldn't be one, I held up my hand to stop him before I lost the courage needed for my quest. You see, I didn't want a trial, but I did want her to go to prison. For a while. I took a deep breath and stated the sentence I'd calculated as being beneficial for all extenuating circumstances. A year, at least. Maybe a little more. To teach her a lesson and see to it that she, and she alone, suffers the punishment for her actions.

George bent his head to an indulgent angle and looked upon me like I'd been reduced to some petulant child.

"Even if I were to be assigned to the case, which is very unlikely given the circumstances, I cannot simply hand down such an arbitrary sentence without the benefit of a trial, and no lawyer would counsel her to confess her guilt."

I impressed upon him again my need to have her put away.

"I'm sorry." And this time, he seemed genuinely so. "I am simply not in the habit of banishing children to prison."

I'd known it would come to this moment, much as I dreaded it. I withdrew myself from being anywhere near the range of his touch and asked if it wasn't true that there were other habits he indulged in rather freely, at least according to the conversations I'd heard between my mother and father late at night when they didn't know I'd slipped down the stairs for a final kiss.

"What habits would those be?" He managed to speak without a breath of fear, though I knew what must have been churning deep within him.

I reminded him of a night, long ago, when I'd been just a little girl and the house teemed with servants. Mother and Father had hosted a dinner party, and due to the lateness of the hour and the amount of liquor consumed, Judge Stephens opted to stay the night in our home.

"There were many such evenings." Already he seemed poised to discredit me. "Before I met my wife. Had my children. I daresay few people would ever connect the person I am now with the man I used to be."

I kept cool, murmuring something about how lovely it would be if that were true. If people didn't have such long memories and insatiable appetites for fresh scandal. But he and I both knew the contrary to be true. After all, there I was, with my recollection intact, and a secret long held beneath the surface of propriety.

"You were just a girl." And there, a crack in his calm facade as our memories found each other.

I admitted that I didn't know why, at first, the young man I knew as Freddy, a footman in our house, went running through our hallways wearing a nightshirt—

"It was a misunderstanding."

I went on as if I hadn't heard him, musing about the fact that it was the first time I'd seen any man in a nightshirt. Not even my father, as he was always so careful to wear a dressing gown and slippers when he wandered around the house. The sight had frightened me, Freddy with his hair askew, nonsensical jabberings coming out of his mouth. The things he said Mr. Stephens tried to do.

At that moment, Mr. Stephens—Judge Stephens—had gone quite pale, and a tiny flickering of pity campaigned for my attention, but I strove on, about how I'd sat on the bottom step, just a jack's toss away from Father's open office door, and I'd heard Father berating him, telling him that what was fine and forgotten as a young man's college hijinks had no place in a God-fearing man's home. And if he garnered one more complaint from a clerk or intern, Father would personally see to it that he was disbarred.

"That was a lifetime ago." The man had aged twenty years since I walked into his chambers. "I have a wife. Children. Grandchildren."

All of whom would be devastated if they ever learned of his previous exploits.

"Why would you ever tell anyone?"

Perhaps, I said, I am simply incapable of keeping a promise.

Silence drifted down around us, and as it piled up, it sealed the veracity of my threat.

"Why should anybody believe you?"

A better question might be, why should anyone believe I would make up such a slanderous tale? I'd quite forgotten it myself until it occurred to me that I might benefit from our old family friend's advancement to the bench. How serendipitous to need from him a favor, and to have such a favor to offer in return: my silence.

He stared at me, clearly rattled, before crossing over to a tall filing cabinet behind his desk and returning with a thick, green folio.

"What do you want?"

I repeated, once again, my request. The girl quickly and quietly locked away. And, happy with my newfound ground, tacked on a new requirement. Two years.

He made one last attempt. "No one would believe you."

I looked at the folder, somehow knowing it held my answer, and drove the argument home. Perhaps no one would believe me, but they would believe my father. He might be dead, but he was known for keeping meticulously detailed journals.

This was, of course, a bluff. Father was known to scribble his thoughts, and his notebooks might very well be stashed away in the attic or in the cabinets beneath the bookshelves in the library, but I'd never once bothered with familiarizing myself with their contents. And I had no intention of doing so now. I held my breath until he opened the folder and took out a crisp, white sheet.

"There is a place . . ."

Before the fire, it was called the Bridewell, but now it was simply the House of Corrections—in Chicago, a lifetime away from our own home. And it was known to house children, often without benefit of trial, sentenced directly by arresting officers. Petty thieves, mostly. Vandals. Most often victims of their own circumstances, but taken to Bridewell—sometimes for as little as a single night, to learn a lesson.

Sweetly, I said it would be like sending her away, using the same indulgent, optimistic tone I might if we were launching her on a European tour or sending her to some refined East Coast boarding school.

"If such a thought helps you sleep at night, yes."

The way he looked at me—from that moment I knew he'd spoken a curse. That I'd never again enjoy a full night's rest. At least, not until the girl was free again, home with her mother, wherever that home might be.

But I know now, too, the curse spoken to me that day reached far beyond a few wretched hours each night of wakeful time to ponder. My physicians could never prove this, of course, and might think me mad to even say so, but as I spanned the distance between us to shake Judge Stephens's hand, I know his touch wakened the disease which even now devours me.

CHAPTER 13
CELESTE, AGE 9

1915

CELESTE WORE HER BEST green wool coat and warmest muffler and hat to guard against the February chill. Mother still laughed at what Californians deemed winter, and Daddy wore only a scarf draped around his neck in deference to the cold, but they were always saying that Celeste had the thinnest blood of them all. She gripped the chocolate bar in her pocket with a mittened hand and gripped Daddy's with the other. Mother and Calvin lagged behind, not nearly as excited as Celeste to see the film.

She skipped to match his stride. "Will there be a talking rabbit?"

He squeezed her hand. "Of course, darling. You can't very well tell the story of Alice in Wonderland without a talking rabbit."

"And will it be in color? Like the other one?" For her seventh birthday party, he'd shown her an *Alice in Wonderland* film, projected with beautiful colors on their own living room wall.

"No, darling," he said, before going on to explain, again, that the film's colorization was a result of tinting individual frames of film. A process far too expensive and detailed to be applied to anything but the most special of projects.

As they approached the theater, the crowd grew dense, until

everybody's steps slowed to a near stop. Tucking herself closer to her father's side, Celeste looked up and around. No wonder Mother wasn't happy. She hated crowds, and moreover, she hated for Celeste to be a part of one, always worrying that she would get lost or snatched away. Now Mother sidled up beside her and clamped a hand on her shoulder with a heaviness Celeste could feel through her coat.

"Still think this is going to be a stupid film," Calvin said. He stuffed his hands in his pockets and looked around, as if fearful to be recognized standing on the street, waiting for a chance to see a film adaptation of a children's book. "A guy's got better things to do of an evening than hang around with his parents and kid sister."

"You didn't seem to be above our company when you were wolfing down that steak at the restaurant earlier," their father said. "And how do you ever expect to learn about the business by hanging out at some pool hall with your hooligan friends?"

"Business." Calvin's dismissive tone raised Celeste's hackles on her father's behalf. She could recite the argument that would follow. How Daddy's patents on his film-developing processes would make them richer than they could ever imagine, countered by Calvin's caustic remarks about Mother's money making it possible for Daddy to "play" at being a scientist.

Film developer today, producer tomorrow.

If film production is the highest goal, might as well work in a camera factory.

Ingrate. Most young men would love to have—

And here, Calvin would explode, spouting off about how all of his friends' fathers have actual professions, while he's saddled with an eccentric who fancies himself equally a scientist, inventor, and entrepreneur, while being nothing more than a womanizing—

And *here*, Mother would step in and hush them both.

Luckily, neither man sought to bring the familiar rancor to the crowded sidewalk. Instead, they merged themselves into the neat, single-file line at the box office window, where Daddy handed money through the oval cut into the glass to pay for their tickets.

Inside, the warm lobby smelled of salted peanuts being dispensed from a roaster one small, white bag at a time. This was hardly Celeste's first time to visit, but still the opulence of the interior struck every young, romantic chord within her. Rich red carpet, stripes of black velvet on the walls, and plush, round sofas with potted palms seeming to grow right out of their centers. Daddy led the family through it with authoritative familiarity, eager, as always, to secure what he said were the only seats worth having in any movie house, anywhere—five rows from the floor, smack in the middle. Having taught the formula to Celeste, he set her free to run ahead and twist her way through the crowd to claim their seats.

She relished the freedom, zigging and zagging, dodging elbows and nimbly stepping over feet. Still, she was far from invisible, as at least three people from the time she left her father's side to the time she found their seats commented on her beauty upon her passing by. She'd trained her ear to the compliments. The sharp intake of breath, the whispered *"Oh, my! What a lovely little girl,"* the cooing and clucking over the richness of her curls or the perfection of her features. When she was with one or the other of her parents, strangers would stop them on the street and declare aloud that she was the most beautiful child they'd ever seen. She liked it best when she was with Daddy because he would beam right along beside her in agreement. Mother, though, would ask the stranger kindly not to fill Celeste's head with such nonsense, lest it grow too big for her own good.

Celeste, however, was so keenly aware of her beauty as to

take it as a fact of being. She didn't have any singular feature shared with either parent. Her father had brown hair, and so did she—almost—with traces of gold, prompting Graciela to declare it *caramelo*. She and her mother had blue eyes, but Mother's turned down at the corners and were prone to a pale, grayish hue, while Celeste's had been described as looking like circles from a summer sky. But that was when she was a baby. Lately, they'd been settling into something more like a mossy green.

She'd once asked Graciela what her mother looked like, and she'd said, *"Oscuro. Como yo."* Dark, like her. Celeste had thought how much easier it must be if everybody in a family looked just alike. Brown hair. Brown eyes. Brown skin. She and Mother and Daddy and Calvin all looked like they'd been assembled from leftover dollhouse families, Calvin with his jet-black hair and Mother's tendency to being fat. And so, when strangers on the street would declare her beautiful, or when photographers on the beach would ask Mother's permission to take her picture, or even when she caught a glimpse of herself in a mirror and spent a minute or so in admiration, she knew it to be a gift that had been singularly bestowed upon her; therefore, humility seemed an inappropriate response.

She walked up the aisle, counting the rows to herself until she reached five, then used her experience to gauge the center. Satisfied she'd picked what would be pleasing to her father, she sat down and began listlessly kicking the seat in front of her, continuing until what had merely been the top of a hat rose up, turned around, and became a face twisted with irritation.

"Hey, kid. Do you mind?"

"Sorry."

She pulled her feet close and pouted, making her eyes as round as she could.

Immediately the man's expression softened. "Say, you're pretty enough to be Alice in this picture. Are you in the movies?"

"Not yet." It was the answer she always gave, followed by, "But my father is in the business, so it's only a matter of time."

If they were ever in the company of somebody who was already "in the business," she knew to say something like *"But my father is working on a colorizing process that will make it so everybody can appreciate the color of my eyes."* Then she'd stare wide and blink so that they couldn't look away. If the inquiry came from one of his university colleagues, she said, *"No, but I hope he makes a breakthrough soon so that he can bring chemistry and art together and make a colorized film of me!"* That one had been more difficult to memorize, mostly because her father had given her so many different versions of the response before landing on something satisfactory.

If she were in the company of her mother and asked the same question, she simply said, *"No."*

"Your father's in the business, eh?" The stranger looked amused. "What's he do?"

Before Celeste could reply, Mother was crossing in front of her, blocking the view of the man, lingering long enough that, by the time she sat down, he'd turned back and was nothing more than the top of a hat again.

Mother leaned close and hissed in her ear, "What have I told you about talking to strangers?"

"I'm sorry." Celeste knew better than to try the wide-eyed routine on Mother.

Daddy took the seat on the other side of her, and Calvin next to Daddy, where he immediately took a cigarette from his coat pocket and lit it with a match struck against the bottom of his shoe.

Mother leaned forward. "Really, Calvin. Must you?"

He shook the match to a glowing ember. "If I gotta sit through this mess, I mean to enjoy it."

A small group of musicians dressed in tuxedos that had seen far better days assembled in the small pit in front of the screen. They set their scores on the music stands and struck a single, strong note. Immediately the conversation in the theater fell to a hush, then to silence as the heavy red velvet curtain opened, revealing the silvery screen behind it.

Celeste scrunched her face, holding her breath and closing her eyes just long enough to say the quickest prayer to God that she might be on a screen someday, and then opened her eyes to see the opening credits fade away into a scene of a small kitchen, a woman baking tarts, and a young girl walking through the door.

That could be me.

As if reading her mind, Daddy leaned over and whispered, "You're a hundred times prettier than that little girl."

Celeste beamed in agreement. The Alice on the screen was tall and gangly, her hair not curly at all. But soon she forgot all about any sort of comparison, getting lost in the fantasy unfolding on the screen, clutching at her father's arm in fear of the evil Queen of Hearts. When it was over, and the theater filled with light to allow a safe exit, she began an immediate recap, extolling the wonders scene by scene. The way Alice's shadow walked away from her body, almost invisible, into dreamland?

"How did they do that, Daddy?" But before he could answer, she'd moved on to how the rabbit's eyes blinked and his nose twitched, the silliness of the Dodo bird, the terrifying Gryphon, and the Walrus, and the Mock-Turtle, and—

"They're all nothing but some two-bit actor in a costume,"

Calvin said. By now they'd reached the street outside the theater, where Daddy beckoned for a taxi to take them home.

"Must you be so unpleasant?" Mother sounded weary and distracted.

"Off with your head!" Celeste hoped to lighten the mood but drew only a scowl from both Mother and Calvin, though several people milling around them chuckled their approval at her display.

Daddy ignored her, stretching his hand out and shouting, "Taxi! Taxi!" His efforts were rewarded by a honking horn as an automobile approached the curb. Upon arrival, it turned out to be a topless roadster packed with four young men, one of whom hung over the side, shouting, "DuFrane!" into the already-noisy street.

"Russel!" Calvin broke away from the family and rushed toward the car, up and over the door, and wedged into the backseat without its ever coming to a full stop. Mother called out to him, but he merely glanced over his shoulder and shouted a promise to be home sometime before dawn as the car wove itself into the pattern of automobiles on the street.

"I don't like those boys," Mother said to whoever might be listening. "I don't trust them."

"They're just boys." Having convinced a cab to take them home, Daddy held open the back door and they all three piled in—Celeste comfortable and warm in the middle—for the short ride home. "No different than I was at that age."

"Surely you don't expect me to take any comfort in that." Mother's voice was flat, without humor or flirtation.

"Take what you will, Marguerite. You always do."

He gave their address to the driver, and the rest of the ride was silent, with Mother and Daddy each staring out their own windows while Celeste stared at the driver's shoulder. Celeste closed her eyes and let the rumble of the engine lull her into a half dream, where she imagined the transparent shadow of herself escaping this car—maybe slipping through that narrow opening at the top of the window—and into the city streets, mingling with the people and the noise and the lights. Anything but this stifling silence. She still had so many questions about the movie. How did they make the Cheshire Cat disappear? How could that old man accomplish all those acrobatics? Questions she knew her father could answer, and would do so with genuine, generous attention. But even as she inhaled, preparing to ask the first one, Mother patted her arm softly and said, "Please, darling. I've developed quite a nauseous stomach," clapping and trapping them to death like the poor Mock-Turtle in his soup.

Rather than stopping at the curb, the cabbie took the car through the rounded driveway and dropped them all right at the front door, where soft yellow light shone through the arched windows. Celeste broke free from her mother and bounded up the steps, opening the door to see Graciela waiting, arms outstretched. Celeste wanted to run into them for warmth, and would have, had her mother not been on her heels crossing the threshold.

"How was the movie, Señora DuFrane?" Graciela's arms became a rack across which Mother draped her coat. She took Celeste's and did the same.

"Delightful," Mother said. "Celeste, I'm sure, will talk your ear off about it as you're getting her ready for bed. Then if you'll please send up some warm milk to my room? I'm quite tired and retiring early."

"Sí, señora."

Daddy slipped in and gave Graciela an apologetic look along with his overcoat. His hand was warm from his glove, and he laid it alongside Celeste's cheek. "We'll talk about the movie a little more in the morning. Maybe Graciela will make pancakes."

He walked off in the direction of his office. At Graciela's prompting, Celeste followed her mother upstairs. Within just a few minutes, she'd washed her face and changed into her warmest flannel nightgown. With her feet tucked down in the sheets, she took her tattered copy of *Alice's Adventures in Wonderland* and let it fall open in her lap, merging the scenes from the film with the words from the story, speaking Alice's dialogue aloud.

"I'm not quite myself, you see." She held her arms dramatically akimbo, not the least self-conscious when Graciela came in. She was carrying a tray with two slices of buttered toast cut into triangles and a tall glass of milk. Celeste puffed herself up and assumed the character of the Queen of Hearts, demanding her tarts.

Graciela didn't miss a beat. "I'm not afraid of you. You're nothing but a deck of cards." They'd read the book together more than once.

Celeste tried to appear fearsome but soon collapsed into giggles. She scooted to the edge of her bed and nibbled on the toast as Graciela ran the hairbrush through her curls, slowly and steadily smoothing them against her wide palm. Between sips of milk, Celeste recounted the film in all its detail, wishing Graciela had been able to come with them and see it for herself.

"Maybe I will go. *Jueves. Semana próxima.*" She paused, giving Celeste an opportunity to translate.

"Thursday. Next week?"

She nodded, confirming. "My day off."

"Can I go with you?" Often, they'd gone to a matinee together after a lunch at a little restaurant owned by Graciela's cousin.

"*Veremos.* You have school."

Celeste wrinkled her nose, even though the manipulative nature of the expression would be lost on Graciela, who sat behind her. "I'll bet Viola Savoy doesn't have to go to school."

"Come on." Graciela got up from the bed and nudged Celeste to do the same. "Let's say prayers."

Side by side, they knelt, elbows propped up on the soft mattress. Eyes closed, Celeste prayed thanks for her home and asked blessings on her family and Graciela. "And please, dear heavenly Father, bring Calvin safely home." At this, she felt Graciela's soft touch on her back. "And, Lord, before I die, let me be in a movie."

Beside her, Graciela made the familiar sign of the cross, saying, *"En el nombre del Padre, del Hijo, y del Espíritu Santo, amén."*

They said *amén* together, though long ago Graciela had discouraged Celeste from making the sign of the cross, saying it wasn't a practice of her family's church, though Celeste had argued that they only had a church at Christmastime.

Prayers said, Celeste snuggled under her covers, at ease with the darkness that settled around her, even as it was softened by a stream of light seeping through the door left open a tiny crack. Graciela kissed the top of her head, and her mother and father would likely come in to do the same later in the night.

Most nights, after all of this, she would succumb to sweet sleep, but tonight a restlessness took root, holding her captive and awake—waiting. Though the image of what she was waiting for remained as elusive as the mysterious Cheshire Cat. Immediately, she supposed, she was waiting for her mother or her father to kiss her good night, even though Mother had certainly gone to bed herself by now and Daddy was known to work in his office until the wee hours in the morning. Calvin's abrupt departure had cast such a pall on the evening, perhaps she was waiting for him, too, hoping there might be some sort of restoration before they all went to sleep. Not that such a scenario was anywhere near likely. She couldn't remember the last time her older brother had apologized for anything, nor when either of her parents had compelled him to do any such thing.

It didn't help that there were clear signs coming from the house that the evening was progressing without her. She heard laughter coming from downstairs, traveling its echoing path, losing words but bringing mirth. Graciela's laughter, low and warm, and her father's, occasionally. He must have been telling her about the movie, the secrets of all the silly moments, not wanting to wait until breakfast time. It wasn't fair. Celeste wanted to talk about the movie. Tried to, until stupid Calvin made everybody mad. More laughter—loud and then hushed.

Imagining her shadow-self, Celeste crept out of her bed and to the door, peering through the narrow opening, seeing the empty hallway and her mother's closed-off room. Safe from detection, she slipped silently down the hall, to the stairs, and winced at the cold tile on her feet. When faced with the choice of running back for her slippers or running down to listen to Daddy's conversation with Graciela, curiosity won out.

"Come on," she whispered to herself, then made her way down, step by step, and sat on the last one. From here not only would she be able to hear them, but she could smell the unmistakable scent of Graciela's cooking—eggs and peppers and cheese. She could hear the spatula scraping against the iron skillet, and her mind filled in the image of Graciela's soft, rounded body swaying with the motion.

At the moment there was a lull in conversation, and Celeste held her breath, fearing they'd detected her presence. She heard a plate being set on the counter and another rustle before her father said, softly, "Thank you."

"You're welcome, *Arturo*. And good night. I'll clean up the dishes in the morning."

Drat. She'd missed everything, until she heard her father say one more word.

"Stay."

He said it like some kind of command, though he was never one to boss Graciela around. Not like Mother, who constantly barked orders from all over the house—get this at the market, clean this, do that. Never with a please or a thank-you. So to hear Daddy speak this one word already brought an uncomfortable unfamiliarity to the conversation in the kitchen. But then, a response Celeste could never have predicted from Graciela.

"No."

It wasn't much more than a whisper. A tiny breath of a word drifting away like so much smoke.

No.

Never, no matter what duty she'd been charged to undertake, had Graciela been defiant. Anytime Celeste had been too demanding, she'd say, "*Más tarde, cariña.* Maybe this afternoon when I've finished the laundry." But as far as her parents were concerned, she'd been pleasantly compliant. Often indulgent. Until tonight.

Stay.

No.

"Just for a little while. Until I finish eating. Keep me company."

"It is late."

"It's not eleven o'clock. Stay with me until Calvin comes home."

"No." Again, stronger this time. "I will see you in the morning, Mr. DuFrane."

Then the unmistakable sound of a chair scraping back across the floor, then something like a whimper, then a new kind of silence. Fuller, and it stirred something unfamiliar within her.

Celeste kept her bottom glued to the step but leaned forward, stretching her neck, hoping to get a peek around the corner. But even if she'd been one of the flamingo mallets from the queen's croquet game, she couldn't have seen into the kitchen. She'd have to get up, walk around the corner, stand in that wide, square doorway, risking her own detection to see something she knew would be best kept hidden.

Still, she stood and took two soft, cold steps, clinging to the banister, as if that would guarantee a quick escape.

"What are you doing up, kid?"

She managed to stifle her scream just in time, turning around to see Calvin, uncharacteristically disheveled, holding a warning finger to his lips. He himself had spoken barely above a whisper, his question more of a feeling than a sound, and when he took his finger away, he too gripped the banister, though clearly in an attempt to steady himself. With his free hand, he gripped Celeste's wrist and pulled her to him and, without another word, led her back to her room.

"Get in," he said, gesturing half-interestedly toward her bed. Silently she obeyed. Then, for the first time in memory, he sat down heavily on its edge. "Were you getting a snack?"

She shook her head, feeling the static against the pillow. "I was listening."

His sour breath let out a humorless laugh. "Dad and Graciela?"

She nodded, and he said something that would have earned a scolding from Mother.

"Why do you have to be so mean all of the time?"

His dark hair was mussed from its usual sleekness, and he ran his hand through it, causing even more disruption. "Am I?"

"Tonight you were. We were all having a lovely time and might have come home to have hot chocolate or something, but you had to go off with your stupid friends and make Mother mad and so nobody said a word."

"We weren't going to have hot chocolate. When was the last time any of us ever sat around to drink hot chocolate? But if that's what Princess Celeste wants, that's what she'll get. I've no doubt Graciela is still in the kitchen."

He said this last bit with a sneer that made him look diabolical in the dim light. She knew he was thinking mean, awful things, and she felt an ugliness growing beyond their usual filial dislike.

"Just go. Get out of my room. Nobody ever really wants you around. They didn't even care when you left. Didn't say another word about you."

He laughed, and the sound of it proved more frightening than any scowl or sneer. "Do you think I don't know that already, little sister?"

There was a hurt buried deep within his words, and she wished she could take her own back.

"I didn't mean—"

"You might be surprised to learn that things were pretty good before you came along. I remember, when I was a kid, Mom and Dad and me. We used to—*they* used to talk to me and each other. We'd spend entire days at the park, flying kites. Having picnics . . ."

He picked one of her dolls up out of the basket by her bed and held it loosely in his hands. "And then you died."

Terrified, both of his words and the eerie, tomb-like emptiness of his voice, Celeste clutched her blanket and brought it straight up to her nose.

"Wait." He brought the doll up and tapped his forehead against it. "You couldn't have died, could you? But you did. I remember. That's when Mom stopped looking at me. When I knew I'd never be enough for her. Because you died for a while. And then—"

He stopped, looking at her as if seeing his little sister for the first time.

"And then what?"

"And then you came back."

CHAPTER 14
DANA SEES STARS

1925

NO FEWER THAN FIFTEEN dresses lay strewn across the bed, each one a masterpiece of silk and beads and fringe. Celeste stood in front of a full-length, gilded mirror, dressed in nothing more than stockings and a garter belt, holding up yet another—this one festooned with long, black feathers—against her pale skin.

"Too dramatic?"

"I'm not one to judge," Dana said. She sat on the upholstered bench at the foot of the bed, idly running her thumb and forefinger along the rippling velvet hem of a rich, red garment. "I've never been to a—what is it called again?"

"A premiere. And neither have I, for that matter. Not as a real person, anyway."

"A real person?"

"An actress. Somebody in the film. I've always been one of those screamers on the street hoping to grab John Gilbert's attention."

"But it's not your first movie."

"It's my first where I get to be an actual woman. I even have a kiss; can you believe that? And for the first time you'll see

Celeste DuFrane on the movie poster in the lobby." She turned her attention back to her reflection and decided that the black dress wouldn't do after all. "It's for a much older woman." Then, inspiration. "Maybe you should wear it."

Dana didn't know if she should be amused or offended, so she offered only a low chuckle in reply as Celeste clapped her hand over her mouth in wide-eyed mortification.

"I'm so sorry." She dropped her hand. "I'm such a dope. That was terribly rude, wasn't it? I just meant that . . . well, you are . . ."

"Old?"

"Really, not so much, but I forget. Sometimes, you seem, I dunno. Older."

"You're getting kinder by the minute."

Celeste made a sound of frustration, threw the black feathered dress on the pile, and cinched her silk robe around her waist. "Didn't you think everybody was old when you were my age?"

At this, Dana *did* laugh, though more bitterly than she'd intended, and her heart softened at the stricken look on Celeste's face. "I don't know that I remember much about being your age. Everything for me is rather a blur. I was a child, I was a child, I was a child, and then—"

"Then what?" Celeste sat on the edge of the bed, mindless of the silks and chiffons piled upon it. "Think back to when you were a child. Before all of this." She waved her hand, as if dismissing nearly twenty years of injustice. "What did you want? More than anything? I wanted to be in the movies. And here I am."

"All Mama and I ever talked about was for her to find a good job as a live-in in a big house, where I could stay and work beside her."

"So your dream was to be a maid?" Celeste had never looked more confused.

"That was my mother's dream. All I ever wanted was to see her happy."

"Nothing for yourself? I remember lying in that room—" she pointed out, toward the room Dana now occupied—"praying to God to be in a movie. I can remember it like yesterday."

Dana smiled indulgently. "A lot more time has passed for me since my childhood."

"Maybe so. But here you are now. Here we both are at this same place. The one thing we have in common is that we were both children, once. And now we're both women. Maybe if we can find something we held in common back then, we can find something we hold in common now."

Dana kept her composure only by imagining Celeste to still be that child, longing to be an actress, playing dress-up with her mother's cast-off gowns.

"Did your mother want you to be an actress?"

Celeste blushed, the pale flesh of her collarbone blotched red. "She hated the idea. Tried everything she could to stop it. Sometimes, and I know this sounds awful, but I don't think she ever forgave me for not being my sister. She saw my existence as being the reason for Mary's death, like the universe had to push her aside to make way for me."

The brash, confident girl who, mere moments ago, had bragged about her name on a motion picture poster all but disappeared, grown smaller and nearly silent toward the end of her revelation. A wave of compassion swept over Dana as she imagined that the only thing worse than being locked away by Marguerite DuFrane's misplaced revenge would be to grow up under it. She needn't tell her that all she'd ever wanted as a child was to live in a house like the DuFranes', surrounded by pretty things she could call her own. And it would be cruel to enlighten Celeste on just where Dana had been when *she* was nineteen—one small, dark cell. Alone and forgotten for a period of time she'd yet been able to measure, and wanting nothing more than an opportunity to speak the truth. Tell her story, and walk out to . . .

What? Where would she have gone had the doors and gates mysteriously opened all those years ago?

Somehow, in this moment, she had all she'd ever wanted.

"Perhaps," Dana said softly, "we have more in common than we think."

Celeste looked up, not understanding.

"I don't believe your mother liked me very much either."

The first giggle snuck out like a mistake, and each seemed to need the other's permission before any laughter could ensue. When it did, it came across with great release, dying away only briefly as both stole a glance at the framed photograph of Marguerite DuFrane on Celeste's dresser.

"When was that taken?"

"Shortly after we moved here." Celeste's brow furrowed in thought. "Just think. She must have been about your age."

Dana squinted, a further reminder that she must see someone about the growing dimness in her eyes. "She looks older."

The second round of laughter had a sweet air of wickedness and died out with a harmonious sigh that led to the most comfortable and content of silences.

"You should go with me," Celeste said after a time.

"Where?" Dana had lost all thread of conversation.

"To the premiere. Tonight."

Before Dana could protest, Celeste had bounded off the bed, calling, *"Graciela!"* at an increasing volume until the older woman's head poked through the door.

"*Sí,* Celita?"

"Do you have time to do a quick set on Dana's hair before tonight? We have to leave at six o'clock. No later."

"Oh yes." The older woman's smile was warm and proud, and if Dana envied Celeste anything, it was growing up with such devoted care. "I'll be back. Ten minutes."

"And I think this to wear." Celeste held up a dress of deep midnight blue. A simple sheath with strands of tiny black beads at the hem. "It's sophisticated without being stuffy. And it'll keep people guessing about your figure."

Dana's mind swirled with fear and possibility, but mostly fear, and she interrupted Celeste in the middle of a thought concerning high-heeled shoes.

"I can't go."

Celeste prattled on a few words before stopping her train of thought and changing direction. "What do you mean you can't go? Why not?"

"You act as though I'm nothing more than some distant friend of the family come to visit. You do remember where I've been, realize how I've lived most of my life. Why do you think I can just put on a fancy dress and go to a party?"

Celeste merely stared, blinking.

"I could never talk to any of those people."

"You never seem to have much of a problem talking to Werner."

Now it was Dana's turn to go speechless, and the expression on her face inspired a knowing half smile on Celeste's as she answered Dana's unasked question.

"Yes, he'll be there. He hates these things too, rumor has it. But he hopes to direct the star of this picture in one of his own, so . . ."

"I've never been to a party. Of any kind. I wouldn't know what to do or what to say."

"Do what I do. Say what I say, unless I drink too much champagne, because I tend to get quite vulgar when I drink. Trick is, stick close to me and you'll be fine."

"But I've never—"

"Jeepers creepers, Dana. Are you going to spend the rest of your life making decisions based on what you've never done? Because if you are, I might as well lock you up in a room right here so you'll feel nice and comfortable."

Despite her tone of gentle encouragement, the words stung like a slap, and Dana flushed with anger.

"You would never say such a thing if you knew, if you really understood."

"Don't be silly. Of course I would. Now . . ." She held the dress out in front of her and shook it, filling the room with the sound of softly clicking beads.

Two beams of light shot straight up in the air. Arm in arm, Dana and Celeste walked straight between them. As if the beams weren't enough, intermittent flashes from the photographers lining the street burned nearly to blindness.

"Over here!" they shouted. "Miss DuFrane?" And Dana would step away to allow Celeste to rest her hand on her out-thrust hip and pout prettily.

"Who's this with you?" more than one asked.

"My sister!" It was the ruse upon which they'd all agreed—Dana, Celeste, and her manager, Roland Lundi. Less complicated than the truth, and a perfect little seed to plant in hopes of growing an interest in their story. All of that had come from Mr. Lundi's fertile, forward-thinking brain. In fact, he was supposed to have been on Celeste's arm this evening as something of a professional date, but had gladly given up his spot in lieu of this opportunity.

"Just wait until they get wind of the whole story," Celeste said, somehow managing to speak without losing a bit of her smile. "They're gonna eat us up like candy."

Dana clutched her beaded purse and willed herself not to run away. Not that she'd know where to go. A chauffeured car had dropped them off in front of the ornate theater and disappeared into the night.

"Isn't it exotic?" Celeste said. It was, with columns and palm trees and images of an Egyptian pharaoh watching over the crowd. "Like walking right into Tutankhamen's tomb."

As the crowd pressed closer, the cameras flashed more brightly, and the questions became more insistent, Dana wished there were a tomb to climb into. At the very least, she was tempted to climb into the backseat of any one of the cars pulling away from the curb and let it take her where it willed. Anything would be better than this, and when Celeste pulled her close, cheek to cheek, the touch of the young girl's cool, powdered face next to her damp, flustered one incited panic, and she cringed away.

"What is wrong with you?" Again Celeste spoke with a frozen smile and a pretty wave out to the crowd. "We need to make it look like we love each other, you know?"

"I'm so—" She meant to say, *I'm sorry*, but the word got caught in whatever mass of air had lodged itself in her throat, leaving Dana unable to breathe, let alone speak. The lights around her became one contiguous blur, and individual voices a single, sustained roar. She had to get away from this spot, this place, and faced with a singular path walled with people, leading either to the street or into the theater, she shrugged from her sister's grip and pushed her way through the crowd, ignoring their protests as she staggered toward the open doors and the golden light of the opulent lobby.

"Dana!"

Her name, his voice, somehow cut through the pressing din of the crowd, but she could not bring herself to lift her head to look for him.

"Dana!"

Again, closer, and she covered her ears, hoping to drown out every other sound. She'd stopped still in the center of the room and allowed herself to be buffeted by the milling throng, each elbow and shoulder threatening to pierce her skin. She would scream if she had breath, but she didn't.

"Dana, darling."

Werner.

He was right beside her now, a protective arm around her shoulder, keeping her from falling to pieces right there in the middle of the Egyptian lobby.

"Come on."

A dark frame had formed a border around her vision, so she turned her face to his jacket, trusting him with every step. They paused for a moment while he fumbled for something in his pocket.

"Go. Get my car and bring it to the alleyway. Fetch me here."

Whatever he'd given the young man resulted in a pubescent exclaim of gratitude and surprise.

"In here," Werner said and, with his hand on the small of her back, guided her past a long wooden counter and through a door into what she soon perceived to be a coat closet. Immediately the clamor of the crowd disappeared as she found herself in a small room lined with all manner of fur coats along a wall.

"Sit down," he ordered, and she obeyed, wondering where the chair had materialized from. He placed his hand on the back of her head and—"Between your knees"—lowered it.

Slowly she felt her body relax, returning to a pattern of deep, measured breath.

"Twenty . . . ," he counted, "nineteen . . . eighteen . . . seventeen . . ."

She was well recovered by the time he got to ten but maintained her posture for the remainder of the countdown to work up the courage to face him after such a display.

"One."

She sensed him crouching beside her and lifted her eyes. "I'm so sorry. I don't know what happened to me. What a fool—"

"Tsch," he chastised with a half grin. "It is a horrible business, all of this for a movie, and each one bigger and sillier than the last."

"Celeste will be so upset with me."

"Nonsense. You've left more of the spotlight for her. She will be in your debt."

Now it was Dana's turn to attempt to smile. The smallness of the room gave an odd sense of comfort, as she felt cushioned by the coats and hidden in its dim light. Her peace deepened with Werner's presence. Close, but not touching. His hand rested on the back of her chair, and he remained at eye level, not towering over. She could touch him if she wanted to, and a restless movement in her fingers made her think that she did. His jacket was made of the lushest black wool she had ever seen, its lapel lined with velvet. Almost in contrast, his face boasted a bit of stubble, indicating he hadn't bothered to shave for this momentous event. With each newly steady breath, she longed to touch both—the richness of his jacket, the roughness of his face. She didn't remember ever wanting to touch anybody this much. Not since the baby.

And with that memory, she balled up her fists and looked away.

"We do not have to stay, you know," Werner said. "Say the word and I'll take you right away from here."

"Celeste is expecting me."

"Celeste, by now, has had two glasses of champagne and is pretending to be annoyed at the flirtations of a dozen producers."

Dana almost giggled. "Still, she might be a little concerned about the antics of her crazy sister."

Werner's brow cocked at the word *sister*. "Is that what she is calling you?"

"We had to say something."

"And why wouldn't an actress want to star in the movie about her own sister's tragic tale. The girl is a publicity savant." He stood and, in so doing, hooked his finger under her chin and raised her face to look at him. "Do you want to stay?"

"In here? Yes."

He gave a gentle laugh. "For the screening. And the party after?"

"I—I don't know." But she did know, and it seemed he did too.

"Come on. I've had my car brought around. We'll go for a drive, get some fresh air, and slip in for the final reel. Nobody will even know we've been away."

"But Celeste—"

"I'll send one of the pages to find her and tell her to look for us after the film."

With an air of decisiveness, Werner charged out of the closet, giving Dana a free moment to take her small mirror out of her clutch and see if any of Celeste's meticulously applied makeup had survived her abuse. Thankfully, there was just the slightest smudging of the kohl outlining her eyes, and her painted lips seemed fully intact. She dabbed her nose and forehead with powder as she'd seen Celeste do countless times, stood, and was smoothing her dress when Werner returned.

He held out his hand. "Come."

Without a word, she took it.

Her sequined headband performed its duty, keeping her hair in place as they drove in the night. Dana held a listless arm out over the car door, twisting her wrist in the breeze. Beside her, Werner drove, a seemingly forgotten cigarette locked between his fingers as he gripped the wheel.

They'd driven first through the city streets, awash in the lights, surrounded by their fellow motorists. Before too long, though, they'd made their way into the hills, and a darkness like she'd never imagined enveloped them.

"Lo, I have brought thee out of Egypt," Werner intoned. "Though it was not exactly the miracle of parting the Red Sea."

"I've never been to the beach."

"There's no time to go tonight."

His reply startled her, as she didn't realize she'd spoken aloud. "I didn't mean—" she stammered. "I wouldn't presume—"

"Someday I will take you to the beach. I have a house there."

His statement disallowed argument. She turned her face up to look at the stars. "I've never been to the moon either."

"I'm afraid I am no help to you there."

A sideways glance showed that he was grinning, and she thrilled at the feeling of being one part of a shared mind. Never before had anybody been so close, not even her mother, who worked far too many hours to ever commit time to such idle thoughts. To say anything more would ruin the moment, so she offered only a grin of her own before returning her gaze to the sky.

After a few more winding turns, Werner steered the car off the road entirely, cut the engine, and turned off the headlights. Below, the city lay like a gathering of diamonds on an endless stretch of black velvet—not that she'd ever seen such a thing. A steady stream of glowing lights showed an endless progression of automobiles, looking so orderly in their journeys from this distance.

"To think," Werner said, "all of this come to pass within our lifetime. Where I come from, towns are dated by centuries. Here? Overnight, it's a city."

She followed his lead, getting up to sit along the top of the seat, making the view even more expansive. *Within our lifetime.* To think of all she'd missed. Until she came to Los Angeles, she'd never ridden in an automobile or listened to a radio or eaten fish or seen a movie. . . . And below, an entire population for whom all of these things were daily occurrences. Werner wasn't the only foreigner gazing out upon a strange, new land.

"Do you imagine this is how God sees us?" she asked, as much to herself as to him.

"No."

She looked at him. "You don't believe in God?"

"Of course I do."

"You don't believe he watches us?"

He shook his head. "Not like this. Not from this kind of distance. How could anybody out there call and be heard? How can we see from here any need or pain?"

"That's just it. I think, sometimes, he doesn't. If he could see me or hear me, how could he have just *left* me there in that place?"

"I was a filmmaker before the war." He spoke out to the city. "And during, too, though mostly a photographer. Easier to capture and hold an image at a time. When you photograph the dead—young men, motionless . . . They tell their own story. It was hard, then, to imagine God looking down and allowing such atrocities to take place."

"That must have been awful," she said, aware of how petulant she must sound in comparison. "And I don't mean to imply any doubt."

"I know." Then, somehow, her hand was encased in his, and he brought it to his lips. She felt the brush of his faint whiskers against her skin, reminding her of a peach she'd had one time, and her mouth filled with the remembered sweetness of it. He laid her palm flat against his chest, pressing it to the point that she felt the sharp corners of his onyx buttons digging into the heel of her palm, and the beating of his heart beneath her fingers. "I think God sees us from here. That somehow he watches the world for its own sake, but for us—for you and me—he watches from within. So he knows our fears, and calms them."

Once again, she couldn't breathe, but it was different from before. Not the panic that constricted her throat back at the theater, but a lifting of a burden. Moments before they'd shared a thought, and now it seemed they shared a pulse.

"There were times," he continued, "when I would be on a barren field, sitting beside a young man whose lifeblood stained the earth, and I would find myself looking at him through the eyes of God. I would feel God inside of me, stronger than I myself could ever hope to be. There must have been times when you felt that too."

She swallowed, feeling silly for her testimony of self-pity. "There were."

"Tell me."

The night's breeze was chilly—more so, it seemed, than when they were driving—and she shivered against it. Werner kissed her hand again, then released it to shrug out of his fine jacket, which he draped across her shoulders before leading her to once again sit down in the seat. Though warmer, Dana drew the lapels close around her, delighting in the weight of the wool, but also thankful to tuck herself away from his touch. She leaned her head back and looked into the vastness of the night, more sky than she'd seen in her lifetime, and let her words drift to the stars.

CHAPTER 15

EXTERIOR: The walls are eight feet tall, solid brick, and continuous save for one break spanned by scrolled-iron gates. Within, children play at makeshift matches, running in a vicious game of tag in which victims are tackled to the ground and buried under piles of flailing arms, only to be separated by the thickset matron who seems more concerned with restoring order than saving skin. No comfort is given to the littlest one under the pile as the matron unceremoniously yanks it to its feet and sends it back into the teeming fold.

CUT TO: In one corner, outside the matron's line of sight, a group of boys pass around a single cigarette.

CUT TO: Two little girls whisper secrets while a third seems poised to slug it out of them.

CUT TO: Dana, hardly a girl at all, but a young woman sitting quietly alone. She wears her hair in a single, thick braid tied with a scrap of cloth at the end. The sleeves of her dress stop well above her wrists, though the fabric hangs on her thin frame. Her stockings are riddled with holes, and a scrap identical to that which adorns her braid is wrapped around one of her shoes, holding the sole in place. She has a wooden cigar box on her lap, which she uses as a makeshift desk. Her brow is furrowed, her face twisted in concentration as she wields a stub of pencil and writes.

CLOSE-UP—LETTER: *To the Honorable Judge Stevens. Dear Sir, I have written twenty letters to you with no response. . . .*

1908

The shrill sound of the whistle pulled Dana's attention away from her writing. She looked up, thinking her ears must be playing a trick on her. Perhaps what she'd heard was an overzealous bird, as eager as the children to greet the spring. But no, there was Mrs. Karistin, striding across the courtyard, waving her arms and charging at the smoking boys as though to bowl them right into the bricks.

With a sigh, Dana placed the paper and pencil in the box and closed the lid. By the second tweet, the children were lined up along the wall, roughly by size and age, the littlest one on the end not more than five years old. He'd arrived three days ago, after planting his boot squarely in the shin of a police officer in the process of arresting his father.

Mrs. Karistin slowly strode the length of them, touching a bamboo rod to the top of each head, counting, One to Seventeen, Seventeen to One.

"Ready to lead us in, then, are you, Little Kicker?"

He gave her a comical salute, and with measured, shuffling steps, the children filed inside. Mrs. Karistin's bamboo stick created a slender but impenetrable barricade across the doorway. Wordlessly, Dana handed the box over.

"Nothing for the post?"

Dana kept her eyes trained on the massive, gray-clad shoulder in front of her. "I didn't get to finish. Might I have more time tomorrow?"

"You know my rules by now, Baby Killer. First Tuesday of the month, you get to write your letter."

Before she could stop herself, Dana protested. "But you blew the whistle early."

Thwack! And the bamboo pole struck her square across the shoulders. Mrs. Karistin could move with catlike speed when she wanted to.

"What did you say to me?"

It was the woman's favorite trap. Were Dana to say, "Nothing," she'd be struck again for lying. If she repeated the offending phrase, she'd be struck a second time for the same offense. Dana had seen it played out time and time again.

Thwack! "Were you running in the corridor?"

Thwack! "Were you whistling in the breakfast line?"

Thwack! "Did you soil your sheets again?"

Mrs. Karistin took a sinister satisfaction in the execution of the conundrum. Most children, after the first or second time, merely melted into tears at the question. Oddly enough, this often saved them from the second blow. But Dana had no tears for Mrs. Karistin or her rod. She'd learned to avoid the question altogether.

"I always have time to complete my letter, ma'am." She dug in her heels and looked straight into the matron's steel-blue eyes. "I write the same thing every month, and I know I don't write any more slowly."

Mrs. Karistin's nostrils flared and constricted throughout Dana's speech, and the smile she formed in response stretched thin and mirthless across her square face. She took the tip of the bamboo rod and touched it to Dana's chin, forcing her head back, angled to look at the sky.

"You see that?" Mrs. Karistin pressed the rod harder, until Dana felt a roughened sliver pierce her skin. "Them look like sunny spring skies up there?"

"No, ma'am." Dana kept her jaw clenched.

"Looks like storms, don't it. And I thought it would be a good idea to get them little'uns in before the storm hits. So's they don't catch a chill. But I suppose you'd rather they stay out in the rain—catch their death—wouldn't you, Baby Killer?"

For the first time in nearly a year, Dana felt the prick of tears and a more familiar burning in her stretched throat. She said nothing.

"Not enough to sneak in and kill some helpless thing in its crib. Now you want 'em all struck down with chills so you can write your precious letter."

As if in confirmation, a single cold, wet drop landed on Dana's upturned forehead and slid down her temple, blending with the first warm tear.

"Look at that." One last prod, and she took the bamboo away. "Mrs. K. knows of what she speaks, don't she? But look at your sad little face. Are you sad?" She'd developed a mincing, condescending tone. "Here." She shoved the box back into Dana's hands and flipped the lid open. "Go on. Stand out there. Write all you please."

Dana took one mistrustful step after another, heading toward her vacated bench.

"Not there," Mrs. Karistin corrected. "Right out there, middle of the courtyard. Sit yourself down." She tapped the bamboo against her palm, leaving no doubt she'd crack it across Dana's back should she refuse to comply.

The rain was coming down in earnest now, splashing onto her exposed paper, making her unfinished words thick and blurred. At this rate the paper would be soaked through, spoiled and swollen, but she dared not close the lid.

She cried openly, freely, her tears mixed with rain. Rivulets ran down into the back of her dress and her body shook with sobs and chill. It had become a downpour, filling her ears with nothing beyond the sound of water pelting against the concrete benches, the windows, and newly sprung leaves on the trees. But then there was another sound, piercing and familiar. The whistle that daily sounded the end of the children's outside play. Dana turned her head; clumped, wet strands slapped against her cheeks.

There stood Mrs. Karistin in the doorway, silver whistle trapped between compressed lips as she ushered the children one by one outside into the yard. Confusion touched each face, and while some of the more rambunctious boys ran out to splash in the puddles, the girls, especially the little ones, clung close to each other and tried to take shelter against the wall.

Dana scrambled to stand, struggling to find purchase in the wet grass, and let her letter box drop to the ground. Sodden sheets of paper spilled out, but she didn't care.

"Go inside!" She yanked at the sleeve of a boy called simply Thief, and pushed him in the direction of the door. "Go!" Running throughout the courtyard, hunched over with her arms stretched out like goose wings, Dana attempted to herd the children, too many of whom took this to be part of a marvelous surprise game, and they ran from her, squealing, heads up to let the rain wash their dirty faces. Her dress grew heavy. Mud and water seeped through her torn shoes. She continued to scream, "Go! Inside, now!" and felt her voice growing hoarse with this new demand.

The squealing sound of laughter interlaced with the pounding rain and with Dana's shouts, the ensuing cacophony enough to draw faces to the windows of the Bridewell. One in particular caught Dana's attention. Third floor, in the wing opposite where the children were housed, a square of warm yellow light within the dark-soaked red brick. A small, plain man with twice as much hair above his lip as on his head. Dana knew him only by sight and by name. She'd never had occasion to speak with him and had heard his voice only once when he came to the dormitory to certify that the nine-year-old girl in the cot next to her had coughed herself to death in the night.

Warden Webb, thumbs hooked into his vest pockets, stared down at the chaotic scene below. Under his watchful eye, Dana stopped and squared her stance.

"She won't let us in!" Her hand was growing numb with cold, but she molded it into a single pointing finger stretching directly toward Mrs. Karistin. Warden Webb, however, kept his eyes trained on Dana as he leaned closer to the glass, brow furrowed.

"She won't let us in! Let us in!" Over and over she shouted, creating splashes with the emphatic stomping of her foot. "Tell her to—"

Warden Webb stepped away from the window just as the shrill tweet of Mrs. Karistin's whistle brought each of the children to a frozen halt. Moving slowly, as if walking in water rather than simply through the rain, the children lined up again, smallest to tallest, all of them made more diminutive under soaked clothing and dark, dripping hair.

"One, two, three . . ." Mrs. Karistin walked the line, counting to sixteen, where she stood in Dana's place, waiting. "Have we stayed out long enough now, Baby Killer?" she shouted across the distance. "Or do you need more time?"

Dana dropped her arms in defeat and, leaving her letter box in the mud, slogged her way to the line.

"Seventeen." Her voice was all sweetness, as if welcoming Dana into some warm, generous fold.

To Dana's surprise, Warden Webb stood just inside the doorway, scowling and saying, "Go directly to the dining hall," above each passing head.

The children's footsteps squeaked and squished against the floor as they marched, creating a puddling trail the length of the hall. They filed in, and each found a place at the long table. Not knowing if they should sit—it wasn't near dinnertime, after all—they stood behind the chairs. Soon the silent room began to fill with the sounds of sniffles and chattering teeth, accompanied by the *plop, plop* of raindrops falling from each drenched child.

Little Kicker began to shake, his tiny body quivering so that he clutched at the back of a chair to steady himself. Dana's eyes searched frantically for something, anything, with which to warm him, finally landing on a dish towel haphazardly draped over the corner of the front table. She bolted for it and ran to the boy, wrapped the towel around his bony shoulders, and held him close. Though she could offer no warmth from her own chilled body, she brought her lips to his pale, tiny ear and whispered, "It will be all right. You'll be warm and dry soon." It was, at best, a distant promise, and perhaps a downright lie, but she repeated it again and again, hoping her breath alone would allay the oncoming chill.

A new chill entirely overtook her as an unprecedented presence entered the children's dining hall. Warden Webb, smaller and milkier than she'd ever imagined. Not much taller than Dana herself, though he kept his chest puffed up and stood to his toes to make up the difference.

"Attention, please." By the timbre of his voice, he must have expected some great battle from his audience. "As of now I am arranging the immediate release of all of you, so as not to bring sickness and fever into this institution." He wagged his finger. "Take this as a warning. I am drafting a letter of explanation to the judge in each case, informing him of the circumstances and requesting that, should you again appear before the bench, your sentence be doubled to recompense the lost time. You are to wait here, and I will send Mrs. Karistin to fetch you each in turn as we find officers to escort you home."

Small sounds of joy came from a few of the children—the younger ones, mostly. The older ones asked if they couldn't please stay until at least after supper.

"I've instructed Cook to put a fire under the soup," the warden said, his voice a little softer than before. "Perhaps you'll have time to drink a bowl before you leave."

Dana buried her nose in Little Kicker's wet head, breathing deep the already-sour smell. She kept her eyes shut tight but moved her lips across the slick, cool hair, whispering, "Thank you. Thank you, God." If, as she'd learned, rain was a gift from God, sent to replenish the earth and bring new life to his creation, then surely this today was his gift to her. She couldn't imagine where the unknown officer would escort her. She'd start at the shabby apartment she'd shared with her mother, to try to find out if she was still alive, and where she'd gone. Or perhaps the DuFranes', if for no other reason than to beg forgiveness.

"Miss Lundgren!" Warden Webb's voice carried the irritation of repetition, but Dana had been so caught up in her reverie, and so unused to hearing her proper name, she'd obviously missed his first calling.

"Y-yes, sir?" She stood straight, keeping her hand on Little Kicker's shoulder.

"Go with Mrs. Karistin to fetch some blankets for these little ones. We'll wrap them up tight while they wait." His words chipped at her hope, as they clearly separated her from the others.

"Yes, sir." Sweet obedience, perhaps, would keep her in his good graces.

"Take one for yourself; then go to the dormitory and change into your night things. Straight to bed with you, and I'll arrange for your supper to be brought to you on a tray. Now, won't that be nice? Like a regular little princess." He twisted his face into a wink, bringing his bushy moustache almost up beside his nose. The stone forming in Dana's heart was heavy enough to throw and knock everything straight again.

"Yes." By now her face was too dry to camouflage tears, so she held them back, promising herself she could weep till morning.

Oddly enough, she didn't. At least not right away. By the time she'd stripped off her wet clothes, laid them to dry on the radiator, donned her flannel nightdress, and crawled into bed under two extra blankets, her body needed every bit of its energy to calm her shivering and warm itself. At some point, her mind pushed guilt aside and allowed her to sleep—a luxurious, almost-decadent occurrence in the middle of an afternoon. She'd awoken to Cookie—a light-skinned Negro woman who, as far as Dana knew, lived in the Bridewell kitchen—standing over her holding a tray laden with a bowl of steaming soup, a not-quite-stale roll, and a tiny dish of rice pudding.

"Had some extra left over, is all," she said, warding off Dana's effusive gratitude.

Left alone, Dana attacked the meal with relish, softening her bread by dipping it in the soup, and finishing it off by mopping the sides of the bowl. The pudding, however, she savored in a series of tiny bites, swiping her finger on the dish to get every last taste. A sense of duty took her to clean the dishes at the washbasin. By the time she crawled back under her blankets, even though it was barely dark and hours before the normal bedtime, she had hardly enough strength to pull the blankets up to her chin before turning her face to her pillow and filling the room with wet, shuddering sobs.

"Awake and alive, girls. Awake and alive."

Dana could feel the swelling of her eyes before she snaked her hand out from under the covers to gently touch the soft, puffy bags beneath them. Her head felt like someone had used an ax to split her skull. More than anything, she felt dry—her lips cracked and salty, her tongue thick.

"Awake and alive."

For once, she didn't leap out of bed. Didn't rush to the wash-basin to splash her face and brush her hair. Her feet were bare and warm, and the thought of stepping onto the cold floor made her curl up in a defensive ball. Besides, what was the hurry? She was alone, after all. The only girl in here. The only kid in the entire wing. And right now the only sound was that of Mrs. Karistin's skirt scratching along the wall.

And then it stopped.

She heard the familiar sound of the iron key turning in the lock, followed by the heavy scrape of the barred door against the floor. No flood of light this morning.

"Up and dressed. Ten minutes."

Dana dropped her arm over her eyes.

"Not moving today?" Footsteps pierced the silence, coming to a stop next to the bed.

Never before had Dana felt so defiant, but somehow her weakness had merged with strength, keeping her immobile in the face of this morning.

"Come on now, you know the routine. Ought to know it better than anyone."

"That was a horrible thing you did." Her lips felt like paste as they formed each word. "Yesterday, those poor children. I don't understand how you could be so cruel."

"Oh, I don't know. Looks like everything worked out for them. And you got a nice afternoon lay-a-bed." The springs on the bed beside Dana's groaned in protest as Mrs. Karistin settled her weight on it. "Now get yourself up, or I'll give you such a beating you won't be able to."

Dana turned, propped herself up on one elbow, and stared at the stocky woman camouflaged in the grayness of the morning.

"I'm not afraid of you." As she spoke, the words became truth. "I'll never be afraid of you again."

The woman's expression remained unchanged. "Might as well. Since you're leaving."

Dana shot straight up, the sudden movement intensifying the pain in her head. "I'm leaving?"

Mrs. Karistin chuckled. "That's just how you looked yesterday when Mr. Webb said you were all going home. Before you knew he meant everyone *else*. That split second of hope. Just like now."

The two sides of Dana's head knit together in a solid mass of pain, and she pressed the heels of her hands against her swollen eyes. "Stop."

"You're staying here, but they're moving you after today. Other side of the yard, where the women are. There was talk yesterday that maybe you're too old to be housed with the children, what with the nature of your crime, and yesterday, no regard whatsoever for their health. Dangerous, you know. On the bright side, you'll get a new dress."

She laughed again, the sound as bone-chilling as yesterday's rain, because with it came the images of what Dana had seen, the few glimpses she'd had of the women on the other side. Drunks, prostitutes—some of the mothers of the children brought here because there'd be no one to care for them while their mothers served their sentences.

"That can't be," Dana said, ready to cry, but she had no tears left. "I have to write to the judge again."

"What a good idea," Mrs. Karistin said, thick with condescension. "And just for that, I have a little something for you."

Dana returned her attention in time to see the matron holding out a token—a wooden cigar box, newer than hers and untouched by rain.

"I can write a new letter?"

"Write all you want." Her grin was not to be trusted. "Look inside."

Dana obeyed, wondering what trick would be inside. Paper without a pencil, perhaps? An inkwell without a pen? Slowly she opened the lid, only to find the contents within much, much more frightening than she could have imagined.

"You didn't—"

"See, I kept forgetting that it costs three cents to mail a letter."

Dana's hands shook as she reached inside the box and closed them around the stack of envelopes. Thirty in all—twenty to the judge and ten to Mrs. DuFrane—and she knew by heart what was written on each one. A plea for freedom. For answers, for forgiveness, for hope.

"Now, that's ninety cents, girl. Almost a dollar. You got a dollar for me? You do, and I'll get them posted right off."

"No . . ." Of course she wasn't responding to the ridiculous question, but answering that part of her heart that wondered if there was a person alive who cared about her future.

"In that case—" Mrs. Karistin reached over and took the box away, meeting very little protest—"I'll just take these right back.

And I suppose there's no hurry, you getting up and getting dressed and whatnot. Might be you need a little more rest."

"Will I get away from you when I go to the women's side?"

"You will, indeed." She stood, and the springs sang in relief. "And then I'll be one more person to forget you're alive."

CHAPTER 16

THE WRITTEN CONFESSION OF MARGUERITE DUFRANE, PAGES 39–53

WITH HEARTFELT APOLOGIES to all other children—including my own—I must tell you, my darling girl, that you were the most beautiful baby ever born. Soft curling hair, a perfect little mouth, and these enormous blue eyes fringed with long black lashes. Beyond all of that, though, you had this intelligence about you that was, at times, unnerving. Almost from the time you were born, you seemed to listen to conversations, as if saving up the words until you were old enough to speak them. No surprise at all, then, how quickly you learned to speak Spanish with Graciela, or that you were in demand for acting roles starting at such a young age. You've always been a chameleon, becoming someone else at the drop of a hat. Born to be an actress, if anyone ever was.

Your first role, of course, was that of my daughter.

I must say, I didn't fully intend for all of this to become the ruse that it did. I like to think that my intentions were simple, even noble. Mrs. Lundgren was in no position to rear another child, and it seemed a kindness to offer you a home. Think of what I promised. Her own daughter returned at my bidding, no record of what she'd done.

If I had to pinpoint the moment of my sin, it would be my failure to fulfill my end of the bargain afterward. I had a healthy new baby, after all—a beautiful little girl to boot. I should have kept my promise, walked into Judge Stephens's office, and told him to send the word to set her free. But when circumstances became what they were . . . well, a new baby commands so much attention, and I simply ran out of time.

I mention the illusion that my motives were noble. The room I prepared for Mrs. Lundgren might have been in a forgotten hallway, but it was fitted with lovely accoutrements, with its own cozy stove to keep it warm and a window to open wide in the afternoons to look out over the park. I carried her meals to her myself, all catered to her particular taste, and I assure you she was not shy about making her preferences known. Cream, not milk, for her tea. Preserves, not jam, for her toast. And never so much as a bite was ever left on the plate.

I imagined myself, when my period of mourning ended, receiving the continued, courteous sympathies of some of the ladies in my social circle, and perhaps one would lean close and ask, "Whatever happened to her poor drudge of a mother?"

At which time I would affect a reluctant air and mention that the poor woman found herself with child, and to deter her from doing something drastic with it, I'd opened my home for the duration of her confinement. And then, later—after—I would send out a tasteful announcement of our intention to adopt.

That is almost how it happened.

I'd managed to meet the needs of Mrs. Lundgren without informing the other members of the household—not even Arthur or Mrs. Gibbons. Shielding her presence from Arthur proved to be easy; he spent so much of his time at the lab or university that he was often home just long enough to fall into bed asleep, and when he was awake, he was barely alert. Always preoccupied and foggy-headed with his ideas and plans and, I like to think, his own muffled grief.

It helped, too, that Mrs. Lundgren herself seemed reluctant to reveal her presence to anyone, especially my husband, saying, "He might not want the baby, especially knowing that it's mine."

I told her there was no need for him to know, as there were foundlings born every day needing a home. I worried, though, that her fear might make her disregard our agreement.

At that, she reassured, "I'll do anything I need to do to get my daughter back."

That statement made me all the more resolute that I was doing the right thing in relieving her of the care of the child she was about to bring into the world. Look, I reasoned to myself, how willing she is to give it away. And it affirmed my idea of the balanced equation: she would have one of her children, I would have one of her children, and God would have one of mine.

Concealing her from Mrs. Gibbons, however, proved a mightier task. I took to giving the woman copious, time-consuming chores that would keep her bound to the first floor for much of the morning—creating inventories of our china and silver, alphabetizing the books in the library, meticulously mending articles of clothing to be donated to the poor. I began to request my breakfast brought to my room, which I promptly delivered to Mrs. Lundgren before going downstairs and declaring I was still famished. For lunch, I made cold sandwiches from whatever meat had been served, along with slices of cheese and fruit. Under the excuse of taking an afternoon nap, I whisked them upstairs in a small basket, along with a jar of cold tea.

Supper, though, proved to be both tricky and costly.

I decided to raise Mrs. Gibbons's wages in the form of renting a small apartment for her close by, saying that, with just the three of us, and Calvin ever more self-sufficient, there was no need for her to confine herself to the tiny room behind the kitchen. Each evening, after washing up the supper dishes, she took herself home. With Calvin tucked away in bed and Arthur not due home before ten o'clock, I might bring Mrs. Lundgren down to the parlor for a game of rummy. We talked to our cards more than to each other, but it was a respite from loneliness. I made her a plate of whatever I'd been served (food reserved for Arthur, but he rarely ate upon his arrival) and, to keep her company, consumed a second plate of my own. Following the meal, we ate enormous slices of cake washed down with milk, for the good of the baby, I said. Both of us eating for two.

"I suppose if I'm to be a prisoner, there are worse circumstances," she said one night after soundly trouncing me on the scorecard. We'd wagered the last almond cookie, which she popped into her mouth triumphantly.

Eyeing the crumb at the corner of her lip, I agreed, saying that her poor daughter most assuredly wasn't sitting beside a cozy fire with such genial company.

I don't know how she managed to swallow that bite. In fact, I feared she'd choke right there at the card table. Tears filled her eyes, and I gloated inwardly at the hollowness of her victory. Truly, I shouldn't have said such things. Such were a cruel abuse of my superior position, but from time to time I felt the need to remind her of our agreement. We were not friends, despite my employment of the euphemism. Later, when I knew the child to be rumbling around inside her, I dropped such comments more frequently. In between, though, our conversations were nothing short of cordial, and I suppose in some way, she helped me prepare for my reentry to society.

Mrs. Lundgren had been a guest in our home for nearly two weeks before I had both strength and opportunity to venture from the house. A missionary newly returned from China had been invited to speak with some of the ladies from my church, and a personal invitation had been sent to me hinting that a glimpse into the hardships of others might help to heal my own sadness.

Make no mistake: my reluctance to leave the house stemmed from my sense of propriety in mourning, but I concede that failure to engage in such an opportunity might earn me more suspicion than sympathy. So when I received the invitation to attend the lecture from the missionary to China, I did not hesitate in penning a response thanking my friend for her personal attention to my well-being and stating that I would be more than happy to attend.

By the time the day of the event arrived, I daresay I felt some sort of excitement at the idea of getting out of the house. Mrs. Lundgren wasn't the only one feeling somewhat like a prisoner, as I'd only ventured out to attend Sunday services since the morning Mary was taken from me. I had graduated from wearing my black mourning gown to simple housebound dresses, and I spent a good thirty minutes surveying my wardrobe to find the perfect suit that would draw the proper balance of compliments and sympathy. I settled on simple, light wool, fawn-colored with black piping, and a black silk blouse underneath.

During my homebound days, I'd allowed myself to roam without cinching my corset to the point of discomfort, and my first attempt to button the blouse made it clear that those days of freedom were at an end. I called downstairs to Mrs. Gibbons, who came immediately, given that she had standing orders not to come up the stairs unannounced, and told her somewhat sheepishly that I required assistance with my lacings.

She tried again and again, but no amount of red-faced tugging would bring my body to the size needed to close the buttons on the blouse, and we had no better luck with the skirt.

Admitting defeat, I instructed Mrs. Gibbons to return the garments to the closet and find something more accommodating. I'd taken to my sofa, exhausted from alternating huffing and breathlessness, and there sat with unbridled girth spilling out around me, when she emerged, a shy, knowing smile on her face.

"Oh, missus, I think it's a grand thing."

I asked what, exactly, was so grand about not being able to fit into one's own clothes.

"I just now put it together. Takin' your breakfast in bed, and nappin' in the afternoon. An' I wasn't going to mention it for fear crowdin' into your business, but I've noticed there's never a crumb of dessert left each mornin' from the night before."

Her words piled up more like accusations than discovery, and I harshly chided her for having the nerve to commend me for growing fat.

"Oh, it's not gettin' fat when there's a child growin'. And I'm so happy for you and the mister. We're all still grievin' for little Miss Mary, but it's a gift from God, isn't it? This new one come to the family. When do you expect it to be born?"

Until this point, I didn't count anything that I'd said to be a lie. Ruthless, perhaps, and clearly outside any rule of law, but truthful in both intent and execution. I sat for a moment, looking into Mrs. Gibbons's sweet, monkey-like face, with lilac powder caked into its fine wrinkles and pale-gray hairs tufted at the corner of her lips, and I calculated.

Spring, I said. Late March or early April. It's hard to know exactly.

She clapped her hands in glee. "Well, that makes you nearly three months gone already, doesn't it? I suppose you'll have to wear some of what you did when you were carryin' Miss Mary, won't you? If I'd known, I'd have taken 'em out of storage yesterday. Now I'll have to press somethin', and I'm afraid it might make you late."

I assured her we had plenty of time, especially once she made clear that the clothes were stored in a second-floor guest bedroom and not in the attic. After sending her off, trusted to find something appropriate without my guidance, I fell to my knees.

I cannot, in this document, recount my prayer. Words uttered to God in our darkest hours are, I believe, sacred, and I cannot say for certain that any fully formed syllables fell from my lips. It was a cry for both forgiveness and favor, drawing on grace for sins I had yet to commit, but fully intended to. My grief granted permission for me to seek his tolerance of my actions and to spare the flesh-and-blood baby any of the consequences of my deceit.

The two mingled together, my weeping and my prayers, until Mrs. Gibbons came back with a pile of garments heaped in her arms.

"There, there," she said, dropping them across the corner of the bed before coming to kneel companionably beside me. I reached for her and held her close, the way I would a mother, if I had one, and confessed to her white lace collar that I was a horrible person, more horrible than anybody could ever imagine.

"I don't blame you for being emotional." She patted my back. "I know you can't just replace Miss Mary with a new baby, but you have to let yourself love it anyway. It's still a child, a gift from God, and we cannot question his timing. Loving this baby don't mean you love your other children any less, not Master Calvin in the house nor Miss Mary in heaven."

My voice hitched as I promised that I would love this baby just the same. Just as if it were truly my own.

"But of course it's your own," she said without a hint of suspicion. "For as long as God allows."

Two hours later, after warning Mrs. Lundgren to rest quietly in the afternoon, as I would be out, I sat in Mrs. Scott's parlor, daintily nibbling on a most delicious lemon cake and sipping apricot punch while wearing a delightfully comfortable elastic-waist skirt and generous blouse. I'd left a similar outfit with Mrs. Lundgren, though ironically, she was nowhere near my girth.

My appearance was met with the reception I'd hoped for. Repeated expressions of sympathy and decorous joy at my obvious condition. In years past, even when I was pregnant with your brother, custom dictated that a woman simply did not socialize when she was so obviously with child. But this was a new century, with the smell of the Vote in the air, and I'd had enough reclusion for a while—such I said with a practiced smile and laugh that served to garner even more compassion.

Each lady in turn echoed the sentiments I'd heard from Mrs. Gibbons, with the addition of Mrs. Phillips, who said that, were she married to Arthur DuFrane, she would spend her life with child for the privilege. I don't know if anything so ribald had ever been said in Mrs. Scott's parlor, and certainly our missionary from China was unused to such raw conversation. Still, we hid behind our gloves and tittered—I more than anyone, wondering what they would think should I share the truth that I'd only known Arthur in a marital sense three times since Mary's conception.

When we'd finished our cake and punch, the missionary from China, the renowned Lottie Moon, stood in the middle of the parlor and calmly waited for our attention. She was a tiny thing, with only the tangible wisdom in her eyes to differentiate her from being a child. Even at her advanced age—sixty, I'd wager, if a day—she sparked with energy and passion as she began to recount the horrors she'd encountered over the course of her work.

"Children, so malnourished as to resemble twigs, cast into the street to beg. Barefoot, wearing rags, their little hands outstretched . . ."

Her words, spoken in this room of silk and chintz, seemed every bit as vulgar as Mrs. Phillips's stated desire for my husband's attentions, but she was very gracious not to call attention to our obvious excess.

"I will be blunt," she said, speaking as if her diminutive form were of no consequence. "We find ourselves experiencing great, great need in China. I cannot enjoy the luxuries of our nation while my heart is so burdened for the lost in that great country. And when I speak of luxuries, I speak not of this." She gestured her tiny hand to encompass the wealth around us. "I speak of the freedom to study God's Word. To worship him freely. To find a Bible in nearly every home . . ."

Oh, how her words gouged at me, my belly full of lies, my home flooded with deception. Others around me were dabbing their eyes with lace handkerchiefs, but I dared not shed a tear, lest I burst forth in confession.

"The harvest is very great, but the laborers, oh, so few."

I looked at this tiny woman, who seemed capable of shouldering the burden of salvation for an entire nation, and wondered briefly how God must see me, gluttonous and shameful, day after day eating my sin. I wished right then that I could go to China.

Take my hat and handbag and follow this woman out of the parlor and onto the next boat. Let Arthur and Mrs. Gibbons discover Mrs. Lundgren in the middle of some night when the woman crept from her room in search of food. Send a letter to Calvin explaining that his mother had to find some way to escape the trap she'd set for herself.

For it was a trap. It could be nothing less. Two women, one child. At some point the jaws would snap, leaving one of us on the outside, and a whole world ready to end my misery.

"How many are there who imagine that because Jesus paid it all, they need pay nothing? Who have forgotten that the prime object of their salvation was that they should follow in the footsteps of Jesus Christ in bringing back a lost world to God?"

"What can we pay?" The impassioned voice of Mrs. Scott spoke first, as was fitting her role as hostess.

"You can all come back with me." Her eyes glittered with humor, allowing us to giggle self-consciously at the absurdity of the suggestion. "But to be direct, you can give money. As the mission board is finding it to be more and more of a struggle to fund our efforts, we are finding it increasingly difficult to meet the physical needs of our workers and the spiritual needs of God's children."

"But we are not Baptists," said Mrs. Scott. Indeed, I'm sure our missionary friend was the first of such to ever step foot in her parlor.

"It matters not to the Lord," she said with good humor. "He loveth a cheerful giver."

A warm round of laughter followed, and Mrs. Scott sat at an ornate writing desk in the back corner of the room, ready to receive donations. Several of the ladies followed; still others crowded our speaker, looking like a host of furred and plumed creatures circling a little brown house mouse. I joined neither group, knowing my delicate condition would explain my inactivity. Soon, such unaccustomed social interaction took its toll on the missionary, and she came to sit beside me, her feet swinging freely from below her plain black skirt.

"You look to be as tired as I feel," she said. I never felt so unworthy to be in the presence of another. "Your friends say you are expecting a child?"

The affirming lie slid out of me, more easily than I could have imagined, turning the remnants of lemon cake bitter on my tongue.

She laid her hand on mine, an astounding strength in even that small gesture. "Do you have other children?"

I told her a boy, Calvin, six years old. And a little girl—here, I choked back a sob—whom God had recently taken from me.

It was the first I'd spoken of Mary to a person who didn't already know, and it felt like a confession of my own sin. That I'd somehow done something to call for such a penalty, and with my voice barely above a whisper, I expressed my loss at knowing just what I had done to deserve such a punishment.

Her worn, thin face became a sea of kindness, but not sympathy. "As it says in the book of Job, 'Despise not thou the chastening of the Almighty: for he maketh sore, and bindeth up: he woundeth, and his hands make whole.' This child, then, is his way of making you whole again."

She'd seen far greater tragedy than this, and through her stories so had I. What was the loss of one privileged child when compared to those masses starving outside of God's grace?

I thanked her for her words of comfort, giving no indication the weight of the burden that she'd lifted.

"Perhaps," she said, "you can find some peace in making an

offering so that one woman, unknown to you, living on the other side of the world, might be spared the same sorrow."

I asked if she really thought that was possible, that one offering would bring peace to my soul?

"In the book of Matthew we hear of a young man who had kept all of the laws of God and had loved his neighbor, and came to Jesus asking what he lacked. And Jesus said to him, 'If thou wilt be perfect, go and sell that thou hast, and give to the poor, and thou shalt have treasure in heaven: and come and follow me.'" She squeezed my hand. "I cannot make that same demand."

I smiled and said I could never attain perfection.

Before I left, I gave Mrs. Scott all of the money I had, nearly thirty dollars, and having obtained the proper address, wrote a check for one hundred more upon arriving home.

"If thou wilt be perfect . . ."

I gave and I gave, every month until you were born, but after everything that happened that night, I knew I would never be able to give enough.

CHAPTER 17

CELESTE, AGE 10

1916

IT WAS A MUCH-ANTICIPATED day in the DuFrane household. One week earlier, Daddy had received a message from somebody called Technicolor, interested in seeing his research on processing color film. He'd torn through the house, clutching the letter and reading its small body of words to Mother and Graciela and Calvin in turn. Celeste had run right alongside him, hearing the missive repeatedly. At the supper table that night, she entertained the family by repeating it verbatim, pitching her voice to that of her idea of a person in authority.

Since then, there had been a flurry of activity. Going through all of his papers to compile years of research notes, documentation of his patents, carefully separating the work he had done while connected to the university in Chicago from that which was a result of many late nights in a rented laboratory or in his own office at home.

Celeste never left his side, eager to do any task, even painstakingly typing the notes scrawled through multiple journals. Though she understood little of what she typed, she prided herself on needing help only with some of the chemical abbreviations. Once all the papers were collected, she numbered each one in her neatest hand, clear up to 357.

"This is why we came to California," he said, gazing raptly on the stack of pages as if it were holy in itself. "This is going to make us rich."

"Aren't we rich already?"

A look passed over Daddy's face, one Celeste couldn't identify. Discomfort, but not quite shame, and he ran his hand over his tome of research. "That is your mother's money. Her grandfather's, actually. This is mine. This is money for the future, before the future even arrives."

She didn't have a clue what he meant, but the tone was clear, and she covered his hand with hers in solemn agreement.

"Now," he said, "help me look through some of the archives and find the right footage to take to the interview."

What followed were nights gathered in the back parlor, a room hung with heavy, dark curtains and a series of small sofas all facing one large, blank wall on which Daddy projected one after another of his experimental colored films. There were minutes upon minutes of nothing more than flickering images of flowers, and the ocean, and a monkey in a red suit furiously turning the handle of a silent music box. One reel showed Mother on a grassy lawn somewhere, sitting on a red-checked blanket and nibbling what looked like a chicken leg.

"Oh, not that one, surely," Mother said as the family watched. "I look big as a house."

Daddy tried to convince her. "But see how clearly the colors of the blanket—"

"Absolutely not." And that was final.

Another reel captured Calvin playing with his toy soldiers, with close-ups of the tiny battles and cutaways to his much-younger face, squinting in youthful strategy. To everyone's amusement, he even puffed at an unlit cigar and studied a giant map with the help of an oversize monocle.

"I remember that day," the now-grown-up Calvin said. "I think that was when we were still back in Chicago."

"It was," Daddy said. "See? The color isn't quite right. Of course, that could be the age of the film."

"But it could speak to how long you've been working," Calvin said, "and show just how far you've come."

"True." Daddy stood back at the projector, but he moved forward until the image of his son was spread across the back of his shirt. "But I'd have to admit to some hand-tinting here—" he pointed to a fallen soldier stained red with blood—"for effect."

"To think of all those poor boys off dying in a real war," Mother said, her words eerily hollow.

"Yes, Mother. To think." Calvin lit a cigarette as his boyish image flickered into darkness. "Although I hardly believe you give much thought to them at all."

For a moment, the only light in the room was the glowing tip of Calvin's cigarette, and it moved in a slow arc, briefly illuminating his face.

"You have no idea what I harbor in my heart," Mother said.

"Enough." Daddy flipped on the light switch, showing Mother and Calvin both preparing to leave the room.

"Just one more," Celeste pleaded. "Please? We haven't seen one of me yet."

"Which is such an impossibility of odds," Calvin muttered, "seeing how you can barely move from one end of a day to another without Dad documenting it on film."

"Shut up."

"Mary Celeste DuFrane!" It was rare for Daddy to ever offer chastisement, but the sharpness in his tone was unmistakable.

"Don't call her that." Mother's defense was equally sharp.

Calvin exhaled a stream of smoke and declared that he was leaving.

"Sit down."

Her father was preoccupied with threading the film from the take-up reel to the feeder, and for a moment the whirring of its rewinding was the only sound in the room. Celeste eyed her brother, who paced the small area between his vacated chair and the door like some sort of caged animal before dropping into the seat. He stared straight ahead, his face sullen as he smoked, mindless of the dry ash that fell to the floor at his feet. Did he really hate her that much? Could he really not stand to look at her image projected on a wall? Ever since the night he'd told her that she'd died and come back again, Celeste had been wary of his presence and haunted by her own. They'd spent little time together, given his tendency to stay out most evenings with what their mother called "mindless California trash." Tonight was the first evening the whole family had spent any significant time together in months, and there he sat, impatiently tapping his foot as if serving out a sentence.

"There," Daddy said, having readied the new film. "One more, and I shall release you all."

He turned off the light and the room echoed with the flickering sound of promise, and then the wall filled with a beautiful shot of their very own backyard, all in bloom. There was Celeste's little playhouse, and a strange woman standing next to it.

"She could be Alice in Wonderland," Celeste said, "after she grows big."

Mother made a dismissive noise. "Not with that painted face." Indeed, the detail of the color clearly showed the woman's pink cheeks and reddened lips. "Just who is she, exactly, Arthur?"

"I've no idea."

Glancing over her shoulder, Celeste thought her father appeared to have been transported back to that afternoon, and when she looked again, she understood why. There she was, in all her cute and curled glory. She remembered being chilly that afternoon, but she hadn't worn a jacket. Rather, a bright-blue sweater, each looped stitch clearly displayed. Her own cheeks and lips were tinted, enhancing what she knew to be a natural beauty. She skipped out of the house and into the woman's arms, embracing her as she would any loving mother. The memory of the moment brought to mind the smell of the woman's heavy, cheap perfume. She wrinkled her nose and announced as much to her gathered family.

"Cheap?" Calvin asked. "How would you know the difference?"

"Because she didn't smell like Mother. It was awful."

"Still, doesn't mean it was cheap."

"I'm sure it was." Whether Mother was finalizing the argument about the cheapness of the perfume or commiserating on the awfulness of the moment remained unclear, but both subjects were dropped.

"You look beautiful, my little Celi." Daddy rarely used the nickname anymore, and the fact that he did so now, steeped in nostalgia, made him all the more vulnerable to her charms.

"Do you see? I keep telling you I should be an actress."

"Don't start," Mother warned.

Celeste ignored her. "If I could pretend that horrible woman was my mother—"

"Don't call her a 'horrible woman,'" Calvin said, seemingly with no reason to defend her other than to be contrary. "She's a stranger. You don't even know her."

"Yes, a stranger," Mother echoed.

Celeste barreled on. "See how I'm hugging her? And letting her kiss me? Most kids would be terrified to have to act like that."

"Most *kids*?" Calvin mocked her choice of word. "Because you're, what, ten years old? Such a young woman of the world."

"And you are too old for this bickering," Daddy said. "Now stop it once and for all."

His words took hold of not only the squabbling siblings but apparently the film as well. It sputtered a bit and the screen went dark—the result of a crudely pasted edit—only to spring to life again with a new image. This time, the entire frame consisted of Graciela's prized hibiscus and the image of yet another woman standing in front of it. Celeste could see she was beautiful, now that so many years stretched between that awkward afternoon and this evening. She ran her fingers delicately along the bright-red petals and brought her nose close to smell their fragrance. Looking mischievous, she plucked one free—this eliciting an irritated gasp from Mother at the viewing of the act—and ran it along her painted lips.

Nobody spoke.

Celeste vaguely remembered watching the film soon after Daddy processed it, but had been unable to appreciate anything other than her own, now rather silly, performance. This, in contrast, was art—a full-color, living depiction of beauty. Somehow, that shrill, painted woman conveyed a loveliness equal to the bloom, but there was something else, too. Something Celeste didn't quite understand, but which had moved Calvin to the very edge of his seat, his cigarette dangling from his lips, forgotten.

"This one," Daddy finally said, his voice thick. "And no other."

Daddy raged around the house, his voice echoing from the high ceilings and shiny tile and empty walls.

"My blue cravat—with the orange! I must have it!"

It was past nine o'clock in the morning, and Celeste, home

from school on the spring holiday, sat in the middle of the staircase, listening to the chaotic morning. Mother appeared, still in her dressing gown, her hair wrapped in a soft pink scarf. She dangled a scrap of blue silk over the banister.

"Here it is." Her voice left no doubt to how little she cared about her husband's dilemma.

Daddy emerged from his study and bounded up the stairs, his freshly shined shoe barely missing Celeste's smallest finger as she scooted out of his path.

"Not this one. I need the navy blue, with the bright-orange dots. *Color!* I need to convey color."

"Well, I'll see what I can do," Mother said, then yelled Graciela's name at the top of her lungs.

Graciela emerged from the kitchen, full of apologies. "*Lo siento mucho.* You asked me to steam press this for you yesterday, and I forgot to bring it up to your room."

"Thank you, Graciela." He spoke with affection and gratitude as he took the tie from her. Rather than going back upstairs, where Mother had watched the finding of the lost treasure with unmasked ennui before returning to their bed, he went to the front hall and used the mirror there to create a fashionable knot, fastening his collar bar beneath it.

"Fetch my vest and jacket, won't you please, Celi? The brown tweed laid out on the bed."

"Yes, Daddy." She jumped up from her place on the stairway and took the steps quickly.

In her parents' room, the shades were drawn against the sun, her mother's form barely discernible in the bed.

Celeste moved gingerly through the semidarkness. "Aren't you feeling well, Mother?"

The reply came in the form of faint affirmation.

"Wouldn't you like to come downstairs and see Daddy off? It's such a big day for him, and I think he might even be a little nervous. It's not like him to fuss so about a silly tie."

"I can't." She shifted from being curled up on her side to her back, with some obvious discomfort in the transition. "Ask Graciela to bring up a pot of tea, once your father is safely out the door."

"Yes, Mother." She found her father's jacket and vest on the large, upholstered trunk sitting at the foot of the bed. Before draping them over her arm, she held them close to inhale the scent of his shaving soap.

"You love him very much, don't you?"

"Daddy? Of course I do."

Mother's outstretched hand beckoned, and Celeste took it, settling on the edge of the bed, fearful of hurting her.

"And me?"

"Of course," she repeated. What a strange conversation to have on such an exciting day. Mother's hand was soft and plump and of so perfect a temperature—neither hot nor cold—that Celeste could hardly tell where her touch ended and her mother's began.

"I haven't always been a very good . . . person."

Celeste leaned over and kissed her dry cheek. "Don't be silly."

"We left so much behind in Chicago. We left everything. . . ."

She often fell into these maudlin reminiscences about Chicago, as if they didn't have everything they needed right here. A home, each other, and now a chance for Daddy to fulfill his dream. She supposed Mother was talking about the baby, the little girl who died before Celeste was even born. The one where Calvin got so mixed up, calling Celeste that baby's ghost. She didn't want to talk to her mother right now, not about anything so sad, so she gave her hand a squeeze and promised to send Graciela up with tea. "In fact," she said, "I'll bring it up myself if you like. And read to you. Would you like that?" She loved to read aloud to anyone who would listen. It gave her a chance to practice her accents.

"No. I have a better idea. You should go with your father."

"Me? Why would I—?"

"You're two of a kind, with all your silliness and dreams."

"But this is an important meeting, with very important men." Hadn't she been listening to a word her father said all these years?

"All the more reason to bring a sweet little girl in tow. They'll be less likely to be unkind if you are there."

"Why would they be—?"

"Do you think this is the first meeting your father has ever had with very important men? Go."

"What if he won't allow me to go?"

"Remind him that you are his daughter. In fact, you're his muse, and then tell him your mother insists."

Thrilled at the prospect and armed with her mother's blessing, Celeste ran quickly into her own bedroom and chose a wine-colored velvet ribbon from her top drawer. Earlier in the day Graciela had given her an intricate braid that began at her crown, which she looped and secured at her nape with the ribbon. She quickly changed from her play clothes into one of her nicest school dresses and grabbed her shoes, thinking she could hook the buttons while Daddy finished dressing.

Her stockinged feet made no sound on the stairs, and she moved slowly with one hand on the banister lest she slip. She rounded the corner into the entryway, announcing that Mother had the most wonderful idea, and came upon her father and Graciela stepping away from each other. Graciela's hands flew to her mouth and tears glistened in her eyes.

"Perdón." She spoke the word behind her silver-and-turquoise

rings as she hustled past without giving Celeste so much as a glance. Her father, too, seemed reluctant to look at her, and busied himself smoothing his already-smooth hair.

"Is everything all right?" she asked. "Were you angry with Graciela about forgetting your tie? Because everything turned out fine. She found it, didn't she? Nice and steamed."

"What are you—?" He looked confused and then at peace. "No, no. Nothing like that. Everything's fine."

"She seemed upset."

"It's fine."

He took the vest and slipped his arms through, but Celeste could tell immediately that he'd misaligned the buttons. She giggled at his gaffe and offered to complete the task for him. He acquiesced and held his arms limp at his sides while she deftly unbuttoned and rebuttoned the vest, happy to be needed.

"There." She stepped back to give him room to pull on his suit jacket and fuss with the lapels. "You look very handsome."

He did, even with the fine lines at the corners of his eyes and the touch of gray in his sideburns. Not like other girls' fathers, those she saw at school functions and in their neighborhood. They were paunchy or bald with sagging faces and puffy eyes. Guilt tugged as she thought—as she often did—that her father was so much more handsome than her mother was beautiful. He was so trim, so *disciplined* in his appearance, while Mother had been to the dressmaker's last week because she'd grown too fat for most of what she had. She'd developed a soft roll beneath her chin and was beginning to move with a kind of breathless lumbering—when she moved at all.

"Mother said I should go with you."

He stopped in his preening long enough to give her a measured look. "She did?"

"Can I, please, Daddy? I'll sit quiet as a mouse, I promise."

"What possible reason could you have for going?"

"I could help you carry your things." She didn't want to share her mother's remarks.

"I can carry them myself."

"The papers and the film?"

He chuckled, and then his eyes sparked with an idea. He tucked his thumb under her chin and raised her face, looking at it from one angle and the next. "Of course."

She rose to her toes. "Do you mean it?"

"When they see you in the flesh, and then what I've done for you on film . . ."

He didn't finish the sentence, but she fully understood. "Does that make us in cahoots?"

"I suppose it does." He stooped to pick up the small leather satchel waiting by the door. "But this won't have to be a secret."

CHAPTER 18

THE WRITTEN CONFESSION OF MARGUERITE DUFRANE, PAGES 67–79

YOU MIGHT BE SURPRISED to know that it was my idea to go to California. Arthur would have everybody believe otherwise, going on and on about how bringing color to film meant the fulfillment of a chemical engineer's dream. Poppycock. I concur that his interest was piqued when he went to that first symposium the week you were born, and I also know by now that his desire to move to that godforsaken coastal village had little to do with making movies. Had I been privy to such future revelations, I might not have urged my husband in that direction. For example, I might not have made it a point, each and every winter, to complain about the bitter coldness or the exhaustion of bundling children up to play outside for an hour. I might not have peppered every dinner conversation about my growing dissatisfaction with our church, and our friends, and the haunted draftiness of our rambling family home.

Somehow I knew, from the day you were born, that I would have to secret you away to keep you to myself. I thought at first we would be hiding from your mother. But even after that fear was allayed, I knew it would be far too easy to simply keep you. You see, I learned when Mary died that we cannot decide what will and will not be our earthly treasures. Only God can keep those accounts. And so, in those first few years, when I had my beautiful baby girl, and a handsome son and husband, and a stately family home with all the privilege that such allows, and a church with my name on a brass plate, and a few friends still willing to adhere to the ever-more-archaic calling hours . . . well, how selfish it would be to think I would pass from this life into the next with all those blessings intact.

Above all, I wanted to keep you, my Celeste, because you had come at such a price. And the price grew and grew and grew.

It is good to remember that I pen this at our attorney's behest, to shine the light on my guilt, my manipulations, my orchestration of the imprisonment of that poor girl, and I wonder if he will let it stand, given the chink it reveals in his own breastplate of righteousness. But it is so important to me, my dear, dear Celeste, that you not see me as some monstrous puppeteer, controlling erstwhile honorable men. Judge Stephens was more than willing to trade her freedom for his reputation, and Christopher Parker, Esquire, for all his nobility, allowed greed to temporarily stay his integrity. But unlike Job, who sat in the ash heap among three advisers who would urge him to look to his own sin, I employed three duplicitous men to absolve me of my own. I've already given full account of one and shall now tell you of the second. The third—Christopher Parker himself—I'm loath to unveil, knowing your affection for him.

Two years before our departure to California, I received a letter from Judge Stephens. Not from him exactly, I suppose, but from his wife, informing me that he had died peacefully in his sleep the week before, and that she had found this letter—enclosed in an envelope with his signature across the seal—and a note informing any who found it to mail it to me immediately upon his death.

I remember Calvin bringing it to me, always one to take on what little responsibilities he could. He loved to take the mail from where it landed on the floor and march around the house to deliver it directly into my hands. In truth, it was a game I'd introduced years before, making believe he was a Union spy, and each piece of mail a secret message to me, General Grant. Not until I held Judge Stephens's letter in my shaking hands did I realize how fortuitous such play would be. I thanked Calvin with a salute, then ordered him to take Private Celeste downstairs for a snack.

The letter was, for all intents and purposes, a confession, much like this I write now, only his begged forgiveness not only for his miscarriage of justice, but also for those hidden sins that made his honor so easily defiled. He also gave fair warning that an identical document was set to be delivered to Warden Webb at the old Bridewell Prison, exactly one year thence.

I can still recall his words: *I want you to have time, Marguerite, to confront your sin and confess your crime before all you hold dear is stripped away.*

When I read that, I felt the weight of my Mary in my arms. So much had been stripped away already. I couldn't imagine what more I could give.

One year. I could live with the sword of Damocles poised over our family's head, or I could make some attempt to stave off disaster.

I must have written fifty letters to Mr. Webb, but each was burned in the ash can. How could I possibly appeal to a man I'd never met? With Judge Stephens, I had the advantage of knowing his proclivities, and with young Parker, I could capitalize on his ambition. But this man? What could I do in one year to prepare for such a confrontation?

First, acting on an instinct as old as the sexes, I put myself on a steady diet of nothing but weak tea, two slices of bread, and one spoonful of whatever supper Mrs. Gibbons had prepared each night.

At first, my body rebelled, refusing to nudge a single inch. Then, after a rigorous course of enemas and certain black, bitter herbs, I found myself melting away. For a time, I smoked cigarettes constantly, finding them to help with the pangs of hunger and generally dull my taste for the little food I did eat. But your father found that to be a vile habit, and once I could fit into one or two of the dresses I wore before Mary, I gave it up completely.

Looking back, I think nothing made it more clear to me just how much time had passed since Mary was taken from me than did putting on those dresses.

And so I went to the old Bridewell.

Never once in all this time had I allowed myself to be within ten steps of the place, not that I ever had to turn down any social invitation in order to keep my distance. Even on this day, I intended to have my hired car drop me three blocks north, but as I clutched my handbag closer and tighter with each step, I turned back and leaped into its safety.

"To the correctional house," I said, and when the driver stopped, I gave him five dollars and told him not to move an inch.

I pause now to say this not to pacify those who rightfully criticize my actions, but to state what became apparent to me in that moment. Had I not known the true nature of this facility, I might have thought myself standing outside a once-respectable boarding school gone past its prime. Long buildings, redbrick walls—even the high iron gate was fashioned with attractive scrolls. The sight, in fact, assuaged my guilt, as it seemed to affirm what I had told Arthur: that she had been sent to a reformatory, and her mother followed.

To this date, I count that as my only outright lie.

I remember thinking that *she* was in there, somewhere, and the thought of a possible confrontation hurried my steps through the visitors' entrance and up the three flights of stairs, where I hoped to have an audience with the warden. I'd made no appointment, not knowing how I could possibly relay the nature of my business, but my upbringing and status had taught me one very important lesson: one must simply comport oneself as if one *belongs*. I decided I was just as entitled to be there as anybody else, and with that attitude I introduced myself to the diminutive woman behind the desk, announcing that I was there to speak with Warden Webb.

Not surprisingly, she hopped right up, poked her head through a secondary door, and in the next minute summoned me inside.

It took no more than one step across the threshold for me to realize that I could have spent the previous six months stuffing myself with Mrs. Gibbons's cream pies. Warden Webb appeared less inclined to succumb to a woman's charm than a hound dog to give chase to a rock. He was a small man composed entirely of droops—his eyes, his jowls, even his stomach over the top of his pants. I'd like to say there was a sternness to him, but that cannot be interpreted as any sort of maliciousness on his part. *Spartan* might be a better word. His office consisted of one desk, three chairs, one window, one filing cabinet, and a candlestick telephone. Not a spot of green or a family photograph. There was, however, a row of photographs depicting six black-robed judges, Judge Stephens among them, and a quaint cross-stitch hanging on one wall with this message: *"And ye shall know the truth, and the truth shall make you free."*

At the time, it seemed a cruel statement, as truth had probably played a role in landing most of the prisoners in this place. Most, though not all. For me, this verse proved to be an inspiration.

Having settled myself in one of the two chairs opposite his desk, I assumed an imploring pose and introduced myself before inquiring as to whether or not he knew of a prisoner named Dana Lundgren.

He looked confused at first, protesting that his facility housed nearly two thousand inmates, and he could hardly be expected to recall the name of a single one. Then he got up and went to his file cabinet, opened it, and—to my relief—found nothing. Going to the door, he summoned, "Mrs. Tooley?" and she stepped right up to be of service. After asking me to repeat the name, she went to yet another drawer and produced a thin, brown folder.

"Dana's one of the young'uns," she said, clucking at the shame of it.

Left alone again, he read through the few pages in the folder as I watched, fingers itching to snatch the papers away. When he'd finished, he looked up. "This is a very serious crime."

I told him it was my daughter who had been killed, and he shook his head in commiseration. I could hear his loose lips flap in the silent office. He himself had not been a part of her processing. "But," he said, "that often happens with the children."

For the next few minutes, I told him one carefully chosen truth after another. That I believed Dana Lundgren to be a deranged, jealous girl, envious of my family. That I had another daughter now, given to me by God to help heal me from my loss, but that I had nightmares of this girl somehow stealing my Celeste away from me. That I had yet, in all these years, to receive a single communication from her in which she reached out for forgiveness. She'd not even been in contact with her mother.

"Is that why you're visiting me today?"

Before I could answer, the first bits of rain pelted against his window, the kind of miserable, cold rain that plagues the springtime, and I told him, yes, that was part of the reason.

"And we are keeping her housed with our children." He didn't say this in any way to invite a comment, so I made none.

Then, having given him time to relish that thought, I opened my handbag, produced Judge Stephens's letter, and asked if he'd received one of the same.

"No," he said, reaching for it, "not that I'm aware."

Handing it over, I told him that I'd found its contents quite disturbing, like the ramblings of an old man caught in the throes of dementia, and asked after the judge's health.

"He's dead these last six months, but went with a sound mind as far as I knew."

I could tell that the man relished being thus consulted, as all bureaucratic cogs fancy themselves as deserving far more power than they are ever permitted to wield.

I asked, then, why would he send me such a letter? Because, surely I had no sway over his sentencing. I'd been far too overcome with grief to even attend the inquest, as the record indicated. I went months without leaving my house. Why, Judge Stephens even wrote me the sweetest note after Mary was killed, saying he would do all he could for me.

(I even produced the note in question. Arthur used to accuse me of keeping every scrap of paper needlessly.)

"Puzzling, indeed." And he puzzled, and he puzzled. "What do you make of this, what he says about the other young men whose lives he may have ruined?"

I took my time there, tapping my chin and watching the rain, as if deep in thought, then suggested maybe Judge Stephens was referring to other young prisoners—children whose lives had been severely impacted from such minor infractions.

"You know, I've often thought the very same thing. That we do a disservice, labeling such young people as deviants. The world is changing. There have been studies, you know."

Feigning fascination with his insight, I leaned forward and reminded him of the fact that there were those who were, in fact, dangerous. Murderously so. And then we heard an awful sound coming from the courtyard.

He went straightaway to the window, motioning for me to stay back in an exaggerated gesture of protection. Still, I moved and stood just behind his elbow, marveling at the sight below.

Her.

Years had passed, but I knew that face, that scrawny little body. Now her hair was plastered wet with rain, and she stood in the middle of the muddy yard, scraps of paper strewn about her, waving her arms and screaming incoherently at the frozen forms of bedraggled children dotting her realm.

"What on earth?" He pulled the curtain aside, affording us both a better view.

I gasped—prettily, I thought—and said I lived my life dreading such a moment as this, followed by a comment about those poor, poor ragamuffins.

"It isn't right." He turned to me. "They'll die of pneumonia."

Unless, of course, she got to them first, I murmured.

As if she heard me, she stopped her wild gyrations and stared straight up at the window. I know for a fact that she had no idea of my presence, but a chill went through me just as if I'd been out there in the rain. I allowed that fear to work through, and I flung myself into Warden Webb's arms, sobbing dryly against his shoulder about my greatest fear being the moment I opened my door to find that deranged girl on my stoop. Or worse yet, in the dead of night in my daughter's room. Again . . .

He patted my back. "There, there, Mrs. DuFrane."

I'd exceeded his limits of physical comfort and stepped away.

He made his way back to his desk and opened the folder, finding the single sheet with Judge Stephens's signature. "This gives an indefinite sentence, which is unusual for a juvenile, but I can only assume he intended further study of her mental competency."

I fervently agreed.

"Still, her legal representation will make a case for parole based on time served, given her age at sentencing." He shuffled through the pitiful gathering of papers. "I don't see that she has a lawyer on record."

I asked what that meant, exactly.

He slammed the folder shut. "It means that, should somebody advocate her case, she will be entitled to the rights of any other inmate, including the right to appeal her case or petition for parole. But until then, rest assured, I will keep her here, safe and sound. In body, at least, if not in mind."

I dabbed at my eyes in gratitude and benediction, for he was doing God's work, really. The poor girl had no one, and nowhere to go.

"No mother?"

No.

"It is a pity indeed when our prisons must act as orphanages. Perhaps that is what inspired Stephens's sentencing." He held up the judge's letter. "May I keep this?"

I smiled and told him he might be getting one of his own.

"If so, I shall receive it with honor. The injustices perpetrated upon these little ones ends today."

And *her*?

He stood to escort me out. "I can only hope to be able to show what mercy we can in the confines of justice."

By the time I made it to my hired cab, the rain was coming down in sheets, and all the children had disappeared. I stood outside the iron gate and noticed one of the strewn papers had blown up against it. For a moment, I considered retrieving it, curious to know what the girl had been so determined to write about. But it was wet with rain, the words nearly blurred away, and I didn't care to have ink run and stain my sleeve.

Once home, after changing into dry clothes, I spent the entire evening complaining about the filth of this city while I watched my family eat dinner. As I did the next night, and the night after, until your father commented on two things. One, that I appeared to be finally losing my baby weight, and two, that we might want to get away from this house full of ghosts and start a new life in a new city. The latter I pretended to protest, then promised to consider.

For the next six months, and the six months after that, I allowed your father to shower me with attention and gifts in an effort to convince me to move, and all the while I waited for my little postal soldier to bring me a new missive from Warden Webb.

Finally, though, in the end, I guess it was neither your father's idea nor mine that we move to this place. One spring day I got a letter announcing that Christopher Parker had graduated from high school and had been accepted into the University of California. I took it as a sign. A way to keep him close to me, but far from her.

A few months later, and we moved into the house you now call a home. *Your* home, my darling. And hers, as I have come to accept, though I thank the Lord I will not live to see it.

CHAPTER 19

DANA PLAYS HOSTESS ON THE PATIO

1925

GRACIELA HAD PREPARED A FEAST. Thin steaks saturated in her secret pepper marinade, grilled to the palest pink, and served with a corn relish salad and a variety of fresh fruit. There was a ginger-ale punch and rich chocolate cake, too—all laid out with the best china and serving dishes on the back patio table.

Dana had never seen a table set so prettily. Since she'd arrived, they'd taken their meals in the kitchen—she, Celeste, and Graciela—companionably, and often with very simple fare. Roast chicken one evening, diced into a salad and served on a leaf of lettuce for the next day's lunch. Breakfast often nothing more than a scrambled egg, though often Celeste slept too late and woke too grumpy for anything more than toast and coffee, hold the toast. Dana, on the other hand, sat down for every meal with a hearty appetite and a grateful palate.

"What did they feed you in that place?" Graciela asked the first time Dana sat at the kitchen table.

"Soup, mostly. And bread. Beans and potatoes."

The first night Graciela made a dish of meat wrapped in round bread called a *tortilla*, served with cheese and sauce. It was rich and spicy, unlike anything Dana could ever have imagined. She ate two platefuls, long after her shrunken stomach warned her to stop, while Celeste laughed.

"Keep that up, you're going to be as fat as Mother. Or at least as fat as she was before she got sick."

"Hush," Graciela chastised. "Do not speak bad about your mama. She was a—"

It was obvious that she was about to say that Marguerite DuFrane was a good woman, but everybody gathered knew that wasn't true.

Having grown accustomed to the constant and informal companionship of the two women, such a feast as Graciela had now prepared, with a late lunchtime set for two o'clock, was strange indeed. Stranger still, the number of settings at the table: four.

"Who is going to join us?" Dana asked. As soon as Graciela was distracted, she snatched a chunk of melon from the fruit plate.

"Ay-yi!" Graciela made a soft swat of her hand. "Now there's a gap." She went about filling in the missing spot by rearranging the remaining fruit, tsking good-naturedly. "There. Take some cheese. I have too much on the plate."

Dana obeyed, helping herself to one more piece of fruit since Graciela was rearranging it anyway. Had somebody told her a year ago that she would be standing on a stone-tiled patio, looking out over a lush garden, and feasting on exotic fruit and cheeses, welcome to all she wanted and more, she would have dismissed him as a cruel, delusional fool. She'd finished most of her snack when she realized Graciela hadn't answered her question, so she repeated it.

"No sé." She'd picked up enough of Graciela's Spanish to translate that she was claiming not to know who was coming to lunch, and she'd lived in the house long enough to learn there

was absolutely nothing Graciela didn't know. This was her way of delaying any delivery of bad news.

"Celeste didn't tell you?"

"That man, Mr. Lundi—him. And someone else, too."

Dana studied the plates on the table. "Two guests. Shall we set another place?"

"When Mr. Lundi is here, I eat in the kitchen."

"Oh." She was about to protest such an injustice, but Graciela's winking delivery made it clear that the choice was entirely hers.

Just then Celeste arrived, wearing a gauzy, peach-colored dress trimmed with silk at the neckline and sleeves. Her head, too, was wrapped in a wide silk scarf, knotted behind one ear and flowing over her shoulder.

"Dana, darling, go upstairs. I've laid out something lovely for you. Celine from Les Femmes en Vogue sent it over with some other things they want me to model. This, for example." She struck a dramatic pose. "But the one I left upstairs just isn't right for me. A bit too matronly, but perfect for you."

Graciela chided her for the backhanded compliment, but Dana took it in stride. "I'm sure I'll be fine." She was wearing a plain skirt and blouse. What the saleslady had called "serviceable" when she went to the department store the day before boarding the train in Chicago.

"Really? Even if Werner joins us for lunch?"

The suggestion brought her to absentmindedly finger the unremarkable cotton of her sleeve, remembering the feeling of silk against her skin as she gazed across the darkness at the twinkling starlike lights in the valley. And then, later, when they returned to the party, he never once left her side, reassuring her that she looked every bit as beautiful as any woman in attendance. He had to lean close to speak into her ear, so close that she felt the faint brush of his whiskers against her cheek, giving the word *beautiful* life as he spoke it.

That was two weeks ago, and while Celeste had been gone night after night to one party or another, Dana had been home, spending quiet evenings playing rummy with Graciela, eating sugar-coated pastel pastries that melted on her tongue as if they'd never existed at all.

"What do you mean by *matronly*?" The word hadn't meant a thing when Celeste first uttered it.

"Honestly?" Celeste bit her lip in a rare show of uncertainty. "It's a bit too big for me. And you've become, shall we say, *healthier* lately."

"Ay! Chica moderna." Graciela made a dismissive gesture. "All of you girls today are too skinny. All bones and elbows, like sticks in all your fancy clothes. This one had an excuse to be nothing but skin and bones, *escuálida*. Couldn't even stand up straight. You remember?"

Dana did. She also remembered the weariness in her bones, but mostly because everything seemed so *vast* here. The walk from the drive to the door had felt like a mile, and the stairs? Only the promise of a bed gave her the strength to mount them, pulling herself hand over hand up the banister.

"I happen to think it will look better on you," Celeste said. "Go see. I left you stockings, too. And feel free to go into my closet for a hat. You'll know the one when you see it."

Dana thanked her and maintained her composure until she hit the stairs. She'd never run up them before, but she did at that moment, feeling lighter than Celeste would ever believe.

Immediately upon seeing the dress, she understood Celeste's reasoning. It was a beautiful garment, deep blue with draping across the bodice and peacock feathers painted directly onto the skirt. Even having lived hidden away from changing fashions, Dana knew this was a dress meant for a woman, not a girl of twenty. In addition to a pair of stockings with a subtle feathering pattern along the seams, Celeste had left her a long string of painted wooden beads and a pair of patent-leather camel pumps fitted with blue ribbon.

Though she watched the transformation unfold in the mirror, the final effect was stunning. Not like the black silk and sequins she'd worn to the premiere. That was Celeste's dress; Dana had been nothing but the body within. This, as far as she knew, had never been worn by anyone, and it touched every point as if it had been designed, cut, and sewn to her figure's specifications.

Figure.

Thirty-two years old, and she'd never given the word a thought. She placed her hands on her hips and studied herself from all angles. "Healthier," Celeste had said. Health in the roundness of her bust and hips. A nipped-in waist, a curve to her calves, and cheekbones hidden beneath a new softness.

Accepting her style guardian's offer of a hat, Dana ventured into Celeste's room to collect. Despite the general unruliness of the closet, she did find the ideal match—a bell-shaped cloche with a ribbon that perfectly matched the color in the eyes of the peacock feathers on the skirt. But trying it on, and tugging it down to the angle she knew to be the most alluring, she was disappointed at the shadow its brim cast on her face. They weren't leaving home, after all, and were eating on a shaded patio. Celeste herself wasn't wearing a hat, but a pretty scarf that showed her face to its best.

I want him to see me. She clutched her stomach at the thought. *I want him to look at me.*

A jar of pink lotion sat amid a dozen other bottles on top of the bureau. Dana took a dollop and, after rubbing most of it into her hands, ran her fingers through her casually unruly hair, bringing new definition. She twisted and shaped and created a part above her right eye, encouraging the curls to follow. Pawing through Celeste's cluttered dresser top and drawers, she found a jeweled hair clip, which she slid into the mass at her left temple.

All the while, she hummed a languid tune she remembered from the party that night. It played on the radio often enough to be familiar, and Werner had caught her off guard, leading her onto the dance floor before she could protest, and holding her close in the gathered mass of people. Just one dance, and she'd insisted on returning to her seat. Whatever terror she felt was now long forgotten.

The chime of the front door startled her from her reverie. Quickly, she powdered her nose and touched up her lips, having become quite adept at the art of makeup. The house knew its share of visitors, but Celeste had driven home the fact that Graciela was to open the door, greet the visitor, and instruct that person to wait until either Celeste came to the entryway, or she summoned the party to be escorted to wherever she'd set herself up for receiving. Apparently it was that kind of thing that made her a star.

At this moment, Dana was grateful for the protocol, as the bravado that constituted her self-admiration soon dissipated at the idea of coming face-to-face with Werner. All of a sudden, her voluptuousness seemed vulgar, her makeup garish, the jeweled clip an overreaching attempt at youth. She glanced at her reflection again, decidedly less pleased with the image looking back at her. She fidgeted with the dress, thinking she might beg off lunch after all. But she wanted to see him; moreover, she wanted him to see her. First, before filling his eyes with Celeste in all her unmatronly, dewy-fresh, peach-gauzy glory.

Three deep breaths, and she descended the stairs. Slowly,

alluringly, as she'd seen Celeste do when she wanted to make an impactful entrance, and was rewarded—somewhat—for her efforts.

"Baby doll! Baby doll, look at you." Roland Lundi, wearing an impeccable pale-pink suit, waited at the foot of the staircase.

Dana smiled, amused, and extended her hand. "Good afternoon, Mr. Lundi."

He pulled her close and planted a stylish kiss on each of her cheeks. His own skin was warm and smooth, like she imaged a lizard basking in the sun might feel to the touch. "Seeing you all dolled up like this, I don't know if I want to get you in the movies or get you down the aisle."

He was somehow more handsome now than he had been the day she met him. His skin a deeper tan, his hair a glossier black, with isolated gray strands few enough to be counted, and artfully placed.

"And wouldn't you be absolutely terrified if she took you up on your offer?" Celeste breezed into their presence, Graciela trailing behind her, and Roland repeated his affectionate greeting.

"You got me there, baby. No offense, sister."

"None taken," Dana assured.

"Besides, I'm holding out for this *mamá*here." He waggled his brows and gave Graciela a playful grin before the two of them launched into a spirited Spanish dialogue that ended with Graciela fanning her blushing face, and Roland twisting his pinkie ring in a gesture of triumph.

"Dame tu sombrero," Graciela said, holding her hand out for Roland's straw boater.

"You be careful with that. Cost me three clams at the pier."

Graciela's retort made him hoot.

The three had arrived at the doors leading to the patio when the bell rang once again. By this time, Roland's witty banter had put Dana completely at ease, and she'd almost forgotten to be nervous about Werner's arrival. She must have expressed her renewed anxiety because Celeste offered a comforting squeeze and said, "You look lovely, really."

The sideboard held four sugar-rimmed glasses and a pitcher of fruit punch festooned with bouncing lemon slices. Roland took on the role of bartender and poured for each of the ladies, and then a third with a splash from his flask for himself.

"Bit early in the day for that, isn't it, Lundi?" Werner crossed the threshold onto the patio, delivering a handshake with the good-natured accusation.

"Or late in the afternoon. Whatever's your pleasure." He poured a glass of punch for Werner and offered to add a bit of liquor to it.

"No, thank you. In deference to our host. I would hate to see Hollywood's newest star in the newspapers for a liquor raid." Werner kissed Celeste's cheek in delayed greeting, then made his way around the table to offer the same to Dana, saying, "You look lovely."

She'd had at least seven steps to prepare herself for his touch and must have felt like a wooden Indian in reaction to his appropriate, friendly embrace. It occurred to her to be annoyed at the fact that nobody took the time to tell Celeste that *she* looked lovely too, which she did—like something pretty enough to adorn the table. But then again, that kind of beauty was a given for Celeste. For Dana, it appeared to be almost the working of a miracle, and she fiddled with the jeweled hair clip in self-consciousness.

"Everybody, please." Celeste invited them to sit, she opposite Roland, and Dana facing Werner. He was wearing a lightweight argyle sweater over a starched white shirt, and though his hair had more gray in it than Roland's, its perpetual disarray made him appear much younger. No more than forty, she guessed, finding him to seem younger and younger with each meeting. Soon they'd be the same age.

No sooner had they settled than Graciela appeared carrying a large wooden bowl and a clear glass pitcher of fresh water. She filled each glass, then set the pitcher on the sideboard.

"Ensalada?"

"Gracias," Celeste said and allowed Graciela to fill her plate with a mixture of greens and peppers tossed with a tangy spiced oil. Finished, she was about to leave when Werner asked her to stay while he, with Celeste's permission, blessed the meal. The four around the table took hands, and Graciela stood just behind Celeste, making her familiar sign of the cross right before and after the brief prayer.

"Thank you, Werner," Celeste said before dispatching Graciela to the kitchen.

Roland watched her exit with exaggerated interest. "Thirty years ago?" he said when she was out of earshot. "When she was a spicy *señorita*? I coulda made her a star."

"She was a star," Celeste said. "She told me she was a cantina singer and dancer."

"Really?" Dana thought about Graciela's familiar, dragging step. "What happened?"

Celeste craned her neck, making sure it was safe to share. "That limp? She was shot by a jealous lover. Here, too." She ran her fingers along her pronounced clavicle. "A bullet went straight through her throat, and she could never sing again. If you ask me—" she pointed at Werner with her fork—"there's your next story."

A polite rumble of agreement followed.

"You know," Celeste said, as if uncomfortable with the idea of silence or, even worse, the conversation veering away from her, "we're actually on the set of my very first movie. Right out there. The little house? I played a girl hiding from her mother. Just an experiment, of course, with Daddy's coloring. And it wasn't my mother in the film. It was some other woman who—"

"If you don't mind, sweetheart," Roland said with fatherly indulgence, "maybe let's talk more about the project at hand. What are you thinking, Ostermann? Going to give this project a go? Turn our little Celi into a proper leading lady? Because I'm lookin' at ya—" his eyes darted between the two women—"and I know you're not related or nothin', but I can see it. Yes, ladies and gent, I can see it."

Dana bristled under his scrutiny.

"You know it is not that easy," Werner said, looking uncharacteristically uncomfortable himself.

"What? Easy. You produce, you direct, our Celi stars, and women weep in the seats."

Werner met Dana's eyes. "I have not yet heard the whole story."

"Story." Roland dismissed the idea. "You've got lady Lazarus, right? Locked away, come back to life. Bring her out into the sunlight and let her fall in love with a hero. What do you think of Eddie Boland?"

"That's not what I meant," Werner said as Dana pondered Roland's idea.

Was that how people would see her? Risen from the dead? She supposed it wasn't too far off the mark. There had been plenty of stretches of time when she'd been confined to the cold and the dark, though she had yet to share those times with Werner. It was those tomb-like times that made her feel most ashamed.

And had she emerged to fall in love? She studied Werner, as

did the others at the table, and felt something like a spiraling coil run the course of her breath. He wasn't as handsome as a movie star—not like the few she'd seen, anyway. The question of whether or not he loved her seemed easy enough to answer. No. Doubtless he regarded her as an object of study. Curiosity, maybe, but most definitely not affection. Still, what more did he want to know? What did he think was missing?

"Your mother," he said, directly to Celeste.

She'd taken a bite of salad and seemed poised to choke on it until she'd taken a generous swallow of water. "Mother? What about Mother?"

"To frame the story," Werner said, "we need to start with that night. The night of . . ." His voice trailed off, and Dana felt the sting of everybody's eyes darting toward her. "That night."

"*She* was there," Celeste said, an unfamiliar iciness to her voice. "Ask her."

Not even Roland had a snappy comeback. He concentrated very hard on his salad.

"I would like to see from your mother's point of view. Did she ever talk about it?"

Celeste gave a mirthless laugh. "Not really. My brother used to torment me, though, telling me I was nothing but the ghost of our dead sister come to life. That Mother found me in the back of the linen closet, where she'd left my poor, tiny, wrapped-up body. I remember being terrified of that closet. He'd lock me in and I'd scream and scream until Mother came, and then she'd beat him for going near it. I think, sometimes, she was as frightened of it as I was. And, oh, you can't imagine, how horrifying to be locked away—" She brought a hand to her mouth. "I'm sorry, Dana. Seems I've always got a foot in my mouth."

Dana said nothing, but sent a forgiving smile as consolation.

The casual observer might think they were just a group of friends—a family, perhaps—gathered for a luncheon on the patio. How easy it was to forget the grisly events that brought them together.

"Anyway," Celeste continued, "to get back to your question. When Mother got sick, all she could talk about was going to heaven to see her precious baby. I don't think she ever saw me as anything more than a replacement. And of course, I didn't know anything about a murder." She said the word in whispered apology. "Practically not until she showed up on my doorstep—rather, *our* doorstep, if the will holds up—and Roland told me all about it."

Werner furrowed his brow as if figuring out a puzzle and looked to Roland. "How did that happen, exactly? That you knew?"

"As Miss DuFrane's agent—" he spoke as if addressing a table full of strangers—"all legal matters necessarily go through me."

Werner clearly wasn't satisfied with the answer, and Roland squirmed under his gaze, making Dana and Celeste mere observers.

"So there was this document."

"What document?"

"Like a confession, I guess."

"Enough!" Celeste jumped up from the table. "Can't we let the dead rest in peace?" She ran off, sobbing into her napkin, leaving an uncomfortable silence at the table.

"Sweetheart," Roland said, taking a slim cigarette case out of his jacket pocket, "why don't you go see if our girl's all right."

"No." Dana felt immobile, lead-bottomed and lashed to the seat. "I'd like to hear this." Although she didn't need it, she looked to Werner for approval and felt a little less weighted when he granted it with a solemn nod.

"Suit yourself." Roland lit his cigarette, then passed the case and the lighter to Werner, who, in turn, sought and received Dana's blessing before taking one for himself. "I didn't want to say anything in front of Celeste. Poor kid, she's got no one in this world. So when I get a call from Parker, and he tells me half of everything is willed to this Dana Lundgren—" he indulged her with a smile—"and on my client's behalf I ask just who this person is, he hands me these papers. This thick. And what I read in them, you don't want to know." He looked at Dana, his eyes filled with something very close to compassion. "You hear me, baby doll? You don't want to know."

But she did. She wanted to know everything, and somewhere, in a file *this thick*, there were answers. Luckily, Werner wanted to know too, and he served as her voice saying, "She deserves to know."

There was a rattle of glass as the French door opened and slammed behind a visibly irate Graciela.

"Matón!" She smacked the side of Roland's head. "You big bully! Our girl is crying her eyes out. What did you do to her?"

"Easy, easy. *Tranquilízate, mamá.*"

From Graciela's stance, it didn't appear she would be calming down anytime soon. "Tell me."

Roland pointed the burning end of his cigarette in Werner's direction. "Mr. World-Class Director started blabbin' on and on about Mother DuFrane. And then it came out—"

Graciela gasped and buried her face in her hands. "*Ay! No!* You told her?" She peeked out from between her fingers. "You told *them*?"

"Just that there was a file."

She continued to moan.

"Not what was in it."

"We agreed." She spoke through clenched teeth.

Years of bitterness, all wrapped up in a bundle of unsent letters, exploded within Dana's core, and she pounded a fist on the table, causing the cutlery to jump in its place. Everyone grew silent.

"Tell me." She eyed Roland Lundi. "You. Tell me everything."

He exchanged a look with Graciela, who shrugged a half-hearted consent before collapsing in Celeste's abandoned chair. After a final, long drag on his cigarette, he ground it out beneath the table and leaned forward, taking Dana's shaking hands in his.

"She was sick, you know? Real sick. Like, I'd never seen anybody like that. Have you ever seen dried fruit before? Not rotten, where everything gets all mushed up, but dried. Like we did when I was a kid. We'd slice apples real thin and lay them out in the sun, and they'd just shrivel up. Then we could eat them all winter long. That was the way with Mama Marguerite. Dried up. Almost as if her body got a head start on dying. It was enough to break your heart."

Dana's heart felt far from breaking. It felt thick, like a mass of concrete, heavy on her lungs, making each breath fight its way around it. How well she knew what it meant to shrivel up to nothing.

"After she passed, we went to the reading of the will, and there you were. Your name. A complete mystery. So I tell Celeste, 'Don't worry, sweetheart. I'll find out what's what.' I go to the lawyer's office and find out he has this file, a handwritten account, telling the whole story. Naturally I read it. You can see her handwriting getting weaker and weaker as it goes on, sometimes little more than a scribble. And in some places—" he looked hard at Graciela—"it's like another person altogether did the writing for her."

Dana turned her hands palms-up to grasp his and get his attention back. "What did it say?"

"I'm not at liberty to tell you."

She released him and pounded her fist again. "What is that supposed to mean?"

"It means it's a confidential legal document, and I'm sworn not to reveal its content."

"Sworn by whom?" Werner asked, just shy of menacing.

"By him. Their lawyer. Mr. Parker."

Werner balanced his cigarette in the corner of his mouth and squinted against the rising smoke as he dug into his shirt pocket for a small notebook and pen. "If it's a part of her final will and testament, it's a matter of public record. What is his name? I'll pay him a visit myself."

"Parker. Christopher Parker. Got an office up in . . ."

The rest of his words were lost as Dana's ears filled with the sound of rushing blood. Not rushing exactly, but thick. The way the water came out of the faucets on the coldest of winter mornings at the old Bridewell, tumbling over chips of ice. The chill raced through her, clear to the tips of her fingers, causing Roland to pause in the middle of his directions and give her his full regard.

"You okay, baby doll? You've gone white as a sheet."

Graciela, too, looked horrified at her appearance, and Werner dropped both his notebook and his cigarette en route to her side.

"Dana? Darling. You look as if you've seen a ghost."

"No." She pushed the word out from the top of her throat. "I've only heard its name."

CHAPTER 20

TITLE CARD: One year later, and most of it spent alone, locked up like a true prisoner, now. Long days spent with her own solitary company, seeking comfort when she can in the words of the Good Book. But with sunset goes the light. . . .

INTERIOR: A cramped, dark cell, lit only by the light coming from a high, small window, its bars casting shadows. Our heroine, now clearly a young woman, reclines on the narrow cot that juts out of the sturdy wall. She wears a long-sleeved striped dress and is propped up on one elbow, reading a book carefully positioned in the sunlight.

CLOSE-UP: A Bible, open to the book of Job, and these words: *"My soul is weary of my life; I will leave my complaint upon myself; I will speak in the bitterness of my soul. I will say unto God, Do not condemn me; shew me wherefore thou contendest with me."*

INTERIOR: The room grows dim. The sun has set, the light is gone. Dana closes the Bible and lies flat on her back, clutching it to her breast. She stares openly at the ceiling above.

TITLE CARD: "God in heaven, thank you for another day, and bring me safely through another night. And if it be your will, tomorrow, set me free. Do not keep me hidden away. Please, send someone to find me."

1909

ANNIE, THE WOMAN IN the bunk below, snored heavily, even though morning sunlight had been pouring through the window for at least an hour. Fine thing it was for her to sleep now, as she'd been awake half the night, forcing Dana to be an audience to her drunken rambling about the men who didn't love her and the children who didn't know her and the cops who had nothing better to do than keep a woman from earning a decent living.

Most nights Dana had the cell to herself, but she had long ago learned to keep the habit of sleeping on the top bunk, as the common factor among her infrequent guests was a moist, sour-smelling essence that permeated the thin mattress and lingered long after their dismissal.

She'd earned the privilege of having a small ticking clock, which she kept wedged between her mattress and the wall. A check of it showed there to be thirty minutes before she and Annie would be gathered and escorted to the dining hall for breakfast. It would be a kindness to wake her now and not subject her to the brutal rousing of a baton beating on the barred door, but she'd been such an unpleasant presence last night, Dana opted for peace.

Her Bible was stashed beneath her pillow. A gift from a group of well-wishing women from the Moody Bible Institute, it had been given to her on her first night in this cell. Not every new inmate got a Bible, she soon learned. Only the ones who were going to stay long enough to read it. Written in the front cover was a note: *To be free in Christ is to be free indeed.*

Her habit since getting the book had been to read one page—the same page—three times a day. Before beginning today's page, however, she opened to the page she'd read yesterday and reread it. Job 10 was page 419.

Thou knowest that I am not wicked; and there is none that can deliver out of thine hand.

Thine hands have made me and fashioned me together round about; yet thou dost destroy me.

Remember, I beseech thee, that thou hast made me as the clay; and wilt thou bring me into dust again?

Dana had pondered these words clear until her dreams last night, and she read them now, her finger with its dirt-crusted ragged edge underscoring each word, until a soft clearing of a throat cut through the sound of Annie's snores. She turned toward the door to see Edna Fontain. As opposite from Mrs. Karistin as could be—small, quiet, and stooped at the waist by the weight of the enormous ring of keys suspended from her belt. It had been Edna Fontain, Effie, who led her across the silent courtyard that day after the rainstorm and into this dark, narrow passage lined with small cells, each with its own barred door. One key for each door, and yet they remained as silent as she, her steady, careful steps discouraging them from clanging together.

"Welcome home," Effie said that first day. She'd stood, watching dispassionately as Dana shed her thin, tattered dress and stepped into the oversize striped garment that had been left, folded, on the foot of the bottom bunk. "This is the best room on the row. Gets the best light, nice cross breeze in the summer. When it gets cold, I'll move you down to the corner closer to the furnace."

It was Effie who brought her little gifts, starting soon after Dana's arrival just over a year ago. Like the small ticking clock, a feather pillow, a third pair of stockings, and occasional candle stubs for nights when the light from the hallway wasn't bright enough for reading the most precious gifts of all—books.

The first, *Alice's Adventures in Wonderland*, made her weep through the first chapter with childhood nostalgia. But as she read, she realized how very much her adventure paralleled Alice's. Always she felt too big, too small, surrounded every day by irrational, incoherent, disconnected women. If only she could wake and find it all a dream.

Then, one month later, the book was gone, another left in its place. Every month thereafter, on her bathing day, something new, delivered in the same way. Most were thin tomes of Western adventure and tragic romance, which Dana read over and over again until the time came when she would leave the book under her pillow and come back to a new one.

Only the Bible remained.

Now, Dana put the strip of silk ribbon—also a gift—in to mark her place and was tying her boots when she heard the faint sound of the key in the door. Quietly she stepped down the rungs and landed on the floor just as the door swung open.

"Good morning, Effie."

"To you as well, Lundgren." Effie, nearly two inches shorter than Dana, looked at her with a wrinkled nose. "She's a stinky one, isn't she?"

Dana sighed. "And a chatter-head. Kept me up half the night. Do we have to wake her?"

Effie considered. "Won't get no breakfast if we don't. But I reckon it won't hurt her to sleep it off. Fellow might show up with her bail before lunch. Save old Bridewell the cost of a meal, won't it?"

Dana smiled gratefully and stepped out into the hall, where she waited with the other women until Effie closed and locked the door again. There were a few who, like Dana, wore the striped dress belted at the waist, and others in the clothes they'd been wearing when they were taken in off the street. These didn't stay long—only until someone who depended on their income came to pay the municipal fine. Whatever crimes they had committed, Dana hardly knew, as Effie addressed them by their names rather than their crimes. More than that, the woman had taken it upon herself to keep Dana as far away from her fellow inmates as possible.

"You're nothing but a little seed yet," she'd said. *"These already gone to rot. But you? Might grow yourself into something someday."*

To say Effie was kind would be inaccurate. She was simply not cruel, and she carried with her a latent insistence that the women in her charge comport themselves with quiet, unquestioning obedience. There had been one or two over the course of Dana's confinement who answered Effie's understated authority with belligerent disrespect, but she'd always managed to find some small token to dissipate their anger. A new, clean comb; a sliver of perfumed soap; fancy, painted buttons for their tattered dresses. And if her gifts didn't inspire subservience, she'd been known to elbow a rowdy inmate in the kidney so hard as to send the woman to the floor in pain. Such displays were rare, but effective.

The women—there were more than twenty of them this morning, a larger crowd than usual—walked in two lines on either side of the hallway, with Effie setting the pace right in the center. Once they reached the dining hall, they wove into a single line to be served from the vast pot of porridge before taking their places at one of the five long wooden tables.

As was her custom, Dana sat alone while the others gathered into tight groups to complain about the food, never mind that they gulped it down like starving dogs and would end the meal fighting with each other for a second portion. They made disparaging remarks about the comfort of their beds after being prodded to wakefulness, and they bemoaned the system that would put them in prison, even though most would be returned to their life's pursuit within a week's time.

Dana merely listened, keeping her eyes focused on the scarred table in front of her. Deemed an "odd duck," she heard snickers and stories whispered around and about her, the essence and details of her crime growing with each new wave of inmates, until she was regarded as something monstrous and vile. It was a reputation that granted her solitude, and she bore it with what mustering of dignity she could.

Suddenly two small hands came into her line of vision, and she looked up to see Effie standing in front of her, hands planted on the table.

"Dana Lundgren, you have a visitor."

The spoonful of porridge turned to paste in her mouth, and she spoke around it. "A what?"

A slow grin stretched across Effie's face. "A visitor. Lady and a gentleman. I'm to take you to the courtyard."

"But I've never had a visitor."

"You have one now, don't you? Finish up."

She could barely swallow what was in her mouth, let alone imagine eating more as her stomach turned into an impenetrable stone. She slid her half-eaten breakfast for Effie to take and deliver to the next table, where the women feigned disdain to be given scraps from a baby killer's bowl. At least one of them, Dana knew—a fat one named Lottie who'd been in residence for three months after beating her husband close to death for eating more than his fair share of a beef pie—would tear into it the minute she left the room.

"Who is it?" They were walking past the empty cells, but she whispered in deference to her bunkmate, whose snores still echoed. "Is it somebody who can tell me about my mother?" And then a new hope seized her. "Is it my mother?"

"You know what I know," Effie insisted, walking so agonizingly slow as to make Dana want to burst forward and leave her behind. "A lady—not much more than a girl, mind you. And a young man."

"What do they want?"

"Ask me more questions and I'll knock you down and send them home."

Effie might have intended the threat to be humorous and empty, but Dana had seen too many instances of her discipline to take any chances. She bit her lip and slowed her steps, walking with her hands clenched at her sides through the familiar corridors to the open courtyard, where two figures sat side by side on a bench.

"You recognize 'em?" Effie spoke from the corner of her mouth.

"No," Dana said, though she squinted as if doing so would spark an idea.

At seeing her approach, the visitors stood. The *lady*, as Effie had so generously dubbed her, was probably not much older than Dana, but quite a bit taller, with an enviable glow of health radiating from her dark-toned skin and impressive stature. Her hair was somewhat contained beneath a crumpled hat, but a few dark, springy curls had escaped, and that's when Dana knew. The last time she'd seen that hair, it had been a mass of braids tied with bright strips of red cloth.

"Carrie?"

In confirmation, the visitor approached with open arms. "I knew it! I knew you'd still be here."

Dana allowed herself to be taken into the unfamiliar embrace, trying not to stiffen against what was clearly intended to be an extension of affection, but she could not bring herself to return the gesture in kind. Her arms remained limp at her sides.

"Do you see?" She spoke over Dana's head. "I told you she'd still be here."

She stepped away to allow Dana a clearer view of the young man accompanying her. He was equally tall, but with a heftier girth, his face almost perfectly round, his head topped with a crop of close-cut curls.

"This is my cousin Christopher Parker." Carrie introduced him with a mixture of hero worship and maternal pride. "He came here to visit from Cleveland, and I told him all about you, and he says he'll be able to help you."

He was holding his hand out, looking expectant, but Dana simply stared, having no idea what to do with such a gesture. She turned back to Carrie, soaking in her familiarity. She'd stayed at Bridewell for longer than almost any other kid—nearly three months—and had been the closest thing to a friend Dana had ever known.

"How are you?" Dana asked, hardly able to believe she was back after all these years. "Where have you been? You look—" tears threatened to choke her words—"you look so pretty."

Carrie laughed a beautiful laugh and took Dana's hand, leading the two to sit on a bench. Her cousin, looking uncomfortable, took a seat on another, and Effie moved to stand behind him.

"As soon as I got out, Mama moved us to Cleveland, near her side of the family. And I tried to write to you a few times, but when I didn't hear back . . ." She shrugged.

"Mrs. Karistin must have kept your letters from me."

"That old cow." Carrie's eyes darted toward Effie, anticipating rebuke, but she became emboldened at the woman's passivity. "I never did trust her for nothin'."

"With good reason," Dana said. She, too, glanced at Effie as her words ran up against a wall strong enough to trap her story.

The older woman breathed a deep sigh and checked the watch pinned to the bodice of her dark-blue matron's dress. "You visit," she said. "I'll be back in thirty minutes."

Once, when Dana was very little, her mother had taken her on a train to visit her father. She remembered standing on the platform between the cars, feeling the wind whip across her face as the landscape rolled by in a perpetual blur. She felt like if she jumped, she would take flight. Now, in this unguarded minute, speaking to a friend who lived outside these walls, she had that same sense of freedom, made all the more valuable by its fleeting nature.

"About a year ago, they said they had to move me because I was too old to be housed with the children anymore. But that same day, the warden let all of the children go home. All of them but me. And it's because, I suppose, I don't have a mother or a family to go home to. At least, I don't think I do. I'm not even sure about that. Nobody talks to me. Nobody has told me anything. I've never seen another child here since, so maybe they stopped locking them up for good. All I know is that I sit in this room all day, save for a little time in the afternoons when I get to come out here and sit in the sun, breathe in the fresh air. But then they take me back, and they lock me up, like I'm some kind of animal. Worse for me, even than the other women, and I know some of them have done horrible things, and I—I—"

Her voice had risen in pitch and volume as she spoke, until the words were tumbling like water out of a bucket. She had to say them all—every one—before the shamefulness of the picture they created called her to hold them back. She clung to the hand of her friend as if she were holding on to hope itself, telling every event of note from the time they'd last seen each other until this very moment.

"It's just like Mrs. Karistin said. Nobody knows I'm here. I've been forgotten."

"I didn't forget you," Carrie said. "And neither will my cousin."

It was the first Dana had thought of him since embarking on her tale, and she turned now to give him her full regard.

"Hello," she said before remembering a long-buried formality. "Nice to meet you."

"You as well." His voice was deep, but unnaturally so, as if he were trying to assume an age he hadn't yet attained. "Carrie says you never had a trial?" It was both a question and a statement, and Dana, quite unused to conversation of any kind, kept silent, puzzled as to how to respond. "You didn't go in front of a judge. Never heard anyone say, 'I hereby sentence you . . .'"

"No!" Dana exclaimed, remembering this exact conversation from all those years ago. "I mean, yes, that . . . no. None of those things ever happened to me. And I understand a horrible tragedy occurred, and I have a price to pay. I simply want to know—"

"What the price is?" Christopher Parker asked.

"Yes," Dana said, whispering now. "And if it's my whole life, I suppose that's fair."

"But nothing is fair without a trial."

"And you can help me with that?"

Christopher's eyes glittered, black as onyx. "I hope to, someday."

She'd been inching forward on her seat, growing more and more invested in the possibility of the answers so long denied, until she heard that word. *Someday.* The same word that had been haunting her own cloudy vision since the morning she woke up in jail.

"He's going to be a lawyer," Carrie said with obvious pride. "First one in our family to go to college."

"Someday." She could barely speak the word.

"That's right." Parker beamed as if Dana shared his family's sense of destiny. "I graduate from high school this spring, and I've already been accepted to three universities."

"Always been the bright one of the family." Carrie continued to hold Dana's hand and gave it a squeeze while gazing in adoration at her cousin. "He's from the good side. That's why I went to live with them after . . . here. I got to go to school, too. For a little bit." Her voice trailed, uncomfortable in the shadow of Dana's unconstrained envy.

"Is there anything—anything you can do for me now?" She hated that she sounded like she was begging. She was not used to asking for anything for herself. Not an extra blanket when she was cold, or a second slice of bread when she was hungry. Her only request had been to Mrs. Karistin, to mail her letters, and once again she saw this as her hope. "Could you mail a letter for me? To Mrs. DuFrane?"

"Of course," Carrie said, looking relieved at the simplicity of the request.

"I don't have one right now," Dana said, wondering just how long she had before Effie returned. Why did she not keep such a missive ready, tucked within her sleeve?

"He'll write one for you, won't you, Christopher? He's one of the best writers in his class. All the teachers said so."

Christopher attempted to look modest under his cousin's praise. "I don't know if I'm the *best*, but I'll gladly write something on your behalf. What should I say?"

Dana closed her eyes, picturing every word. She'd written the same letter ten times on paper, and a thousand on her heart. "Tell her that I'm sorry—"

"Wait a minute," Christopher interrupted. "That could be seen as an admission of guilt."

She shook off his rebuke. "Tell her I would take it back, if I could. And ask if she can forgive me, ever. I could live if I knew I'm forgiven. Live here, even, if I have to. Tell her I don't think God can forgive me if she doesn't."

By now Christopher was up from his seat and kneeling in front of her, looking into her eyes. "I'll do what I can for you. What's best for you, but it might take time. I'm not anybody right now."

Dana sensed movement out of the corner of her vision and saw Effie making her steady, purposeful way across the yard. "You're a friend, aren't you?"

"Yes. I promise."

"Then you're more than I've ever had."

CHAPTER 21

THE WRITTEN CONFESSION OF MARGUERITE DUFRANE, PAGES 54–58 AND 80–85

IN THAT MONTH BEFORE you were born, three fears consumed me. The first, of course, was the idea that you would be immediately taken away from me. I had nightmares of your mother wrapping you up in one of my precious Mary's blankets and escaping with you in the night. *Escape*, I'm sure, is a word my attorney would discourage me from using, as it implies that Mrs. Lundgren was some kind of prisoner in my home, rather than a guest invited to experience comforts and luxuries she could never have known, given her limited resources. Still, those fears pursued me. Daily, friends would stop by, bringing little tokens and gifts—some for me, some for you. Personally, I think they liked the idea of being part of such a dramatic turn of events, this tragedy-turned-blessing, or at least that's what they liked to call it. The way they babbled on, all these words spilling out of their mouths. How this new baby would mend my broken heart. How my Mary's angel would bring celebrations to heaven.

"The Lord giveth, and the Lord taketh away." Over and over again I heard this as they ate my cookies and drank my tea and told me how happy I should be that the Lord was giving me another child. As if I should forget what he had taken away.

Which gave birth to my second fear: that you wouldn't be enough. Oh yes, how a child can heal! Perhaps if you'd truly been my child, growing within me, filling my body with your presence, there wouldn't have been enough room for my bitterness to take root and become the cancerous vine that now chokes out my very life.

I felt it even then, you know. My physicians say that is impossible, but as I watched Mrs. Lundgren grow bigger and bigger with child, I sometimes felt a solid mass growing inside me, flattening my lungs to the point that I couldn't breathe. No one guessed that I wasn't in a family way. Everything about me grew enormously fat, from my face to the swollen tree stump–like ankles that defied any footwear other than your father's leather slippers. Only Mrs. Gibbons, who had been with me through my two pregnancies, hinted that all wasn't quite right.

"If you'll pardon me, missus," she said one afternoon as I wolfed down a plate of scones and a tall glass of buttermilk, "it just don't seem like you have the glow that you did with those other ones."

I assume she referred to the fact that my skin had stretched to contain the extra soft flesh of my face, hanging loose at my jowls and beneath my eyes, where no expensive cream could make it conform to its former beauty. I reminded her that I was still in mourning, and that no mother would be expected to glow with one child in her belly and another in the grave. She never mentioned it again.

And then there was the matter of your father. I remember being pregnant with Calvin, and the two of us would lie in bed, fascinated with the boy's movement within my body. Arthur would fall asleep with his hand on my belly, so eager to meet his son. (Somehow he knew it was a boy.) And he was protective of

Mary even before she was born, hiring nannies to take care of the boy so I could get plenty of rest. I don't think my feet hit the floor during the last six weeks of my confinement with her. The minute he held her, he wept, and did so every time he looked at her for days on end. So steeped was he in grief over Mary that I had to repeat myself three times when I told him we were going to have another baby.

If it matters at all, those are the exact words I used.

We are going to have another baby.

There will be a new little one in the spring.

Calvin is about to get a new brother or sister.

Phrases carefully crafted to absolve me of a lie. Looking back, it seems silly to spare myself that one falsehood when I was near to drowning in deceit.

I remember as a child going to the circus and seeing the woman high above, walking along a single, suspended rope, and the audience gasped each time she tilted to the right or the left. When I could stand it no more, I squeezed my eyes shut and prayed for her, harder than I'd ever prayed for anything in my young life, and when the audience applauded, I opened them to see her safely on the platform, waving to all of us before triumphantly descending the ladder and riding out of the ring on a glorious white horse.

Oh, if only I could have closed my eyes and opened them again to find myself safely delivered of this dangerous trail of deceit. To confess one sin to my husband would have meant revealing another, followed by yet another, until we were bound to each other by only a fragile thread of lies. He would leave me if he knew that a pregnant Mrs. Lundgren rested comfortably in a hidden third-floor room while her daughter had been secreted away at my behest. Indeed, now, looking at my actions thus writ, they appear far more malevolent than when they were mere thoughts in my grief-addled head.

But Arthur—he was not one to employ emotion as a justification for choices, right or wrong. When I had occasion to confront him about his adultery, he wanted me to believe that his decision to dally with another woman was simply a calculated risk based on availability and opportunity. It had nothing to do with his feelings for me, and certainly never implied that he had any affection whatsoever for those with whom he strayed. I'm sure he meant his explanation to give me reassurance, but his utter disregard for the physical expression of our love manifested itself not only in his wanton disrespect for our marital bed, but also in his failure to acknowledge the improbability that the child I "carried" could be his. *Not once* did he question—in word or regard—either the validity of my pregnancy or its source.

And so I kept my eyes open, carefully balancing each of my lies, praying for God to reward my intentions and make a way, though deep down, I didn't deserve a shred of grace. I prayed on behalf of this unborn baby, for the sake of Mary's soul, for the divinely ordained justice that banished Cain for the slaying of his brother.

I have done my initial duty with this document to explain your parentage, dearest Celeste, but I've yet to complete my confession of my role in the imprisonment of Dana Lundgren, even as I indulge my conscience with the insistence that, while I may have been the whisperer of words, if others had not taken action, my thoughts would never have come to anything beyond unfulfilled wishes. Except for the case of your natural mother. Never in my life would I have wished such a thing. God's actions are beyond our understanding.

You, however, were more wonderful than anything I could have conjured in my own imagination. Vibrant, healthy, precocious, and intuitive from the moment you were born. You consumed every moment of every day, not with selfish demands but by being a force of personality that simply could not be ignored. I could watch you for hours—sleeping, rolling on the floor, those first unsteady steps. And your father, too, for all my fears that he'd never recognize you as his own.

One time—you must have been about three years old—it was a wonderful autumn afternoon, and your father and I had taken you to that little park around the corner from our home. It was a rare family outing, with Arthur and I sitting together on an iron bench watching you play with your brother (who never did develop the same doting devotion, more's the pity) at floating fallen leaves in a puddle. The sunlight hit your hair, and I lost my breath at the glory of it. I'm afraid I quite lost my mind, and wondered aloud how two little ugly ducks like us had managed to produce such a beauty.

Silence followed as each of us pondered our own suspicions. Wrestled with our own truth. I sat next to your father, nearly as fat as I'd been before you were born. We couldn't look at each other.

It was one of those moments where I'd completely forgotten how you came to be. Sometimes those moments melded into entire days, and days upon days, when I never gave a second thought to the banished young girl or her mother. I had you, and Arthur, and Calvin. I'd landed on the platform, high above any crowd who would accuse me. And later, of course, California would be the white horse that would come to carry me away.

But that was yet to come.

I'd just packed Calvin off to school, and Mrs. Gibbons was occupied getting you cleaned up and dressed for the day, and

Arthur had already locked himself away in his study—not to be disturbed—when the front doorbell rang. It was far too early for a social call, not that I was dressed properly to receive visitors. Those days, I rarely socialized, claiming a particular frailty that left me sometimes too weak to venture far from my own bed. At home, of course, I remained enthralled with you, responding to your every whim and desire, helping you bump, bump down the steps only to carry you back up endlessly. I'd purchased several serviceable housedresses from the Sears and Roebuck catalog, finding that method of procuring a wardrobe far more appealing than listening to my dressmaker cluck her tongue at the measuring tape. Left with no recourse, as you'd created quite a mess of yourself with molasses or some such thing, it fell to me to answer the door, housedress or not.

You can't imagine the start it gave me to see a Negro standing on our front porch. Our *front* porch. I can't remember a time before that had ever happened, and I can say with almost-absolute surety that had my grandfather, the original owner of the house, been alive, he would have made short work of the young man who took such liberties with our property. Yet there he was. Tall and big as a barn, or at least he seemed at the time. In hindsight, I can see that my girth matched his inch for inch, and he had a moonish round face that offered absolutely no malice. He stood there, wearing a cheap suit not unlike the ones in the catalog from which I'd purchased my own cotton dress, and held a well-worn brown bowler hat in his hand.

"Is Mrs. DuFrane at home?"

That, perhaps, was my opportunity to escape. If I'd just said, "No, sir. She ain't," he might have gone away. Not forever, but long enough. But I didn't. I confessed to my identity.

"I have a message for you from Miss Dana Lundgren."

I told him he must have the wrong house, as there was nobody here by that name.

"Not *for* Miss Dana. *From* Miss Dana. For you, Mrs. DuFrane."

I told him to get off my porch, but he just smiled.

"I already attempted to contact Judge George Stephens, God rest his soul. Terrible thing to die with a secret, wouldn't you agree, Mrs. DuFrane?"

Never had I felt so trapped. I couldn't very well continue this conversation with a young Negro man on my front porch, especially given my state of dress. Nor could I risk inviting him inside, for that would be the one morning Arthur decided to grace us with his presence in the full light of the parlor.

There was nothing to do but to cut through the butter and ask him exactly what he wanted of me.

I could see thoughts piling up behind his eyes, but nothing seemed to make its way into words. "Truthfully, ma'am, I don't even know." But then some understanding seemed to dawn. "I suppose, in a way, I'm here to give you fair warning."

Down the street, the neighbor's maid swept the front porch, as she had been doing from the moment I stepped outside. Must have been cleaner than my kitchen floor by now. I knew she couldn't hear our conversation; up to this point, Christopher Parker (as I would later learn his name was) had been quite discreet, but how was one to know that he wouldn't burst forth in some loud, unfounded accusation?

Still, it was all the more reason to keep my face set in a pleasant expression of neutral congeniality as I asked what, pray tell, would be the nature of his warning?

"I'm going to find a way to get Dana Lundgren out of prison. And when I do, I'm going to bring her right to you so you can tell her exactly what you did to put her there."

My smile froze as he spoke, until any passerby might think this man regaled me with welcome news of friends long gone.

I asked him once again to leave and intimated that I would not hesitate to telephone for the police if need be. His response was an amused invitation to do so.

It was at this moment that I realized I hadn't fully closed the door behind me, as it swung open wide, revealing you, my tiny, sweet Celeste, asking, "Who is this man and why is he laughing?"

Fierce with protection, I swept you to my side.

"Perhaps," he said with a modicum of propriety, "we should postpone this conversation until another time."

I concurred, adding that I highly doubted a proper time or place could be secured for such a conversation.

"There's a park. I passed it on my way here. Perhaps this little one would like to go play later this afternoon? Let's say two o'clock."

At that moment, you began to jump up and down, begging to go to the park, and it was all I could do to keep you from taking his big brown hand and running away from me right then and there. Against every thread of logic within me, I agreed, knowing long before I stepped out of the house that I was putting myself right back up on the tightrope.

CHAPTER 22
CELESTE, AGE (NEARLY) 13

1918

CELESTE DID HER BEST to sit very still while Agnes formed her hair into perfect, bouncing sausage curls. Graciela sat nearby, hands folded in her lap, watching with a careful eye. Despite her obvious role as Celeste's caretaker—she balked at the word *nanny*, being far too old for such a thing—she looked exotic enough to be a star herself. With her dark lashes and naturally rose-tinted lips, she looked like she might have emerged from a dressing room after having makeup carefully applied. She might play the role of a gypsy queen or a Persian princess, not simply a Mexican maid. As such, though, she disappeared in the eyes of everyone but Celeste, who sought her attention and approval at every turn.

"How does it look?" Celeste whispered when Agnes stepped away to fetch the ribbon to be tied at the top of the mountain of curls.

"Qué linda!" Graciela's face radiated approval.

Celeste wrinkled her nose. "I think it makes me look like a baby." She was, after all, nearly thirteen years old—long past this sort of silly style.

"What did the man say? You are supposed to be a child, *verdad*? This makes you look like a child."

Celeste was not convinced and spun around to study herself in the enormous mirror above the dressing table. It wasn't the first time she'd been cast in such a role, playing the movie's star at a young age. It meant a week's worth of long hours, only to appear on the screen for a few moments at a time, doing childish things and being largely forgotten by the movie's end.

"I want to star in my *own* movie."

"Algún día." Someday. And when Graciela said it, it sounded like a promise. Not like her father, who made the word sound like a charge, or her mother, who never said the word at all. To Celeste, it sounded like forever.

"Here we are." Agnes gained some favor in Celeste's estimation by refusing to employ a condescending, singsong voice. She spoke with a world-weariness, as if the length of ribbon in her hand bore the weight of the ages. She fashioned it, pinned it, and with a barely affectionate tap on the shoulder, pronounced her finished and ready for makeup.

That was her favorite part, feeling the heavy cream smoothed across her face and seeing herself transformed in the same way as any other actress. Celeste, but not Celeste. Her own self hidden beneath the surface.

For this film, she played a rich little girl, so her wardrobe consisted of a beautiful silk dress, stockings, and exquisite leather shoes—nicer by far than anything she had at home. Graciela was entrusted with the fitting, including wrapping the first signs of Celeste's someday figure and pinning the pinafore and sash to reflect the form of a much-younger girl. Graciela knelt at her feet, leather shoe on her knee while she meticulously hooked each button. Meanwhile, Celeste studied the script before glancing at the rack of clothing next to them.

"I'm supposed to get a coat."

Graciela made a questioning noise.

"A coat and a hat. The script says I come into the great hall and grandly hand my coat and hat to the maid. Where's my coat?"

Graciela hooked the last button and stood, showing some discomfort in her leg as she did so. A search through the garments produced a fur-lined coat, hat, and muff. The colors were wonderful—the coat a pale sage green, and the fur dyed to a rich burgundy, making Celeste feel almost sad that such detail would be lost on the black-and-white film.

"Don't put this on yet, *mija*. It's too hot."

Celeste agreed but let her fingers caress the silky fur of the collar. She'd played enough poor children to know that her own real family lived a life of relative luxury, but nothing in her world compared to the one in which a child would have such a coat as this.

"If I ever have a little girl," she said, her voice as far-off and dreamy as the concept, "she's going to have a coat just like this. And I will, too, only mine will be *all* fur."

Graciela clucked. "*Qué tonterías.* No child needs such a thing. I grew up with food and a bed, and never quite enough of either one. Don't plan tomorrow by what you envy today."

Celeste pouted and refused to accept Graciela's offer to hold her hand en route to the set, insisting instead on burying them in the rich muff for the walk. Within minutes, she felt the sweat building up against the luxurious silk lining and knew they would be a clammy, drenched mess by the time she arrived.

Today's scene called for the familiar, simple, insipid performance she detested, nothing much more than her impromptu debut in her backyard playhouse. Walk through the door, hand coat and hat and muff to the maid, played by a heavyset German woman with a stern disposition and horrific body odor. On the first take, she did exactly as the script and director asked, but on the third, she decided to make this rich, spoiled girl a little less lovable, and dropped the hat on the floor, then tapped her expensive shoe impatiently while the befuddled woman stooped to pick it up.

"Cut!" the director yelled, and Celeste braced herself for his tirade at having his direction so blatantly ignored. To her delight, though, he exclaimed, "Brilliant!"

The German actress didn't seem to agree, and before clearing the set, she leaned in close enough for Celeste to learn that her breath matched her body in its offensiveness.

"You cannot just do as you please all willy-nilly like that. Make me look like a fool."

"You're an actress," Celeste said without an ounce of fear. "Act."

This time, Graciela gave her no choice but to take her hand as they walked to the second set—a lush Victorian parlor, rich in red and gold, with an enormous fir tree festooned with ribbons and glass bulbs and gold beads. She knew from the script that she was to gaze upon the tree with enraptured joy and clap her hands in delight. Now, as the crew set up their lights and camera, she studied it, trying to find the one remarkable thing that would inspire such a reaction. It was beautiful, to be sure, but brought with it a twinge of sadness, as her own family hadn't put up a tree for Christmas. It didn't seem right, Mother had said, with Calvin being gone to the war. She'd promised to have one as soon as he came home, even if it was the middle of July. But Celeste knew better than to believe such a thing; Mother was never one to follow through on promises of whimsy.

She stared and stared, but the tree presented itself as nothing more than a blur of color and texture. Ignoring Graciela's insistence that she go sit and wait for the director to call for action, she approached slowly, hand outstretched, ready to touch the piney needles. As she got closer, the fragrance grew strong, and she became overwhelmed with memories of being much, much smaller, before they moved to California, when they had a parlor that looked much like this one, dominated by an equally magnificent tree. Upon closer inspection, she noticed that the ornaments were not limited to shiny glass orbs, but small toys as well. Tiny painted dolls and letter blocks and, buried deep within the boughs, a perfect little soldier.

This, then, would be her inspiration, as Calvin had so dearly loved his toy soldiers, waging battles and planning strategies long after other boys had put such things away. His collection was still assembled on the dresser in his room back home. She smiled, searching her heart for delight, but to her horror and surprise, found her eyes filling with tears at the thought of her brother in danger so far away.

She shouldn't cry. She *couldn't* cry. She'd cried once, on her first film, when the director hollered at her for missing her mark. The tears smudged her makeup, and by the end of the day there were whispers about her being "difficult." Tilting her head, she looked up and blinked rapidly.

"Celeste? Sweetheart." The director's voice was softer than she'd ever heard. "Turn around, darling."

She did, slowly, and was surprised to find the cameraman cranking the handle, filming without the call of *Action!* At least, Celeste hadn't heard it. She took a deep breath and forced her face into a smile, bringing her hands together in a halfhearted clap. She had a line—what was it? Her mind remained fixated on her brother while she searched around for the words, trying to picture the script.

"Oh, Papa . . ." That much she knew, though she feared her lips were quivering too much to articulate the words clearly. "I didn't think—" she turned back to the tree, breathed in its fragrance, and, remembering, turned around—"I didn't think you'd remember!"

"Cut!" He was smiling. He never smiled. "Sweetie, that was beautiful. Can you do it again? Let us set up for the close-up?"

Instantly, any urge she felt to cry disappeared, as if her sadness was drying up from the inside. The directions in the script had been clear:

> Young Nellie sees the Christmas tree and is overcome with joy. She spins, claps her hands, and dances excitedly.
>
> YOUNG NELLIE: "Oh, Daddy! I didn't think you would remember!"

An apology traveled to the tip of her tongue. She knew she hadn't done it right; she didn't know the camera was rolling. Given another chance, she'd deliver exactly as the script instructed, but slowly a new understanding of the director's request dawned. He wanted the same performance, *exactly* the same. She knew that look—he was entranced.

"Of course I can," she said, feeling victorious, and she did, six times, including three takes that ended with a run into the arms of the dignified actor cast to play her father.

When the director called the end of the shooting day, Celeste's real father stood beyond the lights, but she didn't run into his arms. That would be a baby thing to do. Besides, he was talking with Graciela, their heads almost close enough to be touching, though they both looked straight at her with a shared expression of pride. At the sound of the crew's impatience, though, she did step lively and presented her cheek for a light kiss.

"Did you see me, Papa?" For such she called him now. *Daddy* was for a little girl. Plus, it's what Graciela called him on her behalf.

"I did, indeed. You were wonderful."

"Everybody thought so," Graciela added, hugging Celeste to her side. "Now, let us go clean your face and change your clothes. Your papa says he has to take you to dinner."

"Not *out* to dinner," he corrected. "Home for dinner, and a meeting."

"Oh," Celeste said, disappointed, and not just because she was hungry. She loved going out to restaurants with her handsome father. He could have been a movie star himself, she'd decided, being every bit as dashing as any of the men ever cast to play the role. Plus, when they went out, sometimes people recognized her as the little girl from one movie or another, and they oohed and aahed until Papa had to chase them away with a charming sternness.

"I think you'll feel better soon." Papa had a twinkle to his eye. "Mr. Parker is meeting us at home. We have a new contract. With Metro Pictures."

Now, unscripted, Celeste clapped her hands and did a small, excited dance. "Is it for the dream movie?" She had auditioned for it weeks ago—the story of a little girl who falls asleep and has fantastical adventures in her dreams.

"It is. And what's more, they've committed to no fewer than ten minutes' color footage."

"Oh, Papa!" Disregarding her maturity, she ran into his

arms, careful to keep her face tilted to avoid rubbing makeup on his sleeve.

"They wanted you, Celi. More than any other little girl."

He was holding her now at arm's length, and something about the way he looked at her chipped at her triumphant joy. "Is that why they agreed to the color?" He'd used such a tactic before, threatening to refuse to sign her contract without a commitment to at least some colorization. Always, when the producers refused, he backed down, but this time . . . "What if they'd said no?"

"But they didn't, darling. It's our dream. Yours and mine, together. Now, go. I told Parker to be at the house at six o'clock to look over the papers."

Deflated, Celeste walked beside Graciela, tugging the ridiculous bow out of her hair and wishing she could wipe her face clean with a swipe of her silk sleeve. They remained silent all the while, until they were back at Celeste's dressing table, the silk dress hanging on the wardrobe rack, and the mass of curls gathered and secured with a simple ribbon at the nape of her neck.

Humming just as she always did in the absence of conversation, Graciela slathered Celeste's face with a pungent cold cream and commenced wiping the makeup away.

"He really is selfish," Celeste offered up after a time, her words distorted as her face surrendered to Graciela's ministrations. "As selfish as Mother says."

"Ah, Celi *mía*, don't say such about your papa. You're always saying how much you want to be the star in your own movie. And here you are."

"They wanted *me*. Not his stupid color. He used me."

"Don't say such ugly things." Graciela made a final swipe, then kissed the tip of her nose. "He has done everything for you, and he loves you very, very much. He feels, sometimes, alone in this family. Share this with him."

The weight of the affection behind those words, if not the words themselves, struck a chord, making Celeste ashamed of her outburst. Her face clean, back in her perfectly suitable dress, she offered Graciela a weak smile. "It is exciting, isn't it?"

"Es maravilloso."

For a moment, Celeste wondered if Graciela was more excited for her or for her father. But maybe it didn't matter. She was right. They could share.

Graciela rode in the backseat of the car on the drive home, with Celeste at her father's side, peppering him with questions about the new movie. When would they film? Who was set to play her father and mother? And what fantastical elements would there be? Would she get to fly on a wire? Wear wonderful costumes? Dance with actors in animal costumes?

Papa chuckled. "All these questions! We haven't even signed the contract yet."

"But we will, won't we? And can I sign this one myself?" She'd been practicing a grown-up signature on all her school papers.

"We'll ask Mr. Parker if we can both sign," he said. "Maybe there's a special way to draw up the papers."

They were driving down Hollywood Boulevard when Celeste looked out the window and noticed a sign advertising the opening of a new restaurant—Frank's Café—and was reminded by her stomach once again of the extent of her hunger.

"I wish we could meet with Mr. Parker at a restaurant," she said. "I'm starving."

"You know that's not possible," Papa said, his voice firm. "I'm sure Graciela won't mind whipping up supper for us, will you?"

"Of course not," she answered from the back. "I know just what I'll make."

"Can we eat first, at least?"

"Celi, dear, Mr. Parker might already be at the house waiting for us. Maybe even for this past hour."

"He can eat with us, can't he?" She knew he couldn't go into a restaurant with them since he was a Negro. That's what Papa had said, anyway. Not a nice restaurant.

"We'll see," Papa said. "But he certainly is welcome."

Nobody, though, would have felt welcome driving up to the DuFrane house just then. The sun had quite disappeared, leaving the world a dusky half dark, and the windows of the stately homes on either side glowed a soft yellow. Yet not a sliver of light shone from within their home. Not on the porch, or through the tall, narrow windows on either side of the front door. Celeste looked up at the row of darkness on the second floor. She didn't expect to see any amber light coming from her own room, but next to it—Calvin's—should have had a single burning flame for the soldier off to war. Every night, she and Graciela met at sunset to pray for her brother's safety and light a new taper to burn down until dawn. Mother must have forgotten. Or more likely, she was too lazy. Given the hour, she might have already retired for the night, having eaten what she could find in the icebox and pantry.

Selfish. Every bit as much as Papa. She might not have even answered the door for Mr. Parker.

Papa pulled the car around back to the garage, revealing the house to be in total darkness on every side. No sign of life in the kitchen and, confirming Celeste's suspicions, nothing emanating from her parents' bedroom upstairs. It wasn't until this point that Papa remarked about the air of desertion, and Graciela muttered, *"Hay alguien en casa?"*

The only explanation other than that of Mother having already been to bed would be to assume Mother had left the house, a far less likely scenario.

They entered through the back door into the kitchen, where Celeste immediately set upon a plate of pastries resting under a glass dome. Graciela barely chastised her for spoiling her appetite before disappearing to her room to deposit her hat and purse.

Papa left, too, hollering, "Marguerite?" He must have been worried, because both he and Mother loathed the practice of yelling from room to room, yet his call echoed throughout the house, unanswered.

Graciela returned, tying an apron around her waist, and set to work pulling down a skillet and rummaging through the icebox for eggs and cheese. She lit the stove with a long match, prompting Celeste's memory.

"Can we please go light the candle in Calvin's room? Mother forgot."

"Después." She cracked another egg into a large mixing bowl. "I already lit the stove. We won't be long."

"Can I do it by myself?" She hated the thought of full darkness descending without the guiding flame in the window, not that Calvin didn't know full well how to find their house in the dark. Goodness knows he came stumbling in plenty of nights without the aid of such a beacon.

Graciela paused, whisk in hand, and beckoned Celeste to her side. "We pray together here, okay? Then you go."

Celeste abandoned the rest of her pastry and walked to the other side of the table. Graciela made her familiar sign of the cross, saying, *"En el nombre del Padre, del Hijo, y del Espíritu Santo,"* before taking Celeste's hand.

"Heavenly Father," Celeste prayed, "please keep my brother, Calvin, safe on the fields of battle. Give him a warm bed to sleep in, and wrap him in your mighty shield. Help him to be brave and kind, and bring him home."

To this, Graciela added what she did every night. *"Querido Dios, te pido que protejas a mi hijo y que vuelva a mí vivo y sano."* Celeste translated: *Dear Father, I ask you to protect my son, and to bring him home alive and well.* That Graciela thought of Calvin as her own son only sealed their prayer.

The two offered *amen* in unison before Graciela sent Celeste upstairs with a new, white taper, a matchbox, and a kiss to the top of her head.

She bumped into her father at the foot of the stairs. "Is Mother already in bed?"

"No, but I did find this on the entryway table." He held up a large, brown envelope, its flap held closed with a red string wound around a cardboard button. "It's from Parker's office. The contract, I'm assuming." The worry on his face eclipsed any excitement from before.

"Maybe she and Mr. Parker went out for a little bit?" She didn't want to offer any undue worry, but she had, on several occasions, happened upon the two of them looking thick as thieves in some conversation that always ended abruptly once her presence was known.

"Doubtful," Papa said, reminding Celeste of the other aspect of her mother's relationship with Mr. Parker. Namely, that she didn't care for him very much at all.

"I'm going to light the candle in Calvin's window. Would you like to come with me?" As far as she could remember, Papa had never participated in the ritual, though her mother did most nights, making it all the more odd that she'd forgotten to do so this evening.

"You go ahead." He hugged her to his side. "I'm going to make a telephone call or two, and then we'll look at those papers together."

She hugged him back before scampering up the stairs. When she got to Calvin's room, she crossed immediately to the window, knelt, replaced the old candle with the new, and struck a flame.

"Don't bother." The sound of her mother's voice startled her so, Celeste nearly dropped the match. She turned the light in the direction of the voice and saw her mother lying prostrate on her brother's bed.

"Mother? We've been calling to you for ages." She lit the candle. "Why didn't you answer?"

"I said, don't bother." By the dim light of the single flame, Celeste watched her mother struggle to turn over and eventually sit up on the bed. "He isn't coming home."

The weight of her words fell straight to the base of Celeste's spine, paralyzing her in place. "Wh-what did you say?"

"I got a telegram." The yellow paper rested as if settling into her clutch. "While that horrible darky lawyer was here."

Barely aware of her own movement, Celeste crawled across the floor and clung to her mother's knee.

"He's dead? Calvin's been killed? Is that what the telegram said?"

"And I'll bet he wanted to laugh at me." Mother seemed to be speaking to somebody far away, as if Celeste weren't there at all. "When I read it. Should have sent him away, always poking his nose in our business."

"Mother, please. Tell me about Calvin. What do you know?"

Their shadows loomed, huge and frightening on the wall, and when her mother lifted her hand to stroke Celeste's hair, the gesture stretched clear to the ceiling. The resulting touch was lifeless and cold, like that of the occasional uncomfortable stranger whom girls were sometimes forced to endure.

"It means another of my children dead and buried."

"Oh, Mother. Maybe there's been a mistake. Maybe he'll come back."

Like I did.

"He won't be back. This is God's justice, his price for my sin."

"Certainly not." She couldn't imagine the magnitude of a sin that would demand such a price. "Besides, Graciela says that Jesus already paid the price for all of our sins. This isn't your fault."

"'Skin for skin,'" Mother said with a chilling smile. "Parker asked if this is what it would take to break me. The weasel. He's in every bit as deep as I am. Threatened to tell your father, he did. Until I reminded him that he, and you—" she propped a chubby finger under Celeste's chin—"are just two more slices of his buttered bread."

Grief had transformed her into a rambling madwoman, her confusing words churning an anger inside Celeste, who wanted nothing more than to learn the details—however gruesome—of her brother's fate. But it became obvious that this was not the time. Later, when Mother's head was clearer, when she could pry the crumpled telegram from her hand, maybe then she'd know. Until then, she would provide what comfort she could; she laid her head on Mother's knee and wept.

Soon, her father's silhouette appeared in the doorway.

"There you are." His voice was thick, the words choked with what could only be knowledge of the fate of his son. "I telephoned Mr. Parker. He told me."

"Oh, Papa!" Celeste used her mother's sturdy, still form to clamber to her feet, then ran into her father's waiting arms. She buried her face in his shirt, mindless of the tears that soaked it through. He, too, sagged against her, and they held each other as Papa wrenched his son's name from the back of his throat, over and over again.

Celeste heard a soft sound coming from behind her father and pulled away to see Graciela standing in the doorway, holding a crumpled lace handkerchief to her mouth, quietly but visibly sobbing. Celeste tried to catch her eye, seeking a secondary source of comfort, an extension of her father's warmth, but Graciela wouldn't look at her. She looked higher, and Celeste knew she was looking at her father. Moreover, she knew her father was looking at Graciela. The strength of their gaze wrapped them all together in the light of that single, glowing flame until Mother, with a single, dry breath, blew it out.

CHAPTER 23

DANA GOES TO THE BEACH

1925

AT DANA'S REQUEST, the driver, Gustav, slowed his speed on what she would describe as the perilous, twisty, turning road. Her stomach was in enough distress with the thought of the afternoon ahead; she didn't need that odd feeling of having her insides sloshing around, not quite in the same place as her outside.

"Lady, I'm telling you if I drive any slower, we'll be crawling backward on three legs."

"Please." She pressed her handkerchief to her mouth before continuing. "I've never been in a car—on a road like this."

That wasn't exactly true. She'd driven through the hills with Werner the night of Celeste's premier, but that was at night, where she didn't have to see the blur of the passing scenery around and, more disturbingly, *below* the car. Also, she'd been in the front seat, next to the driver—next to Werner—and perhaps his comforting presence made the difference.

"If I'd'a known you wanted to go this pace, I'd be sure to charge Mr. Ostermann by the hour instead of the mile. Might I suggest you get a Chinaman and a rickshaw for the trip back?"

"How much farther?"

"Sit back, close your eyes. Ten minutes, tops."

Closing her eyes didn't help at all. It seemed her best bet was to open the car's back window and put her face to the wind. The smell of the ocean was instantly refreshing, almost healing, and she breathed it deep.

Yesterday, when she'd received word that Werner wanted to see her this afternoon—alone—she'd assumed he wanted another meeting in his office. The car arrived promptly at nine o'clock that morning, far too early for Celeste, who had only been home and in bed for a few hours. Even then, Dana suspected that had been Werner's design, knowing the starlet's dislike for early appointments. It wasn't until Gustav made the first unfamiliar turn that she realized they weren't headed to Werner's office at all. By then, she was trapped in the backseat, too late to change her mind, and going too fast to jump. The latter impulse came after learning that she was being taken not to his office, but to his home.

By now, the sound of the ocean wrapped around the rumbling of the car, and she could see the shoreline. They drove past three houses, then four, without the driver giving any a passing glance.

"Do you know which one is his?"

"I been driving Mr. Ostermann out here nearly every day for five years. Yeah. I know. So sit back. When we stop, we're there."

There turned out to be like nothing she'd ever seen before.

The house looked to be a natural outcropping of the craggy wall behind it, the stone taking on purposeful form and structure with the discipline of thick, rugged wood beams. Morning sun glinted off massive windows, and a wooden walkway extended in a serpentine pattern, disguised by the rocks and grass and sand.

"This is it."

The driver hopped out and opened her door with a practiced flourish. She took his offered hand and stepped out of the car, surprised at the wobble in her legs. Smiling self-consciously, she blamed the unfamiliar feeling of sand.

"Allow me to walk you to the door then, miss." He was infinitely more polite now that they weren't moving.

"Thank you," Dana said, though with each passing breath, the idea of ascending to that house became more terrifying, and she wondered if she'd have the strength of mind and body to do it at all. While she pondered the possibility of climbing into the car to be driven back to what was now a wonderfully familiar home, she heard her name on the breeze, and again, until she looked up to see Werner at the top of the walkway, waving.

He looked like she'd never seen him before—his shirt loose and billowing, open at the collar, and his hair freed from any constraint, standing on edge and making him look like one of the little boys set loose to play in the courtyard before that awful, rainy day.

He was coming down the walkway with a quick, not-quite-running step, and to her delight, his arrival onshore was preceded by that of a short-legged dog, who ran immediately to Dana, gave her a quick sniff, then moved on to the driver's equally eager greeting.

"Hey there, Ozzie." He scratched behind the dog's ears and offered his face to its darting pink tongue. Dana wrinkled her nose, though she was fascinated with the idea of such abandon.

"Ozzie! Here." Werner stood at her side, and after one final, circling sniff, little Ozzie stood between them, paws prancing impatiently in the sand. Werner took Dana's hand. "How lovely of you to come."

"You said to."

He smiled, looking younger still. "You can always refuse an invitation, you know." He turned to the driver. "Thanks for getting her out here safe and sound."

"No problem, Mr. Ostermann. When . . . ? I mean to say, what time—?"

"I will telephone this afternoon." Werner spoke as though he were sweeping away an unsightly conversation.

The driver tipped his cap, bade good morning to Ozzie and Dana respectively, and returned to his still-running car.

"Well, then." Werner rubbed his palms together in the first gesture of nervous energy she'd ever seen from him. "Would you like to take a walk on the beach? Or come up to the house first? I have some breakfast laid out. Are you hungry?"

"I—"

"Let's go up to the house, have some coffee. Let the sand warm up a little bit."

At that, she glanced down to see that his trouser legs were rolled, exposing tanned legs and bare feet. Dana couldn't remember ever seeing a man's bare foot before, and the sight of it made her feel more comfortable than she could have imagined. She agreed, and he made a *tschik-tschik* sound to Ozzie, who raced up the walkway in front of them.

"This is beautiful," she said, her words increasingly inadequate with each ascending step.

"Thank you. It is important for me to be able to get away from the city. I keep an apartment close to the studio, but I prefer to be out here most of the time. Lets me think."

Ozzie raced back and forth in front, as if tugging them up.

"And you have a dog."

"I do."

"I don't have much experience with them. Is it a boy or a girl?"

"She's a she, a Welsh corgi, and always so excited when we have a visitor. I think she gets bored with my company."

"I doubt you have any shortage of visitors." Dana might not

have known much of the world, but she was quickly learning, and a man as handsome as Werner with an isolated house on the beach was bound to have his fair share of visitors. The thought of it awakened a sort of privileged fear, making her wonder if she should have been more specific in the note she left for Celeste.

The walkway ended at a wooden deck that jutted out from the house to a free suspension over the beach below. On it, a table was set with a flapping white cloth, held in place by a feast. A platter of fruit—melon and strawberries arranged around a dish of cream—a platter of scones, and a silver carafe.

"I made the scones myself," Werner said. "One of my other many talents. My grandmother's recipe."

Dana fought to hide her amusement. Never had she seen him with anything less than perfected, cool control, and here he was, fidgeting, as if seeking her approval. "It all looks lovely," she said, allowing him to pull out her chair.

As they ate, he talked about the house, listing details of history and architecture, seeming to know every stone personally, intimately acquainted with every beam. "We'll take a tour after we eat. Not much of a tour—it's not a large house; but you'll see how the ceiling . . ."

Distracted by the surf, she heard very little of what he said. Its rhythmic pounding drew her, and she found herself gazing over the railing, food forgotten on her plate.

Werner's voice broke through. "It is hypnotic, isn't it?"

"I never could have imagined such a thing."

"Come." He stood, wiped imaginary crumbs from his chin with his napkin, and crossed to her seat. "Let me show you something."

An instinctual fear gripped her, digging through layers of naiveté, and she reached for her coffee. "I'm not quite finished here. The scones are exquisite. I might like to have another."

"They will wait. I promise."

Dana gave in to her trust and took his hand as he led her from the table and through a paned-glass door. The room inside looked to be an extension of the ocean itself. The walls were made of stone and wood, left to their natural textures, with abstract paintings of cool blues and grays bringing in an extension of the sky. One wall was pure glass, giving the impression that one could walk right out without the benefit of any open door—an idea she found both fascinating and frightening.

A spiraling staircase rose right up in the middle of the room, and it was to this that he led her, sending Ozzie scampering up first.

"Go on," Werner urged. "I promise that Ozzie will defend your honor."

More at ease following the dog than its owner, Dana climbed, arriving at a loft that overlooked the living area below. To the left, she saw a bed—*his bed*—neatly made with a woven blanket of bright design stretched over its expanse. Masculine, without a hint of lace or ruffle and, to her utter shock and shame, utterly inviting. Pausing, she sent a quick prayer of repentance, followed by one for protection from both her thoughts and his intentions.

"Other way," he said from behind her, his voice both reassuring and amused. "Follow Ozzie."

The little dog had scampered to a door identical to the one downstairs, to the right of the landing. She stood on her back legs, pawing at the knob, until Dana opened it onto a balcony that wrapped around the corner of the house, stretching higher, and farther still from the one below, where her coffee was growing cold.

"Go on," Werner urged. "Step out."

She did, and it was like stepping on sky. Only a waist-high railing, formed from uniquely twisted driftwood, stood between

Dana and the vastness of creation. The ocean stretched forever. To the left and right, nothing but sand and water. And sky—always and everywhere, the sky.

"Doesn't it make you feel small?" Though he stood close by, his words whipped to her on the wind.

She shook her head. "No. I know what it is to feel small. This . . . I feel as big as creation. Look." She reached out her hand. "I'm touching the horizon. I'm a titan."

"So you're not afraid?"

"No." She didn't dare turn around. If she looked at him, she would be.

A gust kicked up and threatened to blow her hat clean off her head, and she clutched at it, laughing. "Well, maybe I should be."

He laughed too and held his hand out. "Give it to me." She did, and to her amazement, he squatted and held it out to Ozzie, who clamped it gently in her mouth, barely able to keep the brim above the ground. Werner snapped his fingers twice and said, "Put it away" in a commanding voice, at which Ozzie ran off, taking Dana's hat with her.

"What did you just do? Celeste is going to kill me."

He stood. "Relax. It will be safe in a basket with some of her other toys. It was easier to teach her a trick than to run around picking up after her all the time. She's very tidy."

Dana ran her fingers through her hair, imagining how wild she must look now, and turned her attention back to the view, feeling brave enough to brace herself on the railing and lean out a little.

"There was a woman named Effie," she said, feeling him take his place beside her, "who used to give me little gifts sometimes. Once, she gave me an alarm clock so I could wind it up and hear the ticking. I used to keep it stuffed between my mattress and the wall to muffle the sound. Not because it bothered me; really it was comforting, somewhat. But to smooth it out, like I was spreading out each *tick* and *tock*, running the minutes into each other. Make the time go faster."

Werner said nothing, but moved his arm closer to hers. Not touching, but closer. Had she not been watching, she never would have known.

"Later, she brought me a seashell, this big." She held out her cupped hand. "Said if I put it to my ear, I could hear the ocean."

"And did you?"

"I tried. But then, how would I know for sure? I'd never heard an ocean before. And from what I could tell, it wasn't any different from covering my ears with my hands. But I tried."

"Now that you've heard the ocean, is it the same?"

"No."

"Are you sure? Maybe when you go home, you should get your shell and try again."

"I don't have it anymore." She opted not to tell him of the drunken prostitute who'd taken it in exchange for silence. It wouldn't do to introduce such ugliness into this moment.

"Then perhaps we should go for a walk on the beach and find another for you to take to Celeste. A memento."

She looked up to find him studying her profile, filling her vision with nothing but water and sky and him. "I'd like that."

It didn't seem possible, but he moved closer still, aided by the hand he placed at the small of her back. "It is important for you to know how much I have come to care for you, Dana. Do you believe me?"

She gave a small nod, careful not to bring her lips any closer to his.

"Whatever happens, after today, understand that you have

become something special to me. And I wonder if, at all, you might care for me in the same way?"

If not for the feeling of the railing in her grip, she might have thought she'd drifted straight off into the sky. She wanted this moment to stretch to the horizon and back while her heart thundered with the surf, but the only truthful answer might bring her clattering to the sand.

"I—I don't honestly know how I feel." Immediately she felt a change in his embrace. Not a release, but a subtle retreat. "You're handsome, and interesting. But you know I've never—"

"I know."

"*Talked* to a man. Or driven in a car, or had coffee, or listened to the ocean, or—"

Her list was silenced by his kiss, soft and salty as the air, but nowhere near endless.

"I plan to do that again," he said, drawing away, "when I can be reasonably sure that we are not merely objects of one another's curiosity. Will that be all right with you?"

"Yes." Her heart ticked like the clock, and again she wished for time to speed by.

"Good." He seemed genuinely pleased. "Now, how about a swim?"

She looked down at her dress.

"I have an abundance of bathing costumes. Go back downstairs—the outside stairs, I mean—and go to the right. There is a small white cabana. The ladies' side is clearly marked."

"I've never worn a bathing costume."

He bent to look into her eyes. "You have to stop thinking of your life in the light of things you've never done. Every step is new until we take it. You are not alone in that. There was a time

I'd never held a camera. A time I never spoke English. A time I never kissed a woman. Now I have done all these things."

She was left with the lingering wonder of how many women he'd kissed, and suspected the number might lie in the abandoned bathing costumes in the cabana below. Her wan smile invited another kiss, somehow briefer than the one before, and he released her.

"To the right?" she asked over her shoulder before heading downstairs.

"If you see Ozzie, just say, 'Cabana!' and she'll lead you right to it."

Dana felt a little like Alice in Wonderland, visiting a house that grew from a rock and stretched clear to the sky, let alone talking to the animal that stole her hat. With Ozzie's help, she managed to find the changing room—a small, white clapboard building with the *Ladies* and *Gents* sides clearly marked. Inside, she found four small booths separated by brightly striped curtains, and a row of shelving holding a dozen or more suits. She picked up the first one and held it up. With its red-and-black diamond-print top and black skirt, it looked just like one Celeste had pointed out in a fashion magazine over breakfast the day before.

She stepped out of her shoes and stripped off her stockings, wondering about Celeste's insistence that Dana take a razor to her legs and under her arms. "You know," she'd said, "there comes a time when a girl's gonna take a swim." Did she know? Had Werner asked her permission like some gallant suitor? Whatever the prompting, she was grateful as she stepped into the suit, stretching the top over her shoulders. Funny, once she had it on, she didn't feel any less naked than before. Her legs from midthigh were exposed, as were her shoulders and arms. Moreover, what *was* covered was sheathed in a fabric that seemed determined to cling to her very skin.

She tried to imagine herself as one of those women from the magazine, standing with their chests thrust forward, arms confidently behind their backs, legs angled prettily. In fact, she struck that very pose but, certain she looked ridiculous, doubled over in a fit of giggles.

A knock at the door. "Dana? Are you all right?"

"Y-yes." She composed herself. "One minute. I'm looking for socks?" She'd seen them in the magazines too. Dark ones rolled up to the knee. She pawed along the shelves, finding none, but she did discover a ruffled bathing cap hanging on a hook. That was something, at least, and she tugged it over her windblown hair.

He was waiting when she emerged, wearing a black suit that accentuated the breadth of his shoulders in a way she could never have imagined.

"Look at you," he said with almost-parental approval. "You're a natural."

The fear of being exposed disappeared in the pleasure of his approval, and she resisted the urge to wrap her arms around herself and disappear back into the cabana.

He held up a basket. "I packed the rest of our breakfast, in case we get hungry. Shall we?"

"Lead on." She took a tentative step. "Adventure awaits."

They walked a little way down the shore, their steps in lazy synchronization. Waves sloshed over their feet and splashed up, cold, and she felt her entire body respond in gooseflesh.

"It takes some getting used to, I suppose," Werner said. "And the only way is to run straight in."

"I don't think so—"

But he'd already dropped the basket, grabbed her hand, and was dragging her at a full-out run into the ocean. Dana squealed in protest, but he would not relent, tightening his grip and lifting his legs higher as the water grew deeper, adding his own splash to the white foam, and soon she had no breath to make any sound at all. Thankfully, the water was no higher than her knees, so drowning seemed unlikely, and when he finally stopped pulling her, he turned and placed his hands on his hips.

"What do you think?"

"I th-think I'm f-f-f-freezing."

"That is because, look at you. Half in and half out. The ocean is like love, terrifying if you don't give yourself over."

Before she could protest, he'd grabbed her about the waist and pulled her down. Somehow, she managed to keep her head above the water, but as she stood, spluttering, a wave crashed from behind, knocking her down again.

Werner had the nerve to stand above her, laughing, yet he offered his hand to pull her to her feet.

"Are you all right?" He was doing a terrible job of appearing concerned.

She wanted to be angry, even felt like she had good reason to be, but it was far from the first time she'd been cold and wet, and never had she been under such a vast expanse of sun and sky. Here, she knew, warmth was waiting, and knowing that, she not only allowed him to help her up, she brought with her a generous, satisfying scoop of cold salt water that landed square in his face.

From there it was a game, and Dana, thirty-two years old, found herself playing for the first time since before she could remember. They chased one another, pushed and fell and splashed. At some point, she found the chill diminished, her body warming from within. Breathless now from exertion rather than shock, she communicated in short, gasping, elated sentences until finally, collapsed on the sand, she watched as the tide came in over her toes, lapping clear up to the hem of her suit. It was then the chill came back.

"Come," Werner said, offering his hand one more time. He walked her back to the spot where he'd dropped the basket and reached in, producing a thick white robe.

Effusing gratitude, she thrust her hands into the sleeves and wrapped it tight around her, cinching and tying the belt with a fat, square knot. After donning one of his own, Werner produced a thermos and two tin cups, plopped down in the sand, and commenced pouring coffee.

"Oh, perfect," Dana said after the first sip. She felt her body return to a comfortable temperature, aided by the warmth of the sun on her face. They sat side by side, close enough to touch, but neither making any effort to do so.

"Perfect," Werner echoed.

"Where did I leave off?"

He turned to her. "Excuse me?"

"My story, last time we talked. Where was I?"

"Not today."

"Then why did you bring me here?"

He gestured with his coffee cup. "Drink."

She did, more and more, until the last drop was gone and a delicious warmth surged through her.

"Now—" he took the cup from her—"lie back."

It crossed her mind to be suspicious, but she complied. He manipulated her hands, resting them on the knot of her robe, and removed the sodden bathing cap, tossing it aside. At his final instruction, she closed her eyes. The sand conformed around her body, and the only sound was the irregular rhythm of the surf, until his voice appeared at the edge of her darkness.

"I want you to know peace. To have a moment in time where your spirit is free and you are safe. To do something you may never have even dreamed of doing before."

"Well, you have achieved that." Her words were slow and sleepy. "Thank you."

"And you will let me know when I might kiss you again?"

She opened one eye. "I'll let you know."

He heaved a sigh of mock resolve. "Then, I suppose, the only gallant thing to do now is get you back to the house, as this is far, far too tempting a tableau."

"Just a few more minutes," she muttered, about to remind him that he very well knew how many years' worth of sunshine she had to make up for, when the roar of an automobile invaded the tranquility of the moment.

Dana sensed rapid movement beside her and heard Werner mutter a mild curse without apology.

She struggled up to her elbows. "What is it?"

"Not now," he said, speaking over her toward the car, a sleek, red-and-tan machine that now sat silent in front of his house.

"Werner?" She sat up fully and would have stood had he not clasped her hands in his, imploring.

"Remember what I said to you earlier. That I care for you very, very much."

"Yes, of course. What—?"

"And I would never do anything intentionally to hurt you. Do you believe me, darling?"

She pulled away, saying, "You're frightening me," and stood just as the figure emerged from the automobile.

Even with the distance of years and sand, she recognized him. If the car was any indication, he must be wearing a far more expensive suit, but the round, dark face hadn't changed, and as he lifted his hand to shield his eyes from the sun, she noticed the short crop of dark curls hadn't been allowed to grow an inch.

"What is he doing here?"

Werner stood beside her. "I told him one o'clock. Afternoon."

"You knew?" She swiveled her head between the traitor of her past and that of this present moment.

"He has something for you."

"He has *nothing* for me!"

But at that very moment, Christopher Parker was making his way toward them, looking none too happy about trudging through the sand in a brown wool suit and loafers, until he locked eyes with Dana, standing frozen in place. Then his entire face burst into a smile, and he quickened his step, saying, in a voice that hadn't changed over all the years, "Is that you? Is it really, really you?"

She clutched her robe tighter and set a course toward direct confrontation. Hot tears streamed down her salty skin, and her free hand was clutched into a fist by the time their paths collided. Soon after, she landed a slug squarely into his soft, round jaw. Not satisfied with his reaction, she slapped him for good measure.

"You left me!" She was screaming like she never had before, and the crashing sound of the waves left her dissatisfied with the impact. So she slapped and screamed again. "I trusted you, and you disappeared!"

Her hand was raised to deliver another blow when she was lifted off the ground, giving her opportunity to kick Christopher Parker right in the knee.

"Let me go!" She twisted out of Werner's hold and landed square in the sand. "You knew! I told you about him, and the promises he made. And you . . ." When words failed, she pummeled his chest.

"Darling—"

"Miss Dana—"

"Stop!" She covered her ears, and there it was, the sound of the ocean twice amplified.

CHAPTER 24

THE WRITTEN CONFESSION OF MARGUERITE DUFRANE, PAGES 86–91

I SUPPOSE WHEN I offered to shoulder the price of Christopher Parker's law school, I had in mind my cousin Eugene, who, as far as I knew, had been a law student for most of his adult life. Even with a diploma from the most prestigious of upper schools, the law degree proved to be somewhat elusive, and his poor father—my uncle Elgin—died in debt to Harvard, with Eugene no closer to hanging a shingle than when he played baseball at St. Matthew's Academy.

You know Mr. Parker now as the slick, accomplished young man who has somehow managed to worm his way into every crevice of our lives, but you might be surprised at his inauspicious beginnings. He might even serve well as a lesson in ambition, that nothing is ever truly out of reach, as long as one is willing to stretch in order to grasp it. Stretch your principles, perhaps. Or stretch the truth. Perhaps even stretch the boundaries of the law. Who better to bring in as part and parcel confidant and conspirator than a would-be lawyer?

But oh, his idealism. His sincerity. If you've ever had occasion to bite square down on a sugar cube and felt that tingling discomfort back in the corner of your cheek? Something that, if dissolved in a cup of tea, might bring a perfect balance of flavor, but left to its own devices is altogether unpleasant? That sums up the painful ambition of young Christopher Parker.

How he berated me that afternoon, peppering me with question after question, about how she had come to be there. Angling, he was, as if *I* were on trial, right there in our little park, with you, my baby girl, playing happily not ten feet away. But he found me to be a hostile witness, unable to explain the irrational decision of a now-deceased judge.

"I will tell you this, Mrs. DuFrane." His voice held an unmistakable, if polite, threat. Mindful of our public exposure, we adhered to an unspoken agreement of civility. "I will see that Miss Dana has a day in court. With me as her lawyer, if necessary."

I calculated his age to be about seventeen, giving me some comfort in the space of time to pass before such could be a possibility. No amount of time, however, would change the color of his skin, and I asked him if he truly thought it would be that easy for a Negro from Cleveland to become the voice of justice to set the prisoners free?

"I have written and been accepted to three different universities." One of them in California, where Arthur had spent the months before Celeste's birth. My mind became a spinneret of possibilities.

This time, I calculated far beyond his age, asking if he had secured the funding to attend any of these institutions.

For the first time in our acquaintance, he appeared uncomfortable. "No, ma'am. I figure I'll have to get me a job—a good job—to pay for it."

I suggested that he perhaps would find something on campus. I knew of several such situations, given my husband's occupation. Why, just imagine. Christopher Parker, mopping floors and washing dishes for all the other law students. You might have to wear a sign around your neck to remind them that you belong in the classroom as well as the kitchen, I told him.

Sometimes, I am appalled by my own cruelty. Such was the case as I watched that young man diminish before my very eyes.

While he was puddled before me, I took one more jab, asking just what he intended to do about the unfortunate Miss Dana during his days as a college man.

He kept his face down but looked up. "I'll tell everybody I can about her. I'll write to the warden, the district attorney, the mayor, the governor."

I hadn't yet flinched.

"Your husband."

There. Perhaps our minds weren't so different after all.

I would not beg. I would not ask this boy for a single thing. He hadn't even graduated from his Cleveland high school, and as far as I knew, he never would. Still, I knew I should be mindful of the blessings God had bestowed upon me. When trusted with position and power, one must take opportunities to invest in those grasping to have the same.

As if to remind me of all that was at stake, you came running over to hand me what you claimed to be the most beautiful leaf in the park. And your heart being the purest I've ever known, you had a white polished stone for the person you called "Mother's newest friend."

He was quite sweet and tender in thanking you, and we both watched as you bounded off to new discoveries over by—but not too close to—the pond.

"She's a beautiful little girl," he said.

I reminded him that the young woman he was so quick to champion had killed my other daughter.

"That's for a court of law to decide, Mrs. DuFrane. Or God. Not you."

I told him that I appreciated his dedication to justice, and on some level, it was true. But, I continued, I needed time.

He looked suspicious. "Time for what?"

My eyes traveled to Celeste as I told him that I simply could not bear to be living here, in the same house, with my little girl, should the day come when Dana Lundgren walked out of prison. I granted him full permission to do as he wished, but not until he could do so on his own, with an education and credentials to back whatever claims he thought himself to have.

"It's not right to wait that long. Working and going to school—it could take years. And I happen to think she's suffered enough."

"Suffered enough"? As if he knew anything of suffering. Masking my disgust at his statement, I drew strength simply from knowing that he and I were more alike than we could have first imagined. We both wanted justice. But our interpretations were as different as the color of our skin and the resources at our disposal.

For the first time, I addressed him as Mr. Parker, and I offered, upon his graduation from high school, to finance his college education, all the way through law school, upon the condition that he contact neither Dana nor anyone else until that education had ended.

He at least had the courtesy to look surprised, though I've often thought he might well have been two steps ahead of me, fully expecting to strike such a deal on my front porch.

"That's asking a lot," he said. "From both of us."

But there was more. If he were to see to it that, for whatever might be in his power, nobody contacted *her*, I would include a generous living allowance. Not forever, I amended. Nothing lasted forever. Not college, not a prison sentence, not even, apparently, peace of mind. Only death had a permanence that could not be negotiated.

He held up the small rock you had given him. "I'll keep this, as a promise."

I agreed, as it seemed fair, coming from the one sweet soul worth such a fiendish bargain, but I had one final condition. University of California, where I would do my best to follow, keeping him far away from her and close to me.

Never once did I expect him to become anything more than a casher of my checks. After all, I sent a monthly donation to those missionaries in China, never once believing that a newly baptized Chinaman would show up on my doorstep to thank me for bringing him into the fold. So, too, for years to follow, did I mail off a monthly allotment to the graduate from some unfortunate factory smoke–spewing high school in the slums of Cleveland. On the rare occasion that your father examined the ledger, I explained the money as being a donation to a scholarship fund in Mary's honor, and he seemed satisfied with the idea. Not convinced, mind you, but satisfied. Lord knows he had secrets of his own. And truthfully, I never thought I would see Christopher Parker again.

I underestimated the depth of his integrity.

CHAPTER 25

CLOSE-UP: A framed cross-stitch with these words: *"And ye shall know the truth, and the truth shall make you free."*

INTERIOR: The warden's office, but a new man behind the desk. Younger, stronger, the build and countenance of one who has survived a war, which he has. Warden Brewster, United States Army colonel, retired, is reading what looks to be a letter. By his expression, we can tell that this is an unhappy missive. His brow furrows; he holds the paper closer, then away, then close again, as if doing so might change the bad news within.

CLOSE-UP—THE LETTER: *And so I leave you with stern warning, that should Miss Dana Lundgren not receive an immediate release, we shall have no choice but to seek legal action and have all parties involved face a civil suit for wrongful imprisonment. Signed, Christopher Parker, Esq.*

INTERIOR: The warden crumples the letter and stands to pace his office, coming to a stop along one wall, on which hangs a series of photographs of the honorable men in long black robes who keep him employed.

CLOSE-UP: A photograph. A small metal placard underneath is inscribed, *Judge George Stephens, 1842–1908.*

TITLE CARD: *Some secrets are taken to the grave.*

INTERIOR: Warden Brewster shakes his fist at the photograph, as if to say, "Look what you've done to me!" He returns to his desk, looking despondent indeed, when his attention is drawn to a knocking on the door.

BREWSTER: "Come in."

CLOSE-UP: Brewster is instantly a changed man. His brow is smooth, his countenance all agreeable. Perhaps, in fact, apologetic.

INTERIOR—THE DOOR: Dana walks in, looking far the worse for wear. Her hair is in two long, lank braids, her dress soiled. She is downcast, barely able to meet his eyes.

DANA: "You wanted to see me, sir?"

INTERIOR—TWO-SHOT: Brewster gestures for her to sit down.

1918

DANA COULDN'T IMAGINE why she'd been summoned, but she dared not fan the flame of hope that this might be the fulfillment of a promise all but forgotten. Too much time had passed for her to believe that any force was at work on her behalf. Certainly not Christopher Parker, of whom she'd neither seen nor heard since the afternoon when, after craning her neck to see from her high, narrow window, she'd watched him walk past the black iron gates of Bridewell. Carrie, at least, she'd hoped, would send an occasional letter, as they might have been something like friends. But there'd been nothing, and she'd marked first the days, then the weeks, then a year with the nothingness before cutting loose any expectations and letting herself drift slowly, silently into a mire of complacency.

Until she got the summons and crawled back from death to answer.

Somehow—and she was certain Effie was responsible, but

such could never be proven—Dana had been spared the inconvenience of a cellmate for nearly a year. Instead, and this she knew to be Effie's doing, she'd hosted literary giants, thoughtful essayists, poets, biographers, and world travelers who had taken the time to pen their adventures. Once, she had been hoping to keep her copy of H. D. Thoreau's *Walden* and reread some of her favorite passages but had forgotten to leave it under her pillow. Upon returning from her bath, she found it in its place on her shelf, with a copy of *Don Juan* left under her pillow. Thus began her collection.

On bath day in June, absorbed in what she knew would become one of her favorite books—a collection of Greek mythology—she hopped to the floor, dressed in her nightgown, ready to give herself over to the ministrations of Marvena Gray.

For all Dana knew, Marvena Gray lived in the dankness of the shower room. From what she understood, any new female inmate could request a shower upon arrival, and any day thereafter. By the same logic, she could refuse, as long as vermin and lice were kept at bay. Dana liked it best when she could have the showers to herself, and not be subjected to the uncomfortable leers of the other women as she stood, naked and exposed, under the sulfurous flow of warm water.

This day, she was subjected only to Marvena's eyes, cloudy with disinterest, as she lathered herself with a brand-new bar of clean-smelling soap, even taking the time to wet and scrub it through her hair, clear to the tips. The water seemed especially hot, bringing her to the point of dizziness once or twice. She stretched her hand out to the slimy wall, knowing full well the dim-eyed Marvena would not come to her rescue should she collapse.

Once dried, she was presented with a clean dress and gown, two pairs of stockings, and even gained permission to keep the towel wrapped around her head. She thanked Marvena as she always did and listened to the woman's complaints about everything from bunions to back pain for the entire walk back to Dana's cell.

"Not many of us here today," Dana said, by way of changing the conversation. She didn't feel well herself, but knew Marvena wouldn't be a sympathetic audience.

"Most's in the infirmary." Marvena held the ring close to her face, the better to find the correct key. "Back where they used to keep the childrens. Set it up with cots for them what are sick with that flu."

"I didn't realize."

"Taken its toll on alls of us, it is. Some's died already."

They had arrived at the cell, its door left open, wide and welcoming, and the anticipation of a new book lessened the shame at the sound of its locking behind her. With a final word to Marvena, Dana dropped her fresh clothing on the foot of the bottom bunk and, after verifying that the mythology book remained, reached under her pillow to see what new adventure awaited.

Nothing.

She checked again, just to be sure, though she couldn't imagine where it might be hidden.

The sight of such emptiness brought on a roiling nausea, making her grateful to have skipped breakfast for her shower. She did, however, have a tin water pitcher and cup, and she poured herself a drink, slaking her thirst and settling her stomach somewhat.

Effie had never forgotten her before, but perhaps, as Marvena said, she had been given duties in the new infirmary. No bother, as she had plenty to read. Climbing up onto her bed, she opened her book to a favorite story, that of Oceanus and his refusal to engage in a war with his father. Withdrawing, instead, to become the embodiment of the sea.

Her throat burned with unshed tears; her stomach and head ached in consort with hunger. The words lost their comfort as they blurred in and out of focus. She closed the book, curling herself around it, and fell asleep.

She awoke to fire—a thin blanket of heat stretching the length of her skin, her new, clean dress pressed to her body with sweat. A look at her clock showed the time to be two thirty, long past lunch. Nobody had bothered to come for her, and nothing had been left inside her door. No matter, though, as the sickness she felt in her stomach was nothing akin to hunger. Praying that some water remained, she swung down from her bed and held on to steady herself before venturing out to drink straight from the pitcher. She went to the door, clutched at the bars, and laid her head against the blessedly cool metal.

The hall was empty, as was the cell across from her, and—judging by the decided lack of noise—every cell to the right and the left.

The flu, Marvena had said. And here it had come to roost within her.

Upon her return, the top bunk loomed, an impossible task, and she crawled onto the bottom to lie flat on her back. When she woke up, it was dark, the deep dark of night. She'd slept through supper, through presleep inspection. She'd slept through her own prayers.

There might be water in the pitcher, but she didn't care. Fighting against the aches in her body, she peeled off her dress and nearly shook to death in the moments it took to drop her nightgown over her head. When she reached up to pull her blanket down, her book tumbled with it. Though it was too dark to read, she clutched it to herself for comfort, creating a central, solid space to direct her chills.

She awoke again to silence. Perfect, uninterrupted silence, meaning she hadn't wound her clock, and even if she had the strength to reach it, the face would tell a lie.

Finally she awoke to Effie.

"My word, girl, you've given us all a fright."

"Ef—" But she lacked the strength to say her name.

"Shhh, now. Effie's here. They had me workin' in the infirmary, with all the other sick ones."

In the next moment, a cool cloth bathed her forehead, and Effie was helping her to sit up so she could drink from a cup held to her dry, cracked lips.

"You've got it," Effie said. "Just like all them others." She coaxed a spoonful of thin broth into Dana's mouth. "Going to have to move you. They won't let you stay here sick, you know."

"No," Dana croaked, and risked the pain to grasp at Effie's sleeve.

"It's not far." Effie spooned more broth. "And Effie will be able to look after you. Right now, I'm snuck away. Off duty, even, because I didn't know if anybody would think—"

"No." Her response was stronger now, and she turned her head, refusing another bite. She couldn't leave. She might never come back. This, as wretched as it may be, was her home. She'd been taken from home once before; she wouldn't let it happen again. "Please."

Effie set the bowl down and brought the blessedly cool cloth back to bathe Dana's face. "I can't just leave you here, girl. It'll get us both in trouble."

"I promise I'll get better."

Effie smiled, a rare sight. "You can't do such a thing."

"What does it matter if I die here or there? Don't make me go."

She seemed to consider. "I can only come to you in the early morning and late at night."

"That's more than anybody else." She could have died already, and no one would have known—or cared.

Before leaving, Effie fetched in a wooden crate, from which she fashioned a makeshift table beside the bed. Here she placed a fresh pitcher of water and a stack of soda crackers, moving a bucket close by for any necessities. All of this was a blur to Dana, as was most of the earlier conversation. For two days, measured by Effie's visits, she coughed when she wasn't sleeping, her body shifting in and out of fevers until her gown was soaked stiff with salt. When consciousness allowed, she prayed: thanks for Effie, and deliverance from death.

Unless death would bring her to her mother.

"Oh, Mama." She hadn't said the word aloud since the moment Mrs. Karistin christened her Baby Killer. She said it now again: "Mama." And then, "Father." The heavenly Father in whose hands she placed her life.

For what she'd done, for the greed and envy that plagued her that terrible night, for the anger she held toward Mrs. DuFrane and Judge Stephens, she begged forgiveness.

Take my sin and bring me peace. And if that peace meant death, it held no fear.

"Dana, girl." Effie's voice edged into the darkness of her sleep, and she opened her eyes, feeling rested and whole. "Wake up."

She felt Effie's hand on her brow and could tell the woman was pleased.

"I've brought you some food and tea. Time to get your strength back."

Dana struggled to sit up, feeling a welcome ravenousness. Effie handed her a cup of lukewarm tea; a plate with a scrambled egg and a biscuit sat on the overturned crate. She ate slowly, carefully, finishing only half the food, but drinking all the tea and wishing for more.

"That's my girl," Effie encouraged. "I'm going to try to see you again today, and tomorrow. You need to be better tomorrow."

Dana pinched off one more corner of biscuit. "Why?"

"Because—" Effie's eyes darted, as if someone could be listening—"I don't know if we got ourselves in trouble or not, but the warden wants to see you."

Two flights of steps separated the warden's office from the prisoners, and midway through the second, Dana found herself clinging to the banister, her legs burning with the effort of the climb. A trickle of sweat dampened the back of her dress, and a good, reinvigorating breath seemed as far away as the third floor.

Ahead of her, Marvena offered little encouragement other than "C'mon then," and only the thought of freedom gave Dana the strength to take one more step. And then another.

By the time she stood outside the door labeled *Warden Brewster*, her entire body shook and her legs felt like ribbons beneath her. Marvena opened it and motioned Dana inside, where a woman she had never seen before looked up over a pair of narrow spectacles and blinked incessantly, a thin, sharp pencil poised in her grip.

"And you are?"

"Prisoner Dana Lundgren, here to see the warden."

Blink, blink. "And is he expecting you?"

"I should hope to glory so."

The woman buried the pencil in a mass of graying hair, stood, and went to yet another door, opened it, and peeked inside. Dana, meanwhile, thankful for the delay, prayed for enough strength to walk across the room.

"You can go in now," the woman said, holding up a thin hand to stop Marvena from following. "Just her."

Marvena shrugged halfheartedly and was about to settle her weight on the cushioned bench across from the desk when the woman said, "I'll summon you when it's time to bring her back."

The door to the inner office had been left open, and Dana walked across the threshold trying to look stronger than she felt. After all, at first glance, Warden Brewster seemed so much stronger than his predecessor as he stood upon her arrival and asked her, please, to shut the door behind her.

"I don't believe we've met face-to-face before," he said, extending a hand across his desk. She stared at it, not knowing quite what to do, and he turned the gesture into one indicating the chair in which she should sit.

She'd seen him before, of course, looking out from his window over the courtyard, occasionally walking the halls. But no, they'd never spoken.

"Now, Miss Lundgren." He drummed his fingers on a thin brown folder. "Some issues have come to my attention regarding your stay here, and I believe there has been an error in judgment."

Dana leaned forward, feeling a new beat in her heart. This wasn't about her refusal to go to the infirmary. This was much, much more. "Then you know?"

He opened the folder and thumbed through some of the few pages within. "What I know is that you entered as a juvenile having committed a very serious crime and, without benefit of counsel, have perhaps been improperly transitioned—"

"I never had a trial."

"I have here a coroner's report listing the death of one Mary DuFrane, aged four months, ruled an accident, but I have also your signed confession." He held out a sheet of paper, and she instantly recognized her writing, remembering the moment when she sat in the cozy police station, painstakingly recalling the events of that horrible night. She knew every detail without benefit of reading, since she lived it in her mind as a final thought before going to sleep each night, but she forced her eyes to take in word after word, ascending them as she had the stairs. Though she found nothing in them that spoke of murderous intent, each one brought weakness to her argument for freedom.

"I was twelve years old. I've been here now for more than half of my life."

Warden Brewster scowled. "You've lived far longer than Mary DuFrane. Do not misunderstand me. What I am presenting to you here is an error of clerical oversight, not a miscarriage of justice. Had you been sentenced, properly and legally represented, I've no doubt you would have been given the opportunity to go before a parole board, and they might have had the mercy to end your sentence. But that did not happen."

"No." She choked on the word and recovered. "No, sir, it did not."

"And do you believe, were I to arrange such an opportunity, that you would be capable of exhibiting remorse for your actions to the degree needed to satisfy such a board's desire to act with mercy?"

His serpentine sentence confused her, and she risked asking for clarification.

"Do you regret your actions of that night? Can you, with a clear conscience, ask the state to forgive you of your crimes? Are you sorry for what you did?"

"I am. I wake up every morning wishing that baby hadn't—"

"Do you regret your crime?"

"It wasn't a crime. I only—"

"Do you deserve forgiveness?"

"I know God has forgiven me."

"That is not the same. And it is not enough to grant you freedom from this place. I'll go back. Do you regret your actions?"

"With all my heart. If I'd only realized the baby—"

"Not the baby!" He slammed his fist on the desk and stood, looming toward her once again with his hand outstretched, only this time not in a gesture of welcome, but with a single, accusatory finger. "*You!* Do you understand your actions to be a crime? And do you regret that crime? And can you promise upon what little honor you retain never to commit such a heinous act again? Because that, my girl—" he moved his hand, now shaking, to point at the cross-stitch on the wall—"is the truth that shall set you free."

She followed his finger to stare at the words. "But it isn't true."

"Nonetheless, it will bring to a close what I'm sure has been a sufficient amount of time for you to reflect on your actions and pray for a new path. Am I correct?"

"I have been here a sufficient amount of time, yes."

Warden Brewster sat down, composed himself, and reached for a clean sheet of paper. "Now, then," he said, unscrewing the top of a thick, black pen, "I shall arrange for a parole board to be gathered directly."

"But I won't be able to say that—" she searched her recent memory for his exact wording—"that I understand my actions to be a crime. It was a tragedy, yes. But not a crime."

"We do not grant pardons for tragedies."

"Then perhaps you shouldn't imprison people for them, either."

He stopped the scratching of his pen and looked at her, and for the first time, she saw a flicker of fear in the eyes of authority.

"It does not fall to me to determine who walks in through these doors. I am charged only with maintaining order and overseeing the process of who walks out and when that privilege is granted, in accordance with the sentence imposed by the judge, of course."

"And what sentence was imposed upon me? I've never known."

"It is—" and he squirmed like something trapped as he shuffled the papers in the folder—"indefinite."

What hope she had was extinguished with the word, like a single flame plunging her future into darkness.

"I take it to mean, in light of Judge Stephens's death, that I maintain some discretion. And that should you satisfy the conditions of a parole board—"

"I won't."

"Then it shall have to suffice to grant you a change in status. You are hereby a trustee."

She tilted her head, suspicious. "What does that mean, exactly?"

"It means you are granted certain freedoms within Bridewell, as well as some responsibilities. You may move about unescorted, given that you report to your cell each night for lockup, and to the mess hall for each meal."

"You'll have to remind Marvena to let me out."

"I'll make a note." He crumpled the previous sheet of paper and tossed it to the side before taking out another. "Take this to the children's dormitory. Do you remember where that is?"

"Of course."

"We've allowed it to become a hospital of sorts, for those suffering with this influenza that has the hospitals overflowing. Go, ask what they need you to do, and then do it."

She stared dumbly at the paper when he handed it to her, reading the words as they reflected what he'd just said.

"So I'm free to go?"

"What you are is free to stay and build our trust."

"For how long?"

He tapped his finger on the file. "Indefinitely."

She stood to leave, then turned one more time. "Sir, is there anything in there that would be able to tell me whatever happened to my mother?"

The look that crossed his face came close to pity, and his voice took on what she would have called a fatherly cadence as he said, "No, child. It doesn't. I'm sorry," leaving her no choice but to believe him.

She walked out, fully aware of her change in status, and handed his handwritten note to the woman she now knew to be Mrs. Tooley, who in turn gave Dana a small yellow slip of paper, instructing her to go to the laundry facility (behind the kitchen, 'round left) to receive a new dress. No more stripes. She would have a plain, blue garment. Two if she liked, so as to always have one clean.

Going down the stairs proved to be much easier than going up, and she realized for the first time what it meant to move about without the constant sound of rattling keys behind her. She did as instructed, getting no questions at all from the laundry attendant, she herself in blue, and went to her cell to change. The door had been left open and, once inside, she left it as such, knowing she had no way to get out once it closed.

While changing her dress, she noticed it was shortly past noon, and her newly restored appetite urged her to obey the warden's instruction to take all her meals in the main dining hall. It wasn't until now, strolling unencumbered and unaccompanied through one hallway to the next, that she realized the extent of the prison's emptiness. At least as far as the women's side. The men, she knew, lived crowded upon each other. In her world, cell after cell sat empty, quiet as a series of small, square tombs. There might be tenants toward the end of the week, when laborers received their wages and chose to spend unwisely, but for now, she didn't encounter another soul. When she walked into the dining hall, a few familiar faces presented themselves—some she had known for years, others whose names she hadn't bothered to learn. Feeling disguised within her own skin, she took a tray and walked to where Cookie—the same sweet, dark-faced woman who'd been ladling out her food since her very first supper—greeted her with a comforting smile.

"Got you wearin' the blue now, do they? Bein' a trustee, it the first step out."

In celebration, she gave Dana a serving of shepherd's pie rimmed with oven-browned potatoes, and a molasses cookie purloined from some secret place.

Marvena sat alone at a table, but it felt unseemly to join her, given only a few hours separated Dana from being subjected to her key. Still, with a nearly imperceptible invitation, the woman made room on the bench beside her, and Dana complied.

"So, you're one less thing for me to trouble myself with."

"I guess so."

"Brewster send you to the infirmary?"

"He did." She took up her cookie, broke it in two, and gave the larger half to Marvena.

"I'm headed there myself, if you want to walk with me."

"No, thank you," Dana said, glad to have given a peace offering. "I can find it myself."

CHAPTER 26

CELESTE, AGE 14

1919

THE HOUSE HAD NEVER held so many people. They congregated in the front room, filling the furniture, even perching on the arms of the sofa, much to Mother's chagrin. The few children in attendance had been permitted to go upstairs, where both Calvin's and Celeste's rooms held well-preserved playful treasures. Calvin's treasured soldiers remained in the specific battle formation they had been in when he left for the war, resting under a clear glass case Papa had commissioned when they learned he would not be coming home. But there was also a train set and building blocks, as well as a host of pretty dolls and dishes across the hall for the girls, not to mention the vast backyard with Celeste's beloved playhouse and room to kick a ball.

"Look at them," Mother said, her voice full of disdain. She and Celeste had moved to the back patio both to greet those who congregated there and to escape the crowded stuffiness of the house. "Have their parents taught them nothing? Don't they know where they are?"

"Oh, Mother. They're children. It's good to see some joy, don't you think?" She wanted to add that she couldn't remember the last time she heard laughter in their home. But there was sadness enough this day; no need to dredge from those gone by.

"I'm going into the kitchen to see if Graciela needs any help."

If not for the solemn occasion, Celeste might have issued a laughing challenge. Never in her memory had she known her mother to help in the kitchen, unless one counted emptying the icebox a valuable skill. Without a doubt, she would find her seated at the small corner table, gleaning from the serving trays left by the waiters hired for the afternoon.

"People expect to see you, Mother. You were his wife."

"These are your father's friends—and yours. Not mine. I don't know a soul here."

She left with a more pronounced heaviness to her step, and Celeste's heart went with her. She took a deep breath and squared her shoulders for the burden of the afternoon.

"Was that your mother?"

"Mary," Celeste said with a smile that carried far more congeniality than she felt. Mary Pickford. This little woman might be America's sweetheart, but Celeste knew her to be a ruthless, career-crafting shark, hogging *two* roles in the film *Stella Maris*, in which Celeste had been relegated to the part of an uncredited street hooligan. "Yes, the poor dear. It's been so hard on her with so much loss. My brother, and now . . ."

The word caught in her throat, though she was stronger today than she had been a week ago, when a messenger arrived at their front door with news that her father had been taken away from his office at Technicolor after suffering a heart attack. The intervening time had been spent making arrangements, meeting with lawyers, and sitting vigil at Mother's bedside in perpetual darkness.

"I didn't know your father," the actress was saying, her voice sweet and pleasant, perfectly matched to her persona. "I hear he was a lovely man. I'm so sorry for your loss."

"Thank you." A response as perfunctory as the statement. "I'm just curious, if you didn't know my father, then why are you here?"

Mary patted her arm. "Such a kid. You and I have quite opposite problems. People will always think of me as a child, and you . . . Well, what are you? Fifteen? Sixteen?"

"Fourteen."

Mary cringed. "*Ouch.* Better be careful, or you'll have these lechers giving you quite the chase around. Especially Chaplin. Stay away from him. And Arbuckle." She made a face. "They might call him Fatty, but don't be fooled. When it comes to chasing girls, the man's an athlete. Beautiful dress, by the way, and smart choice pinning up your hair."

Celeste withdrew her arm, increasingly uncomfortable with the conversation. Not that she found it inappropriate, but guilt tugged at her for finding it far more useful than dumbly agreeing upon the sadness of the occasion.

"Thank you," she repeated, this time with something close to heartfelt meaning. "For the advice, I mean. And for treating me like a grown-up."

"Let me guess. Your father acted as your agent?"

Celeste nodded.

"Then you'll need to find a new one, and I'll bet half the people here would angle for the job. I'll send you some names."

"Why are you being so nice to me?"

Mary leaned in close. "I've been in this business a long time, and trust me, you need friends more than you need fathers. I know talent, and you've got it. I don't want to see a bunch of bimbos taking over the films. All this to say, don't let them keep casting you as a kid. Three, four more films, maybe. But once you're sixteen, you need to be playing women. Not a romantic lead or anything, but the best friend. Or maybe a maid if they ugly you up a little."

She left then, disappearing into the crowd—not a difficult thing to do, given her not-quite-five-foot stature.

Left to herself, Celeste scanned the crowd, looking for any familiar face, and recognized few. Like Mother, she'd assumed those she didn't know were here because they knew and respected Papa, but after that conversation, she wondered if this weren't just another occasion for people to see—and be seen by—those who might mean an advancement in a career. With his colorization patents and research, he'd caught the eye of several impressive directors, including Werner Ostermann, newly emigrated from Austria and rumored to be brilliant and aloof. Yet there he was, cigarette in hand, conversing with a tall, thin man Celeste didn't know and one of Papa's colleagues she recognized from her many afternoons spent in his office, offering her face for experimental filming.

"Quién era?" At Mother's insistence, Graciela wore a formal uniform, complete with a white lace collar, the severity of it only accentuating the dark puffs under her eyes.

"Mary Pickford. She's a big star."

Graciela appeared unimpressed and wrapped a strong arm around her shoulders. "How are you doing, *mija*? When should I start scaring people away?"

"You can't do that. They're here for Papa. To pay their respects."

"And eat everything in sight. I came to see if you need anything to eat. I have a *torta* saved at the back of the icebox for you. Come inside? Sit with *tu madre*."

"How is she?"

"Sad." Her brown eyes pooled with tears. "Like we all are."

Celeste knew Graciela had been working through her grief, having come across her more than once reduced to tears while performing her normal chores. Watching surreptitiously while sitting on the corner of her sleeping mother's bed, she observed Graciela touching the clothes in the closet, pulling a shirtsleeve to her face and inhaling its scent. She'd lingered over the arranging and dusting of the objects on top of his dresser—cuff links and collar stays and buttons in a dish. In the bathroom, she'd taken the lid from his shaving lotion, dabbed a bit on the back of her hand, and had even put the bottle in her apron pocket before an attack of conscience called her to return it. She'd loved him, just as all—well, *most*—of the people here did.

Not caring how her mother would react to such an act of affection with a servant, Celeste took Graciela in her arms, for once giving comfort to the woman who had loved her for so long. Not until this moment, and possibly due to her previous conversation, had she noticed that she'd grown taller than Graciela, whose head now rested on her shoulder. The realization prompted her to plant a kiss on top of her head, breathing in the familiar scent of coconut.

Graciela stepped back and took Celeste's face in her hands. "*Ay*, how grown-up you are. *Tu papá*, he was very proud of you, you know."

"I know." She kissed Graciela's soft, brown cheek and sent her in to check on Mother.

Inwardly, she longed for such an escape, but even if her mother dashed all sense of propriety to the wind, she would not. Putting on her bravest face, she moved from one gathered group to the next, receiving their introductions and thanking them for their best wishes.

"Did you sign the guest book?" she asked over and over, knowing even then she would comb through those signatures to learn who had taken the time to acknowledge her father's death. One opportunistic mourner in particular, a dark, handsome, brooding young man, she'd seen around the studios. Every slick, black hair was in place, despite the light breeze.

Valentino. He wasn't a star, but he might be, someday. And when that happened, she wanted to be on that screen with him.

Thinking back to Mary Pickford's declaration that she looked sixteen, she'd just worked up the courage to step off the porch and go thank him for coming, when a soft touch to her elbow stalled her.

"Oh, Mr. Bittick." She'd known him since her father's first visit to the offices at Technicolor, when she'd tagged along and had been made to feel so welcome. "Thank you so much for coming." They exchanged a quick, paternal embrace, reducing all of her previous thoughts about the young Valentino to a puddling shame in the light of this man's genuine concern and affection. Besides, who needed to talk to Valentino? Mr. Bittick was about to introduce her to a director.

The next morning, Celeste awoke to find that she'd fallen asleep in the clothes she'd worn to the funeral, and that someone had come in during the night to remove her shoes and drape a light coverlet over her. That *someone*, she assumed, was Graciela, as Mother had taken to her bed within minutes after the final guest departed, while Celeste tried to lend a hand to the hired staff as they gathered dirty glasses and cups from the side tables, shelves, and any other possible flat surface throughout the house. Even so, she'd wearily climbed up the stairs and into her bed well before dark, and must have slept for nearly fifteen hours, given the brightness of the sun outside.

A soft rap on the door accompanied by *"Estás despierta, mi*

Celesita?" prompted Celeste to sit up and stretch while beckoning Graciela inside.

"I feel like I slept forever." In fact, it was the best sleep she'd had since before Papa died.

"But you feel good, no?"

"Wonderful. How is Mother?"

Graciela dropped her voice and shifted her conversation into Spanish, prompting Celeste to do the same. "I am so worried about her these days. Something is wrong."

"Well, of course something's wrong."

"More than that. Even before your papa, she was eating hardly anything. Not like herself at all."

Celeste studied Graciela with new eyes, in light of what she'd noticed over the past week. She was a beautiful woman—likely the same age as her mother, or close to it, but with the countenance and figure of one much younger.

"Maybe she just wanted to be thin again. Like she used to be, when we first moved here."

"Perhaps," Graciela said, clearly unconvinced. "We'll see." Then she clapped her hands, ready to begin the business of the day. "I drew already a bath for you, with some of those good salts you like, and I steamed your dark-blue dress."

"Aren't I supposed to wear black?"

"Pretty young thing like you, what a shame. There are still some good things about being a child. I stitched a silk band to the sleeve, is all. Mr. Parker is coming this afternoon to meet with you. Do you feel up to it?"

"Of course." Another film, another rich, spoiled child. She couldn't wait to share with him everything Mary Pickford had said.

Later, scrubbed, refreshed, and dressed, she joined her mother in the kitchen with a plate of leftover sandwiches, of which Mother ate uncharacteristically little. In light of Graciela's concerns, she noticed that her mother did seem to be losing weight, with a new hollowness right below her eyes, and loose flesh falling jowl-like from her chin.

Celeste was scraping the uneaten food into the rubbish when Graciela announced that Mr. Parker had arrived, and inquired where he should be shown.

"Arthur's office, of course," Mother said after visibly bracing herself to give the answer.

In all of her memory, Celeste could recall a handful of occasions when her mother had crossed into that room. Nobody ever did without Papa's express permission, and anytime Celeste had occasion to sit in on the contract talks, they did so at the kitchen table. It was a sacred place, accessible only to Graciela for its biweekly cleaning, and even then only after much negotiation.

As Celeste watched Mother get up from her seat and move across the kitchen, she wondered for the first time if her halting gait came not merely from her excess weight, but something else. Pain, perhaps, or a weariness beyond bearing.

"Are you all right, Mother?"

She stopped and gripped the kitchen counter. "Why would you ask?"

"Because you seem—"

"No." She turned, steadying herself. "Why would you ask now? Why today, when I haven't been all right for quite some time."

"I didn't know."

"You didn't *notice*. You and your father, off with your heads together while I'm wasting away. Now that he's gone, you finally have to look at me, don't you? Lord knows he never did."

"I look at you every day, Mother. I haven't left your side this entire time."

"And it only took your father's dying to get your attention."

Before she could respond, Mother left the kitchen, moving at a noticeably quicker pace, leaving Celeste no choice but to follow.

The shades drawn against the afternoon sun cast Papa's office in an amber light, but Mother declined Graciela's offer to raise them. He did not have a desk; rather, three of the four walls were lined with shelves and a countertop, with closed cabinets underneath. Books of all shapes and sizes were arranged haphazardly, some on their sides, some open to pages left waiting to be read. There were all manner of beakers and jars of liquids, photographs in various stages of tinting clipped to suspended string, and canisters of film in every possible corner.

"We should call Mr. Bittick," Celeste said, looking around in awe. "He'd know what to do with all of this. Some of it might be important."

"That's exactly what we will do." Celeste hadn't noticed Mr. Parker standing just inside the open door. She greeted him with a professional handshake, as modeled by her father. "According to his will, all of the contents of this room are to be boxed up and delivered intact to the Technicolor offices. In fact, I'm not so sure we should even be in here."

"This is still my house," Mother said, "isn't it? Or has that been willed away as well."

"It is," Mr. Parker said.

The two looked at each other the way actors sometimes did, while off camera a director yelled, *More! More intensity! More anger! More fear! More pain! More!* It had been the same in the first few days after Papa died, when she'd been shooed from the room while he read Papa's will. Whether it was his race, or the fact that he got on so well with Papa, Mother made very little attempt to hide her dislike for Mr. Parker, and now it grew like a bulbous mass between them.

"Shall we sit down, then?" Celeste said at last, clueless as to the protocol of who should offer the invitation.

While Papa did not have a desk, per se, he did have a good-size oblong table and a collection of mismatched chairs where Celeste assumed he sat to eat all those meals he was too busy to take with them in the dining room. To her relief, they all complied, and Mr. Parker went through the now-familiar ritual of opening his expensive-looking leather folio and producing a sheaf of papers with the recognizable studio logo at the top.

"Now, it's a standard contract, looks to be three to five days' work, with . . ."

He continued delivering information Celeste could almost recite by heart, until it was time for her to take up a pen and sign her name on the final page. Not on the official line, but just below.

"And," Mr. Parker said, "I suppose you'll be signing as her guardian from now on, Mrs. DuFrane."

Mother, seemingly disinterested in the proceedings at first, now sat forward in her seat and said, "No."

Celeste and Mr. Parker locked eyes, each daring the other to confront Mother on her protest. Mr. Parker lost.

"Mrs. DuFrane, if you don't sign, Celeste cannot appear in the film. No contract, no role, and she's not old enough to sign for herself, not until she's eighteen."

"Don't talk to me like I'm stupid," Mother spewed. "I know very well how the law works, wouldn't you say, Mr. Parker? Very well indeed."

Celeste implored, "Then why?"

"I never wanted you to get involved with this movie business in the first place, if you remember. But you wouldn't listen, and your father wouldn't listen, and nothing I said ever mattered. Not a bit."

"Mother!"

"Well, it matters now, doesn't it?"

"Mrs. DuFrane, please." His voice was rich like cocoa, and appeasing. He affected a posture that captured Mother's attention, turning her toward him, making it necessary for her to leave the table if she wanted to escape his gaze. "I understand you're grieving right now. We all are. But we have committed Celeste to play this role. If you want her to discontinue making films for the time being, until you've settled all of Arthur's affairs, fine. But for now, we need your signature."

Mother's eyes began to fill with tears that splashed unbidden into the folds of her face and neck. "Somebody's going to see her." She took on the demeanor of a wild, trapped animal, her gaze darting back and forth as if to find a way around the imposing wall of Christopher Parker, trusted family lawyer and friend. "Somebody's going to see her, and see her name, take her away. Take her away from me, and she's all I have, all I have left in the world."

"Now, there, there, Mrs. DuFrane." He looked as if to take her hand, but thought better of it and laid his, strong and dark, next to hers, pale and puffy, almost touching. "Nobody's going to take her."

"*She* will."

An electric chill ran the length of Celeste's spine, nearly jolting her from her seat. "Who will?"

Mr. Parker tore his attention away from Mother long enough to give her a warning look.

"And don't think I don't know what you get out of this—" Mother tousled the papers—"*arrangement.* What's your percentage?"

"Ten," Celeste said. She knew that, too.

"Well, no more of that, Mr. Parker. Our business relationship is through."

A slow grin spread across his face, and he spoke with an unmistakable sense of threat. "Are you sure you want to do that?"

"You're free." Mother burst forth a mirthless, bitter laugh. "Look at that. I have *freed* you. Forget *Birth of a Nation*. I've given birth to a lawyer."

More laughter, venturing on maniacal, leaving Celeste more frightened and confused than she ever remembered. Mother wiped away hysterical tears with the back of her sleeve, and Celeste felt her own pooling. "I—I don't understand."

"Why don't you go on up to your room, sweetie," Mr. Parker said, bringing Mother to react with a savage fury.

"Don't tell her what to do! Don't call her 'sweetie'! She is *mine*, do you understand? *Mine!* And she is all I have left. All I have left in the world."

Celeste could take it no longer, and she leaped from her seat and ran to Mother, holding her tearstained face to her budding breast and burying kisses in her coarse, neglected hair. She felt the woman physically flinch at the contact, but did not pull away. Not even in the aftermath of Papa's death had they held each other. In fact, she couldn't remember the last time they touched.

She sensed rather than saw Mr. Parker lean back in his chair and set the pen on the table.

"I love you, Mother." How often had she said those words to strangers, women who couldn't even stand to be in her presence? "I will always be here for you. Nobody can ever take me away. I'm not going anywhere; you'll see."

"Oh, my darling," Mother said, holding Celeste at arm's length, "you might not be, but I am."

CHAPTER 27

DANA VISITS THE LAW OFFICES OF CHRISTOPHER PARKER, ESQ.

1925

WERNER RODE IN THE front seat with Gustav, leaving the backseat to Dana and Celeste. With the exception of Celeste's presence, this was very much like the last time Dana and Werner had been together on the long, awkward drive from his home after the violent confrontation with Christopher Parker.

Dana still hadn't forgiven him. Either of them.

"You ambushed me," she'd said that day as the beach and his home disappeared behind them. "How could you?"

"I didn't think you would agree to meet with him any other way. I saw the pain in your eyes when you spoke of him."

This time, all parties involved had plenty of time to prepare, including convincing Celeste to reschedule a meeting with Louis B. Mayer, even under the threat of Roland strangling her if she did. This time, at least, Dana wouldn't be drunk from kisses and sunshine, and most of all, she was wearing real clothes, including shoes, should she be given another reason to kick him.

"Turn left here," Celeste instructed. It had been her idea to meet with Christopher Parker in his office, rather than have him visit in their home. Dana supposed she wanted to keep it all businesslike while she studied up on her mother's hidden life as a monster.

Parker's office resided in the Title Insurance and Trust Company building at the corner of High and Franklin, a prestigious address by any definition, according to Celeste, and only occupied in the wake of Arthur DuFrane's death. Her father had bequeathed all proceeds from his work with Technicolor to Mr. Parker—a fact that made Marguerite furious. When Marguerite died, he worked to pick up Celeste's career where it left off, capitalizing on the contacts he'd made through her father and landing the occasional small role. Sure, he took a 40 percent cut, and she had to endure the shamefulness of the racial slurs slung in the waiting rooms of casting offices, but he worked tirelessly on her behalf, and stepped quietly out of her career after introducing her to an agent he met—of all places—at the same church where Mother had gone in a desperate search for healing.

All of this Celeste related on the drive, relieving Werner and Dana of the burden of conversation, for which Dana was grateful. Still, one question nagged. "Even after your mother died, he never told you about me?"

"No," Celeste said with neither a hint of apology nor defense. "Not until we read the will, of course. He had a fierce loyalty to Mother that I never could understand. Especially because she was so awful to him most of the time. I don't think she ever acknowledged how much he cared for us. You know, he sold all of Papa's experimental film? I found that out later. He used the money to pay off the mortgage on the house so I'd own it outright."

Dana listened, fascinated by the girl's ability to sound like a young woman wise beyond her years.

"And that 40 percent he took?" she continued. "He put it all in a trust for me. Didn't keep a dime for himself."

"Do you imagine Mr. Lundi will be so generous with his commissions?" Werner asked from the front seat, without turning his head.

Celeste laughed. "I doubt it."

It was a light moment needed to break the tension in the car. Even Gustav chuckled, giving the first indication that he'd been listening to a word anybody said.

They slowed past the wide, welcoming steps of the impressive courthouse, turned a final corner, and parked. Werner held the car door open for the ladies to exit onto the sidewalk and instructed Gustav to return in an hour, handing him a folded bill.

Walking into the lobby of the Title Insurance and Trust Company building, Dana decided that Los Angeles must exist on an unspoken promise to emit wealth and luxury in all of its buildings. Here, too, were potted plants, shining floors, and works of art, including a sweeping painting of the unformed city that stretched mural-like in its proportions.

With her handbag tucked under her arm, Celeste confidently led the way to a row of elevators while Werner and Dana lagged behind.

"Are you sure you're all right?" Werner said with a touch to her elbow. "You didn't leave your boxing gloves in the car, did you?"

"Ha-ha. I didn't need them last time, did I?"

He stopped and turned her to him. "I'm being serious now. Are you ready to meet with this man?"

"It helps knowing you'll be at my side, and not with him."

"Oh, darling." His eyes searched her, and even though they stood in the midst of dozens of people bustling about their day, this felt more intimate than any moment they'd ever shared. "I just want you to have the answers you need to put the past behind you."

"Not about the movie?"

"Hang the bloody movie."

He had more to say, she could tell, but Celeste called to them from the open elevator, impatient, though the young man operating it seemed content to hold the door indefinitely if it meant sharing the car with her.

"Third floor," Celeste said as the boy slid the door closed.

Dana, embarrassed to admit this would be her first ride on an elevator, fought her instinct to clutch at the railing on the wall, and instead reached for Werner's hand, bringing comfort in both the motion of the car and the nerves rattling within.

They emerged in a rich, paneled hallway and followed Celeste to the left and down three doors to the frosted glass proclaiming, *The Law Office of Christopher Parker, Esq.* Inside, a stylish woman with dark skin and bright-red lips escorted them to Parker's office.

It was a sprawling room, dominated on one side by a massive mahogany bookcase packed with impressive-looking tomes, and a large window on the other, looking out over a park. His desk, black and lustrously lacquered, sat squarely across from the door, so that the first thing any visitor saw upon entering the room was the prestigious lawyer, hard at work, surrounded by the trappings of success.

When this trio entered, however, he leaped from his seat and hurried to greet them, shaking Werner's hand, kissing Celeste's cheek, and approaching Dana with a good-natured pugilistic stance.

She smiled, despite herself, though she offered no apology.

When they were seated, Parker took his place behind his desk and drummed his fingers nervously. "I'm not sure where we should begin."

"That's understandable," Werner said, "because it would appear you have a lot to explain."

Parker didn't flinch, but he did cease his drumming. "I don't believe I owe an explanation to anyone here, except for you, Miss Dana. And I would offer an apology, but you must understand that every choice I made was with you in mind. To work on your behalf."

"The mills of justice turn slowly," Werner said.

"But grind exceedingly fine," Parker countered. "As they say, 'revenge is a dish best served cold.'"

"I'm not interested in revenge," Dana said. "Or justice. It's too late for that. I only want an explanation. When you visited me that day, you swore you would help me. That you would fight for me."

"I did."

"Really? Because after you left, I spent another fifteen years in that place."

"We were both naive to think it would be that easy. Did you really think a Negro from Cleveland was going to walk into law school just like that? Do you have any idea how few of us there are? Let me tell you: if I hosted a banquet in honor of all the Negro lawyers in Los Angeles, I could feed the whole crowd with a single sandwich. Ham and cheese, because that's my favorite. None of this—" he gestured wide around him—"would have happened without the misguided generosity of Marguerite DuFrane."

"And what do you mean by that, exactly?" Dana asked, though she had her suspicions.

"I mean she paid. She paid my tuition, bought my books, gave me enough money to rent a room and buy enough food to keep me from starving."

"How generous of her." Dana couldn't help but sneer, but stopped herself from saying anything further after Celeste's silent chastisement. She carried an obvious protective affection for this man.

"Indeed it was," Parker agreed. "Unfortunately, there are so many things that no amount of money can buy. Like a seat at the front of the classroom, or in the campus cafeteria. I was thankful not to have to keep a job, because I had to divide my time between studying and explaining to my professors how a Negro could have possibly written this paper with such articulation. When I showed up to take the bar, the proctor told me to come back later, that they wouldn't be sweeping up until after the test. I never asked for a dime more than I needed from that woman, and I couldn't have lasted a day without her."

"So it was like a scholarship," Werner said, "in exchange for silence."

Parker was undaunted. "You could say that. But I told her, straight out, that the minute I had any credentials behind my name, I was going to go back to Chicago and settle Miss Lundgren's case."

"So why didn't you?" This from Celeste, with an obvious intent to bring them all to a place of peaceful understanding.

"I tried."

He produced a letter from the cream-colored file on his desk and handed it over to Dana. The type was purple and faded—a carbon copy, he explained—and a quick read showed it to be somewhat threatening in nature, forceful in its intent. She read it again, more slowly, and then out loud.

"I was ready," Parker said. "Graduated, certified—in California, at least—and knowledgeable. If nothing else, I knew what to say to someone to get them to take up your case. But I heard back."

He produced another paper. "From Warden Brewster. He said you were no longer an inmate at the House of Corrections."

Dana looked at the date. "This was when they made me a trustee." She looked up. "But I was still there. I couldn't just walk out." Though, looking back, she knew that wasn't exactly true. She simply had no place to go.

Here, a crack in his facade. "And that's where I failed, I suppose. I was ready to believe that you'd been released. But I never shared that with Mrs. DuFrane. I figured everybody was better off if she believed you were locked away."

"Why were you still in contact with her at all?" Werner asked, sounding like he should occupy a law office next door. "If she had already fulfilled her end of the bargain."

"Years before, out of the blue, I get a note from her, delivered to the same post office box where she sent all the checks. Said her little girl was going to be in a movie, and she didn't understand the contract and didn't trust what her husband said about it." He looked at Celeste apologetically. "So I said I'd come over and take a look, and . . ." He trailed off, arms wide.

"And we lived happily ever after," Celeste said with such affection, Dana kept a hateful remark to herself.

"And so, here we are," Werner said. "Not quite happily, and not quite ended."

"Not quite," Parker agreed, shifting in his seat. "About a month before he died, almost like he had some sort of premonition, Arthur called me into his office, said he wanted to make a change to his will." He looked at Dana. "He told me about you, and all about that night when the baby died, and how he worried that your life had been ruined from what was a terrible tragedy."

"And did you let on that you knew?" Werner asked, now on the edge of his seat.

"I'm afraid that would have killed him. Sorry." He sent an apologetic glance at Celeste for his gaffe. "Bad enough he thought she was sent to some reformatory school. Anyway, he asked me to track her—you—down, without Mrs. DuFrane's knowledge, of course, and award you with this."

He opened a drawer in the side of his desk and produced a thin slip of paper, which he slid across the shiny surface. When Dana picked it up, she saw it to be a check, written from a Chicago bank, for the sum of two thousand dollars.

"He didn't come into the marriage with a lot of money," Parker explained, "but what he had in this bank was his, and he wanted you to have it."

"Still," Werner said, "that was years ago."

"Six," Celeste said with soft sadness.

"There was a caveat," Parker said and appeared to be choosing what might be difficult words. "Not in writing, just an agreement between friends, to wait until Mrs. DuFrane . . . passed away. He knew—I think we all knew—that she was sick. Very sick, more so than she would say. The way he talked, I don't think he ever believed he would be the first to go."

"Oh." It was a small sound of fresh grief and revealed the child in Celeste that hid behind her bravado. They all afforded her a moment of respectful silence before Parker continued.

"During those last years, whenever I met with Mrs. DuFrane on matters of business, she talked, told me everything. Sometimes, I think she made up reasons to see me, have me read over things she could have resolved for herself. And I told her she should write it all down."

At this, he drummed a single, short rhythm on the thin cardboard-covered folio on his desk. "For legal reasons, mostly. In case, someday down the line, people had questions or wanted to lay blame. A gathering of evidence, so it were, but then, as you know—" he looked meaningfully at Celeste, who returned his gaze with peaceful understanding—"it became so much more. Believe me when I tell you, I haven't even read it myself." He slid it toward Celeste. "She wrote it for you."

He looked to Dana. "When it was clear she didn't have long left, she called me in to amend her will, giving you half of everything. And instructing me to bring you home."

Home. The word still had an unfamiliar ring.

"This time, when I wrote to Bridewell, simply saying I was trying to locate you to deliver an inheritance, I received a much more encouraging response. And *then* . . . well, the rest you know."

"Happily ever after," Dana said, reaching for Celeste, who took her hand and squeezed it.

"The end."

"The end," Parker affirmed before sliding the bundle of papers across his desk. "And now, maybe, you're ready to read the beginning."

CHAPTER 28

CLOSE-UP: A framed cross-stitch: *"The lines are fallen unto me in pleasant places; yea, I have a goodly heritage." Psalm 16:6.*

INTERIOR—DANA'S ROOM: The narrow bed is covered by a square-stitched quilt, and the shelf above it holds a neat collection of books. There is a small writing desk with a glass jar holding a smattering of wildflowers. There are no bars on the window, and a lazy breeze fills the curtains with fluid motion. Three identical blue dresses hang on a hook next to a washstand. Here we see Dana, coiling her hair into a neat bun. She studies herself in the mirror, leaning closer to run a finger across what might be the first of a very fine line at the corner of her eye. She sighs.

TITLE CARD: The outer passes away; the innermost is the same yesterday, today, and forever. ~~ Thomas Carlyle

INTERIOR: She steps back for a final, discerning look, turning this way and that, smoothing her dress, and only when satisfied, puts a clean, starched apron over it and crosses to her door. An ordinary door, no bars, no locks. She swings it wide open.

FADE OUT.

FADE IN.

INTERIOR: A spacious farm kitchen. Cookie, with a kerchief tied around her head, takes a tray of biscuits out of the oven and points to a crate of eggs. After a cheerful "Good morning," Dana takes to the eggs, cracking one after another into a large mixing bowl. Cookie is singing, and after a bit, Dana joins her.

TITLE CARD: "I looked over Jordan and what did I see, coming for to carry me home? A band of angels coming after me, coming for to carry me home."

CLOSE-UP: Dana, her face resplendent with joy, singing the last line of the spiritual.

INTERIOR: The women take platters and bowls of food from the kitchen and into a dining room with two long tables. No fewer than twenty men are seated on the benches, all dressed in striped prison garb. One by one the men are served, appearing grateful each time a plate is filled.

FADE OUT.

FADE IN.

CLOSE-UP: An impressive pile of soiled dishes—plates and coffee cups and saucers, mixing bowls and pans, all stacked up beside a kitchen sink. Zoom out to see Dana and Cookie looking good-naturedly resigned at the task before them. Cookie picks up a plate and plunges it into soapy water, once again singing.

1925

"WHAT'U THINKIN' TODAY? You gon' stay?"

Cookie had asked the same question nearly every day since she and Dana came to the Bridewell Honor Farm. And every day, Dana gave the question some mock consideration.

"Depends. What's for supper tonight?"

"Gon' have to stick around and see."

"Well, then, I guess one more day won't kill me."

Truthfully, being at the honor farm didn't feel much like being in prison at all. There were no bars on the doors or windows, no chains, and most important, no sense of uselessness stretching throughout the day. One single, armed guard presided over the facility during the day and at night, while the inmates, exhausted from a day's labor, slept in the second-floor dormitory.

When Warden Brewster offered her the opportunity to come live and work here three years ago, she'd agreed out of fear.

"I'm afraid you are becoming something of a liability here," he'd said. "We're overcrowded as it is with legitimate prisoners. There's no room for voluntary inmates."

"What would I do?" They were walking the grounds of the courtyard, conversing almost as colleagues.

"I might be able to find you a situation. You'd be given two dollars upon your release."

"Oh, my," she said, feigning overwhelming gratitude. Theirs had become somewhat of an easy friendship, though she calculated that he could easily be her father. Both of them knew exactly why she stayed. She had nowhere to go. Nobody to go to. Nothing to call her own outside of the meager possessions housed within her four walls.

He'd hinted on several occasions that there might be someone, somewhere, interested in helping her revive her life, but she'd refused to listen. After all, at one point, somebody had conspired to steal it away from her. What reason had she to trust?

These days, at the farm, she lived with an almost-continuous sense of contentment. She'd known Cookie for twenty years, the only constant in her life, and now they passed their days in a perpetual cycle of preparing, cooking, serving, and cleaning, with the only difference between the two being that Cookie got half of Saturdays and all of Sundays off.

So, too, did the men, and on Sunday mornings, itinerant

preachers or students from the nearby Moody Bible Institute would come and preach a sermon.

Sometimes, one of the prisoners would try to flirt with her, asking for extra gravy with a wink or, even bolder, with a touch to her hand or just below her apron strings. This, however, was enough of a conduct violation to get the man in trouble with the farm's superintendent and sent back to the overcrowded jail. For her part, Dana did nothing to encourage any such behavior, and having spent one-third of her life alone with her mother, half of it locked up with children and women, and now so many years in this capacity, she knew less about men than any other woman her age could claim. In fact, her mother was just this age the last time Dana saw her.

With the last dish dried and stacked, she added another ladle of water to the beans simmering on their way to becoming the noon meal. A large can of stewed tomatoes sat on the top shelf, and she took this, too, dumping them into a bowl and crushing them with a potato masher before adding them to the pot. A palmful of salt, a pinch of pepper—just as Cookie had taught her—and her afternoon was free. On Saturdays, what they had for lunch, they had for supper, except with supper they got pie. And though Dana wasn't at liberty to leave the grounds with Cookie on Saturdays, she was allowed to roam at will if there weren't any chores pressing for her attention. More often than not, she found something to do.

Such was the case this day, as a mess of snap peas had to be cleaned and snipped to accompany the fried chicken already cooked and waiting in the icebox for Sunday's dinner. Lured by the cool sunshine of the spring day, Dana decided to take her task to the side porch of the farmhouse, entertaining herself with the occasional glance over to the game of horseshoes in the distance.

After a time, she heard the rumble of an automobile. Nothing uncommon, as all manner of prison officials and suppliers came on a daily basis. But this wasn't a farm truck. It was something interesting enough to interrupt the horseshoe game and even provoke a few good-natured catcalls and whistles from the men, all of which were immediately silenced by the stern voice of the guard on duty.

Curious, Dana took the bowl of peas into the kitchen and, wiping her hands on her apron, made her way into the farmhouse's front parlor. She took a damp rag with her, planning to wipe down the windows as a ruse to peek through and see what had caused such a commotion.

Looking through the already-clean glass, Dana surmised that there were two entities that could have provoked such a reaction from the men. First, the car—long and sleek with mirrorlike chrome and paint the color of sweet cream. Second, the man—practically a human reconstruction of the car. He wore a pale suit, pink tie, and straw boater, which he removed as he entered into conversation with Mr. Lyons. When he did, Dana gasped, despite herself. She'd never seen any man quite so beautiful; with his black hair slicked to perfection and a warm olive tone to his smooth-shaven face, he looked like someone who should be in a movie. Not that she'd ever seen one. Still, she could tell he was something special, and as if to reinforce his superiority, at that moment the sun glinted off the ring he wore on his pinkie finger, casting him momentarily in a glowing halo of light.

So fascinated was she, it took far too long for her to realize that the men—the stranger and Mr. Lyons—were actually heading toward the front door, and she hadn't quite escaped by the time they walked inside.

"Ah, Miss Lundgren, there you are." Mr. Lyons always spoke with a kindly air.

She turned and said, "Yes, sir?" trying not to look at the stranger.

"I believe this man has some news you will find to be very interesting indeed." He invited the man to sit down, then asked Dana to do the same.

She hesitated. The parlor wasn't formal or fancy by any standards, but it was understood to be used only by the Lyons family and their occasional guests. Not the inmates. She looked to him for clarification, and he offered a warm smile.

"Go ahead, dear. I think you'll find it to be perfectly appropriate." And with that, he left.

"Please," the stranger said, gesturing to the end of the well-worn sofa.

Still nervous, she complied, and he sat in the chair opposite. He balanced his hat on his knee, then reached into the breast pocket of his suit and produced a thin cigarette case and a silver lighter. She watched the ritual with fascination, every move precise, and imagined it must be something he did a hundred times a day.

"Miss Dana Lundgren?" he said through the first cloud of smoke. "As in, once upon a time there was a girl named Dana?"

"I suppose so. Yes."

He looked at her with a critical eye. "Go figure. You don't look like what I thought. I was expectin' a kid."

"I haven't been a 'kid' for a long, long time, Mr. . . ."

"Lundi. Roland Lundi, and I am here on behalf of one Christopher Parker, Esquire, and the DuFrane family estate."

She turned cold. Ice-cold—like morning wash water in winter—and immediately heard nothing else. The next thing she knew, his ring was winking near her face as he snapped his fingers.

"Are ya with me, kid?"

"I'm sorry." She felt her words climbing to the top of her throat, past years of forgotten hope. "What did you say?"

"I'm here representing the DuFrane estate, on behalf of Christopher Parker, and I'm here to tell you that you have been granted official release. With your consent, I've been charged to take you home."

"Home?"

He took a drag of his cigarette. "I should clarify. To the DuFrane home, in Los Angeles, California, where you have been named coheir to the estate of Mr. and Mrs. Arthur DuFrane." He reached into the pocket opposite his cigarettes and produced a folded paper, which he delivered to her shaking hand. "That is an unconditional pardon and release, signed by a judge and the current warden at the Chicago Correctional Facility, with the stipulation that you will not seek legal recourse for your time spent in their care." He spoke as if reciting a long-practiced speech, but then added a zipping motion across his lips. "No questions asked."

"When?"

"I have two tickets for the nine o'clock train on Monday. But if you want out of here sooner, I have two rooms reserved at the Palmer House. Separate floors, don't worry. You won't be the first scared little lamb I've escorted through the big, bad city."

She barely understood. Not only did he speak at a rate faster than she'd ever heard, but his very words seemed foreign. Maybe not the words so much, but the *ideas*. A nine o'clock. A Palmer House. A lamb.

"D-do I have to?"

Mr. Lundi sat back and stared at her, brow furrowed, through a pillar of smoke. "Do you *have* to?"

"I have responsibilities here. And a home, I guess. And Cookie asked me this morning if I was going to leave and I said no."

He looked even more confused, and not at all entertained.

"I mean," she continued, "if I'm free to leave, then I must be free to stay, too. Right?"

He took a final, long drag of his cigarette and crushed it out in the ashtray on the low table beside the chair. "That is some fine logic, but you understand, you have quite an inheritance waiting for you."

"How can that be?"

He held up his hands in surrender to the question. "Just part of the funny way the world works, I guess. Somebody trying to set something right, you know? Make up for a wrong."

"I never asked anybody to make up anything to me."

"And think how disappointing life would be if we only got what we asked for. Sometimes God likes to send along a little something you never knew existed."

Now it was her turn to be surprised. He looked anything but religious, and his mention of God sparked a new fury. "You don't think I prayed for freedom? You don't think I woke up every day wishing there was some way I could explain, that someone would listen and let me go?"

Mr. Lundi tossed his hat on the table, sat back, and crossed his ankle over his knee. "Where, exactly, would you have gone?"

"Home." No reason for him to know it didn't exist. "And since you know so much, do you know—can you tell me what happened to my mother? I've never heard a word since . . . ever."

"Sorry, kid." He looked to be so, genuinely. "I can't help you there, and I wish I could, honest."

"Then you see? I'm no better off out there than I am here. I'm alone."

"You're not alone."

Something he'd said at the beginning of their conversation came back to her. "You said coheir. I remember the DuFranes had a son."

"Nope, not him. Died in the war. They have a daughter."

"Oh."

"And she's ready to share her home with you, because it's yours, too."

"In California."

"In California. It's where reinvention begins, kid. It's where you go to make yourself a new life."

"I don't need a new life. I just want the one that was taken away from me."

"Sorry, sister. I can't do anything about that. No matter what you do, you can't get those years back. Nobody can."

"And the rest of the family? Mr. DuFrane? And Mrs.?"

"All gone, sweetheart. God rest their souls. You're safe."

"That's not it." She closed her eyes, pressing her fingers to her forehead, trying to gather her thoughts and put them into words. "All I've ever wanted was a chance to tell them, that family, that I'm—I'm so sorry. I put the pillow in her crib because I thought it was pretty. It looked so fancy and so sweet, just like her. I put it *near* her head, but not—I didn't dare *touch* her."

Her body shuddered as she sobbed the last of her confession. Mr. Lundi remained motionless and cool.

"Do you understand?" Her fists were clenched now, and some irrational part of her wanted to pound her words through his crisp, pale suit. "I've had a lifetime to play it over and over in my mind. Like a nickelodeon. I wish to God I hadn't done it, but I know in my heart I committed no crime. And if I'd ever been given the chance to defend myself . . . I've searched my memory.

I've searched my soul. And if it would bring that baby back, I'd give my life. But I feel like I've given my life anyway, and it hasn't changed anything."

Still, he sat like stone while she breathed heavily, as if she'd run a mile with every word.

Finally he raised one eyebrow and lit a second cigarette.

"You know," he said, picking a stray fleck of tobacco from his lip, "they don't have nickelodeons anymore."

Again, he made no sense.

"You said you played that moment over and over like watching a nickelodeon. And I thought you should know, they're gone. The world's turning and changing without you. Now, you don't have to go to California. You can go anywhere you want. You can stay here. But if you want your life restored, bigger and better than you can even imagine, you have three chances. One, you walk out of here today. Two, get yourself to the Palmer House tomorrow. Three, be on the nine o'clock westbound Monday morning."

He perched his cigarette between his lips, reached for his hat, offered her a quick salute with it, placed it on his head at an angle opposite his cigarette, and stood to leave. She sat and watched, craning just a bit to look through the window and see him go to the car, reach in, and come back, walking in without knocking on the door.

"Whatever you decide," he said, "this is for you."

He carried a satchel, crafted in leather and velvet, and set it square in her lap. Otherwise, she would have been too afraid to touch it at all.

"That is a gift from Miss Celeste DuFrane, who says that every woman needs a good travel bag."

"Celeste? Their daughter?"

"One and the same."

"Is she anything like her mother?"

He laughed, smooth as the velvet on the bag. "Night and day, kid. Night and day. She's the sweetest princess you'll ever meet."

As if testing the very idea, Dana unclasped the latch and opened the bag. The hinges creaked enticingly, and the smell of leather wafted up from inside. It was the newest thing she'd ever seen, and it smelled like luxury and possibility. It smelled like *life*, and everything she owned would fit inside, twice over.

CHAPTER 29

THE WRITTEN CONFESSION OF MARGUERITE DUFRANE, PAGES 92–102

BY THE TIME THE DOCTORS finally pronounced the word *cancer*, I was dying, and I had been for quite some time. Just like my mother, and my grandmother before her.

I like to think I stayed alive for you, my sweet Celeste, to see you grown to be a woman. But in those dark times when my body is too racked with pain to grant me any sleep, I think God allowed me to live long enough to see everything stripped away. My baby, my home, my son, my husband, and—I fear—your love, when you are given this confession to read. At least he will spare me from witnessing that day.

It might be that you are wondering, my darling, just why I have decided not to take these secrets to my grave. In part, it is my compliance with Christopher Parker's wishes. He has, in these last years, been as kind to me as any son, and I like to think that, in him, I have done some good in this world. And it is because of his loyalty that I have a final secret to share with you, and from here, you will know all that I've kept hidden.

My sins against you, my precious girl, can be numbered by

your every breath. Even before, as you were born into a lie perpetuated without your consent. Just as I sinned against your father through deceit, and against your brother through neglect, and against that girl out of sheer hate.

It was a relief to me when we left Chicago, and I was thus unburdened from our expected presence at church each week. How awful it was, sitting in the pew with our family name, holding this beautiful little girl in my lap, knowing she was nothing but a lie. Sitting next to this man I knew to be an adulterer. And Calvin, my sweet son, kicking his legs until we were released to go home.

Once here, by some silent agreement, your father and I never bothered going to church. I wouldn't have known where to start, not having the benefit of family and tradition. And so I marvel, my girl, at your sweet good nature, though I suppose our Graciela has much to do with that, as I would hear you nightly saying prayers together. Sometimes, too, now, she prays with me. Rather, over me, as I pretend to sleep. Even in Spanish, her words give such comfort, and the time came when I knew I could no longer ignore my mortality.

Last Christmas, you remember, Christopher Parker gave me a radio to keep upstairs in my bedroom, and one day, turning the dial, I heard a woman's voice.

"Come to Jesus, you who are weak! Come to Jesus, you who carry heavy burdens! Come to Jesus, you who are ravaged by the cancer of sin!"

And I knew she was talking to me, directly *to* me, through that little wooden box on the nightstand.

Aimee Semple McPherson. Sister Aimee. I knew *of* her, of course. Who didn't? She was every bit as famous as you yourself aspire to be. But rather than portraying stories on the screen, she spoke truth. Even though I'd long recused myself from any society, I knew of her church. People lined up around the block, so they said. Thousands of people—different people—every day at her services.

I listened to her daily, fighting my ever-present need for sleep in order to cling to her words. Her voice invaded my dreams, and when the radio sat in silence, I took to reading my own Bible. Or, more and more these days, I have you read it to me, my darling. You have such a lovely, expressive voice, and I admit to sometimes feigning a greater weakness just to hear you. I'll admit my refusal to allow you to continue in film was rooted in selfishness, knowing my days were so few and wanting you all to myself. But I do think you are wasted on the silent screen. With my blessings, sweet child, when I am gone, take to the stage.

One day it was clear that Sister Aimee was broadcasting from her temple. I could hear the faint shouts of the audience as they responded to her. And then she began to call people down for healing.

"You need only believe in the power of Jesus' name! The great physician! The mighty healer! The creator of the perfect universe bids you to believe! Do you have faith? Do you believe in the healing powers of his holy name? Come! Come!"

It seemed as though I was being lifted from my bed, floating free. I was weeping and shouting that, Yes, I believed! I reached my hand toward the radio, bidding it to come to me, thinking maybe if I touched it, the electricity that carried her voice might carry God's power.

Graciela must have heard my cries, for she came running into the room as fast as her lameness would allow. All aflutter with concern, she offered to bring me food, bring me water, bring me fresh pillows or a thick blanket. And I told her no, none of that. Bring me Christopher Parker.

When I told Christopher I wanted to go to Angelus Temple, he seemed skeptical, if only because of my frailty. The cancer by that time had metastasized in my bones, as the doctors had shown me in what they called an X-ray. There I saw the truth of my disease. Bulbous tumors, and holes eaten into my very bones. It is something, I tell you, to be able to see your pain. For so long, I'd intertwined the pain in my heart and that in my body, never knowing where one began and the other ended. In seeing my disease, I saw an end to both. Erase the tumors, fill in the holes, and bring me peace. The doctors said I would surely die; Sister Aimee gave me hope in Jesus. Hope for healing. That I might live.

It was a Thursday afternoon, and you were out. Graciela helped me dress, but as I'd been reduced to this skin and bones you now know, I had nothing that came close to fitting. She managed to find a soft chiffon blouse that didn't irritate my skin, a long skirt, and soft slippers. I'd already bobbed my hair—for convenience rather than fashion—and we'd set it the night before after an evening spent meticulously bathing.

By the time I was ready to leave the house, Graciela and I were both exhausted and joked that we were ready for a nap when Christopher arrived. Straightaway he came to my room, as I hadn't been able to go downstairs in quite some time. Such a *presence* he was, so robust and jovial. He spoke silly flattery to me and made me feel almost womanly again. Not for the first time, I thought it a shame he'd been born a Negro, else he would have made a fine man for you, my dear.

Before we left, he got down on one knee in front of me and took my hand in his. He said, "You know I consider myself a good Christian man, Mrs. Margi—" that was his name for me, when we were alone—"but I don't know if this is a good idea. That woman, she has a strange way about her."

I told him I appreciated his concern, but I felt this as a calling to my soul, and after a bit more reassurance, the most amazing thing happened.

He picked me up. Yes, he scooped me right out of my seat, lifting me as if I weighed no more than a feather, and carried me downstairs.

I tell you, I felt like a girl when he brought me to his car, settled me inside, and tucked a blanket around my legs to fight the chill as we drove with the car's roof folded down. I couldn't remember the last time I'd experienced wind in my face, even though much of our driving took place in the slow congestion of the growing city. I was part of the world again, if only briefly.

When we arrived, a boy (or he might have been a young man—he was tall and thin and black as coal, one of the messengers Christopher employed through his office) met us at the curb with a wheelchair. Handling me with much more dignity than he'd employed at the house, Christopher helped me from the car to the chair, then instructed the young man to take the car and return in two hours. Then he wheeled me inside.

How can I convey the majesty of this place? Of course, I don't have to. You can go, as often as you like. To me, it seemed a preview of heaven itself—grandeur beyond compare. Outside is pristine and white, its roof rounded and soft. Inside, thousands upon thousands of seats, floating clear to the top, where the ceiling is painted to look like sky. Two choirs dressed in white robes stood on either side of the stage, and tall, stained-glass windows showed the stories of Jesus.

Christopher, having made arrangements in advance, conveyed me to a seat on the aisle near the front, close to the stage, and to my surprise, was welcome to sit right next to me.

Within the hour, every seat was filled. Never in my life had

I been in a place with so many people. It seemed the beat of their hearts gave me strength, their breath sustained me while Christopher's imposing presence kept anyone from touching me outright.

The lights shut off, plunging us into total darkness, and the first notes of the choir sounded.

"Would you be free from the burden of sin?
There's power in the blood, power in the blood;
Would you o'er evil a victory win?
There's wonderful power in the blood."

I sat there, sluggish, my own blood ravaged by disease, thinking, Yes, Yes, free me from this burden. And then, a flash of light on the stage, and there she was, like a pillar of silk, wearing a bloodred stole emblazoned with a white cross. Everyone around me leaped to their feet, and I could only weep in solidarity. I worried for a moment that the swelling noise of the crowd would drown out her words, but the moment she took her place behind the microphone, a hush fell, and she spoke.

Five thousand souls in that place, but her words were just for me. *"The time is now. The end is near. We cannot tarry on the path to redemption. We must not live another day without Jesus."*

Unburden yourself, Marguerite DuFrane.

Confess your sins, Marguerite, and be forgiven.

You sin not against your fellow man; you sin against a perfect and loving Father.

Start life anew. Be forgiven, and be healed.

There, feeling utterly alone, I whispered words I'd never said before: I have sinned, I have sinned, I have sinned. I could not name all of my sins, not even if I used every remaining breath to do so, but I carried them with me in the tumors attached to the body of the good woman I'd once been. I begged aloud: Father, heavenly Father, forgive me.

And she said, "Yes, yes. Our Father hears your confession. Our Father forgives your sin. Do you feel it? Can you feel his love and mercy?"

I could. If only I had any one of my many physicians by my side, I would have turned to him and said, I am healed. For in that moment, there was no pain. In fact, there wasn't *anything*. I looked over to Christopher only to see his head bowed in prayer, for which I was relieved, because he would not have approved nor allowed what happened next.

I stood.

With my own strength, without assistance, I stood. And then, I walked. Unbidden and uninvited, I walked—slowly, carefully, as my body seemed to be propelled by a force not my own—to the stage, where Sister Aimee paced, microphone in hand, shouting above the noise of the crowd, lapsing at times into an unfamiliar tongue. Nobody tried to stop me. In fact, when I reached the steps, a lovely gentleman took my arm to lead me. I remember thinking at the time that I might already be in heaven, he was so handsome, dressed in a suit the color of the sky.

He stayed beside me, his hand on the small of my back, more intimate than any touch I'd felt in years, and he whispered, his breath tinged with the scent of cigarettes, "Would you like Sister Aimee to pray over you?"

I nodded, and he asked, "Can you share with me the nature of your illness?"

And I said, simply, I am dying.

The compassion in his face served as the perfect prelude to

any prayer, and he lifted his hand—the ring on his pinkie finger glinting in the light—to catch her attention.

"Sister," he beckoned, and she came.

She looked at me, and all disappeared save for the three of us—she in her milky-white satin, he with his touch, and me with my yearning to live.

Sister Aimee held the square silver microphone in her hand but spoke directly to me. "My sister, have you come to be healed?"

Yes.

"And have you been cleansed of your sins by claiming the saving grace of Jesus Christ?"

Yes, I said. It was by that grace I was able to stand.

"You live with pain?"

Yes.

"Then I ask you, who is it you need to forgive?"

I said nothing.

She pressed on. "From whom do you need to seek forgiveness?"

If not for the strength of that man's hand on my back, I might have collapsed. She looked at me with eyes that seemed to see clear to the end of time, mining my secrets.

"You've lost a child?"

Yes.

"More than one?"

Everything.

"And for that, you hold bitterness in your heart."

I didn't need to tell her; she knew. She handed the microphone to the man behind me, and she laid her hand on my chest. A burning pain seared through me, as there were tumors grown nearly to the point of bursting through my very flesh, but the sharpness of that pain brought a certain, perfect clarity.

Long before this moment, it crossed my heart more than once

to think that I might find healing in forgiveness. Yes, forgiveness, begged for and granted. To grant dispensation to the girl, maybe even offer apology and restitution for the life—the *lives*—I stole from her. I sensed that it would not only temper the bitterness that haunted my every thought, but might even effect a deliverance from this disease before I knew it had a name. My life restored for such a small token. And yet, in that moment, I had only one answer.

I cannot.

Her countenance awash in judgment, she moved her hands to my face, drew me close, and kissed my forehead, my left cheek, and my right. "I would tell you, my sister, to go in peace. But I fear that you shall have none unless you forgive."

It's too late.

"While there is breath, there is hope. God has shown you great mercy so that you can do the same."

By then, she had the microphone, and she wasn't talking to me anymore. The pain returned with a vengeance I could not have anticipated, and I collapsed against the man, who now held me upright.

"It's all right," he said. "I have you."

He turned me around, and there was Christopher, waiting. Weeping. He came up to the stage and, gentle as the Good Shepherd, lifted me. Back up the aisle we walked, as the choir sang:

"I've wandered far away from God,
Now I'm coming home.
The paths of sin too long I've trod;
Lord, I'm coming home."

Abandoning the wheelchair, he shouldered his way through those making the pilgrimage to Sister Aimee's altar, through the lush lobby, and outside to where, right on cue, the young man waited with the car.

The ride home was excruciating, as I felt every twist and turn and bump of the drive. At home, upstairs, Graciela had changed my linens and had a fresh, new soft gown waiting for me. As she helped me change, she said, "I listened, on the radio. I heard every word."

Exhausted, I crawled into my bed, took a sip of the water she offered, and asked her if she thought my forgiveness would save my life.

"No, *mamá*. You are going to die. But you know that. And he keeps giving you day after day to do what is right for your heart. To give you peace before he takes you to eternity. You cannot change the past, but you can make a better future."

My future, I knew, might well be measured in minutes, and I asked her to go see if Mr. Parker still lingered downstairs. When she came back, confirming his presence, I asked her to bring him to my room, along with the other young man (his name was Angus Farland, I soon learned), and once there, with what I was sure would be my dying breath, I instructed Christopher to find her and give her half of everything I have.

It would be my substitute for mercy.

If the girl has given herself over to the mercy of the Lord, so be it. If we share anything, it is the endless source of his grace. I give this confession as an exoneration of my own guilt, not hers.

May God have the same mercy on her soul as I trust he will have on mine.

CHAPTER 30

CELESTE, AGE 20

1925

"'**MAY GOD HAVE THE SAME** mercy on her soul as I trust he will have on mine.'"

Celeste listened to her mother's final written words. Or, at least, this woman who had claimed to be her mother. Neither she nor Dana were up to the task of confronting the long-hidden truth, so Werner, at their invitation, agreed to read aloud for them. The accented depth of his voice gave enough distance from the words to make them bearable. Often, though, she had to urge him to stop as she tried to reconcile the woman she'd known with the woman revealed in this series of handwritten pages. And yet, it answered so many questions, the sadness that seemed always to plague the corners of her mother's life. Her irrational, protective fear.

Still, it left one question unanswered.

The question of her mother.

She looked to Dana. *Their* mother.

They were gathered in Celeste's home, cozy around the kitchen table, with Graciela in the background. She'd said nothing during the reading, save to walk over and clarify Marguerite's penmanship, as there were great passages she herself had written when Mother was too weak.

"And so you knew this?" Celeste had said not far into the reading. "All of this? And you never said a word to me?"

"It was not my place, *mija.* I knew it would be made known to you in God's time. And how beautiful, now, that you can share this with—"

But she'd interrupted herself, before Mother herself revealed Celeste and Dana to be sisters, and as the truth slowly dawned, they joined hands to hear the rest of the tale together.

"She slept so soundly that day when she got back from that church," Graciela said, pouring fresh coffee into a carafe. Nearly a full minute of silence had passed since Werner read the final words. "I kept coming in and checking, leaning close to make sure she was still breathing. Even in the night, and then I saw her up and awake and writing. But when I ask does she want help, like I did sometimes before, she said no. That she needed to finish herself. It took her four days, and then she passed." She made the sign of the cross. *"Dios la tenga en su gloria."*

"God rest her soul," Celeste alone repeated.

"Why don't you take your coffee out on the patio?" Graciela placed three cups, the carafe, and cream and sugar on a tray as if the decision had already been made. "I built a fire in the chimenea. It is such a beautiful night."

Celeste looked to the others, who seemed agreeable, and led the way outside. It was a beautiful, clear night, with enough breeze to bring in the scent of the orange groves and the ocean, but not too cool. Nobody had felt much like eating after the afternoon's visit to Mr. Parker's office, but they'd picked around what was left in the kitchen as a way to stall the inevitable exposure to Mother's pathetic, hidden past.

They gathered the patio chairs to make a semicircle around the chimenea, and though the evening was far from chilly, the warmth from the fire within provided a nostalgic comfort. The crackle of the flames stood in place of conversation. She stole a glance over to Dana, who stared into the flames, and then to Werner, only to see his eyes focused on Dana. Celeste's own heart clutched at the affection laid bare. She'd never once seen her father look at her mother that way.

Again, not her mother, and a new question formed.

"If you two will excuse me for a moment." It was the polite thing to say, though neither acknowledged her.

In the kitchen, she was greeted with the same scene that had been her sign of welcome and comfort since she was a child. Graciela, busy at the counter, preparing food. This time, a dough she'd mixed earlier had been rolled and cut, and the first of the pieces now fried in sizzling hot oil.

"Sopaipillas?" They were Celeste's favorite.

"*Sí*, Celita." Her expert hands worked the dough. "And there is fresh honey in the pantry."

Celeste obeyed the unspoken request to fetch it. Any other day, and she would have opened the jar right away and plunged a spoon in for a treat to sate her sweet tooth while Graciela fried the pastries. But now, her stomach felt full already. Full . . . or shriveled. Either way, there was no room.

She came out of the pantry and set the jar on the table. Graciela, absorbed at the stove, offered a distracted acknowledgment over her shoulder. With the last out of the pan, she would give them a dusting of sugar and cinnamon.

She was everything Mother had never been. Nurturing. Kind. Beautiful.

"Graciela?"

"Sí, mija?"

"Usted y mi padre eran amantes?"

Graciela's hand stilled, and she slowly set the shaker down. *"Qué has dicho?"*

"*Tú y mi padre*—you and my father. Were you lovers?"

"*Ay*, Celita. Your papa, he was a complicated man. He was *embrujado*. Haunted, by that girl and her mother."

"*My* mother. And how long have you known that?"

"After your papa died, when she told me the whole story."

But she didn't meet Celeste's eye with her response. "I don't believe you."

Graciela busied herself with the hem of a tea towel. "In some way, he always knew. He told me once, after your brother . . . that it was almost impossible that you were his child. And that, looking back, you might not even be your—his wife's. But—" she shrugged, helpless—"what was to be done?"

She began to busy herself, moving the sopaipillas to a bright-yellow plate, as if the conversation had ended.

"I'm not a little girl anymore," Celeste said. "I haven't been for a long, long time. What do you know about my mother?"

"Oh, Celita—" her brown eyes filled with tears—"*déjalo.* Let it rest. It is too much for one night."

"Tell me," Celeste insisted with an admittedly childish stamp of her foot.

Just then, Werner walked in and headed straight for the pages left abandoned on the table.

"Dana and I were talking," he said, flipping through, "and it's unlikely that Mrs. DuFrane would simply omit Celeste's birth and the fate of her mother. She spared no details in any other case, and she doesn't allude to any unconfessed sin. It must be that . . ." His voice trailed. "Here, there have to be some pages missing."

He left with the papers, and Celeste returned her attention to Graciela.

"You didn't answer my question. About my father and you."

She sighed, and Celeste braced herself for a truth she didn't want to hear.

"For a time, before you were born, he was here—now that I think, it must have been *right* before you were born. My dancing days had already come to an end, but I was still singing in a little cantina, and your father came in with some colleagues. He was supposed to stay here for a week but ended up staying for much longer."

"With you?"

"At first, he shared a house with some of the other professors, but after we met, he rented a small apartment, not far from here. One night, we borrowed a car and went for a drive and saw this house. He fell in love with it and said if he could have any other life, it would be in this house, with me."

Celeste's face burned with betrayal. "It sounds to me like he *did* have another life."

Graciela didn't look up. "It almost killed me when he left. I knew all along that he had a wife and children. I promised not to write to him, never wanting to bring him any shame. But when he wrote to me that he was coming back . . ." Words disappeared as her face turned into a mask of rapturous joy that lasted long enough for her to say, "I was so happy . . ." before collapsing in fresh grief.

A long-buried memory surfaced. "Papa said you came with the house."

Graciela wore her shame like a mantle. "*Éramos tontos.* Fools, both of us, but he'd convinced me that he did not love his wife. And that if we remained close to each other, someday . . ."

"Someday what?" Celeste thought about her poor mother, surely aware of the treasonous attraction. In the darkest recesses of her mind, Celeste had known too, though she'd been too young and naive to give it words or form. And Calvin, too, surely. Graciela had been just one more competitor for his father's attention, and Celeste knew she didn't speak precisely for him when she said, "We loved you."

"Lo sé."

"We trusted you."

"I know, Celi *mía*. And believe me, it is because of you, and your brother, that I—" She buried her face in her hands for a moment and emerged ashen. "I prayed to God for forgiveness. *Padre, perdóname.* I thought I could go through with this, this—*farsa*—I don't know the word."

"Charade?"

"*Sí.* But when I saw you, my Celita, I saw the children I could never have, and I knew I could stay longer, *para siempre*, forever, as long as your father and I, we didn't—"

Whatever resentment had spurred this conversation began to melt, but Celeste did not move, standing resolute as the woman who had been more than a second mother to her sobbed in a fresh expression of the grief she'd been forced to suppress all those years ago.

"Tu mamá," she said, her eyes red with tears, "before she died. She told me she had it in her heart to forgive one person. Only one, and that person was me. I was writing her papers, and I started to write that sentence, but she stopped my hand. She said, no. She said, 'I will allow you to confess your own sin.'"

A new wave of tears washed over her, doubling her in grief and shame, and this time brought Celeste in with its tide.

And so, there remained just one more question, and the

reappearance of Dana and Werner gave her the courage to ask it. After all, if she didn't, they surely would. Only she could ask Graciela, because she was the only one who loved her.

"Mamá," she whispered into her coconut-scented hair, "*dónde están esas páginas?* The missing ones, that tell about my mother."

"*Por favor!* I loved your papa, but I came to love all of you—your mother, too." She looked past Celeste to the others. "Can you not be satisfied with what you know already?"

Dana stepped forward. "The last time I saw my mother was when I was twelve years old. Locked away in a jail cell. She came to visit me, and we had dinner together. Roast beef and potatoes. She kissed me and said she would make everything all right. That it would take time, and I had to be patient, but in a few months, we would be back together. And I never saw her again. So, no. I'm sorry. I cannot be satisfied."

As she spoke, Werner stepped closer, finally resting his hand on her shoulder, and she seemed to grow stronger with every word. So, too, did Celeste stay connected to Graciela.

"We need to know, *Mamá*. This isn't your burden to bear."

That seemed to break her resolve. After all, they'd both seen the tragic effects of a life dedicated to keeping secrets.

"Go back outside," she said. "I'll bring them to you."

Like children, faces downcast with shuffling steps, they obeyed. The fire had burned down, and Werner tossed in a few thick sticks of wood, and the crackle and scent of cedar drew them in. Celeste picked up her coffee, not quite cool, and took a sip, looking out over the yard.

"I think I want to get rid of the playhouse," she mused aloud. Then, remembering, "Is that all right with you, Dana?"

Dana looked both surprised and slightly amused to be consulted. "I suppose. Why?"

"To put in a swimming pool. Let's redo the whole house, in fact. Top to bottom. Fresh start."

"Whatever you like. It's your house."

"It's yours, too."

It was nothing more than small talk. An idle distraction from what awaited, and then Graciela arrived, holding a bundle of papers folded and tied with a pink ribbon. With a long match, she lit the torches along the patio, bathing them in a soft light, but enough to see the words.

"God have mercy," she said as Werner took them from her. She pulled up a chair and sat, taking Celeste's hand. And together, they stared into the flames.

CHAPTER 31

THE WRITTEN CONFESSION OF MARGUERITE DUFRANE, PAGES 59–66

I STUFFED MYSELF with food while sending hundreds of dollars to those starving in China, and I knew immediately my prayers had been answered when your father came home one day and said he'd been invited to be a guest lecturer at Stanford University. He made it immediately clear that I was not to go along. It was a limited budget; he'd be sharing a house with several other engineers, all of them bachelors for the term.

I asked him how long he thought he'd be gone. Two weeks? Three?

"Twelve," he said.

Three months. He wouldn't be here for the birth of the baby.

When I said as much out loud, he looked—how can I describe it? Relieved? Resigned? If nothing else, there was the inescapable feeling that we both were keeping the same secret. Telling the same lie, and we would for the rest of our lives together. In some ways, my darling, though we both loved you dearly, you were what grew between us. The light of his life, and the light of mine, but our lights never touched each other again.

He asked, "Will you be all right without me?"

What if I'd said no? If I'd been the wife I'd been before, needful and clinging? A bride willing to sacrifice whatever necessary to keep our lives together? I could go with him, share his bed as he shared the house, insisting that he not resume a bachelor's life for three months. Or fall at his feet and beg him not to leave me here in such a vulnerable state.

But I did neither. Instead, I masked my heaving relief as an unfounded fear and forced him to take me in his arms to give me comfort.

I said I supposed I could call him on the telephone when it was time for the baby to come, and he could pace the floors in California and hand out cigars to his fellow housemates. He promised he would do just that.

Three days later he was gone and I felt myself off of the tightrope and safely on the platform. But the solid ground was still miles and miles away.

I began once again to make social calls and receive visitors, and through careful conversation, I learned of a private academy in Lake Forest that allowed students in Calvin's grade to board. I explained to him that it would be best, as I couldn't take care of him the way I should while I was waiting for the baby. I'd be weak and tired, and with his father gone, there might not be anybody here to take care of him when I went into the hospital.

He looked terrified, poor boy. He said, "You didn't go to the hospital when you had Mary."

I said, that's because Daddy was here. And he had been, right outside the door, and by my side before she was an hour old. As disinterested as Arthur was in being a husband, he was a wonderful, attentive, and affectionate father.

I packed up my little boy and delivered him to a formal headmaster, who confiscated his toy soldiers and forbade me to visit for at least two weeks.

That left just the two of us, at least in the evenings after Mrs. Gibbons left for the day.

I suppose it will sound irrational to say that I count this as a special time, but I did. I've never had many close friends. We resumed our games of gin, and Mrs. Lundgren told me all about her daughter. No doubt trying to convince me of her goodness, and I listened as politely as I could. When I asked her what plans she had for the two of them after the baby was born, she said she hoped to find a position as a domestic. Perhaps a live-in situation, where the girl could work also, and they could save up to find a little place of their own.

I asked if she would tell her about the baby, and she said, "No."

And that ended the conversation.

Arthur wrote letters regularly, and once, having come across me reading one by the firelight, she asked, casually, if I would share whatever little quip had caused me to smile. For the life of me, I cannot remember what it was. Something about one of his housemates, an irascible old man who regularly derided his own research. But I shared it, and we laughed, and I went back through some of his other letters and read those, too. Even the few sweet lines he meant just for me, or his thoughts about the baby. Once, he sent a photograph of the ocean, and a tiny, delicate pink shell. He said it made him think of our Mary. I read this to Mrs. Lundgren, unable to continue through my tears, and she took it from my hand and read my husband's words to me.

That's when I knew. When I heard her voice read his words, everything I'd been afraid to suspect came to light. The two of them, melded together. She and I, too, shared a secret and a lie. But not from each other.

Right in that moment, I asked her if Arthur knew she was carrying his child.

She didn't flinch, and she appeared untouched by shame when she said, simply, "No." Then, in the next breath, "Are you going to tell him?"

And I, in the same spirit, gave the same answer. No.

We were, in that moment, simply two mothers, willing to sacrifice bits of ourselves for the sake of our children. Odd as it may seem, I took some comfort in knowing that your father would truly be your father, in every sense. Even more, I admit, it came as a relief to know the source of your paternity wasn't in any way undesirable.

"Perhaps," she said, no doubt bolstered by my calm demeanor, "you could send me a picture from time to time?"

I came close to reassuring her, for as much as she could trust my promise.

I knew it would be far too dangerous to allow Mrs. Lundgren to ever go into labor here at the house, as the unpredictability of babies could mean its arrival right as Mrs. Gibbons was in the middle of cleaning the silver or washing up the breakfast dishes.

So when we knew the time was close, I took Mrs. Lundgren to the Mary Thompson Hospital for Women and Children, which my family has supported with charitable contributions since just after the War between the States, when a Union soldier's widow hemorrhaged to death in the street just in front of our church. I took one of my older satchels from the attic and packed it with a comfortable robe and gown, as well as two dresses I thought might fit well after the baby was born. As a more sentimental gesture, I included a pack of cards, in case she found another woman to play a round with, and in the not-quite dead of night, I called for a taxi to take us straight to the front door.

If I know one thing about the Mary Thompson Hospital, it is that I was hardly the first wealthy woman to arrive with a house servant in tow, and a good number of those would bear children with a strong resemblance to the master. So when I made our introductions, I was met with nary a sideways glance. The prominence of my name at the top of the check assured their discretion, and they were left with the understanding that I, and only I, was to be telephoned when the baby arrived.

I'd arranged for Mrs. Lundgren to have a private room, and believe it or not, we embraced each other before my parting. She actually thanked me for my kindness, and I felt a pang of guilt thinking how cruel her life must have been for her to think me kind and generous in this moment. Still, I reassured her that, once the child was born, and in my home, I would go straightaway to the judge, an old family friend, and I would convince him that my Mary's death had been an inevitable tragedy. She would have her daughter, and I would have, well, whatever God would desire, though I prayed beyond prayer to be given another little girl. A second chance.

That night was the first night in memory for me to be in my home entirely alone. The ghosts were everywhere. My husband's in my bed, my Mary's in her crib with that horrible lace pillow, my Calvin's in his room amid his soldiers, and even my prisoner's from behind the linen closet at the end of the hall. I roamed the night, putting them all to rest, assuring myself that all would soon be set right, this house brought back to life with the cooing of lullabies and the laughter of children. It became my ritual each night, making promises to the house before drifting off to endless, peaceful sleep.

It was just before dawn, one week later, when the telephone in the hallway rang, and I fell upon it, too sleep-addled and dream-ridden to realize, at first, who could possibly be on the other end of the line. It wasn't until I heard the words "Healthy baby girl."

I held the phone as I fell to my knees, so thankful to God for answering my prayers with such perfect precision. But the voice on the other end of the line still spoke.

"Profuse hemorrhaging. Eclampsia. Seizures, shock, and nothing to be done."

I was still giving thanks even as she spoke, until her words overcame my prayers.

In the next few hours, Mrs. Gibbons arrived, and I met her with train fare and a letter to the headmaster of the academy to which I'd sent Calvin, stating that my son was to be released into the custody of Mrs. Gibbons and returned home at the week's end. I also sent funds to allow her to find a place to board during that time, telling her to be sure to enjoy herself and relax, knowing the baby would be here soon after her return, and there'd be no rest for the weary then.

During that day, I went over every inch of Mary's room with a dust rag and pulled the smaller cradle into my bedroom and lined it with fresh, clean linen. The grocer's was an easy walk, and so I went to buy the ingredients needed to mix the baby's formula, which I learned having been unable to nurse either of my children. I also picked up some bread and cheese for the sort of simple meals I would prepare in Mrs. Gibbons's absence.

Then I waited. First for darkness. Then for ten o'clock. Then for just half past for a cab to come and drive me to the hospital, where I saw the same helpful nurse on duty as had been there when I first arrived with Mrs. Lundgren. When she asked if I cared to see the body, I declined, though I assured her that I was to be contacted for all details of the burial. She then produced the satchel, and I urged her to donate the contents to charity but added surreptitiously that she should keep the bag for herself. A woman always needs a good bag.

Having dispatched those details, I was led into a hallway, where I looked through a window and saw rows upon rows of babies. Even if they hadn't pinned a card with your name—DuFrane—to the overhang, I would have known you. You looked like my dream. And miracle of miracles, somebody put you in my arms, and I walked out into the night.

When I got into that cab, I felt as if I rode a white horse. It occurred to me, the divine nature of my plan. You were meant to be mine all along. To be raised by your father openly, and without shame. To be abandoned by the mother who would so willingly give you up. Who would hand over this precious, innocent babe in exchange for freedom of one who had no regard for life?

You didn't make a sound, only looked at me with eyes that seemed to understand it all.

CHAPTER 32

DANA FINDS A FAMILY

1925

"'. . . **ONLY LOOKED AT ME** with eyes that seemed to understand it all.'"

Werner finished the final line and looked up at Celeste, as did they all. Dana hadn't been able to keep her eyes off the young girl, sharing with her the final days of their own mother. Somehow, she had to admit to herself, she had always known her mother's fate. When faced with an alternative truth, that Mama had simply abandoned her daughter to whatever fate awaited, the confirmation of her death came as a comforting relief. For Dana, these missing pages from Marguerite DuFrane's final missive served to answer a single, looming question. For Celeste, it was more likely a rapid-fire sequence of unwanted revelation. Her mother was not her mother. The source of her life was dead. Her father, perhaps, nowhere near the man she'd thought him to be.

"Did you know?" Celeste asked, her eyes showing no hint of the understanding Marguerite had ascribed. "Did you know that your mother was pregnant?"

Dana's mind went back to those final days with her mother,

when she had no idea that they would be final at all. "No. I remember her being tired, but she was always tired. She worked very hard, you know. And I didn't know anything at all about . . . your father."

Celeste looked to Graciela, who in turn studied the pink flagstones in the firelight. "My father," she said, carrying an indefinable fusion of admiration and contempt. "Apparently there was a lot about my father that nobody knew."

"Celita," Graciela cautioned, "your father was a good—"

Celeste burst from her chair. "Don't tell me he was a good man! If anyone should know just how horrible a man he was, it's you! You might be the only person he truly knew and truly loved."

"He loved you, *mija*."

"But he didn't know me. He didn't know who I . . . who my—" She stopped, bit her bottom lip, and dropped her hands limply to her sides. "I don't even know who I am anymore."

Dana stood and embraced the girl's lifeless body. "You're my sister."

Celeste stepped away. "I'm sorry. But that doesn't help me at all."

She turned and ran into the house, leaving Dana to feel emptier than she had before the revelation.

"Forgive her," Graciela said, "and go to her. You are both feeling the same loss."

Dana turned to Werner, who had remained quiet all this time. He still sat, the sheaf of papers rolled loosely in his hands. Now he stood, dropped them on the glass-topped table, and wrapped Dana in an embrace strong enough to fill in all that she lost while his voice read Marguerite's words.

"Go to her." He kissed the words to her temple.

She leaned back to look at him, his face a warm glow in the torchlight. "Will you stay here?"

"As long as you want me to."

Fortified, Dana went inside, looking first in the kitchen, then the front and back parlors, and even poked her head into the room that had been Arthur DuFrane's office, though Celeste had been turning it into her own, feminine and white and pure. In here, she'd said, not long after Dana's arrival, they would watch every movie containing even a single frame of Celeste DuFrane, one after the other, drinking cold bottles of Coca-Cola and eating box after box of Cracker Jack.

But the room was empty, so Dana ascended the stairs, wondering what Mama would say if she knew her daughter—her *daughters*—lived in such a place. She might well have expected such a home for the secret baby she carried, given the snare of promises she wove. But to think that her Dana, who had never known anything other than a one-room flat with a bathroom down the hall, called such a place as this *home*. Not as a servant, not as caretaker, but as a daughter of inheritance.

She paused halfway up and looked at the richness of the display below. Not crowded and dark like the old, grand houses back home. But clean and light, like Mr. Lundi had said that day. A place of new beginnings.

"What would you think, Mama?" Though she spoke softly, her words echoed, and she could hear her mother's answer deep within her bones.

It's too much. Her dreams had always been so small. *A good position. A live-in, where you can work beside me.*

Was that why she shared Arthur DuFrane's bed? Hoping to be brought into the house?

More questions that would have no answers, and it was

fruitless at this point to wonder what her mother would think. "This is mine," she said aloud, stating the fact for the first time. And it wasn't too much. It was exactly enough. Half, shared with her sister. Half sister, to be exact, and that was enough too.

She resumed her ascent and went directly to the master bedroom—Celeste's bedroom—expecting to see her collapsed dramatically on the bed, perhaps draped against the bedpost. But no, the room was empty.

Then she heard her name being called softly from her own room. Celeste was sitting on the window seat, luminescent in moonlight.

"There you are," Dana said, feeling a strong sense of comfort that she'd chosen to come here for refuge.

"This used to be my room," Celeste said, as if Dana had asked for an explanation. "You should have seen it. Everything pink and ruffles and silk and lace. That wall was a mural, and I had tea sets and dolls, and everything you could imagine."

"I'm sure it was beautiful."

"I made Mother get rid of all of it when I was twelve. Right after Calvin died. I didn't want to be a little girl anymore. You know she kept Calvin's room just the same."

"Yes." And by tacit agreement, the sisters kept the door closed.

"I had this horrible feeling," Celeste went on, "that I would die too. My life would come to an end at twelve years old, and she would keep this room forever like it was when I was five, and nobody would know that I ever grew up at all."

Dana approached, and Celeste moved over to make room on the window seat.

"I know what it's like to have your life stop at twelve years old," she said.

Celeste's hand flew to her mouth, a now-familiar gesture

when she made a gaffe. "You must think me the most insensitive thing ever."

"It's all right." She reached for Celeste's hand, porcelain in the moonlight, and after a moment's hesitation, kissed it. "I realize now that it didn't stop at all. It went on. Not always easy, but forward."

"Without your mother."

Tears pricked at Dana's eyes, and she risked only a whimpering affirmation.

"What was she like?"

"It's been so long." She paused, gathering her thoughts and her voice. "She was a simple woman, I suppose. Always just the two of us, and she worked so hard. I spent most of my childhood alone, waiting for her to get back from some job or another."

"Was she pretty? Because—and this is going to make me sound like such a shallow Sherry, but while Papa was handsome enough, I never thought Mother was particularly beautiful. And I've often wondered how . . ."

Her voice trailed off, and Dana picked up the thread. "How you came to be such a lovely?"

"Aren't I terrible?"

"Not at all," Dana said. "You're beautiful."

"So, was she? Pretty?"

"I don't know how to answer that."

"You don't remember?"

"She looks—rather, she *looked* like me. She was just my age now when she died."

"Oh," Celeste said, looking achingly beautiful in every way. The moonlight bathed her in innocence, and the sweetness of her heart lived in the breath of that syllable. Whatever tiny sliver of good there had been in each of Celeste's parents—Arthur,

Marguerite, and Dana's own mother—all of it had converged and molded itself into this girl.

"There weren't a lot of mirrors in—" she caught herself—"where I lived, and I actually went years and years without ever seeing myself."

Celeste shuddered in not-quite-mock horror at the concept, and they shared a swift, soft giggle.

"Then, one day, I might have been twenty-three or twenty-four, and a woman named Effie gave me a small mirror." Dana closed her hand around its imaginary handle and gazed back into the reflection of time. "I looked into it and saw my mother looking back at me. Young, like I remembered her from when I was a child."

"And pretty?" Celeste prompted.

"No," Dana said, feeling like she was disappointing a child in the admission. "Tired. Pale. Worn. I guess her life had been almost as limited as mine."

"Do you think she loved my father?"

To that, Dana found herself at a complete loss. "I knew nothing about that part of her life. I barely remember my own father. I always believed what she told me, that they'd been married, and he died in a riverboat explosion. But now—"

"Now you have no reason to believe otherwise. My father was a charming man. I guess I've known that my whole life. Women have always looked at him, and he encouraged them, to some extent."

"I know Mama was lonely. She hardly ever talked about my father, and I never knew her to have a boyfriend. I always thought she was as happy to have just the two of us as I was."

They sat in silence for a good, long, companionable minute, until Celeste reignited the conversation with a sly little smile.

"What?" Dana asked, intrigued.

"I'm just trying to imagine how different my life would have been if I hadn't been able to come here. If our mother hadn't given me away." The whimsical speculation soon died, however, as they looked at each other, both seeing—Dana knew—the specter of a third sister, taken to God in infancy. She lay there, quiet and still as a lamb, at the place where their knees touched on the window seat.

"All I ever wanted," Dana said, laying her hands on the invisible child, "was a chance to tell your mother—your *family*—how much I hurt for their loss. I would have happily spent the rest of my life in prison if it would have brought her back. I would have given my *life* in exchange for hers if I could."

"Instead—" Celeste brought her cool, perfect hand to her hot, tearstained face—"I was given a life. Can you think of any other paths that would bring us to this place?"

"No." Not outside of the orchestrations of God, though she hated the litter of sacrifices left along the way. She leaned her head against the cool glass of the window and looked down to see Werner silhouetted in the light of the burning torches. He was sitting, elbows propped on his knees, his head touched to his clasped hands. Deep in thought, possibly deep in prayer, and she relished this time to study him openly.

"He likes you, you know," Celeste said, with all the wisdom and assurance of youth.

"Do you think so?"

"And he thinks you're beautiful. I can tell."

"I don't know about that."

Just then, he looked up, straight into the window, and the warmth of his gaze carried like torchlight through the glass. Dana lifted her hand in a small wave.

"Go down to him." She accompanied her command with a sisterly nudge.

"But we still have so much to talk about."

"Do we?" Celeste seemed to gather herself for a declaration, sitting a bit taller before she spoke. "When I make a movie, I'm the same *person* I was in the last film. You know, same me—flesh and bone and whatnot. But I'm playing a new character. So everything I thought and knew about that old character has to kind of die off. Do you understand?"

"I think so," Dana said, but she didn't. Not really.

"The way I see it, you and I—up until this point—we were living a story. And now, tonight, everything's changed. Everything we knew, or thought we knew. Our past—it's different."

"A new story."

Celeste nodded with the exuberance of a child and grasped her hands. "Starring Celeste DuFrane and Dana Lundgren as sisters. Tonight is act one, scene one. Nothing before that existed."

This time, when they fell into each other's arms, it was an embrace grown out of the same root and fused again with affection and promise.

"But we have to promise each other something," Celeste said as they pulled away. "We can't ever lie to each other. About anything. There's been enough of that already."

"Agreed."

"Now—" Celeste gave a stronger nudge—"go downstairs and kiss that man good night. It's getting late, and I have a reputation to uphold."

Dana smiled, kissed her little sister's cheek, and ran down the stairs at a rate twice that which had taken her up, and was surprised to see Celeste right on her heels, saying, "There's just one more thing I want to do."

She moved ahead, and Dana followed her through the kitchen. Celeste scooped the papers containing her mother's confession off the table and continued out to the patio, where Graciela and Werner appeared to be in easy conversation.

"Where are the other pages?" Celeste asked, not mindless of her interruption.

"Oh, Celita," Graciela pleaded with anguished concern, "do not trouble yourself—"

"Here." Werner handed them over without ceremony.

Celeste took them in one hand and, with the other, led Dana from beneath the cover of the patio, onto the narrow stone pathway of the yard, where they could look up into the stars. She held out the folio, and through a mysterious understanding, Dana held it too, until the sisters were joined not only by their grasp on each other, but their grip of Marguerite DuFrane's account of bitterness and lies.

"Mother," Celeste said to the sky, "we have read your words, and we forgive you."

Dana, too, looked to the stars and the moon but knew her answer didn't wait in the heavens. Instead, she closed her eyes, bowed her head, and gripped Celeste's hand ever tighter, inviting her into her prayer.

"Father God, send your Holy Spirit with an anointing of peace to our mothers. And our sister. Until that day when we will find each other in your presence."

"Amen," Celeste said, making Dana's heart swell with expectation of the journey they would take together to fulfill that destiny.

For now, she loosened her grip on the confession but walked hand in hand with her sister back to the patio, where Celeste gave her over to Werner's casual embrace.

"That was beautiful," he said, drawing her close.

Graciela made the sign of the cross, saying, "May all their good souls rest in peace."

"Amen," Celeste said again, this time with stronger conviction. Then, without another word, she threw her mother's tragic tale of anguished deception on the glowing coals in the chimenea. There was an immediate burst of flame, then a blackening and a curling.

"Once upon a time there were two sisters," Celeste said as a latent flame ate the last of Marguerite's tortured script.

Dana watched too. "And they lived happily ever after."

A NOTE FROM THE AUTHOR

THIS IS ONE OF those stories born from the question *What if . . . ?* It's no secret that I've long been fascinated with the 1920s. Such a fabulous decade. Such a decadent decade. And yet we know the roots of evangelism held strong. Whether talking about one of my books or teaching one of my classes, I always visit the idea of the Twenties mindful of the swift, sweeping changes: hemlines, communication, transportation, values, norms, vocabulary—everything made new within half a generation.

But what if you missed it? What if you were dropped, like a time traveler, into this world you knew nothing about? Thus, Dana was born.

I have to admit it was a blast to write a character as deliciously amoral as Marguerite DuFrane. And I've been waiting for the chance to lurk around the movie sets of a newly minted Hollywood. Alas, with this novel, I bid farewell to the very real Aimee Semple McPherson, and I will always be grateful to Bill Jensen (aka Agent Bill) for introducing her to me. Also, sadly, I'll be stepping away from Roland Lundi—a character I've grown to love as much as any romantic hero.

I'm off to new stories, and I hope you'll follow me! Look me up on my website, www.allisonpittman.com, or find me on Facebook (Allison Pittman Author Page) and Twitter (@allisonkpittman).

DISCUSSION QUESTIONS

1. *All for a Sister* is a story of secrets. Discuss the ways in which various characters were hurt by the secrets that were kept from them. Was anyone helped or protected by the secrets? Is there ever a time when keeping a family secret is the best course of action?

2. Young Celeste knows from an early age that she wants to be an actress. In what ways has she been an actress all her life?

3. Would you classify Marguerite DuFrane as a villain? Why or why not? Do you feel any sympathy for her?

4. Do you think that Dana's inheritance is fair compensation for Marguerite's actions? What more could she have done? Why didn't she?

5. After the death of Arthur DuFrane, Celeste is left without a father, and Dana never knew her father at all. In what ways do Werner Ostermann, Christopher Parker, and Roland Lundi help to fill these roles in the girls' lives? Has God ever provided someone to fill a key role in your own life in an unconventional way?

6. Both Celeste and Dana are familiar with the story *Alice's Adventures in Wonderland*. Why would each of them be drawn to this story?

7. Marguerite DuFrane believes there is a connection between her emotional bitterness and the physical devastation of cancer. What role do you think our emotional and spiritual health plays in our physical well-being?
8. What do you think was Graciela's motivation for removing the pages from Marguerite's confession detailing the birth of Celeste and the death of her mother?
9. Graciela presents an ethical quandary. Does the revelation of her relationship with Arthur DuFrane change your view of her relationship with Celeste? How do you think it will affect her relationship with Celeste going forward?
10. Imagine you'd been cut off from all the social and technological innovations of the past twenty years. Which would you find to be the most exciting? Which would be the most intimidating?

ABOUT THE AUTHOR

Award-winning author **ALLISON PITTMAN** left a seventeen-year teaching career in 2005 to follow the Lord's calling into the world of Christian fiction, and God continues to bless her step of faith. Her novels *For Time and Eternity* and *Forsaking All Others* were both finalists for the Christy Award for excellence in Christian fiction, and her novel *Stealing Home* won the American Christian Fiction Writers Carol Award. In 2012, she was named ACFW's mentor of the year. She heads up a successful, thriving writers' group in San Antonio, where she lives with her husband, Mike, their three sons, and the canine star of the family—Stella.